IF I DIE BEFORE I WAKE TALES OF
BLOOD AND FATE

Published by Kooky Cat Books 2023
Copyright © 2022 Martii Maclean
www.martiimaclean.com

A catalogue record for this book is available from the National
Library of Australia.

Formatting and cover design by Kooky Cat Books
Cover art development by Michelle Watson at Empne'o Arts
Project

Duology edition 2023
ISBN 978-0-9876442-4-4 (pbk)
ISBN 978-0-9876442-5-1 (e-bk)

For Trevor and Minerva,
thank you for baking the seagull pies
while I was busy imagining and writing and
learning.

If I Die Before I Wake
Tales of Blood and Fate

A duology in one volume

MARTII MACLEAN

Kooky Cat Books

BOOK ONE

IF I DIE BEFORE I WAKE

*The sleeping curse is genetic and hereditary, passed from
mother to daughter for centuries.
Vreni has slept and woken for more than a century.
Discovering her magical nature and sets out to defeat the
alchemists
and free herself and her family from the evil curse.*

LITANY

Veca Tante and her alchemists have cursed the Lady Ieva
and presume her lost to the darkness of the sleeping death.
But we Pratigs Māsa, the Wise Sisters, have softened the
potion. Ieva sleeps and wakes at the whim of the curse,
as does her newly born daughter.
And so, we fear, will her granddaughters.
These sleeping beauties need protection from
Veca Tante and the world. We pledge to watch over them
for as long as the curse may last.
—Pratigs Māsa, Book of Wisdoms

***

Vreni woke with a shudder. Her heart sprang to life within her chest as though it was a wild creature released from its bindings. Her body tensed in response to the searing pain of her first breath as it entered her long-dormant lungs, which had remained so still during her long-sleep. She wondered if this was why newborn babies cried - this burning breath.

The magical bindings of the curse held Vreni's body frozen for a few more frightening moments. She concentrated on calming her breathing and waited. With each fluttering squeeze of her heart, blood pumped through her body and sent a sensation like burning needles radiating outward in a wave of fiery pain. She tensed again, forcing a breath through her clenched teeth while she flexed her rigid muscles, hoping to speed up the painful transition out of long-sleep.

Her litany always began the same way. 'I am Vreni. I am fifteen years old.' *This is my twentieth awakening.* How much time had passed during her long-sleep this time?

The heat in her lungs began to cool. The burning pain moved down her arms and legs, and then faded, as if flowing out from her toes and fingertips. She stretched slowly, feeling as though she was made of rock.

'I am Vreni. I am fifteen years old. My mother is Gaida, my father is Parvils. Peters was my brother. My younger sister is Rita.' *Or is she my older sister now? Have we both slept? Am I the little sister again?* She knew she was still younger than Mama, but maybe one day she would not be. She would always be younger than Papa.

'Papa!' Her heart tightened into a fist. *Is Papa still alive? Of course he is, or I would already know.*

'Don't fret, sweet one, I'm here,' said her father's muddy voice.

Vreni opened her green eyes. She was so grateful that he was always there when she woke from long-sleep. He looked a little greyer now, and there seemed to be the slightest frailness in his voice. But perhaps he'd always been old like this and she'd just been too young to notice before now.

Yes, her father was old. Vreni watched her father's amulet swinging on its chain as he leaned over her. It glinted in the narrow strip of morning light that slipped through the heavy curtains. She reached out and touched the warm silver. Her father had worn this amulet ever since the day he had married her mother, nearly one hundred and fifty years ago.

The amulet was full of magic. The Pratigs Msa, the Wise Sisters, used the old magic to slow the effects of time on Parvils so he could live three or even four normal lifetimes while he watched over the sleepers he loved, including Vreni.

Not all the men in the family had received the magical gift of power over time. Sons were never sleepers, but no such charm was ever offered to a male child. This charm was only given to those who chose freely, knowingly and out of love, to pledge themselves to the family, as Parvils had done when he married Gaida. Families had to watch their sons grow to manhood and through to brittle old age and death in front of their eyes. This is what had happened to Vreni's brother Peters. She remembered waking to hear the cries of anguish the day he died.

Even though the Wise Sisters had softened the sleeping potion and removed much of the evil and hatred, a horrible cruelty remained, the curse woke the sleepers briefly to feel the pain and loss when a loved one died. Vreni, along with her sister, mother and aunties, had woken when her brother died, but they didn't remain awake long enough to find solace through singing at his funeral. They could only weep for him until the long-sleep of the curse recaptured them.

Her father brushed a dark strand of hair from her face.

'How did you know to be here?' she asked. 'How do you know when we will wake?'

He smiled and shrugged. 'When you've waited as long as I have, you develop a sense for it, a knowing.'

She hugged him to her. He felt frail. He was smaller somehow, but she was sure of it. 'How long this time?' she asked.

'It's been three years. Rita has slept too, so you're still the oldest, for the moment ...'

When Vreni was younger, long-sleep had been confusing. She would wake up expecting familiarity and comfort, but instead see unsettling changes, she people she knew always looked just a little different.

She was the first-born daughter, but as she discovered, in her family age and birthdays did a strange dance around each other. She remembered waking once to see her younger sister Rita, a rosy-faced baby girl, sitting on the hearthrug in front of a cosy fire. Rita had laughed delightedly when Vreni rolled a ball to her. The ball had been crocheted from brightly coloured yarns.

At Vreni's next awakening she again rolled the ball toward Rita, but the ball was faded with age and she herself was older. At first the ball and Rita felt strange to Vreni, but she also felt acceptance—intuition more than understanding—and had snuggled into this older Rita's arms to listen to her tell a story while she toyed with the faded ball.

'Three years,' Vreni echoed. 'And while we slept have, we all been moved again to another strange country?'

'No, we haven't moved again.' Her father looked wounded by her words.

She knew the question had been unfair and she wished she had spoken more thoughtfully. Her father sometimes had to make hard decisions to keep the family safely hidden.

She had once woken to find everything changed. Her home was gone. The family had left Vārve and moved thousands of kilometres away from everything she knew. The journey had taken many months, but to Vreni it had happened in the blink of an eye between sleeping and waking.

I'm acting like a child. I wouldn't want the burden Papa carries. 'That was thoughtless of me, Papa,' she said. 'Forgive me.'

'Always,' he whispered.

Her family had been hidden from the world in one way or another since the time of the cursing, over three hundred years previously. Each new tutor the Wise Sisters sent had taught Vreni pieces of the family history, but to her young ears it sounded like a fanciful tale about other people, in other places. As she grew older she began to comprehend the sleeping curse and what the life of a sleeper was like.

She accepted that this was her story, too. She would have to live as a sleeper, but what did that really mean? So far it had meant isolation, and, as she grew older, restlessness, since her family insisted on staying hidden from the world. *Maybe during my awakening this time Papa will say yes, and I'll get to go somewhere. Anywhere.*

Her father stood up next to her bed and smiled down at her. 'Good morning, Lady Veronika,' he said, using her full name. 'Welcome back among us.' He kissed her hand and bowed like a servant. It was a quaint ritual that had been part of her waking from long-sleep ever since she was very young.

'You'll be hungry when your stomach awakens,' he said. 'I'll see to breakfast.' He squeezed her hand and left the room.

The burning and aching had almost faded from her body. She sat up slowly, feeling a slight dizziness. Stretching out her legs, she wiggled her toes in the plush rug beside her bed. The light-headedness returned for a moment as she stood. She walked across the warm wooden floor, flexing her arms and legs to melt away the last of the stiffness.

Reaching the tall window, she pushed the heavy curtains open and stared out at the dazzling blue of the sea. It seemed to go on forever, fading into the horizon. Closing her eyes, she let the morning sun warm her, melting away the last chills of long-sleep. Then she pushed open the windows and breathed in the fresh salty air. Her lungs crinkled painfully as she forced them to expand fully.

Vreni never tired of watching the ocean. They had lived next to the sea back in Vārve, but here the light was stronger and the water was almost always blue. Many things were different here. Papa had found this remote clifftop house and renovated it until he was sure it would delight his family. He knew it *had* to delight them, because they never left it.

There were many rooms in the rambling house to accommodate the family and staff. A library for Papa, a large kitchen, a conservatory where they had their lessons, and her favourite, the tower, which rose up from the centre of the house. It was a place that was just for Vreni and Rita. Papa had built the tower so they could look out over the 'world', even if their world was only the gardens, the cliffs and the ocean beyond.

She closed her eyes against the glare, feeling the salt breeze on her face.

I am awake again.

EVER AFTER

The tellers of tales like to delight their readers with happily ever-after. It seems I do live ever-after, in a life of predictable, tedious seclusion, but my ever-after is not always lived happily.
—Ieva's private journal

***

Vreni stretched once more, took a deep, pain-free breath and wandered over to her closet. The clothes had changed so much throughout her century. Tight bodices, skirts and petticoats had become stiff woollen jackets and strange little hats, which then became miniskirts and high heels. Vreni had collected fashion souvenirs from each awakening.

'My favourite things from my favourite decades,' she whispered, taking out faded jeans, a mohair cardigan, and a T-shirt with a smiling yellow face on the front.

When she was dressed, she draped a floral silk scarf around her neck and looked at herself in the mirror.

'You look like a gypsy,' Rita said, walking through the half-open door.

'Papa didn't tell ...' Vreni hugged her sister excitedly.

'You're right, I didn't tell you that the fair Lady Marita was awake and with us too,' Papa said to Vreni, laughing, as he stepped through the door. 'You know I like surprises, my darlings.'

'And Mama?' Vreni said.

It was as though a small cloud moved across her father's face. 'She always sleeps longer than you girls,' he said. 'The curse must be becoming diluted with the generations, or maybe my daughters are obstinate and refuse even to be cursed properly.' He smiled.

Vreni threw her balled-up socks at him.

'Breakfast is ready,' he said with a laugh, and pulled the door closed behind him.

Rita sat next to Vreni on the bed, twisting a strand of her sister's hair around her finger, forming a lose ringlet. Then Rita fidgeted with her own hair, which was copper coloured like their mother's. Both had their father's green eyes, but Vreni had soft dark curls like Papa, except that his were always smoothed down.

'How was your waking?' Rita asked, forming another ringlet.

'It hurt, a lot, like it always does.'

'It's a shame the Wise Sisters couldn't have taken away the pain when they softened Grandmama's curse,' Rita said, hugging Vreni tightly.

They both knew it was sometimes hard to lighten the dark mood that lingered after waking from long-sleep.

Veca Tante had put shadowy things in the potion, and not even the combined magic of all of Grandmama Ieva's other aunties could remove all the blackness when the curse was softened.

'Sunshine will help,' Rita said, leading Vreni back to the window. 'Maybe Papa's right and the curse *is* weakening.'

'Wouldn't it be great if the curse weakened and disappeared,' Vreni said. 'Then we could stop hiding and have a life.'

'Well, it hasn't happened in more than three hundred years, so don't get your hopes up. And this life is fine,' Rita said. 'We get to do anything we like.'

'Anything but leave here,' Vreni said. She sighed and forced a smile. 'How long have you been awake?'

'A few weeks,' Rita said. 'I've learned a new thing on the computer. There's a way to shop and order things. You should see what I've been buying.'

'Have you been doing other lessons?'

'Yeah, worse luck, but Sabina's back again, so it's okay.'

'Have you asked her about going out? About leaving the grounds and maybe going to the city?'

'I hinted at it, and I reminded her that you'd asked her the last time you were awake, but I think she pretended not to hear me.'

'She does that to me, too,' Vreni said. 'We'll just have to try harder.'

'Vreni, it's not that bad. We have everything, and if we don't, I can just order it for us. Papa hardly ever says no as long as I address everything care of the family trust so they look like business deliveries. That way the postmistress doesn't ask nosy questions when Uncle Artūrs picks up the packages.'

'But this *isn't* everything, Rita. Don't you ever want to go anywhere?' Vreni snapped. 'It's not like Veca Tante's out there somewhere waiting for us. No magic could keep someone alive for centuries.'

'Are you sure, Vreni? No one knows what happened to her.'

'That's enough fairy tales, Rita. They just use that as an excuse to stop us going anywhere.'

Rita sighed. 'You're just grumpy after long-sleep.' She rubbed Vreni's hand. 'We do get to go places. We go to the beach a lot, and we can take the ponies.'

'Yes, I love riding, especially on the beach, but ... nothing ever really changes.' *My family might be magical, but I never see any magic.*

Her family might live by the magical rules of the sleeping curse, but for Vreni life was sheltered, predictable and boring. There were no surprises, which meant there were few choices that weren't already made for her. She wanted to make her own choices, and take chances sometimes.

Rita broke into her thoughts. 'At least we don't sleep as long as Mama,' she chirped.

'Mama! I must say good morning.'

Vreni left the room and walked quietly to her mother's room. 'Good morning, Mama,' she said, kissing Gaida on the forehead.

Rita appeared beside her and did the same thing.

'Mama still isn't awake. How does Papa endure it?' Vreni said.

'Well, for now he has us, so let's go and distract him.' Rita smiled mischievously.

At the top of the stairs Vreni stopped and looked over the railing into the foyer below. She winked at Rita and boosted herself up onto the banister rail. Hanging on for a moment in anticipation before letting herself go. She slid on the smooth, polished wood all the way to the bottom of the stairs, her stomach lurching.

'Good to see you're feeling more like yourself now,' Rita said, running down the stairs after her.

Vreni's stomach caught up with her at the bottom of the stairs, as did Rita. They linked arms and walked quickly across to the kitchen, pushing the swinging door wide as they entered the warm, delicious-smelling room.

Parvils looked up from his breakfast and gestured towards a plate of eggs and cheese, and another of thinly sliced black bread.

'My ladies,' he said, smiling warmly. 'Sit. Eat. It's so nice to hear happy noise in the house again.' He pushed a cardboard box towards them. 'But maybe you prefer porridge.'

'This is porridge?' Vreni said, turning the mysterious package around in her hands.

'*Instant* porridge, apparently.' Parvils' smile broadened. 'Obviously the people who made it have a different idea of what instant means than we do.'

'Well, we don't see much abracadabra around here ourselves, but what kind of magic do I need to call up to get instant porridge?' Vreni asked.

'Just the microwave,' Rita said, pointing at the appliance.

Vreni shrugged. 'It's nice to see you're so comfortable with these new gadgets, but I'll have an egg.'

'I checked on the computer, Papa,' Rita said as she removed the shell from her boiled egg, 'The weather's mild today. We could ride, all three of us.'

'Or pack a picnic and hike down the cliffs to the beach,' suggested Vreni.

'We could enjoy some time outside together today,' Papa agreed. 'Perhaps we could take a walk in the gardens before Sabina's lessons start.'

'Lessons *today*?' Vreni spluttered. 'But I just woke up.'

'Papa, it's our first day together,' Rita said. 'Surely you want to spend time with your daughters.'

'Life must go on as normal,' Papa said firmly.

'Normal,' Vreni said bitterly. To Papa, normal meant lessons, walks in the garden, trivial amusements, and endless reasons for never going anywhere.

Parvils looked at Vreni, holding her gaze for a long moment. 'Very well, if your legs are awake enough, we can hike down the trail and take a picnic, maybe the ponies if Artūrs has time. I'll call Sabina and reschedule lessons for two o'clock.'

'But Papa—' Vreni and Rita protested in unison.

'They,' Parvils began and then quickly corrected himself, '*Sabina* insisted on starting your lessons again immediately. She said she didn't want to waste time.' He returned stiffly to his breakfast.

Vreni watched him for a moment, wondering what was

going on. Who had Papa meant by 'they'? Why was it so urgent to have lessons?

Sabina's lessons had changed during the last few awakenings. When she was alone with Sabina there seemed to be much less of the usual history and literature now, and more herb lore and similar lessons. Those separate lessons felt strange, like she was viewing them from the corner of her eye and couldn't quite see, or remember, what she learned.

And then there were the strange dreams that always followed the lessons, a mishmash of voices chanting, and pungent aromas and a storm of images. Vreni always woke from them feeling confused and unsettled. She shivered as she remembered her dreams.

'You like catching up on all the gossip with Sabina,' Parvils said, too cheerfully. 'She'll be here soon enough, so eat up. Let's not waste a minute.'

BEACH

All things of the earth and from the earth have their nature
that cannot be changed, only accepted.
True wisdom is to see that our own nature
is no more easily changed than any other thing.
But things can be understood and used to their best purpose.
—Book of Forest Lore

***

Within the hour they had left the symmetry of the manicured gardens that surrounded the house and started along the narrow path leading down to an isolated strip of beach. Parvils followed behind, carrying the picnic things.

The ragged cliff face showed layers of rock worn bare from eons of erosion and exposure by the ravages of wind and ocean storms. The cliff-side trail was steep, and wound in and out of pockets of lush rainforest.

Vreni stopped at an opening in the forest and stood on the very edge of the cliff, looking down as the waves hit the rocks below and surged upward in a forceful explosion of spray. She took hold of a scrawny tree and leaned out over the edge, feeling gravity pulling on her body. She imagined flying, and wondered if the tree would break or its roots pull free from where it clung to the rocky ground.

Not knowing what might happen captivated her. She hung there, watching the waves smash against the rocks. She felt the tree flexing with her weight, heard it quietly creak under the strain.

'Vreni, surely you're not in *that* big a hurry to get to the bottom,' her father said from behind her.

'No, Papa.' She sighed and returned to the path. She walked on down the damp cliff track in silence.

Rita was right. Apart from things they had no power over, like the curse, or being forced to leave Vārve during wartime, her life was good. She and Rita lived like princesses. But now Vreni wanted to be part of the real world. She didn't want to just look at the world from the tower, or on Rita's computer.

The beach was a blinding mass of sparkling light bouncing off the blue-green water. They stopped at the end of the path and removed their shoes, tying the laces together and slinging them around their necks. Their feet sank into the warm sand. Each step they took squeaked as the grains of sand rubbed against each other. They shuffled through the grains, creating a tuneless song until they reached the damp sand nearer the water.

Without speaking they turned southward, as they always did. Vreni wished her mother were here too. How long had it been since they were all together? Her breath caught in her throat. She took Papa and Rita by the hand

and felt her throat relax. They continued along the beach together, following the random, curving line of foam left by the receding waves.

Vreni found a creamy, smooth shell and picked it up, brushing the sand away. 'Is this one good enough to be our keepsake for today?' She held it out to Rita and her father.

They always took one shell home and placed it a glass bowl as a record of their days together on the beach. Back in Vārve they had collected pebbles, and now they enjoyed keeping up the tradition with shells.

'This one is fine,' Papa said, taking the shell. 'Rita?' She nodded, so he placed it in his trouser pocket. 'Let's turn back and find a place to make camp.'

Their father sounded like an explorer. Vreni knew that he would 'um' and 'ah' until he found a suitable position, then he would arrange the blanket and bags of picnic things, all the while looking very thoughtful. Then he would take off his button-up shirt, displaying a white singlet and even whiter skin. Then roll up his trouser legs to his knees. It seemed this was about as adventurous as her father ever got.

'Will you choose a good place for us, Papa?' Rita said, smiling at Vreni.

They turned to walk back and noticed a far-off figure at the end of the strip of sand. The sound of hammering echoed down the beach.

'Too bad,' Papa said, 'looks like we'll have to share the beach today. Maybe we should offer the stranger some help.' Without another word he started jogging up the beach.

Rita laughed. 'Papa's so funny. How many years has he been playing that stranger trick?'

Vreni smiled. 'Well, it might be years since Papa told us that joke, but only weeks, maybe months, since we last heard it. Remember to look surprised. Papa and Artūrs still act like we're five years old.'

The girls followed their father along the beach, thoroughly amused. The sight of him running, even slowly, was quite a novelty.

As they approached the two men they played their part, looking surprised to see Uncle Artūrs. He was leading their two ponies from the float at the rear of his truck.

'Oh Papa, Uncle Artūrs, what a great surprise,' Rita said.

Vreni squeezed her father's arm. 'Thank you.'

'I thought you'd enjoy a ride before lessons,' he said.

'Caramel, have you missed me?' Rita kissed the tan pony's muzzle and patted her smooth neck.

Vreni looked at the deep brown face of her pony. 'You're not my Chocolate Soufflé, are you?' she whispered. 'But you're still beautiful.'

'Very observant, Vreni,' Papa said. 'No, these ponies aren't Caramel or Chocolate.'

'They're their daughters,' added Artūrs proudly. 'Fudge and Crackle.'

'They were born a few years ago. We trained them while you were sleeping,' Papa explained.

'So, do you like your father's clever names? You know, Caramel Fudge and Chocolate Crackle.' Artūrs tapped his finger against the side of his head. 'Your papa is a clever man.'

'Absolutely, Papa.' Vreni hugged her father tightly.

'Well, don't keep the ponies waiting,' Artūrs said.

The girls took the ponies' reins, and with a boost up they were sitting high on their smooth, bare backs. With a soft tap of a heel, the excited ponies trotted off along the water's edge. Their hooves made gentle splashing sounds as they moved through the shallows and each girl got to know her pony's moods.

Vreni sat tall on Crackle's back. The deep-brown mane flicked against her hands as they rode into the breeze.

'Let's go, Crackle.' She gave Crackle a firm nudge in the flanks, and the pony cantered down the beach. Each hoof-fall in the shallow surf sent up fine splashes of cool water onto Vreni's legs.

Fudge and Rita had come alongside, so she dug in her heels and Crackle lit off down the beach. She gripped the pony with her legs and took a tighter grip on the reins. Rita was catching up behind her and she felt Crackle's excitement grow.

Vreni leaned forward. 'Let's beat Rita to the end of the beach,' she called over the noise of hooves splashing in the foamy water.

Crackle snuffled her pleasure and breathed deeply. Vreni could feel the large ribcage expand under her. The pony let out an excited whinny and took off along the sand.

The wind buffeted Vreni's ears as she raced down the beach. Crackle's hooves made thumping, heartbeat sounds on the wet sand as she moved from a canter into a rhythmic gallop. Vreni leaned in close to her neck, smelling the salty mix of the sea air and the pony's sweat. Her heart danced in her chest. Her skin prickled with the heat of excitement.

Rita tried to pull ahead of them, but Crackle surged in front, enjoying the chance to be free, as did Vreni. She savoured the adrenaline of this moment, the unfamiliarity of the new pony.

Without warning, Crackle stopped abruptly and reared up. She thumped her hooves down on the sand, changed direction and moved back into the water. Vreni, caught off guard by the sudden change of direction, began to lose her balance. Crackle waded out into deeper water and skittered playfully as the cold waves tickled her belly.

Vreni gripped harder with her legs, but it was too late. She slipped sideways. Crackle gave one last squirm of delight and Vreni plunged into the surf. The unexpected cold of the water forced a groan of surprise from her lungs. A small wave broke over her head, washing her hair over face.

She cleared the tangles from her eyes and felt the playful nudge of Crackle's nose rubbing up against her cheek. 'So now you're my rescuer, hey?'

Vreni stood up in the waist-deep water. The soft swell rocked her and pushed her against Crackle's shoulder. Crackle's eyes sparkled playfully, and the pony shook her head as if mocking Vreni.

'You look pretty happy for someone who just got thrown off her horse,' Rita called from the water's edge.

'Crackle surprised me,' Vreni said. 'She has a restless soul.'

'Just like her rider,' teased Rita. 'Does this mean I win?'

'Maybe,' Vreni said, leading Crackle back out of the water.

Rita came closer and offered a hand so Vreni could climb back up.

'Thanks, Rita.' Vreni sat dripping and smiling on Crackle's back. 'First one to lunch is the winner.' She kicked Crackle's flanks and galloped up the beach to where Parvils and Artūrs sat on a deep-blue blanket, leaning again two smooth rocks.

'We trained Crackle to dump you like that, you know,' Parvils said, laughing, as the girls tied up the ponies.

Parvils and Artūrs had begun eating already, and were congratulating themselves on the pony-breeding project. The blanket was covered with bowls and plates that contained chicken, potato salad dressed with sour cream, meat-filled pastries called pīrāgi and rye bread. There was also a small tray of cheese and dill cucumber. Vreni knew the round tin contained sweet apple bread to go with the milky coffee they would have later.

'Come, eat, we have a feast,' Parvils urged.

They had barely finished lunch when Parvils looked at his watch. 'We should brush down the ponies and get back up to the house.'

'That's it,' Vreni whispered into Crackle's ear as she brushed the pony's neck. 'Back to the corral for us both.'

Vreni slumped in the back seat of Artūrs truck and brooded on the way back to the house. She knew she was returning to the tedium that trapped her. She longed for … not knowing what might happen next, like when

Crackle had thrown her into the surf, or when she had held herself out over the cliff edge, wondering if the spindly tree would break. Vreni wanted to go somewhere, do something, *anything* but the ever-after of lessons and time-filling drolleries.

Sabina's car followed the truck as it turned into the grounds and stopped at the front door.

'Stop here,' Parvils said to Artūrs, waving at the tutor. 'I want to speak to Sabina. You go on and settle the ponies, girls. Then tidy yourselves and get ready for your lessons.' He got out of the truck and walked stiffly toward Sabina.

From outside the stables, Vreni watched what looked like an argument between Sabina and their father. Even from a distance, the tension between them was evident. Their raised voices drifted on the breeze, but Vreni couldn't hear anything but the emotional tone of their discussion.

LESSONS

The young Veronika is showing great potential.
She could be the one.
Continue with her instruction in the old magic,
but hide it from her until we're certain she is the one.
—Instructions to Sister Sabina

***

Sabina showed no sign of the mysterious argument with their father when the girls met her in the conservatory.

'Hi, Sabina,' Rita said.

'Hello, Sabina.' Vreni hugged the tall, dark-haired woman warmly. 'I'm glad it's you again.'

'I'm so pleased you've woken, Vreni,' Sabina said gently. 'And you're both awake together. That's wonderful for you.'

'So, tell me all the gossip,' Vreni said, trying to delay the start of lessons.

'Let's have some tea and a *little* gossip, and then lessons,' Sabina said. A flash of seriousness crossed her face before she smiled and took the girls by the hand.

They sat on cane chairs at the end of the conservatory,

beside the tea tray. Lessons had always been an inevitable part of Vreni's life, but in truth she enjoyed the company of a tutor, especially when her mother slept so long. Sabina made them work hard, but she also tried to help fill the gap when she noticed that the two sisters were missing their mother.

Once Vreni was old enough to be curious, each of her tutors, sent by the Wise Sisters, had also become her link to the world, especially before there was the internet. She loved seeing how the world of women had changed while she slept. The tutor's clothing was always different, along with the outside world.

'Sabina, your dress is beautiful,' complemented Rita.

'Thank you.'

'Did you buy it *online*?' Rita asked, sounding proudly expert on the topic.

'Online? Please tell me you're using that computer for study and not shopping,' Sabina said.

'Well, I had some time on my own, and I was bored. You should see what I ordered last week, Vreni. The parcels should arrive any day,' Rita said.

'I know I've only been asleep three years, but apart from Rita's shopping what changed during that time?' Vreni asked Sabina. 'What's new? Has anything amazing happened? Have they gone to the moon again?' She laughed. She always asked this question.

Sabina smiled. 'No, no one's been to the moon lately.'

They shared questions and answers about music and fashion, gossip and world events until the tea went cold.

Sabina fidgeted a little before saying, 'I'd like to instruct each of you separately sometimes, like we started doing in our previous lessons. That way you can each concentrate on the subjects that interest you most.'

'The herb-lore lessons we started were interesting,' Vreni said. She shrugged apologetically. 'But I don't seem to remember much from them at all.'

Sabina's eyes flicked around the room in an odd manner, and then she smiled. 'Don't be too hard on yourself,' she said finally. 'The Pratigs Māsa, the Wise Sisters, train for many years to develop their skills and knowledge. We have time enough for you to learn what you need to.'

'Learn what I need to? But I'm not one of the Sisters.'

'Well, think of it as a ... family tradition.' Sabina looked uneasy for a moment. 'In this technological world, they want us believe that the time of magic is in the past, but nature still has amazing resources to offer, if you learn how to use them.'

'But it's not just nature.' Vreni said. She felt that Sabina's answer was a bit shallow. 'What about the charm the Wise Sisters gave Papa? Surely magic that strong can't be brushed aside so casually. The power must still be there or Papa would be dead and gone by now, like Peters.' She pressed her lips together firmly.

If there was no magic, the curse would disappear and their family would be free. What was all this double talk about?

Vreni decided to play along with Sabina and her superficial answers. 'Of course I want to learn more about herbs. Then maybe I can make a love potion and get a boyfriend, or make a charm to convince Papa to let us go somewhere.'

Sabina stood abruptly, looking serious. 'Vreni, it's herb lore for you. And, for Rita, art and design. But for now, let's concentrate on history.'

Sabina had ignored her hint again. 'Sabina, could you plan a trip for us,' she said, 'to the city maybe? Somewhere that would help with our studies, of course.'

'We went to the zoo when we were younger,' Rita added, 'two tutors ago.'

'I'll give it some thought,' Sabina said.

Vreni sighed. Sabina had said that before and nothing had happened.

They settled themselves at a large round table in the centre of the conservatory where they spent several hours studying most days. Over the years they had studied languages, history, geography, mathematics, science, the arts and literature.

History and geography had always been the most interesting to Vreni. The world had changed so much over her own, century-long lifetime, and the stories in her family's journals wound back for hundreds of years. People and events from history intrigued her.

Sabina began as she always did, by retelling some version of the family history.

'Many centuries ago, before the cursing, your family traded within the Hanseatic League. They had developed strong skills for investment, so over the centuries their wealth grew enormously. This monetary power allowed us—you,' she corrected sharply, 'to pick and choose where and when to move, so the family stayed hidden from the world. The Baltic was the world back then, and it was so big that hiding was easy ...'

Vreni's thoughts drifted. What would it have been like if the curse had never been put in place, or if it could have been removed somehow? But then she would have lived all her years back in a different time. She would never have seen all the changes throughout her century. Her family would have lived a different life, and she would never have been *this* Vreni, living in *this* time.

Sabina coughed loudly and Vreni focused again.

'... the family was very influential, trading and travelling the rivers of Europe,' Sabina was saying. 'Then the cursing caused them to turn all of their endeavours inward, to protect and conceal their own, but their generosity had bred staunch loyalties and many people helped the family seep into the forests and take up a reclusive life.'

'But they had the magic,' Vreni challenged.

'They did,' Sabina agreed, 'but so did Veca Tante, and she was enraged when she heard that the Wise Sisters had softened the curse. She still wanted your grandmother Ieva dead, and if she couldn't do it with magic, then she, and her alchemists, would find a more direct way.'

'But when we sleep, aren't we ...' Vreni's question trailed off.

'When you sleep, you don't age or die, but if you're harmed enough the injury becomes fatal when you wake,' Sabina said quietly.

'So they hid Grandmama Ieva from Veca Tante.'

Sabina nodded. 'There were other concerns, too. The

Christians made pilgrimages into the northlands, and they wouldn't have taken lightly to meeting women who seemed to stay alive forever, nor would they have looked kindly on women with the unexplainable *powers* the Wise Sisters possessed. As the Son of God grew in importance, the word *witch* replaced the name Pratigs Māsa, or Wise Sisters. The family needed to stay hidden, and their caretakers became secretive although they remained loyal to them throughout the centuries.'

Vreni knew most of the family history, but each retelling added another layer.

'Over those earlier centuries people always desired to invade and control,' Sabina said, 'but in this last hundred years since you girls were born, there have been weapons and technologies that seem to have shrunk the world down to the size of a colourful toy ball.' Sabina held up Vreni's yarn ball and threw it toward her.

'Many nations have claimed the Baltic territories since your grandmother's time,' Sabina said, 'but there were still places to hide back then. When the Soviets swept in with cruel indifference and greed, seeking a coastal port that wouldn't freeze their ships in place in winter, they wanted everything. It seemed they could see everything, so the Wise Sisters and your family decided to hide in plain sight among the refugees fleeing the war, and we travelled to our new life, here.'

When the time had come to flee, Vreni and Rita had been in long-sleep, but everyone else was awake so the travel plans were finalised quickly, and they had walked away towards a new life. Parvils had called it luck that they were both asleep, because many border officials thought they were ill and hurried them through in case they caught the sickness.

Their father told them they were wonderful actresses, trying to make light of the huge changes, but at times Vreni still felt panic at the strangeness of having woken in this weird new place, with its topsy-turvy seasons, bizarre animals and plants, and everything she had known gone.

'Enough history for now,' Sabina said. 'Vreni, I'll work with you today. You can go, Rita, but no more shopping.'

Rita made a quick exit from the conservatory before Sabina could change her mind.

Vreni's stomach lurched as she remembered how dizzy and out of control she had felt after her last private lesson with Sabina.

Why can I only remember fragments of those other lessons? If it was some kind of family tradition, why wasn't Rita doing them too?

SIGNS AND SECRETS

For the magic of the glimmer to continue to hold strong,
Veronika needs to freely agree to the beginnings of her
preparations. Invite her to join us someday, and
her acceptance will add strength to the glimmer's spell.
—Instructions to Sister Sabina

***

'Why doesn't Rita get the same lessons as me?'

Sabina gathered her thoughts for longer than she usually did before she spoke. 'The Wise Sisters are your heritage, Vreni. The first of us were your grandmother's aunts, so it's in your blood, and we see potential in you.'

'For magic? But I—'

'The Wise Sisters employ many types of knowledge, and practise many skills to keep the old magic alive.'

'And you'll teach me? But why not Mama or her sisters? What about Rita?'

'We've watched all the sleepers and waited. We, the Wise Sisters, see in you the signs of something the others don't have. For reasons you will understand later, it has once more become important that the magic stays strong, and grows even stronger still. I—we—would like you to learn our ways so that one day you will add your strength to the Wise Sisters'.'

'Me, become a Wise Sister?'

'It will be your choice, one day. Can I ask you, out of tradition, not to share this conversation with anyone?' Sabina said.

'I-I won't,' Vreni stammered.

'Thank you, Vreni,' Sabina said. 'And now, enough of this chatter. We'll continue with herb lore. Let's see ...' she said, thumbing through a thick notebook with a rich blue leather cover.

Vreni's head spun with the strange newness of what she had heard, with the idea that she might join Sabina and someday learn all about the magic and become ... what?

'Sabina?'

'I know, you're full of questions.' Sabina closed the book and took Vreni's hands. 'I've been kind and cruel to you all at once, so I'll tell you just a little more about being a Wise Sister. There's a lot to learn, and you need patience and self-control, so start practising those right now,' Sabina said, smiling.

Vreni groaned as Sabina pointed to the blue book.

'You've been learning about using gems as charms for strength and protection ...'

Sabina's voice started to sound distant, full of echoes.

'... and how to use cloves to ...'

The words bounced in and around in Vreni's awareness. They were slippery. It was hard to hold their meaning.

The room became hazy around her. It tilted and seemed to lose its edges.

'... use your voice to release your intentions, to influence or enliven a spell ...'

Vreni heard many voices. She could feel her throat vibrate with song. Her ears throbbed, they were full of chanting. Was she a part of this music? She wasn't sure. Her heart beat in time to the strange phantom rhythm—she could feel swaying movement all around her—and then all was quiet again.

'... fragrances from herbs and oils can soothe, persuade, defend ...'

The air around Vreni was now a hazy tangle, thick with cloying aromas. Her nose twitched as each new fragrance drifted past her, twisting on the meandering air. She breathed in the sweet vapours. Words, fragrances and images became a confusing broth in her mind.

'Liquorice brings new love and clove for compliance ... burdock and caraway will offer protection ... geranium is a healer ... courage from cardamom ... pine and sage for the sacred wisdom ... beech is wish-magic ...'

Vreni became aware of the conservatory again.

'Well done, Vreni, that was a great afternoon's work,' Sabina said.

'Thank you.'

The lesson writhed and squirmed just out of reach of her memory. No matter how hard Vreni tried to hold it clearly in her mind, it faded away, just as the others had before it. She didn't tell Sabina. She didn't want her tutor to change her mind and think Vreni wasn't worthy of training as a Wise Sister.

***

The days and weeks after Vreni woke crawled by. Sabina came and went from the house. Vreni overheard more hushed arguments between her and Papa. They tried to make it look like Papa was walking her to her car, or helping her with a task, but the tension between them and their heated conversations were evident.

Vreni had asked Sabina again if she would take them on an outing, maybe to a natural history museum, or the botanical gardens. No plans were made.

The private lessons continued, and remained misty and confusing. Sabina assured Vreni that she was pleased with her progress, but Vreni felt increasingly confused and frustrated by her forgetfulness.

Between lessons there was time for music, books, the internet and the ponies, but even with all these distractions Vreni felt like a bird in a cage, unable to stretch her wings and fly.

Parvils had noticed her restlessness, and he was spending extra time with her, engaging her in long discussions. She loved debating with him as he had a knack of taking an opposing view in everything. But she didn't want to just observe the world, or debate about it, she wanted desperately, to be part of it.

Yes, she had a history, a past, and a present that never

changed, but she didn't seem to have a future—not one that she had chosen anyway.

When yet another day's lessons had finished, Vreni mumbled goodbye to Sabina and went to the tower to be alone.

The room at the top of the tower was an octagonal glass chamber ringed with low window seats. During the day it was flooded with light and the changing colours of the sky. At night, the glass became a strange kaleidoscope, reflecting and re-reflecting the room. Some nights she would turn off the lights and the room became an observatory, surrounded by the jewels of stars, and the creamy light of the moon.

At least up in the tower she could look out over the world and pretend she had a chance of being out there one day.

The sky was filling with angry clouds. She watched the sea turn from a calm sparkling blue into a thrashing hideous monster, rearing and howling as the storm winds came. She had a storm inside her too—twitchy, discouraged, fuming.

She flung open the windows and let the storm gust in and mix with her own angry tempest. Her tears mixed with the cold, stinging raindrops.

The storm passed. She tried to shake off her feelings of frustration as the afternoon sun broke through the thinning clouds. Standing in the centre of the tower room, she turned slowly, looking at the cliff edge and the sea, then the fruit trees and stables, next the pine grove to the west, with glimpses of the road beyond that led to the world.

She kept turning, her eyes skimming across the organised patchwork of the garden beds and back to the sea. Staring out the tower window at the calming waves, she waited for her composure to return.

MONSTERS

We never know when the sleep will call,
so birthdays make no sense at all.
Count the days you've been awake,
to know when it's time for gifts and cake.
—Family rhyme

***

'Looking for sea monsters, Vreni?' Rita said as she appeared at the top of the tower stairs.

Vreni huffed out a weak laugh and turned toward her sister. 'Maybe we're the monsters now. Freaks.' She sighed and looked back at the sea.

'Come on, Vreni, think of all the things we've seen because of who we are,' Rita said, trying to lighten her sister's mood. 'What about cars, Vreni, *automobiles*? They're not as friendly as horses, but there are no droppings to pick up.'

Vreni smiled and sat on the narrow top step next to Rita. 'I remember how frightening cars seemed when I was young, but you held my hand and I felt safe,' Vreni said.

'Well, I was your big sister for a while back then, and that was my job,' Rita said.

'So many changes.'

'Electricity.' Rita nudged.

'Radio.' Vreni nudged back.

'Television.' Rita covered her face with her hands. 'I thought you'd captured fairies and put them in a strange glass cage for me.'

'Well, *I* was the big sister then.'

'I cried when Papa turned off the TV.' Rita laughed. 'I thought the fairies had died.'

'The moon landing!' Vreni grabbed Rita's hand. 'Rita, I wish you'd been awake in 1969. I watched as they landed on the moon. I couldn't breathe as Neil Armstrong stepped onto that new world. I thought that by now we'd *all* be able to go to the moon any time we liked.'

Rita laughed. 'Earth to Vreni! What about the dresses, shorter, and shorter, and shorter,' she said, pulling up her skirt.

'Jeans!' Vreni said. 'I could kiss the genius who invented jeans.'

'Neil Armstrong and the jeans genius ... Vreni, I think you need a real boyfriend.' Rita ducked and laughed as Vreni swung to slap her.

'I wish,' Vreni said. 'Anyway, I've been looking through my journal and I counted my days awake. Since 1904, I've been awake for five thousand, eight hundred and thirty days. I'll be sixteen soon.'

'Me, too,' Rita said. 'I was born two years later, but I've

counted five thousand, eight hundred and twenty-seven days awake, so we're twins now.' She laughed.

Vreni was enjoying listening to Rita buzzing with gossip and girl talk. They weren't often awake at the same time, so these moments together were a pleasure. Who else would understand her daydreams about boyfriends, or of spending time alone and out in the world, away from her family's always-watchful eyes.

'We have birthdays coming up,' Rita said, nudging her out of her daydream. 'Let's shop for presents. Thank goodness they invented the internet. How boring was life before online shopping.' Rita opened her laptop.

'But what about *real* shops?' Vreni said. 'Going to real shops, or out to eat lunch, or the cinema, or dancing, a party, an art gallery, a concert, maybe even travel. I want to be part of the world, Rita, not just watching it on that thing.' Vreni pointed to the laptop, its screen flickering with bright colours.

They planned a fantasy day of shopping in the city. Rita flicked from one website to another, all showing images of shops with their windows crammed with fashion, and streets crowded with people. Vreni imagined walking from shop to shop, surrounded by the excitement of the city, people everywhere, eating, talking, laughing, holding hands, sharing a kiss.

'How could we be almost sixteen and never have made any ordinary decisions on our own?' Vreni said. 'We've never even had to decide when it was it safe to cross the road.'

'Well, let's decide now. Come on, we'll make a list of

birthday presents and order something special,' Rita said, shoving the computer into Vreni's lap.

'What I want, when I turn sixteen, is to be able to *act* like I'm sixteen. To go *there*,' she said, jabbing at the images on the screen, 'and not be trapped here, having the world delivered in postage bags.' She slammed the laptop closed.

'We could ask Papa if we could go to the shops instead of having presents delivered,' Rita said sceptically.

'I've already asked Sabina about a study trip and she acted like she'd never heard me, so I can't imagine how Papa would react if we asked.'

***

Vreni tried to forget about the city and concentrate on her studies, but one afternoon, during a private lesson with Sabina, she was distracted again by the idea.

'Vreni, you look troubled,' Sabina said.

Vreni sighed. If anyone were going to be sympathetic, surely it would be Sabina.

'I'm just restless,' she said. 'It's always lessons and crafts and amusements. I can't make you understand, because you are part of the world. You can't know how trapped I feel, and Papa seems satisfied to stay in his own private world, so how could I convince him? I want to go somewhere. I want to go to the city.'

'You've seen a lot of the world on the computer,' Sabina said gently. 'It's different for you girls now, and I can understand your feelings, but remember your unique situation.'

'I'm sure it *is* unique to be a prisoner in your own home,' Vreni said bitterly.

Sabina squeezed her hand.

'It's not like it was for Mama or Grandmama. Things are different now. Please, Sabina,' she whispered.

'Things are changing now,' Sabina said, more to herself than Vreni. 'I've been talking about such ... things with Parvils.'

'I've seen you and Papa together.' Vreni hesitated but continued. 'What are you two always arguing about?'

For a moment Sabina looked like she'd been caught out in a secret, and she looked down at the ground before answering. 'He's your father, so he's interested in ... how your lessons are progressing.'

'Papa could come and join in with the lessons anytime he wanted to,' challenged Vreni.

'He's protective of his daughters, of course. He isn't very happy with the ... interest we have in your future.'

'About me joining the Pratigs Māsa?'

'He has some reservations.'

'Why would he be worried? The Sisters have always protected us.'

'Well ...' Sabina looked at the floor.

What isn't she telling me?

'He's concerned about you having an outing.'

'So, you're trying to arrange something.' Vreni heart galloped and she forgot her concerns.

'I have a few ideas in mind,' Sabina mumbled.

'Like what? The city?' Vreni squeezed Sabina's hands.

'I need to talk more with your father.'

There were more heated conversations between Sabina and Parvils over the next few days. Vreni could never hear what was being said. She hoped the debate was about the trip to the city. She thought she would feel better if she told Rita about her conversation with Sabina, but after she did, she had to listen to Rita's endless chattering what-ifs, which seemed to double the agony of waiting for Papa's answer.

FLEDGLINGS

I know Parvils has been reluctant, but the world has
changed too much, and secluding the sleepers
is not a viable strategy with this generation,
or for our plans to free the family from the curse.
Arrange an outing, but plan it well. We need
to see what our bird is like when she leaves her cage.
We may need her to work with us very soon.
—Sister Anna's counsel to Sister Sabina and Parvils

***

'I've been ... talking with Sabina about an outing,' Papa said, sipping his coffee.

'Finally,' Vreni whispered. She squeezed Rita's hand under the table.

'Most fathers don't wait a century before their daughters come to them seeking permission or his blessing to venture out into the world.'

'Well, Papa, surely you don't mean to keep us prisoner here forever,' Vreni said jokingly.

'All this was so much easier in the old times,' Papa said.

'Back then there were so many rules about what a young woman couldn't do that a father didn't have to be the one saying no. The whole of society said it for him.'

Parvils toyed with the magical amulet hanging around his neck as he looked at his daughters, who looked restless and determined. He had listened to Sabina talking about her plans for Vreni's training. Even though he was concerned, he was not in any position to resist the guidance of the Wise Sisters, so he had agreed.

Parvils smiled at Vreni. He had known many years of waiting, so he understood her restlessness too well. Rita was a squirrel out to gather pretty things, but Vreni was a bird that was becoming too big for the nest. He knew she needed to spread her wings and fly, even just for a short while. This moment was always going to come, the moment when his daughters would seek a world bigger than family and home.

'When I met your mother back in 1867, just having a husband was adventure enough for her.' He smiled. 'But things have changed. You've seen glimpses of what you're missing. This internet is a bad thing for fathers because it shows you the world. But how can I stop my fledglings from wanting to fly away from the nest?'

'So we can go?' Vreni held her breath.

'Yes, you can go, but there are rules,' he cautioned, 'lots of rules.'

'Thank you, Papa,' the sisters said in unison. They hugged their father, spilling his coffee.

'I'll be in danger if your mother wakes while you're away in the city shopping.' He smiled, mopping up the mess. 'Uncle Artūrs will drive you into the city and stay outside every shop at all times.'

'Of course, Papa,' Rita said.

'Whatever you think best,' Vreni said.

Artūrs was her father's trusted companion, and the protector of his most precious things. Vreni knew that without Artūrs watching over their every move, there would be no shopping trip. She told herself it would be enough freedom—for now.

SHOP TILL YOU DROP

Archangel root and thistle to safeguard against danger,
sage for wisdom, cardamom for courage, clove and a
grain of liquorice for friendship, and garnet for protection.
—*Vreni's glimmer journal*

***

Vreni woke early, too excited to sleep. 'The city.' The words rang in her ears. 'The amazing, mysterious, exciting city,' she whispered. She imagined wings unfurling as she stretched.

She may have travelled halfway around the world with her family, but she had never even bought herself a coffee on her own. Finally Papa was allowing them to go to the city and she had her chance for a little freedom.

She quickly washed her face and bundled her hair into a knot on top of her head, then rifled excitedly through the decades within her closet, choosing boots, her favourite washed-out jeans, T-shirt, scarf. As she pulled on her jacket, she smiled at her memories of the strange things women had considered fashionable throughout her century, and what might come next.

She checked herself quickly in the mirror, grabbed her bag and hurried to Rita's room, thumping on the door.

'Shop till you drop, sister,' she called.

'I'm way ahead of you,' Rita called from halfway down the curving stairs.

Vreni chased after her and they burst into the kitchen together.

'I fear for the family fortune, letting you two modern young ladies loose near real shops,' Parvils said. 'I've seen the accounts from your spending through that awful device.' He passed over two steaming bowls of porridge.

'Online shopping, Papa,' Rita said, trying to convince her father of the virtues of the computer as they ate. 'It brings us amazing things from far away, just like the travelling traders who used to call in the summers in Vārve.'

'But back in Vārve,' Parvils said, 'I got to decide which traders to turn away from the door, or at least I could strike a bargain. Sometimes poor Artūrs can barely carry all your parcels from the post office. Be kind to him on your trip today, and make sure you leave something for other people to buy.'

Parvils smiled as he watched his daughters eating breakfast, chirping excitedly about their adventure like a pair of baby birds.

***

The car ride to the city only took an hour, but to Vreni,

fidgeting in the back seat, it felt far longer. As they drove through the deserted coastal scrublands towards the edges of the city suburbs, she pinched herself once or twice to check she wasn't dreaming. It all felt as though it might be magic. She thought about what Sabina could have said to make Papa agree. Maybe she *had* used magic.

Vreni was wondering more and more about magic, especially when she thought about the strange private lessons she was having. There were no secrets in the family about things like the Pratigs Māsa softening the curse, or Papa's long-life charm, but apart from that her family didn't feel magical, and neither did her life, but the lessons were strange.

When would the Wise Sisters ask her to join them? She was finding it so difficult to remember the lessons and feared she wouldn't be good enough after all.

Vreni shivered and turned her attention to her sister. 'Do you know what you're going to buy?' she asked Rita.

'Shoes are the hardest thing to buy online,' Rita said, sounding like an expert. 'I've bought so many pairs and returned nearly all of them.' She rolled her eyes at Artūrs as he groaned from the driver's seat.

'I'm too busy for shoes,' Artūrs said, smiling over his shoulder. 'And the postmistress winks at me now when I say hello.'

'Don't worry, Uncle Artūrs, I'll try on every pair of shoes I can to save you from the postmistress,' Rita said.

'Shoes would be nice,' Vreni agreed. She flicked the corners of a thin bundle of money, and then shoved it back in her pocket. 'But not those heels you wear, they look dangerous. All the colours are so bright now, it'll be hard to choose but definitely a red pair and maybe—'

'We don't have to choose,' Rita said, as she waved a small plastic card in the air between them. 'We have cash and this card. Do you remember the PIN?'

'Of course I do,' Vreni said.

Rita laughed. 'It'll be like we have Papa with his pockets full of money right beside us in every shop.'

'I saw some beautiful chains on TV, very long silver chains with amazing charms on them, and necklaces made of crystals,' Vreni said. 'I want to go to jewellery shops to look at all that sparkling stuff.'

'Bling.'

'Bling?'

'Bling,' Rita said knowledgably. 'Accessories.'

Vreni nodded and shrugged. 'I'd love a scarf.'

'*Another* scarf?' Rita tugged on the scarf around Vreni's neck. 'Don't you already have seventy-five?'

'And don't you already have enough shoes?'

With their list completed they became quiet. Staring out the car windows, watching the sea of houses crushing more closely together, and the roads becoming wider and busier.

The buildings of the approaching city loomed high into the sky. Vreni's heart was fluttering at the thought of even this small amount of freedom.

***

Vreni was used to the space of home. The city was like

a dense forest of buildings, sprouting lights and signs. It expanded until it was almost too large for her to comprehend. The computer had shown her city scenes and she had felt eager to be part of it, but now she was here everything seemed so frantic. Crowds of people raced up and down the sidewalks, and darted in front of the car in such a hurry.

She flopped back onto the seat and stared out at the sky for a moment. She opened the car window and her ears filled with roaring engines and honking horns. Clanking, disharmonious music was blaring from a group of street performers outside a crowded cafe. The air had a gritty feel, and smelled of dust and exhaust fumes. But drifting over it came the delightful aroma of freshly baked pastries, and the sweet fragrance of a flower shop with buckets of blossoms spilling into the street.

Everything was so fast and so loud, she felt the energy of the city all around her.

Artūrs manoeuvred the car through the traffic while the girls gave him directions from Vreni's phone. Vreni liked the phone more than the computer, it felt like a symbol of her independence. After finding a place to park, Artūrs told them he would wait for them and then take them to the next place they wanted to go.

Vreni glanced at Artūrs. Today he was Papa's most trusted eyes and ears, and their protector. People like Artūrs had served with love and loyalty through the centuries following the cursing, but Artūrs seemed the closest and most loyal of all.

Vreni wondered again about magic. Did Artūrs give his loyalty freely?

The question vaporised as Rita opened the car door and pulled Vreni by the arm onto the bustling footpath and into the first shop.

***

By the end of the morning's shopping, they had almost filled the car with purchases. Vreni's confidence was growing with every hour they spent in the city.

Artūrs insisted that he would not eat burgers and fries for anyone, so they conceded and let him choose a more stylish restaurant where they could buy food more like the type of midday meal he favoured, something heavy, spicy, and piled generously on a large plate.

After lunch the shopping continued. The girls' goal was to visit every shop on their list. Sometimes they bought things, but often they just looked and talked to all the people they met, soaking up the hype of the city.

***

The very last of the day's light flowed crimson-orange between the city buildings. Shop lights were starting to glow. As the sun had almost set and the long summer day was melting into a warm evening, they persuaded Artūrs to let them stay in the city into the evening, for as long as the late trading lasted.

Artūrs was happy to accommodate them. He had

enjoyed an easy day of reading and napping, and the temptation of choosing another restaurant for dinner before they returned home was all the encouragement he needed.

The girls entered a store called *Thing*. On the back wall was a huge screen showing music clips, with people dancing in a sea of brilliant strobing colour. The music washed over Vreni as she and Rita danced in and out of the racks of clothes and accessories, holding up outfits.

'The purple or the green?' Rita called, doing a quick turn to show off a top, with a second one draped over her shoulder.

'Green.' Vreni danced past with an armful of clothes, blowing a kiss as she went into the changing room.

As Rita returned the purple top to the display, she saw a man walk into the shop and move over to a wall covered with posters for concerts and dance parties.

'So, do I look like a gypsy now?' Vreni said, coming out of the changing room.

She saw the man near Rita, and watched him for a moment, gathering details in a series of glances. Tall, spikey fair hair, nice broad shoulders. She smiled at herself and her thoughts, and breathed out slowly.

He looked toward her. When she caught his eye, he quickly looked at the wall again. He wore a long brown coat, which hung down to his calves. The coat lay open, showing a white T-shirt with the word PARADOX printed on the front in orange lettering.

Vreni could not look away. His eyes were a piercing blue-grey, like a stormy sky.

He looked towards her again, and smiled. 'Well, I don't think you look great, stylish,' he said. He held her in his gaze as he walked toward her. 'Hi, I'm William, not really a fashion expert, at your service.' He offered his hand, and his smile broadened.

'I'm Vreni, thank you for the kind words.' She shook his hand, and her breath caught in her throat. 'This is my sister Rita.'

'Are the new clothes for tonight?' He pointed at a dance-party poster on the overcrowded wall. 'If you're going, maybe we could get some food before it starts. It's only five blocks east of here and the night markets are on, so we could look around there and eat.'

William still held Vreni's hand. Her heart was thumping. She stood frozen, caught up in his smiling gaze, not wanting him to let go. She could hear lots of good advice circling on the edges of her thoughts—advice about making sensible decisions—but she decided instead to go with her impulse.

'Yes, we'll be there tonight,' she said, her mind racing. 'We have a few things to do on the way, but I promise you a dance.' *What am I doing? But I might never get a chance like this again.*

Rita squeezed her arm, hard, but Vreni ignored her.

'Just one dance? But I've got loads stylish moves,' he said comically, still staring at Vreni. 'See you tonight.' He lifted the hand he was still holding and kissed it lightly, then turned and left the shop.

Vreni looked at her freshly kissed hand, which was trembling.

'What is your problem?' Rita said, punching Vreni's arm hard. 'How can we go to that dance party? Have you found some spell to send Papa to sleep, and Uncle Artūrs as well?'

Vreni felt as though she was being squeezed. She saw this as a single chance to escape the cage she had been held in until today.

'What, so you're telling me that lessons with Sabina and endless shopping is enough for you?' she snapped. 'Well, your carriage awaits.' She jabbed a finger toward the window, where they could see their uncle dozing in the parked car in the dim evening light.

Vreni walked over to the sales assistant and paid for the new clothes they were wearing. 'Is there a back door from the shop we could use?' she asked the shop assistant.

'Sure, through there.' The woman pointed, only half paying attention.

Vreni checked the address and time on the poster and stuffed her old clothes into her bag. 'Tonight, sister, we will *not* be sleeping princesses.'

She eased open the shop's back door and stepped, determined, into the alleyway. She stood holding her breath until she heard Rita grumble and slam the door behind her.

DANCE PARTY

A bird can be safe in a cage, but if it cannot fly,
is it ever really a bird?
—Pratigs Māsa, Book of Wisdoms

***

The girls stood close to each other for a few moments in the gloom of the alley.

'You've lost your mind, Vreni,' Rita snapped.

'Maybe I've lost my mind, but I've still got my brave sister.' Vreni looked at Rita. 'We have this chance, Rita, to be normal, to do things other girls take for granted.' She pecked Rita's cheek to lighten the mood. 'Anyway, we have some money, a mobile phone, and brave Uncle Artūrs to rescue us when we're tired of dancing with handsome guys.'

'And Papa?' Rita asked.

'Just a few hours of living, real living, and we'll return to our jail.'

'Jail?'

'Come on, Rita,' Vreni said, grabbing her sister's arm.

They moved to the end of the alley and stopped. All at once Vreni felt very alone. Her hands were suddenly clammy. She wiped them on her jeans and turned east, following the people that she guessed were moving towards the night markets.

The evening streets became noisier and more congested as they walked. Crowds were gathering in the vibrant market square that had been set up in a blocked-off street. People stood about, clogging the footpaths, talking and listening to music. They were clustered around stalls and food vendors. Tables and chairs caused lumpy blockages outside restaurants, and spicy aromas filled the evening air.

Vreni led the way through the confusion of sensations, pushing through the frantic joy of it all. They stopped at stalls selling trinkets that Rita had called bling. Vreni found a new scarf, made of silk and bordered with lace and fringing.

Rita pointed. 'Look at her.'

A street performer was standing frozen like a statue while people tried to distract her and make her move. The audience rewarded her skills by throwing money into a wooden box at her feet.

Rita laughed. 'You could stand me here next time I'm in long-sleep and I'd earn us thousands.'

'Then you could buy even more shoes,' Vreni joked.

An acrid, chemical odour caught Vreni's attention. She heard a strange noise behind her, and saw the crowd disappearing out of the corner of her eye. She braced herself for trouble. She grabbed Rita protectively and turned them around.

The crowd had formed around a wide space, and in the centre of the circle were two shirtless men spinning flaming metal staffs around their heads and throwing them into the air across the circle to each other. A few people carrying drums pushed through the crowd. The first drummer offered a rhythm and the rest joined in, laying down a frenzied fast–slow of pulsing beats as if they were one mind, or one raucous beating heart.

The fire twirlers were now moving in time to the beat. Two girls joined the fire-dance, spinning burning balls of flames on the end of a glinting silver chain. The moving flames painted arcs of orange on the night sky.

The glorious noise and the dancing flames filled Vreni's awareness. Her heart took up the beat and calmed the racing nervousness she had felt ever since leaving the shop.

The two girls bounced through the street market until they became aware of their hunger. They found a sparse, brightly lit cafe filled with battered old tables and chairs that were unoccupied.

Vreni nudged her sister. 'We can have the burgers we missed out on at lunch.'

'Hello, beauties,' said a crumpled old woman sitting behind the counter. 'What will you have?'

'Burgers?' Vreni realised she wasn't sure how to order. 'And coffee with milk, thank you.' 'Pick a table Rita,' she said as the crumpled woman had written down their order and shuffled off to the kitchen.

'Do you think Uncle Artūrs has told Papa yet?' Rita asked as they slid into a booth.

Vreni's stomach clenched. She smiled and shrugged, not mentioning the times her phone had vibrated in her pocket over the last couple of hours. 'The dance party will be starting soon. I have to see it, but then we'll call Uncle Artūrs straightaway, okay?' she said, trying to sound reassuring.

The burgers arrived, but they ate half-heartedly, their stomachs too tight for more than a few mouthfuls. Soon they abandoned their meal and left the quiet cafe. Vreni found the warehouse on her phone and they zigzagged the last block and a half east.

***

The aging warehouse, now a dance club, glowed in a storm of flashing colour. The whole building pulsated with sound, sending waves of vibration through the streets. Vreni felt her heart change its rhythm to match the beat of the music.

'Vreni! Rita!'

William waved from beside the front door. He jumped between them and wrapped an arm around each of them as though they were old friends. Vreni also received an unexpected kiss on her cheek, causing her heart to rebel against the rhythm of the music.

Kiss, her mind sang, *kiss, kiss, kiss.*

William gave a friendly nod to the man at the door,

who nodded back and waved them into the dark musty shadows of the foyer.

'William.' Vreni finally found her voice as they walked toward the door. 'You really wanted your dance, then?'

'Still just one dance?' William said, leading the girls inside. 'Very funny.'

They stepped through the door and the music hammered at Vreni's ears. The massive vaulted space was a jungle of light that flashed and twisted as if it was alive. People danced in and out of the light, appearing and disappearing from view. Friends were clustered together on the edges of the dance floor, or at small tables, smiling and laughing, and trying to hear each other talking.

Vreni noticed couples in the shadowy places away from the crowd, enjoying a space all their own. Vreni thought of William's kiss, and her cheek felt hot.

'I'll find us a table,' William said. 'Do you want me to take that so you can dance?'

Vreni patted her pockets to make sure she had the phone, cash and card, then eased her backpack from her shoulder and handed it to William.

The girls took excited, unsure steps out onto the dance floor. For Vreni, it was amazing to be surrounded by the music, feeling the rhythm pulsing deep into her bones. No matter how loud they turned up the music when they danced up in their tower, it didn't compare to the energy of sharing this experience with a crowd. The thrill she felt pushed away any last morsel of nervousness she had.

Moving in and around the sea of dancing bodies, she noticed the looks some of the guys in the crowd were giving them. It felt strange. Vreni knew she was blushing. She felt flattered, and returned some of the looks with smiles.

She grabbed Rita, and moved to join a large crowd of girls who were laughing and dancing with their hands up in the air. The girls welcomed them, and they all bumped happily into each other as they danced. Vreni could smell all the different perfumes as she moved closer to the dancers. The feeling of belonging was delightful.

William's face appeared within the circle and he danced towards Vreni. He moved in close to her and took her hands. Her heart became acrobatic. He continued dancing, moving her backward until they had left the crowd of dancing girls behind.

Looking over William's shoulder, Vreni saw Rita laughing and pointing at her, kissing the air, before smiling and turning back to the circle of happy dancers.

William danced close to Vreni. They made their own private circle and people moved around them. The lights flashed and the music throbbed, but it all seemed to fade around Vreni until all she could see was William's face. She felt him close to her. It was dreamlike, but when she reached out to touch him, he *was* real and right there.

He wrapped his arms around her waist, leaned in and kissed her lightly. She felt giddy, amazed by everything that had happened. The absolute joy at being free and normal, and the kiss.

'You're wonderful,' she yelled.

He kissed her again.

Rita danced in between them and leaned in close.

'Three songs,' she said to Vreni, laughing. 'Enough dancing and definitely too much kissing.'

William winked, pointed to a table and walked over to it.

Vreni danced close to Rita and hugged her tight. 'This is all amazing.'

'Thank you, Vreni,' Rita said, 'for being brave and bringing me here.'

'It was nothing, just a small adventure for two sisters.' Then Vreni added, more seriously. 'I'll tell Papa it was all my idea.' She pointed across the dance floor. 'Little girl's room.'

Rita nodded and danced away towards William at the table.

***

Vreni stood for a moment in the gloom of the narrow hallway, giving her eyes time to adjust after leaving the bright lights of the toilets. An arm reached across her shoulders and she turned, expecting to see William next to her, but it was one of the many male faces that had ogled her on the dance floor. She smiled, moving away.

The man grabbed her and pulled her further down the dark hallway. She tried to cry out, but he pushed her against the wall. The air was squeezed out of her lungs, leaving her gasping. She pushed back against him, trying to free herself, but his broad body seemed to surround her.

'I've been watching you dancing.' His words felt sticky

and hot against her neck. 'I like your moves,' he said in a whispered growl.

She drew in a ragged breath. Her blood burned with a flood of adrenaline. Then her fear suddenly boiled away, leaving anger in its place. *Well, how do you like this move?* Leaning her head to the side and bracing herself, she smacked her head into his temple.

The surprise of the unexpected head butt earned her a moment. She tried to free herself, but he grabbed her again, rougher now, and pressed his body hard up against her. Her lungs seemed frozen with returning fear. When she had gathered enough breath, she screamed.

He responded by shoving her. Her head hit the wall. She felt dizzy. She swallowed down the vomit rising in her throat. He leaned into her again. Then the heavy, stinking presence of the stranger was gone.

She felt light. *Am I dead?* Her body crumpled to the floor.

When she opened her eyes, she saw William slamming her attacker against the opposite wall. Then he lifted his knee with surprising force into the man's groin, causing him to collapse onto the floor and vomit violently on the carpet.

William scooped Vreni up into his arms. 'You're safe now, you're safe. It's all right.'

She sobbed like a frightened child, gulping air. She'd thought long-sleep was the worst fate she had to face, but now she realised there were many more curses in this world. William's arms felt like a place of refuge.

Two large uniformed men grabbed the vomit-covered menace. Taking an arm each, they dragged him towards the front door. Some of the dancers offered up mock cheers as he was delivered to the police.

William got a glass of water from the bar and offered it to Vreni, and they slowly returned to their table. Rita was sitting with her head leaning into the corner, her eyes closed.

Vreni sat down heavily and let William's arms surround her. She sipped the water slowly, and with each sip her mind began to clear. She looked at her watch. She would need to face her father soon. At least Papa's wrath would never seem as frightening, ever again, after what had just happened. She sighed deeply, shuddering.

'Thank you, William,' she said. 'I don't want to think about what might've happened if you hadn't been there.' She felt the tears welling in her eyes again.

'But I was there. Don't let some weird creep like that stop you from dancing.' He smiled, trying to lighten the mood. 'Or I won't get to dance with you anymore.'

Vreni thought about how wonderful the night had been, dancing with William, kissing him. She let herself imagine, for a fleeting second, that her life was somehow different. She pretended that a night like this one could happen again. But the weight of the curse fractured the brief dream.

'I'll give you my email address,' William said.

'Great,' she said, knowing she would probably never use it but wishing she could somehow see him again.

She could imagine William being part of her life, the way her father was part of her mother's life. She thought for a moment about William watching over her, and waiting while she slept. But then reality intruded. How could she do that to someone? How could she begin to explain to William what her life was like?

'Rita, come on, it's time to go,' she said, nudging her sister.

Rita didn't move.

'Wow, she's a sound sleeper. I can't imagine nodding off in here.' William looked around the chaotic dance space.

Vreni's mind froze on one thought. *Sleep. Rita was asleep.*

'Wake up, Rita, we've got to go home.' Vreni shook her sister wildly. 'No! Not here, not now. Please, wake up.'

IF I DIE BEFORE I WAKE

*The body of a sleeper undergoes total cellular cessation
during long-sleep.
It does not decompose; it will not heal.
Whatever happens to the body while in long-sleep
will take effect once the sleeper wakes.*
—*Pratigs Māsa, New Records*

***

'What do you think she took?' William asked.

'What?' Vreni wheezed.

'You know, maybe she took a pill or something. You can get anything in a place like this.'

'No, not Rita, never.'

'Maybe someone slipped her something.'

'What? I need to call our ... driver.' Vreni reached for the phone in her back pocket. The screen was smashed.

'Use mine.' William handed her his phone.

'I don't know the number. I've never had to call before.' Vreni felt like a child.

'No problem, my car's up the road,' William said.

He scooped Rita up into his arms and leaned in close to her face. Then he looked at Vreni with a strange expression. He turned and raced around the edge of the dance floor to where the security guard stood near the entrance.

Vreni grabbed her bag and scrambled after him.

'Call an ambulance,' William was saying to the man, 'I think she's overdosed.'

He lay Rita on the matted shag-pile carpet in the foyer and checked her pulse, then her breathing. Then he locked eyes with the guard on the phone and indicated 'hurry up' with a rapid circling of his index finger. He turned back to the lifeless Rita, checked her breathing and pulse once more, and started to give chest compressions.

'No!' Vreni screamed and threw herself over Rita's sleeping body. 'You can't do that.'

This is all so totally wrong. Rita should be hidden away by now. Vreni knew that Rita looked dead. All victims of the curse always appeared dead when they were in long-sleep. She whispered the words from the ancient tale. 'No breath or warmth or flutter of heart ...'

'What?'

'Just get us out of here, please. Take us to your car. She'll be fine. I've seen this happen before,' Vreni begged. 'Please, now!'

'She won't be fine, Vreni. Let me help her ...'

The rest of William's words were drowned out by the sound of a siren. Moments later two paramedics burst into the foyer.

'I think she's overdosed,' William said, stepping out of the way.

The paramedics closed in on Rita. Their presence stripped Vreni of any remnants of control she might have had over the situation.

'Just leave her *alone*,' Vreni screamed.

William placed his arms around her, but now they felt more like a trap than a refuge.

'*Help* me, William. Don't let them take her. They'll hurt her.'

On the stretcher, Rita was disappearing into the cool neon evening outside the club. The paramedics slid her into the back of the ambulance.

'No!' Vreni howled again, jumping in after them, staying close to her sister.

When William tried to follow, one of the paramedics stopped him, saying, 'Family only.' William showed the man a small card, which Vreni couldn't read, and sat down beside her as the ambulance doors slammed shut.

The smell of antiseptic and adrenalin in the cramped space was almost suffocating. Bright lights and the buzz of urgent conversation mixed with the endless screech of the siren. Vreni sat frozen, trapped in the unreality of it all. She could hear William talking to the paramedic, but the words held no meaning for her numb mind. All she could see was Rita's shiny pink stiletto heels and the tangles of her copper hair, everything else that was happening was hidden behind the hunched paramedic.

Vreni heard a ragged sigh escape William's chest. She saw the paramedic sag as though he'd been deflated, and then he leaned over and signalled the driver. The siren fell silent. The paramedic looked at William, who looked back knowingly.

'There was nothing they could do, Vreni. I'm so sorry.' William squeezed her hand tightly and leaned back against the side of the ambulance.

'I know,' she said, with a detachment she hoped would be taken for shock and disbelief.

What was I thinking? Why did I ever believe we could be part of the real world? She stared at Rita, feeling as small and fragile as a glass bird. *I have to fix this.*

'What will happen now?' Vreni needed information so she could try to form some kind of plan. She had to get Rita home, hidden and safe, or her foolishness would cost her family dearly.

'We'll need to tell your family,' William began gently. 'There'll be paperwork. They have to find out why she died, so they'll have to do an autopsy.' William looked at the paramedic, who nodded confirmation.

'Autopsy?' Vreni's mind came suddenly awake. Sleepers are suspended somewhere outside of time, but if something happens while they sleep, the harm simply waits until they wake. Rita would never survive having her body opened and pieces removed for examination.

'That can't happen,' she said, 'I need to get her home.'

TRUST

The aroma of cloves, when warmed by the heat of the body, will compel a person to do the bidding of someone they hold in affection.
—Pratigs Māsa, herb lore

***

William and Vreni followed as the paramedics wheeled the gurney carrying Rita through the emergency department doors. The surreal parade moved down the noisy corridor and stopped at a small, brightly lit cubicle.

Vreni stood close to Rita, brushing wisps of hair from her face.

'Vreni, she's gone,' William said.

'Just for now,' she answered. 'But if I don't get her home soon she may be gone forever. William, *please*.' She gripped his shoulder and whispered urgently into his ear. 'I would offer my own life to keep my sister safe. We—*I* need you to help me get her home. Then you'll understand everything.'

William hugged Vreni. He noticed her perfume. He

breathed deeply and considered her request. Then he walked over and spoke quietly to the orderly, who turned and left them alone in the small white cubicle.

'We're lucky, I know the layout here.' He held out his ID card: *William Masters UNL*. 'I've been doing some lab stuff at uni. My father is obsessed that I study science—whatever, the details can wait until later.'

'So you'll help us?'

'Okay I'll help you, but for now you need to trust me. In a moment we're going to leave Rita here and walk out.'

'But—' Her eyes stung. 'She softly touched Rita's smooth cheek.'

'Trust.'

They walked out of Rita's cubicle and down the corridor past the triage desk, towards the exit. Vreni's feet felt like lead. William waved as they passed the desk. The staff looked at Vreni, then quickly looked away.

As they approached the main doors Vreni resisted the urge to run back to her sister. William took her arm and pushed her around the corner into a darkened corridor, and led the way towards the rear of the emergency rooms.

They re-entered Rita's cubicle. William quickly lifted up her limp body and they retreated into the half-lit hallway, hiding for a moment behind a storage cabinet before quietly moving back along the corridor. William looked from the main door to the fire door. Vreni wondered how they would get outside without being seen by the staff or setting off the fire alarm.

They stood in the shadows for long, agonising seconds. Vreni's heart thumped in her ears.

There were angry shouts as a scuffle broke out between two drunks in the waiting area. With all eyes focused on the fight, they took their chance and slipped out the main door and into the cool evening air.

'Help me with her,' William said. They each took one of Rita's arms and held her sagging body upright. 'Now she just looks like she's been drinking too much,' he said.

They walked as fast as they could with her dead weight between them. After a couple of blocks William veered into the same stark cafe Vreni and Rita had stopped in for dinner. The air inside the cafe was now thick with the rich aroma of roasted coffee and cinnamon.

They eased Rita into a booth. Her head lolled against the wall.

'Coffee, please,' William said to the crumpled woman who was reading a newspaper at the counter.

'Big party night, eh,' she grunted, nodding towards Rita.

'Yes, but she'll be no trouble,' Vreni said.

The old woman served a steaming pot of coffee, and a smaller jug full of warmed milk. She flicked a strange glance at Rita and placed three cups on the table.

'She might smell my coffee and wake up,' the old woman said. Then she turned and shuffled back to her newspaper.

William poured a cup of coffee and gulped down a large mouthful. 'My car is maybe three blocks from here.'

'But—'

'Trust. I'll be back in ten minutes.' He pushed through the door and disappeared down the street, his long coat flapping as he ran.

Vreni poured a cup of milky coffee and watched as the old woman flicked slowly through her newspaper. People trailed in and out of the cafe. Vreni forced herself to sip at her coffee. She counted the sips and watched the clock. Twenty-seven sips and she'd finished her coffee. No William. She added milk to his half-finished cup.

Fourteen sips later headlights flared outside. William walked in the door and Vreni let herself take a deep breath. They eased Rita from the booth and headed for the door.

'You take Sleeping Beauty home, eh,' said the crumpled woman. She looked up from her paper and caught Vreni in her gentle stare. Vreni shivered as she felt the woman's gaze remain on her as they left the cafe.

With an effort, they manoeuvred Rita safely into the back seat of William's car.

'South,' Vreni said, slipping into the front seat.

William looked at her and then at Rita's reflection in the mirror. 'What the hell have I done?' he whispered. 'They'll know it was us. They know me at St Mark's. I spend time in the labs for uni, and my dad's corporation gives heaps of cash for research so they'll remember I was there for sure.'

He looked at Vreni, who hadn't heard anything he'd said. She was staring straight ahead into the night.

'Trust,' he whispered and headed for the motorway.

WILLIAM

The young man is unaware of his lineage, but because of it,
he can be instrumental to our cause. It's also useful that he's
highly susceptible to the subtleties of herb and fragrance.
We cannot make him act against his will. We're
fortunate that his unconscious desires
align with our goals of attaining the potion.
We must thank the fates for sending him to us.
—Discussion between Sister Anna and Sister Sabina

***

Once in the car, Vreni spoke only to give William directions.

During the ten minutes since they had turned east off the highway William had been watching the set of headlights following in the rear-vision mirror. 'I didn't think we'd see anybody out here tonight.' He pointed over his shoulder.

Vreni turned her head quickly and looked. 'How long have they been behind us?'

'Not long,' answered William. 'Do you know who it is?'

'I think it's our driver, Artūrs.'

'How would he have found you?'

'Lucky coincidence?'

An image of the old woman from the cafe flashed into Vreni's mind. She could only speculate on how Artūrs had known they were heading towards home. She hadn't thought about what precautions he, Papa or the Sisters would have put in place to keep them safe.

A sudden flood of paranoia swept her. How far would her family go to protect them? What were they capable of? Suddenly feeling hot, she opened her window. The salty freshness of the sea air was cool on her face.

She knew things would never be the same again after this, but right now she didn't want to share any more weirdness with William. He was going to learn all about her family soon enough.

The road became narrower and darker as they drove closer to home. Vreni watched William's face in the glow of the dash lights. The whole day was starting to feel fictional and far away. She reached out and touched his hand. He twined his fingers through hers and they drove down the narrow, dark road without speaking.

They rolled slowly up the gravel drive and pulled up in front of the house. Vreni saw her father waiting at the front door. He took a step towards them, but then he slowed and froze.

The dark blue Mercedes pulled up close, too close, behind them. Papa's face was stony. He opened his mouth to speak but the words seemed stolen.

Artūrs broke the silence. 'Parvils, they're safe,' he said,

getting out of the Mercedes. 'Rita is ... sleeping. This young man has brought them back to us safely.'

Vreni couldn't bear seeing the look on her father's face. She pushed open the car door and ran to him. 'Papa, I'm so sorry. I encouraged Rita to go on this foolish adventure with me. It was just meant to be an hour of dancing. My phone broke and I couldn't call when I needed to.'

'My daughters are safe,' Parvils managed to say with a forced, faraway voice. He took Vreni into his arms. 'It seems a new chapter is opened.' He nodded at William across the roof of the car.

William could only nod in response. He lifted Rita from the back seat and stood in the darkness waiting.

'Follow me.' Artūrs led him up the stone stairs and through the wide front door.

Vreni watched as her father took third place in the procession. She tried to speak again, but her words were trapped in her throat. What could she say to make the situation better? Who else now knew about their family and its secrets? Papa, Artūrs and many others had worked so hard to keep the family safe, and she couldn't even resist the impulse to run off and go dancing.

She wished she could travel back to the beginning of the day and do things differently so her father could now see her as a young woman and not a childish spoilt girl. She swallowed the sob rising in her throat and fell into line behind her father.

Artūrs led William up the curving stairs and along the carpeted landing towards Rita's room. Her eyes stayed on William's back as he carried his burden. As he turned a corner, Vreni saw him look through the open door of a softly lit room. On the bed inside was her sleeping mother. Her mama had slept for so long now that Vreni could not remember when she had last been awake.

She felt flushed with guilt. She couldn't even remember when she and her mother had last talked. *All I've worried about is my own selfish wishes.*

William's eyes locked on Gaida's sleeping form and his chest heaved. Then he looked down at Rita, and finally turned back to Vreni with a look that was full of questions.

They entered Rita's bedroom, which felt cramped with so many people standing in the girlishly lavish space. William laid Rita gently on the bed. *What happens to William now?*

'I must thank you properly for protecting my daughters the way you did,' Papa said to William. His words were strong and gracious again. 'Let's sit in the library for a while, and enjoy some food, a drink.'

As the men left the room, Vreni finally let her bubbling emotions surface. Fear mixed with excitement, and guilt with pride. The feelings weighed heavily, and she sagged and sat next to her sleeping sister.

'Rita, I'm so sorry, I just meant to have a small adventure.' A slow tear rolled down Vreni's cheek. 'I never thought you would fall asleep. I should have stayed with you. No, I never should have made you go with me.'

Suddenly she was sobbing, and her words spilled out. 'You didn't see, but there was this horrible guy outside the toilets. He grabbed me. He wouldn't let me go. I was so scared I couldn't breathe.' Her tears splashed onto Rita's face. She wished the tears would wake her sister so she could be comforted. She curled up on the bed next to Rita, pressing her face into her sister's shoulder, and wept.

But Vreni had cried on sleeping shoulders before. She knew Rita would not wake and that she would have to deal with this alone.

When her tears had stopped, she sat up tall and wiped both their faces. Remembering all the good things about the day, she chatted with Rita as though she was awake.

'It was amazing, Rita. We had more excitement than I'd ever dreamed of before this day began. I didn't mean it when I said shop till you drop.' She sighed and smiled, then squeezed Rita's arm, leaned over and kissed her cheek. 'Sleep well.'

Though it was a childish superstition, Vreni whispered their private prayer.

'Now I lay me down to sleep,
I pray the Lord my soul to keep.
And if I die before I wake,
I pray the Lord my soul to take.'

'But you didn't die.' She walked to the door, dimmed the lights and looked back at her sleeping sister. 'But you didn't die.'

***

The library was warm. Flames ribboned up from the logs in the fireplace, and the familiar smell of books and woollen wall tapestries made Vreni breathe in deeply.

William and Papa were sitting in armchairs, facing each

other, each of them holding a glass filled with dark red wine. She walked slowly across to join the conversation. Artūrs entered the room behind her. He was carrying a heavy tray of supper foods.

Papa smiled. 'William has told me about your ... evening, Vreni.'

Vreni felt herself unclenching, but she didn't trust herself to speak yet. She sat on a chair next to William. 'He saved us,' she said quietly.

Artūrs took the other two glasses from the small tiled table, handed one to Vreni and sat down opposite her. Vreni looked back at her father. He was staring at her and running his fingers across the pattern cut into his crystal goblet. For now, he didn't look like her Papa. Instead she saw Parvils, and felt she didn't really know him.

He leaned over and took hold of her hand. 'Please, Vreni,' Papa said. She was suddenly tense. 'Please forgive yourself for today. I am proud of my adventurous daughters.'

She gulped. 'What?'

'I'm not proud of the deception, but I am proud of your spirit. This family is full of strong women who know their own hearts. Following your heart is not always easy, but it's the only way to feel alive. I know a lot about following your heart.'

Papa leaned back in his chair for a brief moment and rubbed his silver wedding amulet between his fingers. He smiled. 'Everyone is safe now, and we have a new person to add to our family, such as it is.' He reached across and patted William solidly on the shoulder.

Vreni's eyes widened. Add to the family? She didn't know what to say.

'Thank you so much for helping us tonight, William,' she stammered. 'I hope everything will be all right with the hospital and—'

Artūrs interrupted with a cough. 'All the loose ends at the hospital have been tidied up,' he said quietly to Parvils.

As the two men nodded at each other, Vreni wondered how they knew about the hospital already. How had Artūrs known they were on their way home?

Vreni could see William's face filled with the same questions.

'We've always been a family with ways to ... influence others,' Papa said to William. 'Our network, both private and in business, is wide reaching. We have eyes and ears everywhere, especially where my precious daughters are involved. To the world, this night never happened. We can make things happen, and un-happen, as if by magic.' He laughed softly.

Vreni was shocked. What was Papa thinking? He never spoke so openly about family matters, not even to them. Why was he doing this?

Vreni watched her father. He looked so at ease, so gracious, yet business like. She felt like an outsider watching a meeting between three businessmen discussing matters in a detached, amiable manner. But this was not just any discussion. It was a secret that so many people had worked so hard to keep for such a very long time. Why was Papa telling this stranger everything?

'So, William, you have noticed by now that our family is unique.' Parvils relaxed back into his chair and stared into his half-filled glass. 'Let me tell you the story of the burden we've carried for more than three centuries. How to begin?'

Parvils paused. 'Of course,' he said with a smile, 'as it should be started. Once upon a time, several centuries ago, there was a fair aristocratic lady named Ieva who loved a kind and wise knight. When they married, she was given rule over her family's province. Ieva's evil aunt, Rozālija, was overlooked in the line of succession, and because of this she raged and brewed dark magic, placing a curse on Ieva. When Ieva pricked her skin on the poisoned pin of Rozālija's brooch, she would be trapped in a death-like sleep. No breathing, no heartbeat. Not dead but never to wake. Rozālija, also known as Veca Tante, wanted Ieva trapped forever in an *un-place* between life and death, but the other aunties heard of the curse in time to soften the potion—'

'But isn't that the story of Sleeping Beauty?' William said, looking sceptical.

'Yes, Sleeping Beauty.' Parvils nodded. 'That story is our history. Lady Ieva is—was—Vreni's grandmother.'

Artūrs refilled William's glass, and he drank its contents quickly.

'Ieva was my wife's mother. She died seventy years ago, aged sixty-two.' He looked at Vreni. 'Vreni was four years old when her grandmother died. Or were you five?'

'I don't remember, Papa, I was too young.' Vreni

watched for William's reaction while she answered her father.

'Seventy years ago, but that would mean ...' William stopped and stared at his empty glass. Artūrs filled it once more.

What is Papa doing? Vreni stared at her father, but he simply gestured for her to explain.

'I was born in 1904, and Rita was born two years later,' Vreni said.

'But that's more than a hundred years ago.' William stood and strode across the room. Parvils picked up the bottle and followed. William let him refill his glass while he stared at the fire.

'I told you my daughters were special, and what a shame Gaida, my wife, is asleep. She is so beautiful, like her daughters. She would have enjoyed meeting you. Another time, perhaps.' Papa smiled, but William was still frowning.

'I study science, biochemistry, and this just can't happen. How ...' William blustered. 'There isn't any therapy that can extend life like that.'

'Yes, there's some of what you call medicine in the potion—well, herb lore and alchemy—but there's also magic,' Parvils said.

'Magic.'

'Of course,' Parvils straightened his shoulders. 'There was more magic in the world then. We don't need it now that we have science. Science is the world's magic now, so the old magic has been diminished, but not for us.'

'Who else is sleeping, Vreni? Why aren't you?' William asked.

'Grandmama Ieva was the first of us.' Vreni felt giddy to think that this discussion could possibly be happening, but she was energised enough to be able to tell her tale and maybe gain William's acceptance.

'In the story, the fairies, Ieva's aunties, softened the potion but there was no magical kiss,' she said. 'Ieva did wake, sometimes after sleeping for months or years. When she was awake, she had a normal life, with children and grandchildren. There are five sleepers now- Mama and her two sisters, and Rita and me. We all wake ... whenever.' She shrugged. 'And then we return to long-sleep without warning.'

'Like Rita did,' William whispered. 'What about the husbands? What about you, Parvils?'

'Only the women sleep,' Parvils said. 'The men ... wait. Ieva's aunts became the Pratigs Māsa, the Wise Sisters, and they gave Vreni's grandfather a precious gift. I received mine when I married Vreni's mother.' He held out his silver amulet. 'With this, the Sisters have slowed time for me.' He blew a kiss toward Vreni. 'Our beauties live a very long time, asleep and awake. The men have a normal life span, but by wearing this charm we're granted several lifetimes so we can watch over our beloveds and wait for them to wake.'

Vreni listened to her father talking lovingly about his loyalty to her mother. She thought of dancing with William, and kissing him, and how he had saved her from the attacker. She remembered the feeling of William's kisses on her lips, and wondered how many details Papa knew about their time together. Why was Papa telling William all these secrets?

William returned to his chair. Vreni moved to stand beside her father, who was staring at the painting of her mother hanging above the fireplace.

'Papa, why are you saying all this?' she whispered. She glanced towards William. Artūrs was refilling his glass, offering him a tray of cheese, asking him something about horses. 'William seems like a good person but he's still a stranger. Last week you wouldn't even let Rita and me use our real names on the computer and today you're explaining all our secrets to an outsider.'

'When I first met your mother, I needed to learn the secrets of this family so I could decide if I was willing to share the burden of the curse,' Parvils said. 'I knew that one day it would be my duty to do the same for another young man.'

'But Papa, we only met *today*,' Vreni hissed.

'And how do you feel about him?'

Vreni thought about spending more time with William, going out dancing again, being normal. Her heart skipped.

'Your eyes are showing me what your heart is starting to feel, and his eyes hold a similar look,' Papa said gently.

Vreni shook her head. 'This doesn't make sense. What if William thinks we're all crazy and decides to tell someone what he's heard?'

'Parvils, the young man is asleep,' Artūrs said, taking the glass from William's limp hand. 'He'll remember nothing. I'll take him home and arrange for his car—'

'What? No!' Vreni cried. Her heart thrashed inside her chest. 'Is this why you told him everything, knowing he would remember none of it?'

'I had to be gracious. The young man rescued my daughters.' Papa sounded cool and businesslike again.

'I was not *rescued*, Papa, I was returned to my prison.' Vreni ground her teeth together tightly, and heat flowed up her face and formed as burning tears. 'I had one normal day, *one day* of living like everyone else does. You said you were proud of having strong daughters, but you punish me so cruelly.'

She clenched her hand around the stem of the glass and flung it away. An explosion of shards flared across the floor. She heard noises behind her and turned to see William being carried from the library.

She crumpled onto a sofa. Sobs rose up in her like crashing waves, threatening to drown her.

***

The fire was dying in the stone hearth when Vreni felt her father's hands on hers. He offered her a soft handkerchief.

'On this day, sweet Vreni, I needed to be the best and the worst father. I am always guided by my loyal promise to protect this family, even if there is pain in my decisions, but no father can watch his daughter's heart break.'

Parvils wrapped her warmly in his arms. 'What we did to William is not your punishment,' he said, 'it is his test. It's the same test I went through. He won't remember when he wakes up, but the memories will still be there, hidden away while his heart decides, and he may remember our secret one day.'

'But he's gone. He's forgotten me.'

'He has not forgotten you. He still has memories of meeting you and dancing,' he said, wiping her tears, 'but he won't remember the rescue or our conversation tonight unless, one day, his heart decides he wants to be part of this life—your life. And then the hidden memories, everything we told him tonight, will be revealed to him.'

'What gives you the right to treat people this way?' Vreni pushed him away angrily.

'It's the way it happened for me when I first knew your mother. I've told your William enough about our family that he might choose to accept his role, and his fate, without any falsehoods, if his heart desires it. The men who join our family need to make their commitment with all of their hearts and minds—no coercion, no secrets. That's the way the Pratigs Māsa insist it must be for the amulets to work.'

'The Sisters?'

'They see something in him,' her father said.

'When did the Sisters see him?'

'This day was full of many watching eyes, and I've come to appreciate the unique quality of the Sisters' perception.'

Vreni thought of the crumpled woman in the cafe who had called Rita 'Sleeping Beauty'. Had she been one of the watchers? Vreni struggled with these stinging truths. The more she knew the more like strangers her family seemed to her.

Vreni looked up at the sound of Sabina's voice. 'This is the way it must be.'

'I will walk in the garden,' Papa said, and left the room. Sabina took his place beside Vreni.

'So, the Wise Sisters are involved in this, of course,' Vreni said. She felt even more naive.

'Yes, Vreni, we needed to make sure that you remained safe.'

'You watched us?'

'Yes, a few of us kept watch while you shopped. Not as well as we would've liked, but your protection charms did their job.'

'So, what else am I too young, or stupid, to have worked out about my own life?' Her eyes were hot with new tears.

'You may feel you know nothing, but that's because you haven't needed to know any more until now.' Sabina took her hand warmly. 'Our lives were all changed by the sleeping curse, but life is still life. Even though your life is unique, it's still filled with hope, desires, frustrations and love.'

'Life? What life?'

'This *is* your life, Vreni, but everyone's life has rules and challenges. You're starting a journey towards who you will become. You'll get many chances to make your own decisions, starting tonight.'

'I don't understand,' Vreni said.

'All those centuries ago, the Sisters made a two-fold pledge to your grandmother. Firstly to watch over the family, and secondly to one day free you from the sleeping death. We believe we're closer than we've ever been to success in reversing the effects of the potion, but we need to ask you to join in our efforts. We believe you're the one to help us succeed.'

'What good would I be to the sisterhood?' Vreni said bitterly. 'In my one day of independence I put my sister and myself, and our whole family, in peril. I don't believe my efforts would bring you anything but failure, and besides, what does Papa think about all of this?'

Sabina hesitated. 'He sees how important this is and he's proud of you.' She kissed Vreni's forehead tenderly. 'You are much more than you realise right now. You can decide in the morning, but for now you should sleep.'

'Are you staying here tonight?'

'I am.'

Vreni walked with Sabina to the bottom of the stairs. Her tutor headed towards the guest rooms at the back of the house and Vreni watched her walk down the dark hallway. The evening's feelings of betrayal and doubt were now tangled with curiosity and an excitement about working with the Sisters and what that could mean. Her feet were heavy on the stairs as she walked to her room. Before today she had felt she didn't belong in the world, and now she barely felt she belonged in her family, but the Wise Sisters were asking her to become another thing.

How could things change so much in one day? What could she possibly do for the Sisters? She didn't even know who they were, except for Sabina. It would be easier to stay in the tower, to stay a sleeping princess. Vreni wondered what the Sisters would ask her to do.

A cool breeze blew off the sea. She watched as the

heavy curtains billowed slowly in the moonlight. Finally, she slept and dreamed.

MY SOUL TO TAKE

All is well - young Veronika's resourcefulness and
spirit surpassed our expectations. Parvils is understandably
reticent about one of his daughters facing such challenges,
but I have asked her to join us.
She will tell me her decision tomorrow.
—Sister Sabina's report to Sister Anna

***

Almost awake, Vreni lingered in that magical place at the edge of dreaming. She loved real sleep, there were no dreams in the long-sleep of the curse. She drowsed in the warmth of her blankets. Slowly the music in her dream faded and a disturbance somewhere in the house roused her. There was screaming.

She was fully awake now. No, not screaming, wailing, long drawn-out agonised sounds, like an animal in pain.

Vreni was out of her bedroom and running for the source of the sound. The thud of other feet running came from places all over the house, converging on the library.

Pushing through the clot of people in the library

doorway, she saw a long-feared scene before her. Her father sat pale and unmoving in his ruddy leather armchair. His eyes were closed. His book, still held in his hand, lay against his chest, open at the last page he was reading.

'Napping, he's just napping.' Vreni whispered.

The stricken wailing coming from her mother was undeniable proof that her father was dead. Gaida had collapsed at her husband's feet, her body convulsing with unspeakable pain. On the other side of the chair, Rita sat curled in a tiny weeping ball, holding Parvils' hand. Vreni's two aunties sat together on the sofa, weeping bitterly.

Vreni wanted go to her father and shake him awake. Then they would all laugh together about acting so foolishly.

'Now I lay me down to sleep,' she whispered as she walked over to her father. She leaned in and kissed him gently on the forehead.

Rita reached up and took her hand, and they finished their prayer together.

'... I pray the lord my soul to take.'

'Oh, Mama, I'm so sorry.' Vreni knelt next to her mother. Holding her, she crooned comforting sounds in Gaida's ear.

'Vreni,' her mother sobbed. 'How horrid this curse is, that it traps me in sleep so long but wakes me to see my Parvils dead. What depths of evil must we endure?'

Vreni held her mother as she shuddered with sadness. They lay together, both leaning, one last time, against the man they loved.

After a while, Mama finally quieted and lay still in

Vreni's arms, so still, too still. She realised that her mother had returned to long-sleep. The aunties and Rita were sleeping again too.

The cruelness of the curse struck her again. Even the softened potion brimmed with evil, taking the sleepers away from so much of life's pleasure but waking them to experience pain. Vreni knew that when Mama woke next, the pain of her husband's death would be fresh once again, like an open wound. Gaida would not have the solace of a final goodbye at her husband's funeral.

Vreni stared down at her mother's sleeping eyes, swollen from weeping, the tears of grief still wet on her quiescent cheeks.

'I will not live this way,' Vreni hissed.

She untangled herself from her mother and walked to the corner of the library. She watched Artūrs scoop her sleeping mother into his arms to take her back to her accursed bed.

Who will watch over us now? Vreni wiped away her burning tears.

'I will not live this way,' she whispered again as she followed Artūrs out of the library.

She rushed out the front door into the cool morning mist. 'I will not live this way,' she shouted.

Sobs rose up in her throat, and she gulped them down. Her chest heaved as if her heart might disintegrate with grief. She ran stumbling through the garden until she reached the small pine grove her father had planted. She wrapped her arms around the thickest trunk. The bark spiked her face as she pressed hard into its roughness, weeping.

'I will not live this way!'

***

Finally, Vreni returned to the house and went up to the tower. She stood staring out at the sea. She watched the birds diving for fish and remembered other times on the beach. Frosty walks on the gritty beaches near Vārve, bracing against a sudden chill wind and sheltering behind her father. She thought of their last day on the beach together with the new ponies. Days like that would never happen again.

Her breath came in sobs. *Did my choices yesterday do this to Papa?* She had run through the garden trying to run from the pain, from the way her life would be now, but she knew she could not run from her life, only change it. Her tears dried into salty streaks on her face as she watched the gentle rise and fall of the sea beyond the cliffs.

I need to do this thing Sabina has asked me to do, whatever it is, if it will free us. Without Papa, it's up to me to keep us safe.

'Vreni, I cannot know your pain, but I can share your loss,' Sabina said, appearing at the top of the tower stairs. She took Vreni in her arms and they sat down together on the top step. Rocking her gently, Sabina began to hum.

Vreni let the quiet music soak into her and fill some of the emptiness. 'I can't live this life.'

'We don't want you to live this way, either. We believe we can lift the curse, but we need you to help, so on this day, when I know you're already carrying such a heavy load, I must add to it by asking you to decide.'

Sabina wiped away tears from both their faces.

'How can I help you?' Vreni asked. 'I've never even noticed who, or what, you really are.'

'For as long as your family has laboured under the curse, the Wise Sisters have promised to protect you and to someday free you from it. Our Watch-Haven Trust has traded and invested to ensure we have the funds to keep our promises. Through the trust we have woven a far-reaching web, and we have seen that the Alchemists Guild, which Veca Tante brought into being to serve her wicked purposes has also endured, although it is now called AlGuild. We continue to watch them and soften the corporate harm they cause when we can.'

'What do you need from me?'

'We're very close now, Vreni. We're sure we can reverse the potion completely and free you all from the sleeping death. What I ask is for you to help us achieve this wonderful thing for your family and for you.'

'But I don't have anything to offer.'

'There's more to you than you can know yet, young Vreni. It's time for you to come and join the Wise Sisters at Mežs Mājas, our forest home. Let us teach you and show you who you really are.'

Vreni looked out at the darkening sky and realised that this saddest of days was ending. 'I will join you,' she said, leaning her exhausted body into Sabina.

They descended the tower stairs without speaking and walked to Vreni's bedroom. Sabina tucked the blankets tightly around Vreni and sat next to her with the light of the waning moon shining weakly through the curtains. Sabina hummed quietly until Vreni slept.

CHOICE

When the cage door lies open, what choices does
the bird make by spreading her wings to take flight?
—*Book of Questions*

***

Vreni stood in the early-morning stillness of the house that had been her haven and protection ever since arriving in this new country with its harsh sun and topsy-turvy seasons. She let her thoughts drift off to the snowy winters left behind, and could almost feel her cheeks burning from the icy wind dashing across her face as she rode in the open wagon.

How long ago was that? At least half a century, if she went by the way everyone else measured time. Perhaps soon she would measure time in this way as well.

She walked slowly through the house. It felt like a mausoleum, with all the people she loved trapped in the cocoon of long-sleep. She climbed the stairs to the bedrooms until even the small noises from downstairs melted away, leaving nothing but a stifling silence that seemed to eat at her spirit.

She stood looking down from the top of the stairs towards the library door.

Her father would lay forever in the pine grove he had planted to remind him of his old home. He had spent years in this house, and in their chalet back in Vārve, watching over his wife, longing for her to wake and be with him.

Did he jump at every unexpected noise, hoping it was one of them waking? Vreni tried to imagine the stillness her father had lived with as he marked time. He had been their protector, but now it was time for her to take his place. She vowed to do whatever it took to free them from the endless heartbreak of the curse.

Fragments of memories from Sabina's lessons had started to reveal themselves. Songs, curious rhymes, the ancient traditions of nature craft and folk lore bubbled into her awareness, and she felt there was more hiding just out of reach. Apprehension made her hands damp, but she felt eager to discover how the old magic of the Wise Sisters would change her life.

Sabina had said the Sisters would teach Vreni the skills and secrets she needed to play her part in creating the cure. All she could do now was put her faith in them, she had no other choice.

Things had to change. Papa was gone. Artūrs would safeguard the sleepers for now, but she would have to become their protector soon.

She imagined William waiting, guarding her. She couldn't ask anyone who loved her to wait and wither while she slept. Maybe one day he would love her enough to wear the amulet, but she knew she would not ask that, not after watching her father live as love's prisoner, and seeing the pain in her mother's eyes as she watched Papa growing older and older each time she woke.

What an obligation Mama must feel. Vreni knew she would hate being weighed down with such a debt.

Her footsteps fell silently on the thick carpeting as she walked along the landing looking in at her family. She said her goodbyes to her sleeping aunties. It was much simpler that they all slept, leaving her awake and freer than she had ever been before. She took it as a positive sign that her quest with the Wise Sisters would be successful. Even if it didn't succeed, to try anyway and fail would be more acceptable to Vreni than doing nothing.

She entered the silent room where Gaida was sleeping and lay down next to her mother as she sometimes did when she missed her very badly.

'Stay asleep, Mama. If you wake now, you'll stop me doing what I have to do. Stay asleep a little longer, and when you wake the curse will be over.' She kissed her mother's smooth forehead and walked from the room.

Rita's room was full of colour and comfort, with walls of posters, shoes strewn on the floor and too many cushions. Rita lay in her bed looking like she might wake at any minute.

'Hey, Rita, do you want to come with me? I'm getting out of the house again, and this time I get to stay away for a while.' She looked at her sister, wishing that shaking her would wake her up. She pressed her hands into tight fists, feeling her fingers tingle when she relaxed them. 'If the Wise Sisters are successful, this might be your last long-sleep.' She sat down and pushed up close to her sister. 'I wish you would wake and come with me. I know I'd be less scared if you were there.'

Vreni let out a slow breath, and leaned over and kissed her sister's cheek. Tasting a trace of saltiness from Rita's tears for their father, she stiffened, stood quickly and rushed to the door. She turned and forced a smile.

'I'm sure I won't be going shopping, so I'm sorry, but I won't be able to bring you any shoes. I'll see you soon, Rita.'

She walked back down the silent stairs. She was leaving the sanctuary of her home for the unknown that lay ahead. Could they all die, sleeping here like this? Vreni had never thought of her family being unsafe before.

'Now I lay me down to sleep,' she whispered, 'I pray the lord my soul to keep, and if I die before I wake, I pray the lord my soul to take.'

Vreni knew her family was safe for now, with Artūrs and the few others who ran the house protecting them, but she was also their guardian now.

Possibility was power, Sabina had told her. A person's intentions hold power and when those intentions were combined with faith and action, miracles could be achieved. That would mean the intention placed on a spell, and then woven into the words spoken over a potion or an amulet, could turn the desire of the spell maker into reality.

Am I a spell maker? I need faith, like the bird that sings before the sun rises. I need to believe because belief is the true power.

She shuddered as another clutch of forgotten fragments from Sabina's lessons popped into her head. What else would she need to become? All she could do was ask Sabina.

MEŽS MĀJAS

Even in the dense summer forest, the birds
that should be together can always find each other.
Together they are always stronger.
—Book of Wisdom

***

Now that it was time, Vreni could not close the front door behind her.

'Artūrs and the others are here,' Sabina said soothingly, 'and the Wise Sisters will watch as they have always watched.' She put her hand on Vreni's and, as the car sent from the sisterhood pulled up in the driveway, they closed the door on the only life Vreni had known.

They stood for a moment outside the closed door in the morning sun. Vreni thought that Sabina looked different now than she had done during lessons. She was softer somehow, as though she had taken off a rigid mask of herself.

Sabina smiled and warmly clasped both of Vreni's hands in her own. 'Welcome, Sister Veronika, I am Sister

Sabina,' she said as though they were meeting for the first time. 'May our strength be your strength.' She kissed Vreni on one cheek and then the other.

Vreni felt the honour in this formal greeting, like she was becoming part of something astonishing. The sense of otherness, the feeling of being isolated she had known for so long, was disappearing. She belonged with the Sisters, not as a child but as the woman she was becoming.

***

Vreni was quiet in the car as it sped through the stark landscape. The unforgiving glare of the sun seemed to bleach the colour out of the scrawny trees and bushes that struggled to push up out of the dry ground. The brightness even threatened to fade the blue from the sky itself.

She opened her window and felt the blast of dry air in her face. It smelled of overheated dust and some un-known woody spice. Her ears rang with the ceaseless squeal of some mysterious insect. She closed the window and returned to the cool quiet of her thoughts.

The car finally turned from the smooth black strip of highway and began snaking its way up through a cluster of parched hills. As they rounded a dusty bend, Vreni could see that the narrow road passed between two large boulders. Beyond the boulders she saw a glimpse of green, not organised and potted colour like at home or in the city, but greens of every hue, stretching on and on. She sat forward as the car passed through the gap between the boulders and dropped down into an immense, lush valley. Her breath caught in her throat. These were like the colours of summer in Vārve.

The thin road swept through pine and birch and moss that cascaded down the slopes on all sides. Shaded patches full of summer mushrooms were surrounded by thick tangles of emerald ferns. Here and there she saw woody, dark green canes laden with glistening red berries. There was bird song and bumblebees, and the smell of the dampness in the earth after the snow has melted.

But this should all be decades ago and half a world away from where we are now. Vreni gazed around, devouring the sights. She hadn't realised until now how much she had hungered for this. The car followed the curving road and eventually emerged from the deep teals and jades into a rolling grassy field dotted with small yellow flowers. At the centre of the field sat a ring of buildings.

'Welcome to Mežs Mājas.'

'Forest home,' Vreni whispered.

Sabina squeezed her hand. 'We thought you would enjoy how this place looks.'

'You're right, but how is this possible?'

'At Mežs Mājas, and at some other places where we prevail, it's up to the Sisters what the world we weave looks like. So we create what we desire. We seek our comfort by weaving a place like this that is truly ours. For so many centuries the Wise Sisters lived as part of the old forests. We knew the secrets of the plants, spoke the language of each creature and shared the songs of the birds. It's all part of us and we could not be removed from it all so easily. The forests and the creatures they nurture are within our hearts, and therefore they are ours to weave as we desire.'

'Magic,' Vreni said.

Sabina shrugged and nodded, then looked into the rear-vision mirror and caught the eye of the woman driving, as if looking for reassurance.

'You will learn to be a weaver of worlds too, Sister Veronika,' the woman said, 'a bringer of victory.'

Not Vreni, but Veronika. A bringer of victory? She felt hot. Her heart leapt in her chest. 'I will be her,' she whispered. *I want to be this person, this bringer of victory. I've lain sleeping too long.*

The car slowed and stopped in front of a long stone cottage, the pitched roof a thick blanket of thatch that pointed up into the lavender-blue sky. Woven baskets full of vibrantly coloured geraniums hung from the eaves.

At the edge of the circle of cottages stood a tall windmill, its sails rotating lazily in the gentle breeze. Vreni tried to see inside the cottages but the rows of lead-paned windows only mirrored the trees. She stepped from the car, her footfalls crunching on the gravel driveway. She caught herself looking for a stork's nest in the chimney pots. Storks were bringers of harmony and good fortune for the households where they choose to nest.

'Yes, we even have storks,' said the driver, the woman who had called her Veronika. 'Welcome to Mežs Mājas, I am Sister Anna. We want this place to feel like home for you. Sabina and I will make sure you feel happy here. We'll also guide you as you prepare for your ... task.'

Vreni cringed. Guide and prepare her for what? She

met Anna's fiery blue eyes and, reached out with both hands, greeted Anna and kissed her. 'Thank you, this is already more than I'd dreamed of.'

'If you can dream it then it can be so,' Anna said. 'Welcome home.'

Flanked by her new companions, Vreni walked to the door of the cottage.

The interior was filled with soft light that rippled through the uneven glass in the windows. The walls were white and roughly plastered. Colourful tapestries hung on the walls, showing scenes brimming with the birds and animals of the forest. The colours were bold and lively, and the animal figures seemed almost to be moving and going about the job of gathering food and feeding their babies.

A wooden table ran the length of the room underneath the windows on the far side, beyond which was a sun-drenched courtyard garden. The long table was covered with a beautiful white cloth that had an intricate pattern woven into it. Along the centre of the table sat numerous platters and dishes, some made of wood, some of silver, and laden with meats, chicken and cheese. There were bowls of steaming soup and baskets of bread, dumplings and sweet pastry.

Vreni had eaten very little since her father had died. Grief had filled her stomach with rocks. But she knew that refusing to eat, or eating like a mouse, would be ungracious of her, and the aromas rising from the food were unexpectedly tantalizing.

A noisy gaggle of young girls suddenly burst through the door. They were laughing and jostling each other.

Sabina followed behind them. 'Young sisters, please settle yourselves, you chirp like hungry chicks,' she called over the noise. 'Come and meet our newest fledgling, Vreni—I mean Veronika—is Sister Sabina's niece. We all know how first days feel, so please help her feel welcome.'

'Hello,' Vreni said nervously. 'This is all so beautiful. I'm so pleased to be here.'

She braced herself, wondering if the girls knew who she was, and how they would react. But they rapidly surrounded her, offering outstretched hands to shake and warm pecks on her cheek. She was relieved and pleased to just be one of the new birds.

Their voices grew louder again as they swept Vreni towards the table. They sat down, surrounding her, and started eating. Vreni felt lighter inside because of the warmth of their welcome, and the rocks she had felt in her stomach were replaced with her old appetite. The food was divine and Vreni was relieved to realise that all of the young sisters were far too busy interrupting each other to ask her any questions. It was like being at a table full of Ritas, all talking excitedly at the same time.

***

After lunch the young sisters invited Vreni to join them as they went for an afternoon of practising what they had learned in the morning's lessons. The girls dawdled through the circular garden to another low building they called the lab.

Inside, the lab was cool and sparsely furnished, with tall stools circling a large, heavy marble-topped bench. In the centre of the bench were piles of dried herbs tied in bundles, jars of seeds and spices, and bowls of dried flower petals. A metal box contained small glass bottles, a few of which were filled with coloured liquids. Each girl had a heavy stone mortar and pestle in front of her.

Vreni took a seat at the bench.

'Dill seed in your bath water makes you *irresistible*,' a girl named Sofia said, and giggled. Her blue eyes shone as she lifted a few dill seeds and sprinkled them onto the table-top, and then passed the jar of seeds around the table.

Vreni inhaled the fresh smell.

'The scent of cloves on your skin, and your love will do whatever you ask him to,' another girl, Emma, said with a laugh.

They passed the afternoon mixing ointments and fragrant herbal potions, mostly useful only for attracting boys. Vreni felt familiar and confident with the work. Again, there were flashes of memory from Sabina's jumbled lessons. The fragrances she worked with that afternoon smelt similar to some that belonged to her mother or her aunties. She and Rita had dabbed them on themselves when they were younger and played dress-ups, and she had worn one of them on her trip into the city.

Cloves? William had taken risks to help her that night. Maybe the fragrance had come from the Sisters. Maybe William had only been attentive and helpful because of some potion. Vreni shook her head, feeling overly suspicious.

'You're Sabina's niece,' Sofia said.

'Yes,' Vreni said, relieved that she didn't need to create a story. 'And she's my ... tutor,' she added.

'You've had extra spell work then, lucky you. Has she shown you the chants for growing things yet? I can't wait to get my own whisper birds.'

'No,' Vreni said, wondering what Sofia was talking about. 'We've been concentrating on herbs.'

'That's why you're so good at these,' Emma said.

Vreni looked down and realised she had been mixing while she was talking, and the lotion in her mortar was glowing with energy and resonating with a quiet hum. The girls fell silent and joined with the tone of the hum.

'They're always more powerful if we all give voice to the intention,' Sofia said. 'Seal it in the jar while it's full of energy.'

Vreni wasn't sure what she had intended, but she spooned the humming mixture into a blue glass jar and sealed it. *I have magic inside me, and all around me.*

Vreni worked and watched, getting to know the other girls, who were mostly the daughters of the Wise Sisters. The end of the afternoon's experimentation was signalled by the sound of song rising throughout the gardens.

The young sisters quickly packed away their herbs, petals and bottles, and left the lab. They joined in the singing and followed behind the older women. Vreni followed and copied. She knew the songs as soon as she heard them and wondered how this could be, but the questions were washed from her mind by the rising music.

As the sun set, the Sisters gathered together in the circular courtyard garden and sang for the blessing of the day and to welcome Vreni. She felt the rhythms and the power of the songs became part of her.

**

The days that followed were a whirl of old traditions, charms and magic. Vreni realised that Sabina had somehow been weaving lore and magical skills into her daily lessons for a long time, because the concentrated training at Mežs Mājas seemed to trigger a knowing deep within her. She felt as though she was discovering new but ancient things, gifts from the past that had lain dormant inside her until being here had stirred them into life, but she still felt sure there was more that remained unknown to her.

GLIMMER

A glimmer will only hold back hidden memories
if the glimmered mind allows it; once a person wishes
the memories to surface, the glimmer will not hold for long
against their free will, but a guided awakening
is always kinder.
—Book of Wisdoms

***

'Tell me what you've hidden in me,' Vreni said to Sabina as they walked among the curving rows of fruit trees.

Sabina looked across at Anna, who was walking through a small orchard gathering ripe fruit. Vreni also watched Anna as she murmured words of thanks to each tree for its gifts before placing the fruit in the basket. Anna looked up from her whisperings and started towards them. Sabina nodded, and then guided Vreni through the garden.

'Understand, Vreni, that we're all linked by the wisdom of the old magic. I trained you and Rita during your recent awakenings in the hope that one of you would show the strength and skill for our undertaking. This training would have been a large burden to place on a child who already carries so much, so we decided to conceal your lessons within a ... glimmer. The magic could remain hidden in the back of your awareness until we knew you were ready to embrace your potential.'

'Glimmer? Training?' Vreni's mind tumbled with questions.

'Be patient, and you'll be able to answer all your own questions once the glimmer is lifted.'

They reached the edge of a still pond, which was ringed with heavy square stones. Anna joined them and lowered her basket to the grass. Sabina beckoned Vreni to sit on a stone bench that faced the unmoving water. Vreni placed her palms on the cool stone, watching the colours of the garden reflected on the water.

'We can see the smooth water, but some things are hidden just below the surface.' Anna's voice was smooth.

'If the surface is all you seek, then that is all you will see,' Sabina added.

'Within your glimmer lies wisdom and power ...'

'... insight and control ...'

'... burden and challenge ...'

Vreni felt encircled by the Sisters' words, as though she was contained in a bubble. Everything was still.

'Do you choose to see below the surface of your glimmer?' Sabina said. 'To see who you can be?'

'I do,' Vreni whispered.

A faint hum began to rise from Sabina and Anna, their voices overlapping in a weave of tone upon rhythm. The rhythm seeped into Vreni's chest and she felt her heart following its beat. Anna began to lay her words on top of Sabina's echoing chant. Vreni felt the bubble surrounding her filling with the power of the words. She breathed them in.

'Look beneath to see within,
to where true vision hides.
See beneath and look within,
to where your truth abides.'

When Anna finished speaking, she picked up a smooth pebble and handed it to Vreni. Vreni rubbed the pebble slowly between her thumb and fingers, and threw it. It dropped into the glassy surface of the pond.

There was a sudden release of pressure as the bubble that had surrounded her burst. Her awareness was flooded with the hot energy of knowing. Secrets sprang from their hiding places in the back of her mind, and she could now hear echoes of songs and chants and words of power.

Images of what she had written in her forgotten journal flashed into her mind. She saw pages filled with spells, and formulas for gain and influence. She could smell and taste—*dill seed, clove, sorrel*—the herbs and unctions that she had mixed and laced with the intent of her heart's desire. There was a fresh knowing, of the secret hiding places in the linings of her clothes, where she had hidden her personal talismans—*garnet for protection, cat's eye to remain unseen*—and the words she had used to enchant them echoed in her ears.

She drew a sharp, painful breath. It felt for a moment like she was awakening from long-sleep.

The smooth coolness of the stone bench was the first thing Vreni noticed as the flood of revealed knowledge ebbed back into the places it had been stored, but now it was no longer hidden from her. She felt remade but also familiar and complete. She sighed, rising from the stone seat.

'I will become Veronika, bringer of victory. I am no longer just Vreni, sleeping princess.' She stood tall.

'She remembers,' Sabina said.

'You've done well, Sisters.' Anna smiled at them, and from within her basket of fruit she took a thick tattered book with a bright blue leather cover. 'This is yours, Sister Veronika.'

When she handed Vreni the blue book, Vreni remembered that it held all the knowledge from her hidden lessons.

NOW I LAY ME DOWN TO SLEEP

'It is recorded in the Book of Wisdom *that a youngling will travel into the dream realm and return safely.'*
'But how can we be sure that the traveller is her?'
'We cannot be sure, but we can hope.'
—Conversation between Sister Sabina and Sister Anna

***

On the night of the first full moon since she had arrived at Mežs Mājas, Sabina and Anna led Vreni out to the central courtyard that was lit by the milky light of the newly risen moon. They walked through the lush garden to a darkened corner where a doorway glowed. Inside it looked like a small rock grotto. Sabina beckoned Vreni to enter.

As Vreni's eye became accustomed to the soft light, she saw that she was at the top of a helical staircase that led below ground. She thought of the spirals hidden within seashells, and stood for a moment, letting her eyes blur and play tricks with the shadows and dimensions of the glowing helix.

Sabina placed a hand on her shoulder.

'What's down there?' Vreni asked.

'A place where we have access to the Realm of Dreams that connects us all across place and time.'

'Dreams?'

'Come, we'll show you,' Anna said.

Vreni felt the warmth of the rough stone steps against her feet as they descended in silence. At the base of the stairs was a doorway filled with warm light. Vreni felt the slight resistance of an unseen wall of energy as she stepped over the threshold. A circle of Sisters stood in the centre of the room. Their singing filled the air. The rhythmic threads wove in and out of each other, creating a fabric of sound that rippled around her.

'Spirals within circles, within circles making spirals,
Dreams circle our hearts and spiral from our minds.
We spiral within so we may circle without.
Journeys within journeys, endings and beginnings.'

Vreni walked around the chamber, running her hand along the smooth, curving stone wall. It was alive with colour, paintings of trees, flowers, herb plants and animals were all part of a beautiful circular garden. Within this colourful garden, painted women were dancing, their faces full of joy and their hands raised up to the sky. Vreni expected to see them move and join in with the other voices in the room.

She followed the gaze of the painted eyes that were looking towards the ceiling, and saw a spiral of sparkling light that started near the door and wound around and around, growing finer as it coiled towards a glowing crystal at its centre. Vreni moved to the rhythm of the music and muttered the songs as she followed the curving wall back to the door.

'What is this place?' she asked.

'It's a dream room,' Sabina said. 'We're here to continue your preparation and training, and to give you your first challenge.'

The circle of Sisters parted, and Vreni noticed a raised platform in the centre of the room. She shuddered and looked quickly to Sabina. 'Dream room?'

'Yes, we're going to make you sleep,' Sabina said. Seeing Vreni turn pale, she added, 'Not long-sleep, just a nap.' She took Vreni's hand.

'By entering the Dream Realm,' Anna said, 'you can travel back to the time of the cursing, feel the power of it, and, we hope, find the original potion. We've tried sending others to find it, but they can't sense it.'

'You are your dreams, and your dreams are you,' Sabina said. 'We believe you will feel the potion because you have the traces of it in your blood. You need to seek out the original potion and hold it in your hand, to feel and remember the dread.'

'But why?' Vreni asked.

'Because that memory will bring us a little closer to the cure,' Sabina said.

Vreni's heart fluttered as she looked at the sleeping platform. 'What will happen? What will I do?'

'We believe the alchemists hid the remainder of Veca Tante's potion once they had painted it on every sharp object they hoped Ieva might touch.' Anna patted Vreni's hand and smiled. 'In the dream realm you'll visit your grandmother's palace. The alchemists had secret chambers that faced the setting sun, and the potion will be hidden somewhere in there. You will appear to be a scullery maid, one of many, expected only to scrub and fetch, so you'll be able to move about unnoticed,' Anna said reassuringly.

'Just a few weeks ago I couldn't even rescue my own sister without help.' Vreni's throat was tight. 'There'll be no one with me this time, so how will I do it on my own?'

'You'll have tools and spells to aid you,' Sabina said soothingly. 'The sisters always left a cache of charms and spells in case one of their own was caught in need. Our chambers were—are—on the side of the castle that faces the morning sun. In those chambers, look for a box within a box within a box.' Sabina pointed toward the ceiling. 'It will be marked with a spiral that only Sisters can see. Inside you'll find a veil of silk, a circle of mirrored silver, a pouch filled with what look like tiny seeds.'

'Cloth, a mirror, seeds? How will those things help?' Vreni snapped. Her stomach churned.

'The seeds are the eggs of whisper birds,' Sabina said. 'Sprinkle some into your hand, whisper your heart's desire and they'll hatch and grow to do your bidding before they fly to freedom. When you wear the mirror charm around your neck, you'll be invisible to all but those skilled in old magic. The silk veil is infused with a taming potion. It will calm beasts and people when it's laid upon them. You are of the Pratigs Māsa, Vreni, the time for doubt is gone. The time of magic is here.'

Thoughts of running back up the stairs tempted Vreni. She stood frozen for a long moment, and then walked towards the raised platform. Lying on the warm stone, she stared up at the glistening spiral. The rhythmic chanting of the Sisters rose up and filled her awareness. She felt the heaviness of sleep approaching.

Now I lay me down to sleep ...

REALM OF DREAMS

The Realm of Dreams allows us travel to other
places and times, but these places and times are
not just dreams, they are real,
and so are any dangers the dreamer will find there.
—Pratigs Māsa, Book of Wisdoms

***

This awakening was different. There was none of the burn-ing like after long-sleep, and no warm dreaminess either, she was suddenly awake and alert. Vreni lay with her eyes half closed, listening to the clatter of cooking and many busy voices. Her nose twitched at the stale-smelling pile of straw and cloth remnants that made up her makeshift bed on the floor next to a warm stone hearth.

'Wake up,' said a voice next to her. 'Hurry, *steigā*, the day is half over already.' A hand shoved at her and she opened her eyes fully.

'Come on, my lazy friend,' said the smiling girl.

'Good morning,' Vreni said, expecting the girl to

question who she was, but she just gestured towards the crowded worktables.

I am me, but I am not me. Vreni stood and smoothed her rough woollen dress, brushing the straw from its folds. Sabina had said that while she travelled in the dream realm she would just be a suggestion at the edge of peoples' minds. And how could she be anything else when she wouldn't even be born for centuries to come? But this place was real enough. If it weren't, the Sisters wouldn't have told her about the box of magic left ready in case she needed it.

Vreni followed the smiling girl and copied her actions. She took a boiled egg and ate it hurriedly, washing it down with a cup of clabbered milk, wincing as she swallowed. It was Papa's favourite drink, but she had never liked the sour taste.

'These are for the high table,' the smiling girl said.

Vreni watched closely and again copied. The girl took a tray of breads. Vreni took the second tray full of smoked fish and cheese, and followed her through the stone doorway towards a large hall.

As they approached the table, Vreni caught sight of her grandmother. Grandmama Ieva was so beautiful, so full of grace and kindness. The tray Vreni was carrying tilted and almost fell. She struggled to calm herself.

Grandmama Ieva sat next to her husband Carls, and there were others seated around the table. She could not take her eyes from her grandmother. Their gaze met for a moment as Vreni placed the tray on the table.

'Thank you, sweet one,' Ieva said as she smiled and picked up the tray to serve her guests.

Grandmama looks so young and happy. Vreni kept busy with small jobs so she could stay and watch for a while, and then walked back to the kitchen smiling.

When the flurry of breakfast was over, Vreni picked up rags and a wooden bucket and made her way outside. She stood at the well as if gathering water, all the while using the direction of the sun to orient herself to the location of the apartments in the east and west of the palace. She set out first toward the morning sun in search of the box within a box within a box that could contain her salvation if today's searching became complicated or dangerous.

Watching to ensure she remained unnoticed, she made her way steadily eastwards through the cool, damp passageways that twisted through the palace. Away from the cooking fires, the air was chill, and the slender arrow-slits in the thick stone walls allowed only choked rays of light to penetrate the gloom. She carried her rags and bucket with an air of purpose in case she was being observed.

Door after locked door yielded nothing. Finally, she saw a faint glow in an alcove up ahead. On a door was a small spiral, it was there for a moment and then faded. She turned the door's handle and it opened for her.

Inside, the room was flooded with morning light. She stood like a startled animal, waiting for her eyes to adjust to the brightness. Although she believed she would have been welcome, she was still relieved that the room was empty. This day and this challenge were hers alone. She was the girl who did not belong here, and she did not want to cause complications or danger for the Wise Sisters who had been—or would be—so loyal and protective of her family.

Vreni calmed her mind and opened her perception to the search.

'A box within a box, within a box,' she muttered. But there were several boxes in the room. This room could be the first box. Out of the corner of her eye she saw a spark of light as a second spiral flared and glowed, then faded swiftly. 'Blessings!'

She ran towards the chest by the window and opened it. Inside were two rough woollen dresses, a bundle of linen rags and a leather journal. She lifted these items gently and discovered a small birch-wood box. She ran her hand over the smoothly polished lid, which glowed momentarily with a spiral.

Lifting out the smaller box, she closed the larger one and sat on its lid with the small birch-wood box on her lap. Her heart sank when she opened it, the box contained nothing but herbs. Why was this box marked for her to find if its contents were useless to her?

Vreni searched into her newly remembered training and stopped herself before fear and doubt could cloud her thinking. 'Show the truth I seek.' She spoke the words quietly.

Around the edges of the box, she saw a faint glow. She loosened the herb tray and lifted it out. Underneath was a compartment holding a cloth of silk, an amulet and a small pouch, just as she had been told.

But how could they be here? The box wasn't deep

enough to have a hidden compartment. Vreni shook her head in wonder. 'I have much to learn.'

She was about to leave when she recalled another thing. She must give a sign of thanks to the Pratigs Māsa for providing her with these charms and potions. She knelt next to the chest she had been sitting on and, using the tip of her finger, drew two circles on a polished lid, a smaller one inside a larger one, with the two circles touching at a single point.

'It was given freely, received with gratitude,' she said, 'and it will return to you three times over.'

With the small box placed in her bucket and covered with cleaning rags, Vreni left the peaceful room belonging to the Sisters she would never meet and, with hesitant steps, started westward in search of the alchemists' chambers.

***

After the quiet of home, and even the purposeful bustle of her time at Mežs Mājas, Vreni was amazed by the crowds that filled the palace. So many people were engaged in household tasks and running messages. She realised that she was looking at this world through her modern eyes. Without technology and machines, it took a lot of people to do all the work.

While everyone was busy dealing with visitors coming and going, Vreni entered a room. She gasped and hid herself in a shadowy corner. Her grandmother was there, overseeing preparations for her guests. She looked so happy. Today Vreni had seen that being welcoming and hospitable was a pleasure for her family, and she knew from family stories that for Ieva, being taken from all this was the greatest tragedy of the curse. Was there a chance she could stop it all happening?

Her mind raced with possibilities. She searched for a secluded place to think. In a corner in the palace's central courtyard was a kitchen garden. She sat among the scraggy, overgrown herbs out of sight and pondered.

Grandmama's not sleeping yet. I could find the potion and destroy it before we're cursed. My family would be free. 'Why didn't the Sisters speak to me about this possibility?' she whispered.

Vreni opened the borrowed box. She took out the mirrored silver amulet, tying the smooth silk ribbon it hung on around her neck. She unfolded the silk cloth and draped it around her hips so it appeared to be an apron. Then she loosened the string on the pouch. It was filled with small, pale seeds. She let one seed fall into the palm of her hand.

Placing her lips close to the grain in her hand, she whispered, 'Show me. Teach me.'

The surface of the seed smoothed and was now an egg. The minuscule egg cracked open. A tiny robin hatched out, fluffed up its minute feathers and doubled and redoubled in size until it was fully grown. It turned to look at Vreni for a moment and, nodding its tiny head, flew from her hand and landed on a flowering sorrel bush.

'Amazing,' Vreni said, as she tucked the pouch of seeds into the pocket hidden in the fold of her dress. 'Thank you for the lesson, young robin.' She gestured the sign of thanks on the lid of the box and left it to be found in the garden.

The palace was a maze of darkened passageways that opened out unexpectedly into light-filled halls and galleries that were filled with the sound of banter, talk of business and trade, domestic scuttling, laughter and music.

Vreni made her way westward. With the freedom of invisibility that the amulet offered her, she allowed her curiosity to rule her for a short while. She watched the girls in the kitchen, who looked to be about the same age as her. They were talking about new dresses, gossiping about a look from a boy, or a flower left as a token of love. Gossiping, just as she and Rita did.

Many hours seemed to pass as Vreni explored the palace, observing her family's history while she hid behind the mirror amulet's magic.

In the westernmost wing of the palace, she rounded a sweeping curve in the passageway and heard voices. Daring to look, she saw a stick-thin old man talking to a young guard. She saw from the ornate pin on the collar of the old man's robes that he was an alchemist.

'No one enters or leaves without my word. Except Rozālija, of course,' the alchemist said.

'Of course, sire, the old aunt pleases herself,' the young guard replied.

'Indeed she does.' The alchemist laughed as he walked away down the passageway, his laughter diminishing.

Vreni stepped forward around the bend, waiting to see if the amulet made her invisible to the guard. She came so close to the man that she could smell the smoked fish he'd eaten for breakfast on his breath. She wrinkled her nose. He couldn't see her, but he was blocking the door and stopping her entering the alchemists' chamber.

Recollecting a spell for casting voice, she prepared to conjure the alchemist's words to play with the guard's perceptions. Taking a slow, quiet breath, she recalled the tone of the alchemist's voice and then spoke, sending the conjured voice far off into the dim passageway.

'I have stumbled, damn these uneven stones,' the conjured voice echoed.

The young guard turned his head toward the voice and walked into the gloom.

Vreni took the moment and pushed open the heavy door just wide enough, slipping into the chamber.

The room was lit by a single stripe of pale light coming from a tall, arched window. Motes of dust drifted across the band of sunshine. The walls of the chamber were lined with shelves laden with books, boxes and bottles. Wooden benches were cluttered with strange pieces of equipment that looked like they belonged in some frightening black-and-white movie. The air smelled of an odd blend of sweet oils made by crushing herbs and flowers, along with something much less appealing, something that reminded Vreni of the smell of sweaty horses.

She heard a muffled rasping sound and walked forward slowly, straining to hear it again. She scanned the room cautiously, and her throat tightened.

Lying asleep on a small bed under the window were

three children, girls. *These girls can't be here. What will they do to them?*

She rushed over and sat on the bed, shaking the girls' shoulders. She put her mouth close to their ears. 'Wake up,' she whispered harshly, trying to rouse them without alerting the guard.

Then she knew they could not have made the noise she had heard. These girls would not wake, not ever. The potion had been used on them, not the softened one but the true sleeping-death potion.

'They sleep alone. No one knows to watch over them,' she whispered. A warm tear ran down her cheek. A sudden wave of outrage washed over her. How many more girls like this were there? She wiped the tear away roughly, determined to find the potion.

Moving back across the room, she began scouring the shelves filled with bottles, searching for markings that would identify the potion, reaching out with her intuition to feel with her heart and her mind.

At last, Vreni felt drawn towards a small tear-shaped bottle made of blue glass. On the outside of the bottle was a stained leather label, on which had been drawn a picture of a sleeping face. The rest of the figure in the drawing was shown bound tightly with dark rope.

'Binding the victim in the prison of the sleeping death.' Vreni muttered, picking up the almost-empty bottle.

A burning cold crept up her arm. Her heart trembled with uncertain, fast-slow rhythms. Dark sounds wailed in her ears. She wanted to drop the bottle and be free from the cold of it, but her hand was frozen and would not release its grip. The bottle was nearly empty, and the potion had already been put where it would do its evil deed.

CATCH ME IF YOU CAN

Weave and blend the unnatural opposites,
knit them together in such a way
that they cannot be undone.
Rozālija insists these opposing creatures cause
torment for each other.
She enjoys seeing pain and suffering in her pets.
—Alchemists Guild instructions

***

'Ah, someone else who will sleep and never die,' a voice boomed behind Vreni.

Her face flooded with heat. The alchemist had returned. He was standing by the closed door. Next to him stood a willowy woman with burning amber eyes that stared directly at her. Vreni suddenly realised she was not invisible to them.

The tear-shaped bottle slipped from her sweating fingers and tumbled in the air. The woman crossed the room in a silent blur and her thin hand wrapped around the glass before it hit the floor. Then she gazed at it and ran a slender finger gently across the glass before placing it back on the shelf.

'Veca Tante.' The words froze in Vreni's mouth even as she spoke them.

The old aunt leaned close, sniffing at Vreni's face. She moved closer again and rubbed her rough cheek against Vreni's, making Vreni think of a cat.

'Another experiment, Rozālija, my love?' the alchemist asked. His eyes sparkled as he looked between Veca Tante and the sleeping girls.

'Not this one, she smells more like ... food.'

Veca Tante sniffed Vreni again and looked puzzled. She raised her hand to Vreni's face, and ran her papery finger-tips across her cheek. Then she flicked her nails. Vreni felt a burning pain and the stinging wetness of blood. Next there was a strange, damp roughness on her face, and Vreni realised the old witch was licking the blood from the scratches she had just made. The woman smacked her lips together, savouring, but then stopped. She stared, bemused, searching Vreni's eyes.

'You taste like something that you cannot be ... yet,' she said, shaking her head and licking her thin lips again. 'But you do taste like food, and my little Bruno must be so hungry by now. Would you feed my little Bruno for me?' she asked the alchemist as she walked back to stand by his side.

'Of course, my darling Rozālija,' he said.

Veca Tante leaned in and kissed him lightly on the neck with her bloodstained lips. The alchemist moved towards her, but she raised her hands to stop him. 'Bruno is waiting, and I need to deal with our guard.'

She left the chamber, pulling the door closed behind her.

Vreni could hear the young guard's shaky voice through the door. 'Yes, my lady, I know, but I didn't see her. No, it will never happen again.'

The scream entered Vreni's ears like a sharp knife. There was a thump against the other side of the door, and Vreni heard footsteps clicking on the stones, fading down the passage. She felt the remnants of her boiled egg rising from her stomach. She coughed and swallowed hard. *I am responsible for that man's death.*

The alchemist was busying himself unfastening a thick leather belt from around a barrel. He lifted the tattered hide and Vreni could see that it was not a barrel but a circular cage.

Inside the cage was an emaciated wolf, covered with uneven clumps of ragged fur. The creature was circling the cage, and with each turn it looked from the alchemist to Vreni. Its understanding seemed to grow as it circled, and it began to salivate, running its long pink tongue around its ragged mouth. It grinned, showing slick white teeth. The air in the room was pungent with the smell of sweaty fur and rancid drool.

The alchemist hooked a timber lever through a loop in the top of the cage; at the other end of the lever was an empty basket that hung high in the air. 'When the basket fills with grain it will lift Bruno's cage, and you ...' He shrugged, took a knife from his pouch and stabbed a hole in a large sack hanging from the ceiling.

Vreni watched as the grains of rye started flowing out. She heard the door click shut, followed by the heaving *thunk* of the key locking the door.

The wolf was growling, a low and threatening sound, like the rumble of distant thunder. Above the growl came another sound that did not belong. Vreni heard a child's voice. Her eyes flashed to the sleeping girls. Would they be eaten too?

She heard a voice again, no it was two voices, coming from near the wolf's cage. She watched the wolf, trying to understand what she was hearing. There couldn't be voices. There was only the wolf circling, but the voices were there and growing louder.

She could see movement beneath the wolf's tattered fur, lumpy swellings growing and rippling beneath its skin. Within the matted tufts of the wolf's fur, little faces pushed through and looked around, blinking. The eyes darted here and there, searching until they saw Vreni, then each one strained, taking turns to watch her as the wolf paced and circled within the cage.

If this is the old woman's pet, what else is she capable of? 'I'll never know now,' Vreni whispered, her voice unsteady.

She was entranced by the confusing horror of this creature and the tiny faces imprisoned within its fur. As the wolf turned in its cage, she could hear the children's voices rise and fall.

'Be careful,' said a singsong voice.

'Don't go into the woods alone,' scolded another.

'You shouldn't stray from the path,' warned a third.

'Say your prayers,' came a fourth.

Together they chorused, 'Run!'

Vreni's heart thundered in her ears. The wolf was pawing at the tiny gap between the stone floor and the bottom of the heavy iron cage.

It couldn't end like this. She wanted to send her birds through to unlock the door, but she looked at the sleeping girls and realised she must protect her sleeping sisters. She reached for the pouch in her pocket and sprinkled the whisper-bird eggs into her palm.

'Torment, anguish, agony,' she whispered. 'The eyes, peck at its eyes.'

The eggs cracked one by one. She saw the wolf's cage lifting up as it forced its muzzle underneath, slavering and biting at the floor trying to wedge its head through the narrow opening.

The minuscule birds stared at Vreni as they ruffled and flapped, growing and growing. The wolf growled and panted, chewing at the stone.

'Don't go into the woods alone,' chanted the entrapped children.

Finally, the birds took flight from Vreni's clammy palm. They circled in the stagnant air between Vreni and the wolf.

With a frantic last effort, the wolf pushed under the heavy iron cage and burst out in an unsteady tangle of paws. Its growls were combined with the panicked screams of the tormented children. *How many murders have these wretched young prisoners had to watch over and over again?*

Before the wolf had a chance to turn its attention to her, Vreni dived behind a large wooden bureau that stood in the centre of the room. She heard flapping and chirping. The wolf yelped and growled. It sprang up with its jaws snapping, trying to capture its tormentors and swallow them whole. It leapt about madly, crashing back down to the hard stone floor after each attempt.

Above the tormented clatter, she could hear that the children had started giggling. Then, unbelievably, they started singing.

> 'Little robin red breast sat upon a tree,
> Up went vilks and down went he.
> Down came wolfie, and away robin ran.
> Sings little robin redbreast, 'Catch me if you can.'

The birds had formed a cloud of screeching feathers. They circled, taking turns to dive at the wolf, stabbing their sharp beaks into its eyes. Pearls of blood appeared on its mangy face. The wolf continued to snap blindly at its attackers. It yelped and howled in frustration. The captive children giggled and sang, delighted at the creature's anguish.

Vreni unknotted the taming cloth and pulled it from her hips, knowing that this square of fabric was infused with calming herbs and magic. She hoped it would work on this poor, cursed creature. Maybe these were the children the wolf had eaten, and they had come back to torment it. As vile as this creature was, and as tormented as the poor children must be, Vreni knew she could not kill them. She knew they had no more choice about how they were made than Vreni did.

She crept around the cabinet, approaching the wolf from behind. The birds dived and pecked. The children teased and chanted. Vreni threw the flimsy silk cloth onto the wolf's back.

The cloth seemed to wrap itself around the wolf's flanks, and then, with a ripple, it slithered up to cover the animal's shoulders and head, smothering the children's voices. The wolf struggled and growled, trying to free itself from the grip of the cloth. It circled in panic. Small spots of blood began to stain the pale silk. The birds circled quietly above the panting wolf, as though waiting to see if they were still needed.

Slowly the wolf gave up its snarling and collapsed onto the stone floor, its half-starved form looking barely more than a fur-covered skeleton.

The muffled voices of the children had ceased their chanting and were quietly mumbling, 'Good wolfie, good *vilks.*'

With a shaking hand, Vreni reached out and lifted the cloth from the wolf's eyes. It looked at her with sad confusion. 'Veca Tante curses us all in different ways,' she said, as she lightly patted its muzzle with the back of her hand. It whimpered.

She reached for a joint of meat in a box that had been placed close to the wolf's cage where the animal could smell it, but it remained cruelly out of reach. The wolf took the meat gently from her hand and gnawed into it noisily.

The circling birds lifted higher into the chamber,

singing cheerfully, and then they found an open window and flew into the sunlit sky, their magic task completed.

Vreni hesitated before slowly lifting the cloth from the wolf's flank. The small faces whose singing had added to the animal's torment were now being pulled back into their horrid prison.

The wolf stopped its chewing for a moment and stared up into Vreni's eyes. It lifted its head so that its face, and teeth, came frighteningly close to hers. She held very still. The wolf nuzzled gently against the wound on her cheek, as if they now shared the pain that Veca Tante had inflicted. They both sighed.

Letting the cloth fall again, she left the wretched creature to feast on the raw, meaty bone and looked again at the young girls lying on the low divan. *What can I do for them? I don't even belong here myself.* All she could do was what she had been asked to do.

She walked away from the girls and picked up the tear-shaped bottle one more time, holding it until the icy menace of the potion inside crept up her arm. She made sure she would remember exactly what it felt like. If it still existed in her world, she would now be able to feel its presence and, she hoped, bring it back to the Wise Sisters so the cure could be made.

Vreni took the key for the door from where it hung inside the wolf's cage. She knew she could do nothing about the sleeping girls. She was a visitor and couldn't take anything from this place except wisdom.

A message. She could leave a message for the Sisters to find. *Perhaps the Sisters can save the girls the way they had saved—will save—Grandmama and everyone else by softening the curse somehow.*

Vreni unlocked the chamber door. The weight of the guard's body pushed the door towards her. There was no visible sign of what had killed him, only thin lines of blood running from his eyes, nose and mouth.

I caused this. She felt the weight of his fate heavy on her shoulders.

She kneeled down beside him and her tears fell on his face. They mixed with his blood as she tried to wipe it with the hem of her dress, as if that would somehow help. 'I'm sorry for what happened to you,' she said. 'Maybe your sacrifice today will make a difference one day.'

She closed his frightened eyes and traced a sign on the dead guard's tunic, and another on the door. If it was the Sisters who attended to the body, she knew they would see the magical message and be guided to find the girls.

With heavy feet Vreni retraced her steps back towards the kitchen, wondering for the first time how she would return home. All at once cries erupted and rippled throughout the palace.

'The Lady Ieva, she is struck down.'

Screaming and weeping followed by the thudding of running feet echoed through the passageways. She followed the commotion to its centre. She saw her grandfather Carls lying with his face pressed against Ieva's death-still body. He was weeping wretchedly, as her mother had done when her father died.

It has begun.

'My lord, please forgive me,' begged a handmaiden.

'The brooch was a gift, it had just arrived. The lady asked me to pin it on her gown. It was an accident, just a little blood, but now this. I don't understand what's happened.' She sobbed and collapsed to the stony floor. The brooch was pinned to the gown surrounded by a small dark stain of blood. 'I could do nothing.' She crumpled to the floor, shaking.

A woman wearing a spiral pendant, the sign of the Pratigs Māsa, bent over Ieva and spoke privately to Carls. He stared at her with swollen, disbelieving eyes. Then he swiftly scooped his wife up into his arms and followed the woman towards a door at the far end of the vast hall.

Vreni stood and started to thread her way around the edge of the crowd to follow after them. She felt a firm hand on each shoulder.

'This is not your place or time, young sleeper, home you go.'

'But this is my family,' she pleaded.

'This is not your story yet.'

Vreni's two escorts kept a firm grip on her as they walked back through the chaos of the palace towards the bed of straw and rags next to the hearth. As they walked, they started humming gently. Their music surrounded Vreni. She remembered the sleeping girls in the alchemist's chamber.

'Veca Tante has girls, sleepers,' she thought she heard herself say as the two Sisters lay her near the hearth, but the humming voices swam around in her mind and the world of the palace faded from her vision.

Vreni woke with a gasping breath and cried out. 'The

girls, they are sleepers, they are trapped. I tried so hard to wake them.' Her words tumbled out. 'I saw Grandmama. I saw it happen. Veca Tante clawed my cheek, she licked me, licked the blood. She was going to feed me to her wolf, and there were children in its fur, singing.' She sobbed bitterly.

Sabina and Anna sat close and held her while they sang. Their song followed on from the one sung by the Sisters who had sent her back from the dream realm. She felt the rhythm of the song taking control and slowing her heartbeat, the soft rise and fall of the music soothing her outrage, and her nightmarish thoughts faded.

'The magic left for me by the Sisters saved me,' she said at last.

'The wolf was cursed to suffer the singing of the children it found lost in the woods and killed,' Anna said. 'We have records of such grotesque, tormented blendings in the *Book of Wisdom*. Veca Tante enjoyed watching the pain of others. She designed magic to lock her victims in an eternal struggle. It wasn't enough to kill them, but the agony made them prefer death. She was filled with so much loathing and desperation that she needed to surround herself with the agony of others.'

'I'm sorry, Vreni,' Sabina said. 'We didn't know of other sleepers, but it stands to reason they would have trialled the potion.'

'So where are they?' Vreni cried. 'Buried? Entombed for all these centuries?' She felt smothered.

'The sleeping girls have you now,' Anna said. 'And they

have us. We'll search the ancient records for clues to help us find them.'

It wasn't enough. Vreni wanted the Wise Sisters to find them *now*. They had slept too long with no one watching over them. No father. No warm, safe bed.

Sabina and Anna began the humming again. They supported Vreni and walked out of the chamber and back up the spiral stairs into a cool night filled with sparkling stars. The moon was high in the sky.

'How long was I dreaming?' Vreni asked.

'Not long, it's around midnight,' Sabina said.

Only a few hours, but Vreni felt exhausted.

The sisters led her to her room, helped her dress for bed and tucked a soft feather quilt around her.

Sabina rubbed some sweet-smelling oil on her temples and touched the raw red line beginning to raise itself into a scar on the side of Vreni's cheek. 'No more dreams tonight,' she said.

COMPANION

We have been observing him. His behaviour indicates that the glimmer Sabina placed on him has loosened.
He desires understanding about the glimpses of surfacing knowledge, and this shows us that he is the one.
—Message to Mežs Mājas

***

Vreni had slept late. When she washed her face next morning, her cheek was stinging and tender. *I might not have returned from the dream realm at all.*

The morning sun flowed over her as she sat at a small table near the window in the dining room. She watched the steam from her tea drift in and out of the beam of sunlight as she slowly peeled away the shell from a boiled egg.

'Vreni,' Sabina said, coming to sit opposite her, 'how are you feeling? I hope your cheek isn't too painful. We applied ointment last night, and with luck it should heal without a scar. You showed great bravery and skill facing what you did in the dream realm. We feel you're now ready to help us with our challenge.'

Vreni's breakfast suddenly tasted sour. Her memories of the dream realm poured over her. She squirmed in her seat.

'I touched the unsoftened potion,' she said. 'I can still feel its blackness clawing towards me through the bottle. Wouldn't my knowledge of that be enough to help you create a remedy? Surely I'd be able to feel something in your new potion that would let you know it would work.'

'We'd be blessed if that were true, Vreni, but no,' Sabina said. 'We still need you to seek out the remaining potion and bring it to us. We can only be successful in reversing the curse completely if we can analyse whatever remains of it. You're the one who can bring it to us.'

'Bring it from where?' Vreni asked.

'The alchemists were forced to flee as we were, but they've continued to conduct their business. They're a corporation now, called AlGuild. Although they're quite secretive and hide themselves away, we also know a lot about hiding so it's hard to stay hidden from us.' Sabina's eyes sparkled. 'Some of their staff can be boastful when they're flattered by a charming woman. We know where their headquarters are, and we're sure that's where they'd keep anything of value to them.'

'So I just go there? Just walk in and feel around for the potion?' Vreni said. 'What makes you so sure about all this?'

'Others have gone there before you,' Sabina said. 'And they found out a lot about the building and the grounds.'

'But they didn't bring back the potion?'

Vreni decided she didn't want to hear the answer.

Instead she thought of her mother, Rita and her aunties, held captive by the curse. She remembered her day in the city, seeing normal people with lives that flowed like streams, not frozen ponds, the way hers often seemed to. Finally, she thought of the lost girls, who had no one. The anger and determination she felt last night returned in a flood.

'I'll go to this AlGuild place and search, but am I really ready? How can I manage such a task on my own?'

'You won't be going alone.' Sabina looked towards the door.

As Vreni followed her gaze, Anna walked through the door, followed by a tall male shape silhouetted by the morning sun.

'Where's the dance action around here?'

'William! How? Why are you here?' Vreni jumped up and hugged him. He was solid, real.

'Small world,' he said. 'Anna asked me to help with a research project.' He looked around and shrugged. 'Uni likes to send field researchers to build up its reputation, and they also like to get their hands on new research findings first. So I'm here, wherever here is, to help with your work.' He eyed Sabina and Anna questioningly.

'How fortunate that I realised you two seem to know each other,' Anna said from the doorway. 'Please, William, help yourself to some food before we start work. And Vreni, would you give William a tour of our lovely gardens and make him feel welcome? Bring him to the laboratory in about an hour.'

'I'll leave you two to catch up,' Sabina said, following Anna out of the dining room.

'It's great to see you.' William hugged her tight. 'What are you doing here?'

'I'm here studying, too.' Vreni wasn't sure what to say, not knowing how much William remembered.

'How's Rita?' William asked.

'She's about the same. We haven't been doing much. No dancing.'

So much had changed, and Vreni struggled to make small talk. She was glad William hadn't asked about her father, but from what she understood, William's memories of that evening stopped with the dance party. He would have no memory of even being at her house.

She walked over to the breakfast counter and filled a plate for him. 'What are you studying at university?' she asked, even though she knew the answer.

'Science,' he said, getting to work on his breakfast. 'Bio-chemistry. My father insisted I follow the family tradition. The way he tells it, you'd think our ancestors *invented* chemistry. He's a big corporate hotshot.' William's words seemed tinged with anger. 'But I can't tell you much about him or his work. I've barely seen him over the last few years. He's always working when I'm home, which hasn't been very often, not since I was old enough to be sent away to school. Education is everything to my father. He says that he wants me to join him and work at his company when the time's right. He says it will be an "irresistible" offer. He can be very dramatic. He goes on about how important the work is, but he never tells me anything else.'

'So will you join his company?'

'Not likely.' He pushed his half-empty plate away. 'He's decided everything else for me, but he's not deciding my career path.'

'What about your mother?'

'I never knew her. She died when I was young.'

'That's sad, I'm so sorry,' Vreni said.

'Thanks. It is sad, but I never knew any different. I had a sister as well, she was born two years before I was, but when she was tiny, she died in her sleep, you know, SIDS. And just after I was born Mum also died in her sleep. I believe she was unwell after the birth.'

'How horrible.' Vreni reached out and squeezed his hand.

'I was lucky, really, because I was too young to realise. But it must've been unbearable for Dad because he's hardly ever spoken about her. There's not even a photo of her or my sister in the house. It's like they never existed.'

'So he works to fill the space your mother left.'

'Well, something drives him to work all the time, but I'm not like him.'

'In that case, let's take a walk through the gardens before you start work today.' Vreni directed William out into the warm morning sun.

Because of the old magic used by the Wise Sisters, the grounds surrounding the cottages and the laboratory buildings at Mežs Mājas were kept in a state of perpetual late springtime. The grass was lush and damp. The trees were thick with leaves and buds, but somehow also loaded with ripening fruit. The moist, cool air was heavy with sweet fragrance, and noisy with the buzz of insects and the songs of birds.

Vreni guided William along the gravel paths that wove between the overcrowded garden beds and glinting ponds. He took hold of her hand and she felt a spark. She wondered if he would remember the things that had been hidden by her father and Sabina. But would it really be fair on him to remember them?

'This place must have great irrigation because there's nothing but dry scrub for kilometres all around outside the valley,' William said. He seemed to accept this strange place without question.

He stared at her for a long moment, smiled broadly and pulled her off the path.

'Where are we going?' she asked.

'Over there.' He pointed to a small grove of pine trees. 'I heard there was a dance party in there.' He jumped into the clearing at the centre of the grove and started dancing, stomping around like an overwound toy.

Vreni laughed and gave a mocking round of applause.

'Would you like to dance?' he asked, walking over and taking her hand.

Vreni smiled. 'Yes, but just one.'

'We'll see,' William said, pulling her close to him. They stood, swaying together on the spongy carpet of pine needles. He offered a soft kiss, which she accepted.

As they danced in each other's arms in the cool shade of the small clearing, Vreni didn't care if he remembered everything or not. He was here with her and that would do for now.

Then William faltered for a moment, tensed slightly and pulled away from her, staring out towards the trees. He wobbled slightly, looking dazed. He shook his head and lowered his gaze to the ground.

'How's Parvils doing?' He choked out the question.

Vreni's stomach knotted. 'You remember?'

'Well, I'm not sure. I've had weird, random flashes of things, and that name ... I don't know, I thought it was my imagination. The note you pinned to my shirt said you got your driver to take me home because I'd been drinking too much. I didn't remember doing anything except dancing with you. Then all these other things have been flashing up.' William squeezed her hands. 'I did meet your family?'

'Yes.'

'I remember pieces of a very weird conversation, but I don't remember getting home, so for a while I believed your note.'

'The conversation was real, and weird,' she said. 'My father and Artūrs, our driver, gave you drinks that made you forget and fall asleep. Then Artūrs drove you home.'

'So the ... sleeping-curse thing is real?'

Heat rose in Vreni's face. 'It's real.'

William lurched and leaned against a tree, then slid down the trunk and landed heavily at the base. He stared at the ground, shaking his head. 'How is Rita, really?' he said.

'She's still sleeping, and safe, because of you.'

'When will she wake up?'

'Whenever she does. We never know how long we'll sleep.' Vreni shrugged. 'We just wait.'

'Unbelievable. How could that possibly happen?'

'You heard the fairy-tale my father told you that night. Trust me, it's true. I'm proof,' she said, spreading her arms out wide. 'Ta-da.'

William shook his head again, shrugged and then smiled. 'How is Parvils? And what was in those drinks?'

Vreni felt herself sag. Her knees buckled. William reached and caught her. She sat next to him, feeling the roughness of the tree's trunk through her shirt. 'Papa died.'

Each time she said the words, it became more real. Her throat ached and wouldn't let her say more. William wrapped his arms around her and waited.

'He was very old,' she began in a whisper. 'The Wise Sisters in Papa's tale have magic that can extend life, but no one outlives a sleeper. You already know that our lives span centuries. We leave so much behind us because we're trapped in the cycles of long-sleep. Papa waited, and protected us while we slept, and now he's been left behind by us.'

Vreni leaned into the warmth of William's chest and cried quietly. Surrounded by the cool freshness of the pine grove, she told him about the other astounding things that had happened since she arrived at Mežs Mājas.

'What an amazing world I've danced my way into,' he joked, kissing her lightly on the forehead.

'Speaking of amazing, you seem *amazingly* okay with

all the things you've found out. You must have a high strangeness threshold.'

'Honestly, Vreni, I don't know. Maybe I don't believe it all yet, maybe I just wanted to hear you out, to hear the whole story.' He nodded slowly. 'The scientific, logical me wants proof, but the dancing me is fascinated by it all. And I'm fascinated by you too, of course,' he added dramatically.

'Of course,' Vreni joined in. 'Maybe you're under my spell.' Her father said that the Wise Sisters saw something in William. Or had they done something to him, something they hadn't told her about yet? The Sisters were good at secrets.

Sabina appeared, walking towards the grove of pines. William fell silent in mid-sentence, looking awkward.

'She's a Sister, William. She knows it all.' Vreni gestured to Sabina. 'The Pratigs Māsa, the Wise Sisters, are part of my family's support, part of the circle of influence Papa talked to you about that night.'

'So, am I really here to do research?' William asked.

'Do you want him to go with me?' Vreni asked Sabina and shook her head. 'This is not William's problem.' But she couldn't help thinking how much she wanted him to be there with her. First date: steal a body. Second date: unknown danger. *Maybe I'll never be a good girlfriend to have.*

'Go where?' William asked.

'Yes, if he's willing, we'll send him with you,' Sabina confirmed.

'But it'll be dangerous,' Vreni protested.

'What will be dangerous?' he asked.

'There have been previous attempts,' Sabina said, 'and because of those efforts we're better prepared now. Your glimmer is gone. Look inside yourself, at the training, the magic. You'll see how truly ready you are, *Sister Veronika*.'

'What?' William asked loudly. He stood up. 'What? Where? What danger? I'm right here, you know.'

'I'm sorry, William, everything will be made clear soon,' Sabina said. 'For now, know that you will play a vital part in this. I need to show you both what we know, but let's talk more inside.'

PLANS WITHIN PLANS

William will open the door for us.
He believes it's only our magic that allows him to do it.
It's better that he believes this for now.
—Mežs Mājas, strategy discussions

***

The laboratory was clean and white and ordered. A few sisters were working quietly on something that looked surprisingly uninteresting to Vreni, considering how magical everything else had been so far. The lab workers nodded towards them as they followed Sabina past the benches and through a heavy stained-glass door at the end of the lab.

The room behind the door was vastly different. At its centre was a broad wooden table covered with antiquated bottles and bowls, and lush bunches of herbs that filled the air with a sweet, spicy aroma.

Anna sat stiffly at the table studying the yellowing pages in a heavy, leather-bound book. Sabina indicated that they should sit.

Vreni glanced at the book's mottled pages. She could see by the changes of penmanship that the text must have been written by many sisters over the years. The pages were peppered with diagrams, runes and colourful illuminations. Anna turned the page and Vreni saw a highly decorated drawing of a labyrinth.

Anna looked up from the book. 'Are you two are willing to help us?'

'Help you do *what*?' William's voice had an edge now.

'To help us free Vreni's family from the sleeping curse once and forever,' Anna said.

William started to speak, but Anna raised her hand to stop him and continued. 'We've travelled and hidden alongside their family throughout the centuries, and we've watched as the Alķimķi Gilde also manoeuvred and concealed themselves. We know they've continued to grow their riches and power. They've become the AlGuild, and, like us, they've developed a necessary corporate structure to continue their true purpose.'

Anna rubbed her hand thoughtfully over the painted illumination of the labyrinth. 'We need you two to enter the AlGuild compound and retrieve what remains of the original sleeping potion. Over the years we've studied and developed our knowledge. All we need now is the last remnant of the potion and we can fully reverse its effects and free you all.'

William tried to joke. 'Happily ever after.'

'Yes, but without the *ever*,' Vreni said. 'Our family's had more than its fair share of ever after already.'

Anna continued, ignoring their attempt at banter. 'We

believe the AlGuild would keep anything they prize inside a remote centre for research and development. It wouldn't do their corporate image any good if people discovered their true nature, or their grisly history. You saw some of that, Vreni, in the dream realm, and you need to know they haven't changed much over the centuries. The AlGuild continues to profit from destruction and misery, and we, through our holdings, endeavour to diminish and soften the harm they do to people and the environment.'

Anna glanced at Sabina, who continued. 'We've learned from previous attempts that the internal layout of the R&D building is in the form of a labyrinth. If this holds to tradition, you'll find what you seek in its centre. There's only one path in, and we presume with as much certainty as we can have, that there'll be a shorter, direct path out.' Sabina smiled weakly at Anna.

'A labyrinth is not a maze, one path in and one path out,' Vreni said. 'So why have you failed before?'

'It's true that there's no choice but to follow the single labyrinthine path,' Anna said. 'The labyrinth is like life, and in life we sometimes face challenges along the way.'

'You'll do well against these challenges, Vreni,' Sabina said. 'We know. We watched you in the dream realm.'

'Watched? How?' Vreni asked, amazed.

'Mention of you is in here.' Anna patted the book. 'There's a story of a girl that fits your description, who came and went on the day of the cursing. The sisters took note because this girl knew where to find the box of spells, and how to use the magic it contained without needing any instructions.'

'We sent you to the dream realm already knowing you would be successful,' Sabina said.

'But I'll be travelling in the real world now,' Vreni said.

'The dream realm was real enough while you were there,' Sabina said, touching the scar on Vreni's cheek. 'And you used your magic with skill and bravery.' She took both of Vreni's hands in hers. 'Have faith, Sister Veronika, bringer of victory,' she said formally.

'If I'm going to be victorious, why does William have to come with me?'

'To enter the main building there's a new bio-lock, a touch pad,' Sabina explained. 'We've created an amulet, a key, that allows the wearer to open the door, but if *you* touch the panel, Vreni, the system will sense the magic in you and you won't even get inside. William will open the door for you.' She placed a silver, key-shaped amulet around his neck.

'The compound is fenced but not guarded,' Anna said. 'They've created elemental pets, like the wolf you saw in the dream realm, to defend the grounds around the building. We don't know what these defences will be because these pets tend to destroy themselves or each other frequently and new ones replace them. We just know what we've seen in the past.'

'We also know that the members of AlGuild are complacent,' Sabina continued. 'They presume their defences will kill any intruders so they don't monitor the grounds in any other way. They won't be expecting anyone to survive the trip through their Pleasure Gardens and come picking their bio-lock.'

'If they follow with traditions about labyrinths laid down in the ancient writings, once inside you'll meet further challenges as you move through the building,' Anna said. 'We're making every preparation possible to support you. You'll have William, but we'll be with you as well, in our own way.'

Anna looked at Sabina and tilted her head questioningly. Sabina widened her eyes and gave the slightest shake of her head in return.

'We're making final preparations tonight,' was all Anna said.

'All will become clear for you both in the morning. Go and rest. Spend some time together. I'm so glad you've found each other again.' Sabina squeezed Vreni and William's hands, and smiled. 'Go, we'll see you both tomorrow.'

***

The evening was cool and quiet in the garden. The daytime frenzy of bees and birds had given over to the slow, regular sound of some unseen insect that thrummed quietly to welcome the rising moon.

Vreni and William found a shadowy, hidden place that was separated from the rest of the garden by a tall curving hedge. They sat on a smooth polished bench, the wood still held the last of the day's warmth. The black glass of the pond mirrored the golden light that spilled from the cottage windows and into the darkness. Laughter and chatter rose and fell.

They sat for a long moment, held by the evening calm.

'Are you sure you want to do this?' Vreni asked quietly.

'It could be the start of something beautiful between us,' William said in a mock-romantic voice.

Vreni realised that he wasn't going to be serious about what lay ahead, not tonight, so she joined in with his joke. 'Maybe you're a little too old to be my boyfriend,' she teased. 'You're at university already.'

William burst out laughing. '*I* am too old for *you*?' he snorted. 'If my estimations are correct, I won't be too old to be your boyfriend for approximately eighty-two more years. You look great for your age, by the way. And what is that, one hundred and how many?'

She punched him. He kissed her and everything else faded. There was only the kiss. She rested her head on his shoulder, remembering all the details of all their kisses, and locking the happy thrill of them safely in her heart so she would have them forever.

'So you just freeze in time during long-sleep?' he said quietly after a while.

'That's what happens. Everything stops.'

'You must've seen so many changes in one hundred years,' William said.

'I suppose that's something good about the curse, I've seen some amazing things. If people had said that such things were possible back when I was young, we would've questioned their sanity, and now I've seen more than I could ever have imagined.'

'It must be like having a time machine.'

She smiled. 'I suppose so. When I was young it was still

mostly horses for travel and fire for cooking, especially in the countryside. Since then I've seen cars appear and reinvent themselves, getting sleeker and faster with each awakening. I've seen television and telephone. What marvels they are, where sound and images can be sent along wires, through the air, to be shared by thousands, and now millions. I remember being terrified when I first saw planes roaring through the sky, and even more amazingly, the next time I woke humans had ripped themselves free of Earth and sent men all the way to the moon. I watched it, you know, I watched *my* Neil Armstrong walk on the moon.' She sighed.

'Oh, *my* astronaut hero,' William said, putting his hands over his heart.

'Ooh, jealous,' she teased. 'You know, I vowed I would go there one day, and with all the fantastic things that had already happened I thought it would just be a matter of time, but I'm still waiting. Maybe one day. Computers are the most astounding things of all, but they gave Papa lots more excuses to make us stay at home. He said we could shop online and see any place on Earth at the click of a button.'

'You all just sleep and wake and ...' He shrugged.

'That's the way it's always been for me. Sometimes Rita's awake, sometimes Mama, sometimes all of us together, even my aunties. Sometimes Rita is older than me,' she laughed. 'Now, that can feel strange. But I guess nothing will seem strange ever again after tomorrow. That will be—'

'What about all the magic?' he interrupted before she could finish. 'Where does that fit in?'

'Grandmama had many aunts: Magrietina, Dālija, Lilija, Efeja and Rozālija, that was Veca Tante's name. They were the original Wise Sisters. They spun the old magic. Grandmama inherited everything instead of Rozālija, so the old aunt became filled with envy and hatred, and she looked for the darkness in the magic, fear instead of faith, cruelty instead of love, and death instead of life. She wove death, spun it into a potion. You know the rest.'

'This AlGuild, they're really still operating after all this time? What about Veca Tante, could she still be alive?'

'Maybe. Rita and I wonder about that sometimes. Her sisters used magic to extend their lives, but I doubt any magic would work for four centuries.'

'And you? You're quite beautiful for an *old* lady.'

'That's because I get plenty of beauty sleep.' She nudged him hard in the ribs with her elbow. She stood up, leaned down and kissed him. 'Speaking of sleep.'

She took his hand and led him to the small gardener's cottage that had been prepared for him. Then she kissed his cheek and turned for her own bed, drawn by the echoing lilt of the Sisters' voices as they filled the evening air with the sound of their humming.

AMULETS

*William has responded well to the recovery of the hidden
memories we folded into his glimmer. His allegiance
appears strong. Our suspicions and hopes about him have
proven correct. He is the key. He's the one to breech the
door to the labyrinth. He may falter when he
learns his lineage, but I feel the goodness in his heart.
Others might presume his fate is predestined,
but we all have free will. We will proceed.*
— Anna and Sabina, strategy planning

***

Early-morning sunlight sliced through the violet shadows
within Vreni's room. The brightness penetrated her eyelids and blended with her dream of the cool garden the
evening before, where she had sat with William. In the
dream the moonlight dappled her face, but the moon-
lit dream was gradually solidifying into day, the day she
would walk into AlGuild.

Her hands tightened into fists. She was fully awake.

When Vreni reached the dining room, William was

already sitting in a block of bright sunlight at the table by the window. He was picking curiously at a platter of black bread, cheeses and fruit-filled pastries.

She realised her hands were clenched again and she made a conscious effort to relax them. *Whatever this day brings, it will happen soon enough without me talking about it now.* She crossed the room, hoping that William would be pretending too.

'I could ask the kitchen if they have porridge instead.' She lightly kissed the top of his head.

'No, no, I'm just glad you're here. I was wondering if I was expected to eat all this myself.'

'Of course, it's all for you,' she joked, 'and lots of coffee to wash it down.' She poured two cups of coffee and put one in front of him. *'Ēst! Baudīt!'* She gestured dramatically towards the platter. 'Eat! Enjoy!'

'I heard you mention porridge,' the cook said, placing a large, steaming bowl on the table.

'Thank you,' they both said, laughing.

'Don't mention any more food,' William whispered, 'or we'll be here until lunch.'

'Shhh, don't say *lunch*,' she whispered, laughing.

***

After a breakfast filled with fake small talk, they walked slowly through the gardens towards the lab building. Vreni remained silent, not trusting herself to talk about what might be coming soon. She didn't want to hear what

William might say in reply. She knew everything would change once they went inside.

The lab door squeaked open. They nodded polite greetings as they walked past the Sisters, who looked as though they'd been sitting at the workbenches since yesterday.

Vreni walked slowly to the other end of the sterile white room, looking at the stained-glass birds and flowers that were all that was left between her and this day starting. She breathed deeply and pushed open the heavy door.

Inside, she was surprised to see that Sabina and Anna were not sitting at the table. Instead, an ancient Sister sat there, reading and scribbling notes. The old woman stopped and looked up at them as they entered. Her piercing blue eyes stared out through folds of papery skin. Without introducing herself, she started speaking as if William and Vreni had only stepped out of the room a moment ago.

'We're as sure as we can be that the AlGuild building conceals a labyrinth.' She was drawing a labyrinth on a small scrap of paper as she spoke. 'Because the path through the labyrinth winds around on itself, wheels within wheels, the passageways fold, wrapping around each other, offering maximum protection to whatever is at its centre. So the centre is where you need to go.' She began tracing a path on her drawing with her crooked finger. 'There's only ever one path to the centre of a labyrinth, so there can be no shortcuts and the way will be defended.'

She looked up. 'You have visited the dream realm, Veronika. You've seen a small example of AlGuild's beginnings. You have first-hand knowledge of what they're capable of. We can't predict what might await you once you enter the labyrinth, but we'll be with you. All the Wise Sisters here at Mežs Mājas have gathered what they need from the earth and the animals to form magical charms and amulets that hold the power of nature within them, ready for you to bring to life, to do your bidding as you see fit. Along with this nature magic, the Sisters have stored magic from themselves, which they give freely as their contribution to your quest.'

Vreni shook her head. 'I don't understand.'

'Remember the talismans and charms you discovered hidden in your clothes that gave you protection? You'll wear something similar but many times more powerful.'

The old Sister reached for an ornate box on the table. She lifted the lid and gently removed a thick ribbon of silk that was knotted to form a large crimson loop. Threaded onto the ribbon was a cluster of small glass spheres that glinted, reflecting the soft light of the desk lamp. She laid them gently in the palm of her creased hand.

Vreni leaned in to look more closely at the necklace. The spheres contained whirling colours and what appeared to be tiny objects. She tried to see inside the glass balls. Some were filled with what looked like coloured smoke or mist, swirling and twisting as if it were alive and straining to be free of its glass prison. Others seemed to contain liquids. Some of the liquids were transparent and others appeared to have tiny particles floating in them. Two of the spheres shone like pearls, one golden and the other cool silver.

'The magic in the charms on this necklace hold the

tools you might need to complete this journey, young Sister Veronika, but they're only tools. You'll need to use your powers to realise the potential within each sphere. It'll be up to you how and when you use them. They will obey you. Your intentions will become their undeniable purpose.'

'But how will I—' Vreni's question was cut short.

'You will know, Veronika. Reflect on the lessons you discovered when we lifted the glimmer. That was a life-time of training for you, and almost a century of careful preparation by us. You are the one, look inside and see that it's true.' The old Sister grasped Vreni's hands and locked her in an icy stare. She drew closer and began humming quietly.

Vreni leaned heavily on the edge of the table as felt the old woman somehow visiting her thoughts. The memories of her training began shifting around inside her mind, flashing vividly as she was guided to recall them all. With each rising memory, Vreni felt the strength of the magical influence build within her. She felt sure this ancient Sister was adding her own strength to Vreni's skill.

The old woman finally released Vreni's hands from her grip and smiled.

'Thank you for reminding me,' Vreni said, as she caught her breath and reached towards the necklace.

The old Sister's eyes sparkled within the soft folds of her smile and she placed the necklace into Vreni's hands. 'The green liquid in this charm is the softening formula we used to save your grandmother.' She touched the gold and silver pearls, and a third, which was blood red. 'The silver one is filled with the powerful chanting of your Sisters, and the gold is their glorious singing. Never forget how powerful our words are. The red one is filled with the strength of all the Sisters here today.'

'And these?' Vreni asked, touching the spheres that seemed to contain something alive.

'All of these ones are full of things that wiggle and squirm and fly and hop,' the Sister said. 'Nature's creatures ready to do your bidding.'

Vreni thought of the whisper birds. They were such tiny creatures, but they were still able to defend her against the wolf.

She cast her eye across the other charms. They created an amazing glistening rainbow, but her eyes were drawn to the two spheres that hung in the very centre of the cluster. One contained a bright turquoise-blue eye that stared out knowingly at her, and inside the other was a pair of rosy, disembodied lips that looked to be drawn into a sad smile.

'These ones are different,' Vreni said.

'With those charms you'll never be alone,' the crinkled face answered.

Alone. Vreni felt dizzy and cold. 'Where are Sabina and Anna?' she asked.

'They are ... preparing.' The old Sister took the string of charms from Vreni and touched them gently. 'It's time for you to go to them and complete final arrangements before you leave.'

The old woman stood with surprising agility and placed the loop of silken ribbon holding the amulets around

Vreni's neck. Then she gripped her shoulders, smiled at her warmly and kissed her on the forehead with her soft, wrinkled lips. Without saying anything more, she turned and pushed open the door behind the table and walked through, leaving Vreni and William to follow.

In the adjoining room the air was filled with singing and chatter and the Sisters moved purposefully to and fro. Details about the room seeped into Vreni's awareness. First, the singing and chanting was too quiet for the number of sisters present, and a group stood motionless at the edge of the room, fixed in a trance-like state, holding bowls and baskets full of insects and animals.

Sabina and Anna were still nowhere to be seen. Why weren't they here preparing with everyone else? Her breath quickened as she searched the room for them again.

'Tell me what they're doing,' Vreni said to the old Sister, walking towards the group of entranced Sisters who were holding equally spellbound creatures.

'Those amulets you're wearing all need physical substance to work,' the old woman said. 'We took the creatures and placed them within the charm you're wearing. These Sisters stay here giving their comfort, calmness and resolve to each remaining insect and animal in their group. The Sisters will stay with them like this, not eating, drinking or sleeping until your task is done. By doing this we're offering one of our Sisters to take the place of the missing members of their swarm, or army, or flutter. It's the exchange we make for their sacrifice.'

'And the silent singers?' Vreni stared at the group of

swaying Sisters. They appeared to be singing but they made no sound.

'You have amulets, the gold and silver pearls that contain the powerful songs and chants we have used in our magic for centuries, so of course these singers have given their voices,' the old Sister said, smiling.

'But they can't give up so much for me.' Vreni's eyes burned with tears.

'Calm yourself, young Sister Veronika. They're fully committed to this cause, and their sacrifice is only temporary. All will return to normal at the end of your quest.'

'But what if I don't—'

'Hush, girl, the balance will always be restored in its own way.' The old woman gently wiped a lone tear from Vreni's cheek.

All at once Vreni's resolve crumbled. Her breakfast started churning in her stomach. She let out a long sigh, as if she was deflating, and crouched down close to the cool stone floor. 'Where are Sabina and Anna? I can't do this alone,' she whispered.

William leaned down and gently helped her stand.

'You're never alone, Sister Veronika,' the old Sister said. 'Look around you. You have the talent, magic and love of all the Wise Sisters with you always. You have William bearing the magic of the key, and our magic will ensure that Sabina's eyes will see what you see, and that the words from Anna's lips will guide you and advise you on your journey through the labyrinth.'

'What does that mean? Where are they?' Vreni felt hot.

Her stomach was a storm. She searched the room, willing Sabina and Anna to appear and comfort her.

Finally, she saw them enter. As they came closer, and Vreni could see their faces, the meaning of the old Sister's words became frighteningly clear. One of Sabina's eyes was gone. Where her right eye should be, smooth, pale skin had grown over as though the eye had never been there. All that remained was a hollow covered with taught skin, framed by a curved line of long dark eyelashes. The eyelid appeared to be sealed closed, covering the empty socket where her eye used to be.

Next to Sabina was the unbelievable sight of Anna. Yesterday, Anna had had a serene smile and a mouth always full of song and wise words, but today there was nothing but a tiny, shrivelled fissure where her lips used to be.

Vreni heard a sobbing groan rise in her throat. Sabina and Anna held their arms open, and she ran and hugged them.

'Why have you done this thing?' Vreni said with a trembling voice.

'Because we promised to be with you, just as the aunts promised to be with your grandmother centuries ago,' Sabina said, 'and it's these promises that makes the Wise Sisters stronger with each challenge we face. We will travel with you through our amulets. We want to be with you.'

And we want to keep an eye on you two lovebirds.

Vreni gasped. Anna's voice came from somewhere inside her own head. She placed her hands to her temples and looked at Anna, whose eyes were smiling even if what was left of her mouth could not.

'She can speak with you and answer your questions,' Sabina explained quietly.

'But how will you hear what I say?' Vreni looked among the charms and saw a tiny ear. 'Oh no!' She quickly ran her hands across Sabina's cheeks and under her long, dark hair, and felt an unnatural smoothness where her right ear should have been. 'I can't ask you to do this thing. Undo it now,' she begged.

'Hush,' whispered Sabina, holding Vreni close. 'This is my choice. I, we, want to be with you.' Sabina stared at her. The sealed eye twitched as she smiled. 'I will serve as the eyes and ears of your Sisters, to watch out for you, and Anna will relay our messages and be your advisor along the journey.'

They each took one of Vreni's hands. 'The Wise Sisters are never alone,' Sabina said reassuringly.

Vreni felt the enormous weight of the amulets she was wearing. Her Sisters had made unthinkable sacrifices to aid her on this quest. Their faith was their true gift to her. They believed she was Sister Veronika, bringer of victory. They believed she would bring the potion to them. Then their faith would be rewarded, and they would all be restored and made whole again.

The Wise Sisters had lived with this lore throughout the centuries. They knew that for someone to achieve a thing they needed to be willing to sacrifice something towards that achievement. *I hope I can repay their sacrifice.*

'William, you have your amulet,' Sabina said, touching

the key-shaped charm that hung around his neck. 'When you reach the door of the building, hold this with one hand before you place your other hand on the bio-lock pad. We'll try to get you as close as we can to the boundary fence at the south side of the AlGuild compound, but you have to travel through the surrounding grounds by yourselves. As we told you, they're defended but not guarded. Though these defences will be dangerous enough. You only need concern yourself with overcoming them, as the only guard we've seen is at the building's front door. If he doesn't see you, there won't be anyone else outside the building to raise the alarm.'

Three of the young Sisters came in and mumbled their blessings. Sofia gave Vreni her favourite scarf, and William his coat. Emma offered a small bundle, which William stowed in an inside coat pocket.

'Bring the potion back in this,' Emma said, handing Vreni a small pouch on a silk ribbon.

Vreni linked arms with Sabina and Anna as they made their way back through the lab and out into the morning sunshine. They crunched reluctantly across the gravel path, and after forcing cheerful goodbyes and good-lucks Vreni and William slid into the back seat of the car and drove away.

THE PLEASURE GARDENS

The AlGuild has power over nature and the elements,
as we do, but they only achieve destruction. Their pets
wait within the grounds of the compound, and defend
it as their form and nature permits. The AlGuild is satisfied
and complacent, and posts only one human guard.
—Pratigs Māsa, quest records

***

Vreni and William landed lightly on the grass inside the high but otherwise undefended fence that surrounded the AlGuild compound. They looked around cautiously. There were no guards in sight.

Vreni heard Anna's disembodied voice: *The fence doesn't need to be a barrier. You haven't met the real defences yet.*

To the north, the flat steel roof of the imposing AlGuild building was just visible behind a grass-covered ring of mounded earth. East of the building, they could see the security gate, which was closed and unattended. A pathway ran from the deserted carpark outside the gate through a break in the miniature hills. They guessed the path led towards the building's entrance.

They walked east for a short distance along the fence line, then turned and walked west again, trying to decide how to approach. It would have been reassuring to have satellite photos of the compound but, not surprisingly, the Sisters had not been able to find any.

The gardens were vast and quiet. The building and its one human guard were a long way off, but they didn't know who or what would be guarding the door. Vreni thought of the wolf in the dream realm and shuddered.

'I wonder what they use for defence out here,' she said.

'I guess we'll know soon enough,' William replied.

Walking northward towards the raised, grassy ring, they had taken no more than a dozen steps when a strong wind blew up from the north with such force that they had to lean into it to keep moving at all.

'Their defence is to blow us back over d'fence,' William joked. He took Vreni by the hand and together they pushed into the now howling wind.

Vreni could see a faint stain gathering in the air above the ring of low hills. It seemed to hover, as if waiting, preparing itself. She looked on, captivated, wanting to keep watching even though she knew it indicated nothing good.

The distant, stained air coalesced into a small dark tornado. The funnel took on a solid shape and then started moving south, not on a random path as might be expected, but aiming directly at them.

'They do mean to blow us back over the fence,' she said, tightening her grip on William's hand.

As the outer edge of the tornado reached them, they

felt the sting of dust and dirt that was being blown around by the wind. The particles gave the swirling funnel a red-brown colour. Small pebbles and tiny sharp fragments stung the skin on their face and arms.

Suddenly they were inside the tornado. It howled and screamed around them. Vreni closed her eyes tightly. She could feel needle-like shards stabbing at her eyelids as if they were trying to reach her eyes and blind her. Her nostrils filled with dust. The dust smelled of blood. She wondered if this dust had mixed with the blood of others who had failed to breech the AlGuild's defences.

William and Vreni clung to each other. They could no longer see which way they should be walking or what other dangers might be hiding inside the dark screeching vortex.

The shards were larger now, and sharper. They were digging into their skin, cutting them. Vreni felt an unexpected coolness on her skin as the wind blew over it, and she realised her blood was being cooled by the menacing wind.

She felt an abrupt coldness, and her mind was suddenly bombarded with images of battered bodies spinning around, being twisted and contorted by the wind. She tried to open her eyes but the red dust blasted at them. She tried to push away the vision of horror, but failed, and she stood frozen.

The images in her mind were of bodies tumbling endlessly, ragged flesh being shredded, and droplets of blood being blown away by the unceasing gale, arms and legs being pulled and snapped, the flesh stripped from their bodies until there was nothing left except pieces of bone worn down into tiny chunks of rubble, and tiny sharpened needles that sliced and ripped and whirled in the frenzy. She imagined piles of bones, polished clean and left lying in the tornado's wake, shining in the sunshine as the only remnant of the tornado's passing.

She was drawn from this ghostly vision by the pain of sharp objects that pelted her rigid body. She realised with a shudder that the tornado had given her a view of their fate. They were to become what she had seen, mashed flesh and broken bone.

William leaned heavily against her. He was pulling down on her arm, on her shoulder. She thought he must be so badly hurt that he could no longer stand. Her knees buckled under his weight and she fell onto the grass. He was pressing into her back with his hand, pushing her down. He didn't stop until she lay flat on the ground.

She noticed the sweet smell of the grass for a brief moment and then she felt the great weight of William lying on top of her, his arms encircling her face. The screech of the wind lessened slightly as his arms blocked the noise. She realised that William wasn't injured, he was protecting her.

They lay together as the bloody storm raged around them. Within the howls of the wind Vreni was sure she heard screams, voices crying out in anguish. She wanted to raise her head because she was so sure she would be able to see the tortured faces, but William held her down too firmly. The screams pushed their way into her mind until she wanted to jump up and join in their tortured howling, but she remained on the ground, and at last the screams and the faces faded.

Everything became still. The wind had stopped even more quickly than it had started, and the silence buzzed in her ears.

'Vreni, stay down, it's just the eye of the tornado,' William said.

She struggled free of his protective arms for long enough to see the red wall of the spinning funnel surrounding them and a tiny circle of blue sky far above. She felt for the necklace, making sure the charms were there and wondering what action she should take.

She heard Anna's voice: *No, Veronika, no magic, not out here. If they don't see evidence of magic, they'll assume their pets have dealt with the problem and they won't even come and look. Wind is just breath. We can only breathe out for so long. It will exhaust itself soon enough.*

'Anna says it will end soon,' she said to William.

'But not until—'

His words were lost as the gritty winds started to lash them again. He pushed her face down into the grass again and covered her. She could feel his body tensing as the chunks of bone struck him. They lay huddled together, faces pushed into the ground, listening to the howling wind. At first Vreni cringed every time she felt William's body tense and flinch, but as the onslaught continued his recoiling gave her comfort. If he was reacting, he was alive. She was not going to be left alone...yet.

***

Anna was right. The wind did finally blow itself out. Finally, they dared to raise their heads, and then rolled over and lay on the grass staring up at the peaceful blue of the sky. There was no sign of the maelstrom except for a circle of flattened, bloodstained grass where the tornado had touched down.

Vreni's face felt stiff, as if she was wearing a mask. When she moved her mouth to speak her face stung, her skin felt as though it had been burned, and she could see bruises already forming where her arms had been struck with pieces of bone.

William's face was smeared with red, and his coat was tattered and ripped. Vreni thought of the shredded bodies she had seen in her vision and knew it could have been much worse.

'We could've been ripped to shreds,' William said, helping her sit up.

'That's what I saw, in some kind of vision,' she said. 'I saw the others, the ones who've already died inside that storm.'

'I saw some of them, too, like some kind of hallucination. Interesting strategy using the visions so we'd stand, frozen with fear, while the tornado ripped us to pieces. It didn't work, though.'

'No, but that was because of you. I was overwhelmed, but you could still think, still act. Thank you.'

'You're welcome.' He shrugged and brushed the dust off his coat sleeves. 'It makes sense that you're more sensitive to it, with all that magicky stuff you do.'

'Magicky?'

They stood slowly and checked themselves for any injuries before heading north again.

The ring of mounded earth now blocked their view so they moved cautiously through a low point to check what lay ahead. Within the ring of hills was a wide band of manicured lawn, bordered on the far side by an equally broad ring of flowers, and beyond that a ring of trees, and beyond the trees the building, almost fully hidden.

The circle of lawn curved away in both directions, as did the hills. Midway across the ring of neat green lawn was a series of ponds, spaced evenly around what could be seen of the grass circle. Each pond was decorated with a few glass statues that had been placed at the water's edge.

'It seems oddly unnecessary to have statues here where no one will see them,' Vreni said, staring at the nearest pond. All she could think about was the cool water, washing off the blood and dust, and cooling down her burning skin. She stepped forward.

'Wait,' cautioned William, grabbing her arm.

'What, sea monsters?'

She shook off his hand and kept walking. She kneeled at the edge of the pond and scooped up handfuls of cool water and splashed her face, then rinsed the red crust from her arms. She kicked off her boots and socks and plunged her feet into the water. She laughed at William, who was standing back from the pond as if he was on guard duty.

'You look like you've been lost in a murky forest,' she

teased. She took her scarf, wet it in the pond and threw the wet ball of cloth at him. 'Wash off the dust.'

William caught the wet scarf and sat down, wiping red grime from his face and hands. Vreni lay back on the grass and closed her eyes. She would take advantage of William guarding her for just a moment and rest. The water felt cool on her feet. It felt almost too cool and she felt a chill seeping into her bones.

'Come on, Sleeping Beauty, it's time to get going,' William called.

'I know.' Vreni pulled her feet out of the water and stood up. 'My feet feel frozen anyway.' She laughed and reached for her boots, but as she went to take a step, she found that her feet would not move. It was as if they were planted in the ground.

'William!' She lost her balance and fell over.

William was by her side in a second. Gelatinous ribbons of water trailed up from the pond's surface, reaching out of the pond and wrapping around Vreni's feet and ankles. He looked at the strange unfrozen ice holding her prisoner and then at the icy crystal statues standing around the pond.

'No way!'

'What is it?'

'Another defence,' was all he said.

'But I can't move.'

William ran to the pond's edge and grabbed a large rock. He lifted it high into the air.

'What are you doing?' she cried.

He didn't wait to answer but brought the rock down

with full force onto the ribbons of crystallising water on her feet. They shattered, became liquid again and splashed onto the grass.

'Move!' he yelled, pulling her away from the pond.

Vreni stumbled and had trouble standing. William held her, bearing her weight, and forced himself to look at her feet.

'What was all that about?' she asked, stifling a sob.

'Did I hurt you?'

'I don't think so,' she said, wriggling her toes.

'Thank goodness. I hoped I'd broken the crystal and not your feet.' He hugged her.

'What? Why?'

'The water from the pond was hardening around your feet,' he explained.

'You mean those statues are ...' She groped for her boots and scuttled further away from the water.

'Yep, victims of the second defence,' he said. He supported her as she tried to calm her shaking legs.

'Earth and water,' Vreni said. 'The defences out here are created from the elements.'

'Earth. Well, dirt and bone, swirling at lethal speeds inside a tornado, and water that freezes you into a crystal statue.' William shuddered.

'Only air and fire to go,' Vreni said, pulling on her boots.

'Only,' William said quietly, handing back her scarf.

***

Everything remained still and quiet in the garden. So

far Sabina and Anna's theory had been proven right. The defence system seemed to work independently of any guards, and there was no sign they had been noticed yet. They kept walking steadily northward. They watched and listened, alert for the next elemental defence.

'Fire is obviously dangerous, but at least we'll see it coming,' William said.

'We can't see air, but I don't know how air could be dangerous,' Vreni said.

They walked cautiously across the last of the neat green lawn. The next ring of the garden was filled with wildflowers, scattered randomly among a shaggy carpet of green. Long, spindly stalks supported swollen yellow-green flower buds. Some of the flowers were open, dotting the waving sea of green with bright colour.

Beyond the wildflowers Vreni could see a circle of trees planted close together to create a dense shady arbour, and beyond the treetops she saw glimpses of the AlGuild building.

The labyrinth was inside. Would the potion really be there? What else would they find? But they weren't there yet, so she focused again on the flowers, watching for any sign of danger.

William led the way into the wildflowers. Up close, the buds looked like swollen, misshapen tulips, balanced on top of over-tall stems that were green-brown and thorny. The blooms swayed in the light breeze.

Vreni heard Anna's voice: *Do you still have your knife?*

'Yes.' Vreni touched the smooth leather handle of the knife hanging at her hip.

Good, you'll need it soon.

'Why?' Vreni gripped the handle, and her hand was suddenly clammy. She scanned the sea of flowers again. Nothing. 'Why?' she repeated. *Those flowers have been conjured.*

William strode on ahead with his long coat flapping and the hem catching on the thorny flower stalks. He paused for a moment to pull it free, bent down and picked a flower. 'For you.' He reached out to hand Vreni the bloom.

The petals quivered. She was sure of it. Yes, there it was again, the slightest movement rippling across the flower. Then the petals appeared to come loose from the stalk, flapped gently and stretched, ruffling and unfolding. The flower transformed into an oddly proportioned butterfly.

Each of the butterfly's petal-wings was larger than Vreni's outstretched hand, but its body was tiny, almost hidden between the oversized wings. There was movement all around them. Twenty or more flowers were opening and transforming. When each was fully open it rested on the thorny stalks, the wings rising and falling in unison, with a rhythm reminiscent of breathing. Every butterfly had one large eye on each of its wings. Some pairs were blue, others green or brown.

'It blinked.' William stared at the butterfly creature on top of the stalk he still held in his hand.

Vreni watched the eyes on the wings blink once, then again. 'This can't be a good thing,' she said, as the eyes on each wing of every one of the woken creatures blinked in unison.

William's butterfly blinked again and ruffled its wings. Then it flapped gently into the air and hovered level with his face. The others followed and soon the small rabble of creatures was flapping and hovering around him. The leader was watching, looking at William and Vreni in turn. It landed lightly on William's head. Vreni was captivated. They seemed to be lingering in the air so peacefully.

Another blink and everything changed.

In a swift blur of wings, the creature had wrapped itself around William's head, covering his face. At least five of the creatures followed the first, moving with blinding speed, wrapping themselves, layer upon layer, over William's face.

Vreni heard his stifled screams, and watched as he clawed at the wings that gripped his face. He thrashed and contorted in his effort to pry them loose. Then his cries faded and he sank to his knees, collapsing onto the ground.

Vreni stood frozen for a disbelieving moment, trying to make sense of what she was seeing. Then she reached out, prying at the wings that seemed glued to William's face.

Your knife, Vreni, Anna said.

As Vreni pulled the knife from its pouch, she felt the first feather-soft wing brush her own face. She grabbed for it and pulled the creature from her skin. Slicing madly at it with her knife, she separated the body from the wings, and the creature shrivelled and turned brown. She reached for another that had landed on her head and then stabbed at the others waiting in the air. She sliced again and again. Each severed corpse withered where it fell.

She lunged for William. He had stopped fighting now and his legs shuddered weakly. She pried her fingers under the top butterfly, severing its wings from its body.

'Get *off* him,' she yelled, tears blurring her vision.

He still lives, Anna said. *You're doing well. Keep going.*

Vreni clawed each creature loose and cut away its body, stopping only to slash at those that flew towards them for a fresh attack. Time seemed to drag. She urged her fingers to move more quickly through the layers that entombed William's head. Finally, she cut through the last set of wings, watching them desiccate against William's pale skin. He gasped a ragged howling breath, then coughed and sobbed.

'You're safe, they're dead,' Vreni said, pulling him close as she fended off the last of the circling creatures. She realised how desperately she needed to hold him after watching him struggling on the ground.

Anna's voice came urgently in her ear: *Smother-flies. Old magic and strong. Smother-flies are drawn to the rhythm of the breath. You'll wake more of them if you can't quiet William's breathing. Try to hold your breath as you walk through them and they won't be able to sense you.*

William needed time they didn't have, but Vreni let him rest a moment longer. She hummed quietly to disguise the rhythm of his breathing, and added a soothing charm to the quiet tune.

When he was still, she quickly told him what Anna had said. 'We have to go now.' She loosened her arms from around him, and then stood and reached out her hand.

William's hand was cold and damp in hers. His eyes

still shone with fear as they walked through the field of sleeping smother-flies. Vreni held her breath until it burned and she was lightheaded, then stifled a shallow half-breath.

At the edge of the field of flowers they stood for a moment, staring back at the deadly blooms, not willing to chance filling their hungry lungs. When Vreni finally allowed herself to take a deep breath, it was sweet and energising, and painful.

William walked on beside her, silent except for the sound of his breathing, which was deep and long, like he was feasting on the air.

'Air,' she said. 'The *absence* of air as a defence.' She shuddered.

'Only fire left,' he coughed, squeezing her hand tightly.

'Only,' she said quietly.

***

They were close to the building now, but the densely planted grove of birch trees that encircled it hid them from the eyes of any guard. They tried to check their position so that when they came out on the other side of this ring of forest, they wouldn't be too close to the main entrance and the guard.

It was shady and cool as they stepped under the trees. The sunlight and shadows made dappled patterns on the leaves that blanketed the ground.

'Trees and fire,' William said. 'It's a bit of a no-brainer, I suppose.'

This last defence shouldn't offer much of a challenge, Anna said. *At least I hope not. They would be expecting most people to be dead before they got this far.*

'Anna said this last defence might be small. Just one extra precaution,' Vreni said, crossing her fingers.

As they walked on, a light shower of orange-and-red leaves fell from the thick canopy above, touching them gently before landing with the others that thickly covered the ground. The rust-coloured carpet of leaves crunched quietly with each step.

As they reached what they judged to be the halfway point through the small forest, the fall of leaves increased, although they still fluttered down slowly. Then the leaves that landed on their shoulders began to burst into flames.

'This is it. Still got your fingers crossed?' William brushed a burning leaf from Vreni's shoulder.

They walked on underneath the trees. The rain of leaves grew heavier. Now it was many more leaves, burning on their clothes, landing in their hair. They swept them off each other but the shower of fiery leaves was increasing. Now the burning leaves were reaching the ground and setting fire to the ones that already lay there. William took off his coat and pulled Vreni under it, shielding them from the leaves that ignited as soon as they touched down on a surface.

'We need to get out of here,' William said. 'Soon the fire on the ground will be a huge problem.'

The leaves on the ground feel your footfalls, Anna explained. *They tell the other leaves to drop from the trees. Whether you move fast or slow, the leaves will know you're there.*

William watched Vreni, knowing she was listening to Anna's voice. 'Any advice?'

'Run,' Vreni said.

They huddled close under the heavy coat and ran towards the tree line, leaping over patches of burning leaves as they went. The air around them was thick with acrid grey-blue smoke that couldn't escape through the thick canopy.

They burst out of the trees. Their eyes burned and they could hardly see. Throats scorched and breathless, they ran across the innermost circle of lawn and threw themselves onto the ground close to the wall. They were a long way around the southern curve of the building, far from where the guard was likely to be, but they waited, trying to stifle the sound of their coughing.

LABYRINTH

... single-minded dedication to discovering the full potential of nature and the human condition.
Mastery over the mystery, for our greater good.
—Excerpt from the AlGuild mission statement

***

The flames had smouldered low and quickly burned out, and the smoke seeped away into the leafy treetops. Vreni and William clung to each other and waited, hearts racing. Nothing. They dared a cough. Nothing. It seemed, for now, that they hadn't been detected.

'So those were the AlGuild pets.' William looked back over the grounds towards the south. 'What next?'

'Have you had enough?'

'No, but why didn't you use the charms?'

'Anna said not to use them yet,' she answered. 'She said that using magic out here would draw attention to us.'

'After that back there, I suppose anyone who was watching would believe we were dead.'

'And we still have the charms to use once we're inside,' Vreni said, as much to reassure herself as William.

'Those charms, will they really work? The Wise Sisters don't seem to do much abracadabra sort of magic. Will we have what we need to keep ourselves alive in there?'

'While I've been at Mežs Mājas I've learned that the magic works because of the contributions made by so many of the Sisters. The old magic is more about intentions of the Sisters, rather than *abracadabra*.' She smiled. 'It's about unity. So many of them—of us—have made sacrifices. Mine is to walk the labyrinth and use my power to release the stored magic of their spells. I have to believe that all these sacrifices will be rewarded and the charms will work.'

Rest a while, Anna interrupted. *Eat. Drink. If William still has the bundle Emma gave him, open it now.*

'Anna says you have a bundle that contains food and drink,' Vreni said.

'What, this?' William pulled a small cloth-bound bundle from the inside pocket of his coat. 'I hope you're not too hungry.'

'The sisters are very good at ... storage.' She laughed, thinking of the tiny whisper-birds.

She pulled at the wax seal that held the parcel closed and felt a tingling in her hands as she pried away the thick wax. A tiny ball of energy sparked where the seal had been broken, fizzing and flowing, trickling inside the wrapping.

She laid the parcel on the grass and pulled open the cloth. The contents inside gave the slightest quiver before expanding and taking form, growing just as the whisper-birds had done. When the transformation was complete, the bundle contained a simple meal of cheese and black bread, a mound of juicy red berries and a bottle of water.

William stared disbelievingly.

Vreni took one of the berries and held it gently between her fingers. She looked closely at the perfect red spheres clustered together. 'I love summer berries. They taste so good. The only berries that taste better than these are the ones you find for yourself.'

She offered a berry to William and took another for herself, eating it slowly.

'When I was little, in the summertime back in Vārve,' she said, 'we used to go looking for wild berries and mushrooms in the forest. We would pack a lunch, and take baskets and buckets and the dogs. We'd walk for hours in the dappled shade. It was always so cool inside the forest.' She smiled. Her eyes were looking back through time. 'Our tutor, a long time before Sabina, of course, showed Rita and me a secret way of finding the best, juiciest berries.'

'How?' he asked, handing her some cheese and bread.

'We used to ask the birds,' she replied. 'Well, we didn't *ask* them, we eavesdropped on them. We learned how to walk quietly under the trees and listen. It's easy once you know what the birds are saying.'

'You talked to the birds?'

'No. We listened. When a mother bird found a stalk heavy with ripe fruit she would sing and sing. She was saying three things when she sang.'

'What did she say?'

'First the mother bird would be saying thank you for the berries, because today her babies would not be hungry. Second, she would be bragging and celebrating being so good at finding berries. And third, she would be calling to all the other mother birds to share her luck with them. All the birds share like that, because they know that it's the nature of good times and bad times to come whenever they please. The birds know that a challenge is made easier by sharing it. That's how the Wise Sisters do it, too. They work together to achieve far greater things than any one of them could accomplish alone.'

Thank you, Vreni, Anna said quietly.

'Do you miss Vārve?' William asked.

Vreni gave a tiny nod. 'But I think that at Mežs Mājas I have something that feels the same. No, better. Home is a different thing now than I thought it was.'

'We could go there one day, if you like, to Vārve. You could show me how to search for berries and mushrooms. One day, when we're both free to make our own plans.'

'Why are you doing this?' Vreni asked quietly. 'This is not your fight.'

William stared at the ground for a long moment before he spoke. 'Two reasons, I think. First, because I'm selfish.'

'In what way are you selfish? Look at all you've done for Rita and me already.'

'Well, yeah, but I want to be here for *me.*' He smiled at her. 'I've met this girl who can do magic and seems to live forever, and then she invites me on the adventure of my lifetime so far.'

He stopped and looked back at the ground and then

continued, more serious now. 'You're not the only one who's been controlled by your family, Vreni. I've done what I've been told all my life. I was sent to a boarding school with high walls when I was young, and now my new walls are my father's expectations to study, and follow in his footsteps. Now I'm finally getting to do something that hasn't been planned for me.'

'You've got the dancing,' Vreni said, trying to lighten the mood.

He smiled. 'I wonder what my father would say if he knew about the dance parties.'

'And what's the second reason?'

'Well, that seems less clear, but a feeling that I wouldn't be anywhere else but here, and that I need to go wherever you're going.' He rubbed his hands together and smiled. 'I don't know, maybe you've put a spell on me.'

'You've caught me out, but it was only a spell to make you dance with me.' Vreni laughed to cover the slick of dread that was flowing through her mind. Could the Sisters make William be here against his will, by magic? She had to believe they hadn't done that. After all, she'd been told that the magic would only work if the sacrifice were given willingly.

They finished their meal in silence.

***

Looking out from where they sat, there was no sign of their passage from the fence to the building. The lawns and gardens of the compound seemed ordered and peaceful.

The scene was the public image of the AlGuild. It was scenes like this that appeared on the corporate website for AlGuild research and development, with lots of glossy photos and some very vague corporate information. Anything useful like projects, or current staff and management, were only available with a password.

From the fence, the building blended into the low hills that surrounded it, but up close it loomed over them like a smooth, circular monolith. It was as wide as a football field, with a roof perhaps six or seven metres high. The outer surface of the building was dotted with evenly spaced windows, which sat high on the walls to allow in the light but were too high for anyone to see in.

Or see out, Vreni hoped. She felt relieved to know they probably hadn't been seen.

The large rectangular windowpanes mirrored the now peaceful gardens. The shining patches of glass continued around the curve of the building. None showed any evidence that they could be opened.

They stayed close to the wall as they moved towards the east side of the building, edging closer to the entrance. A pathway, elaborately paved with the AlGuild logo, linked the entrance to the front gate and the still deserted carpark.

'You can't fault them on corporate image,' William joked.

'Well, not unless you take a walk through their Pleasure Gardens.'

After a few more silent steps, the front entrance came into view around the curve of the building.

'There's the keypad, but what can we do about the guard?' William whispered.

'I'll call him off.' Vreni remembered the guard in the dream realm, and hoped her skill with voice would work again. 'We won't have long.'

She took a calming breath and watched the guard for a long moment, preparing to send her false message around the far side of the building.

'Hey, Harry, I thought these windows were toughened glass. This looks like a crack,' said the false voice.

'What?' The guard looked surprised. He hurried away from the door towards the unexpected voice.

'You knew his name was Harry? You do have some skills,' William said.

'Yeah, reading skills. He had a nametag.'

She pulled William toward the polished glass door and the bio-lock pad. He held his key amulet in one hand and placed the other, palm down, on the sensor pad. The door clicked and released a hiss of air. They opened the door just wide enough to slide inside and hid themselves in a shallow alcove at the side of the doorway.

Vreni watched the door, which was still slightly ajar. It hissed as it closed maddeningly slowly and then finally clicked.

Through the window they saw the guard return to his post outside the door, looking confused. Vreni remembered the fate of the young guard she used her voice on in the palace and shuddered, hoping Harry wouldn't meet a similar fate because of her.

The foyer of the building looked just as corporate as

the entryway outside. It was furnished with sleek leather sofas and low glass tables. One white wall contained an oversized painting in a weighty gold frame, and the other was adorned with the AlGuild logo and its vague mission statement. The reception desk was unattended and there was a layer of dust on it, and also on the coffee machine that sat unused in the corner.

'This looks like it's all for show,' William said.

She nodded. 'They just need it to look normal from the door.'

She pointed past the dusty, overgrown potted palms to where the glaring white facade ended suddenly, not far inside the corridor that led into the rest of the building. She chanced a quick look through the glass door to make sure they remained undiscovered, then grabbed William's arm and they moved quickly into the passageway out of sight.

HOARD

If you keep a thing hungry you will keep control of it.
There are so many things that can be hungered for and
the greater the hunger, the greater our control.
—*Notes from the AlGuild manifesto*

***

The corridor leading out of the foyer changed abruptly from smooth white plaster to rough damp stone. It reminded Vreni of the walls in her grandmother's palace. She stood listening, straining her ears for any sign that they weren't alone, but the space inside the passageway was filled with a thick silence. It was so quiet she could hear her hand moving over the rough stonework wall.

'That was definitely all for show,' she said, pointing back to the foyer.

She inhaled, curious. The air smelled moist like earth and bark after rain, but lingering on the still air was the scent of something else. The faint odour made her think of burnt spice or strong vinegar, something sour and acrid.

She looked as far as she could along the corridor. She

held her breath, expecting someone or something to appear and stop them. After the Pleasure Gardens, she could only imagine what might be done to stop them in here.

She nudged William. 'Let's go.'

They set off cautiously, still expecting to have been discovered and confronted at any moment. The narrow passageway ran straight for a short distance, then turned to the left and curved in a clockwise direction. The roof was much lower here than it had been in the foyer. They had moved away from the light at the entrance, but it wasn't any darker. There was light, but no light source was evident.

Because of the curve of the passageway, they could only see a few metres ahead. They soon lost any idea of the distance they had come. It was silent within the labyrinth, and even the words they dared utter seemed to soak into the walls as they spoke them. The passageway remained unchanged, continuing to sweep clockwise.

'Candles,' Vreni muttered.

'Where?' William's voice was urgent.

'Not here, in the dream realm. The hallways of the palace had small alcoves in the walls every few metres holding candles. If we had those here, we could judge how far we'd come.'

'I'd rather know how far we have to go.'

There was nothing to do but continue. The cobbled floor consumed the sound of their footfalls as they walked.

***

The curve of the passageway began to straighten out. Suddenly Vreni was alert again. She threw her arm across William's chest defensively.

'Stop,' she whispered.

'What?' William looked up with wide eyes.

'Something's new, slow down,' she said, scanning the path ahead, watchful for threats.

It's a turning point, Anna said. *Try to remember the drawings of the labyrinth we showed you.*

Vreni moved cautiously up to the end of the wall. The passageway turned back on itself. The turning point was decorated with vines, leaves and budding flowers that had been carved into the stonework. The designs twisted their way up into a shallow, domed roof that rose from the passageway they were standing in and then dropped down again as the corridor switched back on itself and departed the turning space.

Vreni turned slowly. Her eyes followed the trailing vines across the dome. She finished her circling turn and found herself face to face with a creature staring down at her from the high ledge of an alcove at the end of the wall. She jumped back, gulping down a sourness that rose in her throat, and reached for her knife.

William rushed to her side. Following her gaze, he also jumped at the sight of the peering stone face.

It's a grotesque, Anna said, *a stone creature.*

'Carved in stone,' Vreni said, laughing at their over-reaction.

It was more likely turned into stone. The alchemists would rather conjure and entrap a thing than create a thing.

'Its eyes seem to follow you around the room,' William said.

Vreni looked at the grotesque and shivered. Light glinted from its polished stone eyes.

They turned away from the staring goblin and entered the stone passage at the other side of the turning. Now the path swept in an anticlockwise direction, with the same seamlessness as before.

Vreni thought back to the diagram of the labyrinth in the *Book of Wisdoms*. She tried to draw what she remembered in her mind, adding in the details she was discovering. Those details could be useful later. Perhaps what she was seeing would be more meaningful to Sabina and Anna than it was to her at the moment.

William was walking ahead of her, counting steps. Their eyes met for a moment, but he turned forward again and continued counting silently to himself.

The anticlockwise path was longer than the first clockwise curve. The labyrinth was a set of concentric circles that folded back on themselves. First it would take them deep into the building, and then back out to its edge before they would finally turn inwards again, to reach the very centre where the alchemists would be hiding their most precious possessions. That was where the remaining sleeping potion should be. Vreni wondered what else they would find there.

William nudged her. He pointed up ahead. The light was brighter there, and the passageway straightened again, but this time it also widened slightly. They flattened themselves against the wall and listened.

They heard a snuffle, then a mumbled growl. The noise sounded like words being spoken. They strained to hear if they were real words, and if so, who, or what, was speaking.

'... seven, eight, nine, ten, eleven ...' There was a metallic rattle then a shuffling noise. The voice faded and returned again. '... twenty-two, twenty-three, twenty-four, more of those is nice, yes, Hoard needs more of those.' There was a loud snorting, sniffing sound, then the voice was weeping. 'Yes, food is nice, too. Hoard is so hungry.' The voice sobbed for a while and then quietened, but the sniffing remained.

They stood pressed into the last curve of the wall. William caught her eye and then reached down and touched her necklace, his eyes asking if she really could use the magic they had been promised was contained in the charms.

She was glad she couldn't answer. She trusted the magic in the charms, but she had less trust in her own ability to call the magic into being. She leaned towards William and kissed him. He pulled away from her abruptly.

It took her a moment to realise that he hadn't pulled away, he had been snatched away. She stifled a scream when she saw a large creature silhouetted in the bright light dragging William into the circular space ahead.

It hasn't seen you, Vreni, Anna said urgently. *Stay hidden.*

Vreni pressed herself hard against the wall. She held her teeth tightly together to stop herself from crying out, and strained her eyes to the side to get a better look at what had taken William.

William had been lifted off the ground and dragged away as though he was a doll. Now he was thrashing and kicking into the creature's filth-encrusted lower limbs, trying to free himself. The creature didn't look right to Vreni. It appeared to have four arms, and four legs, or maybe more. *Maybe there's more than one of them.*

Vreni stayed nailed to the wall, feeling the rough stone pressing sharply into her back. She dared to turn her head and stare as the monster shambled back into the light. She heard a metallic rattling. Then she thought she could hear humming and quiet laughing.

She prised herself from the wall and moved forward slowly. At the edge of the circle of light, she came to a large pile of rags and tattered cushions. The sharp stink of urine and some unimaginable filth jabbed at her nostrils. She gagged as she crept up close to the pile and pulled the rags around her, creating a hiding place.

As she scanned the area more carefully, she realised she was at another turning point in the passage. It had been made wider here to make room for this thing, whatever it was.

On the other side of the circle, William struggled against the gruesome shambles of arms and legs. The creature stood on several mismatched legs, but there were some other, stray limbs dangling down from the lower part of its bloated body.

Vreni could see now that it was only one creature, but it had four arms protruding from its front, which were now tying William to a metal loop that hung from the far wall, and more arms sticking out the back of its body.

Many of the arms were withered and twisted, and the skin of each was different—pale, dark, smooth, hairy.

Vreni tried to count the arms as the creature loped about awkwardly. The fleshy collection of half-dead arms was crowded at odd angles all around the lumpy body. She finally counted eight mismatched legs, three of them flopping, too misshapen to reach the floor, but she couldn't count all the arms on the patchwork abomination. Its skin was crisscrossed with puckered lines where the pieces had somehow been fused together.

William continued to struggle, but the creature had tied his hands to the wall above his head. He was stretched out, his feet barely touching the floor.

The monster huffed at him and shuffled to the centre of the floor. It was dragging a heavy chain. The chain, which was manacled to the ankle of one of its thick legs, stretched out across the floor and was firmly attached to a steel ring on the wall above the stinking pile of rags where Vreni was hiding. She realised this must be its bed, and this bend in the passageway was its home and all the life the creature knew.

The wretched thing began to hum again, and then it started singing. 'You heard me crying!' The creature tilted its head and sang out towards something or someone who wasn't there. 'Hoard was so hungry. Food is so nice. Hoard wanted to be more, more of Hoard is so nice. Now Hoard can collect more pieces and not be so lonely.'

Vreni watched, horrified and amazed. As the creature sang, she noticed its faces. Just like its arms and legs, the hoard had many faces, or parts of faces. Its mouths sang out. The tuneless music came from one of the mouths, which was surrounded by the pudgy folds of its face, but as it sang the ghastly song, the lips of other mouths, dotted here and there around its head, neck and shoulders, moved in unison in an attempt to join in the grisly chant.

For every mouth that adorned the bloated, pale body there were pairs of eyes and ears in measure. Not arranged in sets that became simply a misplaced face, but a collection of misshapen and mutilated ears scattered around the head and shoulders, and as many shrivelled, suppurating eyes, some milky and dead, some staring off in all directions.

And there was a tail. On the monster's back, a dog's tail wagged.

The creature kept singing. 'Hoard is thankful, Hoard has food, food is so nice, and more parts for Hoard, and more parts makes Hoard happy. Thank you, master.'

William finally cast his eyes towards her hiding place and she risked a wave. He responded with a minute half-smile.

To have created a hoard, how heartless, Anna said. *A hoard's hunger for food is insatiable. The only thing greater is its hunger to belong, to be near others. It's the loneliest of all creatures, so it collects pieces of its victims to form a crowd around itself, in the hope that it won't feel so lonely. Before this happened to this hoard it would have been a good man. The alchemists captured him and emptied out his heart. Now the hoard needs to devour flesh to stay alive. It then knits the remnants of its victims into itself to ease the aching loneliness that torments its heart.*

Vreni lifted the charms that were strung around her

neck, hoping that Sabina would see her question. What charms would she use?

Sabina had seen, and Anna replied. *The hoard will be fascinated by the sound of a voice, but being trapped in here means it lives with silence most of the time. You have the singing and the chants of the Sisters to fill the air with sound, and you need something to catch its eye, to distract it.*

Anna's voice ceased. Vreni wanted to be told more. It was all so cryptic.

She steadied her breathing and stared at the charms. The final choices and the speaking of intention was her contribution to the spell. She knew she must decide for herself and will it into being. The songs of the Sisters swirled inside the glass capsule. Then Vreni remembered the swarm of bumblebees that sat frozen inside another charm.

She signalled William to talk to the hoard.

The hoard leaned in close to William and sniffed at him. All the noses joined in the sniffing. Next it licked the side of his face. The other mouths made feeble sucking noises. All William could do was hold his breath against the stench of the beast's drooling mouth and step as far to the right as his bonds would allow him.

He coughed and started to speak. 'Hello, I'm William,' he choked.

The creature drew back and smiled at him. 'You talk to Hoard. Talk is so nice.' The hoard leaned closer again for another noisy sniff, and licked its very wet lips.

'So, your name is Hoard. Do you have another name?

'Once I did, a name that was so nice, but the silence took

it and the others that are Hoard mumbled lots of names.'
It danced around as if to show off its gruesome collection.
'Their names got in the way. But we are all Hoard now.'

'How long have you lived here?' William said, trying to
hold the hoard's attention.

'Long, so long, and so alone, and so very hungry.' The
hoard came closer again and bought its foul mouth up
to William's face. Its lips and tongue lightly touched its
captive's skin to taste him once more.

William shuddered violently.

The creature continued to lean over him. There was a
rasping noise as it sharpened its yellow nails against the
stone wall. 'So hungry.'

It inspected the razor-sharp claws that curled from
each fingertip before pushing a bony knuckle into the
flesh on William's belly.

'Hoard has food, food is so nice,' it said, and licked its
lips. 'Hoard can be more now. More is so nice.' It ran its
sharpened claws lightly over William's arms and face, as if
trying to decide which parts of him to add to its collection.
'Hoard has food, food is so nice, Hoard can be more.'

The hoard appeared to be dancing with excitement. It
gripped William's arms and shook him.

Vreni knew she had to act now. The hoard's chain
wasn't very long. If she could free William they could run
and get out of its reach. She took three charms from her
necklace.

The hoard continued its strangled singing, which would
cover the sound of her voice. The charms full of swirling
music would be first. She held them in her palm. She

found the words somewhere within her and let them spill over the shining sphere.

'Canon and cadence, sweet voices singing out,
The melodies will fill the air until they are a shout.
Sing my sisters, sing with all your hearts.'

The skin of the tiny orb split and peeled away as Vreni's words moved across it. Through the mist that spread across her hand, she heard a quiet chant. The voices grew louder as the mist lifted into the air and drifted towards the hoard.

It looked around, its eyes darting in all directions. 'Who's there? Stop singing!' it growled. The freed voices filled the circle that was the hoard's world. 'Enough! Hoard is singing.'

Its arms swung heavily as it twisted and turned. It tripped over its bulky chain as it looked for the source of the sound. The voices swam around it. The chanting was now accompanied by singing. The hoard moaned from all of its many mouths.

Vreni reached for her second weapon, a swarm of tiny bumblebees that had been held in mid-flight inside another of the small glass spheres. She rolled the bauble gently between her palms to warm the bees and wake them.

'Awake now and take to the wing,
Fly and buzz, swarm and sting.
Distracting, enraging and saddening,

Tormenting and maddening.'

The glass of the charm dissolved in Vreni's palm. The bees began circling in a miniature hive dance. Like the whisper-birds, they doubled and redoubled in size as they danced around on her palm. They lifted from her hand and swept around the room, spiralling up towards the hoard. The singing and chanting grew to a crescendo.

The hoard reached feebly with its malformed collection of hands, trying to cover its numerous ears. 'No more singing,' it pleaded to the unseen voices. 'Silence is so nice.' It twisted and staggered around. 'No more singing.'

The bees swept past the hoard. It wailed, swatting at them as they swarmed around its head. It yelped as the bees started to sting. It was slapping wildly at itself, trying to fight off the fast-moving attackers. Its arms and legs took on the fight without waiting for the hoard's direction. It stumbled and faltered, tripping again and again on its heavy chain.

The air was filled with the rhythmic chanting and harmonies of the Sisters, the unceasing drone of the swarming bees, and the frantic bawling of the hoard as it continued to fight its unseen menace.

Vreni knew the hoard's chain only allowed it to reach a short way into either passageway. As long as it couldn't pull hard enough to wrench the chain free from the wall, they could be outside of its reach soon enough. She took her chance and ran from the pile of rags towards William.

The hoard's arms continued to beat the air, trying to swat the bees. She ducked under its flailing hands, the needle-sharp claws just missing her face. As it turned, one of its stunted legs swung freely and struck Vreni in the ribs. She staggered, landing hard on the floor. Her knee burned and her eyes stung with tears. She pulled herself up from the floor and limped to William.

She looked up. No! She couldn't reach William's hands tied high on the wall. Trying to block out the hoard's distracted yelping, she took a step back and threw herself at William.

He groaned.

'Sorry,' she whispered.

Finding a small foothold in the stone wall, she clambered up his body and rested her knee on his shoulder. She pulled out her knife and cut through the frayed rags that bound his wrists to the iron ring. He lowered his hands. She lost her balance and they crashed to the floor. He bent quickly and pulled her to her feet.

The hoard spun around and saw that William was free. 'No!' it roared. 'Hoard's food! Hoard's more!'

Vreni pulled William towards the narrowing passage-way on the far side of the stone circle that was the hoard's prison. Just a few metres and they would be out of its vile reach. They ran, stumbling as they clung to each other. The hoard's demands dissolved into angry bellows of frustration. Its feet made heavy, arrhythmic thudding sounds on the stone floor behind them.

Vreni felt William suddenly slow down behind her and looked over her shoulder. The hoard was pulling on William's flapping coat with one crooked arm. Then she saw a second arm, with its hand filled with razor-like claws, sweep across William's face. The claws caught on his cheek.

William screamed and dipped his head, trying to avoid the worst of the gouging attack.

Vreni pulled William's arm with all the strength she had left.

The hoard caught a foot in its chain and tripped, toppling into the wall and smacking its gruesome head against the stone. It staggered as it tried to get to its feet. Vreni used the moment to haul William into the narrowing passageway that had turned back on itself and was sweeping clockwise again.

The hoard was howling in defeat behind them, its calls growing more distant with every step. Vreni couldn't bring herself to stop. They ran on for some distance until William misjudged the curve of the wall and hit it heavily.

'Stop, Vreni, we're safe here,' he panted.

'But—' She turned and froze.

William's face was slashed. Three deep gashes oozed blood that dripped down his left cheek onto his neck and soaked his collar. A fourth cut above his right eye had somehow, luckily, glanced over the eye itself before scraping across his right cheek. He staggered and slid down the rough wall. He sat shaking violently.

Vreni sat beside him and took a closer look at his face. He winced at her touch, but remained silent. She pushed into his coat pocket and retrieved the cloth that their lunch had been wrapped in. She gently placed it across his wounded cheek.

'I wish I could do more.' She squeezed his hand.

He smiled weakly. Placing his hand on the makeshift bandage on his face, he stood up. 'Let's get going,' he said quietly.

She took a breath to speak but then changed her mind. He grabbed her hand and they continued along the curving passageway.

TEMPTATION

*Our deepest desires are treasures. We hide them inside
ourselves, where we believe them to be safe.
These desires can be our greatest strengths,
or our most vexing weaknesses.*
—*Pratigs Māsa, Book of Wisdoms*

***

The arc of the cobbled passageway swept on. Each stone in the wall melted into the next, and the ones behind them fell away into nothing as the curve devoured them. They trudged on, each step heavy with effort. They walked together but were somehow separate.

Vreni knew from the map she had contrived with her mind's eye that this ring of the labyrinth would be slightly longer again than the one that had led them to their encounter with the hoard, but knowing it would be a greater distance to the next turn didn't ease the dread she felt about what they would meet there.

She wanted to talk to William, to discuss strategy and calm her fears about what they might face next.

She glanced at him out of the corner of her eye. He was stooped over, his head bowed, clutching his face tenderly. She decided he deserved the consolation of the little time they might have to be alone with his pain and to settle his thoughts. *I can't burden him with my fears now.*

Vreni knew Sabina would be listening, but if she asked questions or spoke her fears out loud so the Sisters could hear her and offer advice or words of reassurance, William would hear her too. He would hear her fear and her crumbling confidence. She didn't want to force him to withdraw from his fallow, thought-filled state just to help her feel better.

She watched him, but left him to his thoughts for a little longer. He was the injured one, while she was only scared. She had chosen to do this thing rather than wait for someone else to do it for her, so she must do it, even if it was frightening. She hung her head and concentrated on their feet shuffling slowly on.

***

The mysterious soft glow of the passageway was growing stronger. In front of them the curve was straightening and the space glowed more brightly. Vreni couldn't leave William to his thoughts any longer. She slid her hand into his and squeezed.

His shuffling steps stopped and he looked up, wincing as he straightened. 'What next?' His voice wavered.

'Stay here. I'll go and look.'

Vreni let go of William's hand and nudged his shoulders

firmly against the wall to reinforce the idea that he should stay there. She hoped doing this would make her look more confident than she felt. She walked slowly but purposefully towards the brightening light, not trusting herself to look him in the eye in case she faltered.

The warmly lit space ahead was about the same size as the last turning point. She heard water flowing somewhere. She could smell the freshness of it. Her throat suddenly ached, feeling incredibly dry. Her mouth tasted brackish. All she could think of was drinking cool, clean water.

She flattened herself against the last curve of the wall and dared to look out into the space. It was deserted. There was no one and nothing to be seen. Her attention was drawn again to the sound of running water. A small spigot was trickling water into a stone basin carved into the far wall. In the centre of the circular space was a collection of low leather sofas and velvet stools strewn with silk cushions, surrounding a large, highly polished wooden chest that was inlaid with brass.

Vreni's legs suddenly felt limp and she found it hard to lift her feet. The music of the flowing water filled her awareness.

She turned to signal for William to join her, but he was leaning against the wall with his eyes closed. She quickly walked back to him, feeling happy that she could offer the hope of some comfort and a place to rest, even if they could only stay for a while.

'William,' she whispered, rubbing his rounded shoulders. 'So far, I can't see any trouble up ahead. Seeing as there was no danger at the first turn, we might be lucky.'

She led him, quiet and stooped, to the circular space of the third turning point. She heard him inhale deeply and knew that he had smelled the water. His uninjured eye opened more fully and took in the scene.

'I'm so thirsty.' He flopped down onto a sofa, sagging against one of the oversized cushions. He patted his pocket and reached into it, retrieving the water bottle he had kept from their lunch bundle. It had miraculously survived without breaking during their encounter with the hoard.

'You first.' William handed Vreni the bottle.

She wanted to argue but her tongue was burning, sticky and sour.

The water trickled from the spigot maddeningly slowly. She filled the bottle three times and drank each thirstily before she began to feel the dry bitterness in her throat washing away. She filled the bottle for William and took it back to where he rested among the cushions.

She trailed backward and forward between the spigot and the sofa, bringing him water, continually scanning the space as she did so, alert for danger.

This turning point was about the same size as the one that had served as the hoard's prison. The space was decorated similarly to the first, except with much more elaborate detail. There were pools of indigo shadow around the room, but where there was light, intricate designs and details were visible the walls. There were carved vines and flowers, but instead of the staring face of a grotesque, there were birds.

On the bottom half of the walls were geometric designs creating borders that framed scenes of gardens and landscapes. From these frames, the carved vines twisted and curved up the smooth stone walls towards the domed ceiling.

Vreni's eyes followed the creeping vines upward and saw that the ceiling of the chamber held a sea of gemstone stars. She thought for a moment of the dream room back at Mežs Mājas and could almost hear the Sisters' voices singing. She allowed herself to float away, surrounded by the warm sea of imagined sound, and some of the tension slipped from her shoulders.

'Nice,' William said quietly.

'What?' she asked absentmindedly.

'The tune, very nice.'

'Thanks, I was just daydreaming, I must've started humming out loud.' She felt a little self-conscious and confused because she couldn't remember starting to hum, even quietly.

'Come and rest,' he urged.

Suddenly Vreni felt exhausted. She filled the bottle once more and drank slowly. 'I need to clean your wounds.'

She removed her scarf and wet one end in the stone basin, then returned to the sofa and finally sat. It felt like paradise. The coolness of the leather against her arms was soothing and mounds of velvet cushions surrounded her, cradling her tried muscles. She breathed deeply, feeling her body go limp at last. She would have been happy to curl into the generous softness of it all and turn her back on everything. She sighed deeply and closed her eyes for just a moment.

William fidgeted restlessly next to her. She reluctantly lifted her head from the cushions and shook it gently to focus her thoughts. She leaned towards him and timidly pulled away the cloth that had been covering his wounds.

Gently, she cleaned the filth and dried blood away from the cuts. She was relieved to see that the cut that ran across his right eye was mercifully slight. His sight would be safe, but the gashes in his left cheek were deep and angry looking. They had stopped bleeding, but they were now oozing a yellow watery mess that didn't look like stopping any time soon.

'Am I still your handsome prince?' he joked quietly.

'Indeed, sir,' she said. 'We princesses like our heroes to look rugged and adventure-worn. Now keep still, brave prince, so I can sooth your wounds.'

She cleaned the gashes as well as she could, and then bandaged them using the only thing available, her scarf. She wrapped the scarf around his forehead, covering the cut above his eyes, and then circled it around once more, this time below his eyes and across his nose, binding the deep gouges in an effort to pull the ragged edges together and soak up the liquid that oozed profusely from them. The makeshift bandage covered most of William's face.

Now that the wounds were covered, she looked at him and smiled. He looked like a bank robber or a masked hero from an old black-and-white movie. She tied the two ends of the scarf together to secure the bandage and kissed him gently on the lips. His eyes sparkled through the swelling.

Vreni rested her head against the soft cushions again. She felt the hardness inside her stomach softening a little. Her thoughts drifted to the first time she had kissed William on the darkened dance floor, surrounded by music and flashing colour.

'Yes!' William exclaimed joyfully. 'I am so hungry,'

She opened her eyes. William had lifted the lid of the wooden chest and was picking through the boxes and bundles inside. He opened a few of them.

He laughed. 'Bananas, nuts, bread that's not black.'

'There's nothing wrong with black bread,' Vreni scoffed. 'Mmm, black bread and liverwurst.'

'Delicious, I'm sure.' He pulled a face and reached for a crusty bread roll.

'Should we take a chance on eating any of it, considering where we are?' she asked warily.

'I'll take it slowly.' He pulled a small piece of bread off the corner of the roll and put it in his mouth without chewing. 'I know it's not much of a precaution, but feeling for a mouth reaction can help identify dangerous plants and things in the bush, so maybe it'll help here. So far it feels okay.' he said, talking around the bread.

'Maybe there'll be some apple bread in there, or cheesecake, something sweet,' Vreni said wistfully.

'Turkish delight,' William added.

'My prince, you are indeed exotic.'

'Your prince?' His eyes sparkled again from within the bandages.

Vreni shoved her shoulder into his. 'Seeing as you're not poisoned yet, let's try something else, but slowly.'

They lifted the boxes and bundles out of the chest and closed the lid, using it as a table. Inside the parcels they found berries and cheese, small savoury pies, a pot of smooth liverwurst and a loaf of heavy black bread.

They opened the lid of a round silver tin and a delicious sweet smell rose up, dancing on their nostrils. The tin contained a dazzling array of sweets: tiny bite-size portions, each nestled in colourful paper wrappers. There were fruit jellies, fine biscuits, cubes of Turkish delight studded with pistachio nuts, even tiny round cheesecakes and chocolate truffles.

A glass bottle held a deep plum-coloured liquid, which stirred with tiny bubbles when the lid was opened. It smelled of berries and cinnamon, and tasted sweet and refreshing.

At first, they explored the picnic with caution, nibbling tiny pieces of foods and waiting for any sign of danger, but with each morsel they sampled their cares diminished. They paid attention only to their hunger, and ate.

***

Vreni looked across the remnants of food sitting on the lid of the chest. She was surprised she had eaten so much without remembering having eaten it, and stunned that at some time during their meal they had abandoned their caution about poisons or spells. But nothing had happened except for twinges from her overstuffed belly.

'Want to dance?' William stood, and without waiting for an answer took her hand and kissed it, leading her to a small space between the sofas.

She thought briefly about continuing their journey through the labyrinth, but when he pulled her into his arms she felt warm, and let herself drift into the soft, pulsating rhythms. She fell into step with his gentle swaying. The music swelled and the pools of light within the chamber dimmed, making way for the glow of slowly strobing colours.

They rocked and turned in each other's arms, so close that their heartbeats fell into rhythm, and then matching the beat of the music that seemed to flow out of the walls.

Small thoughts flicked through Vreni's mind, but before she could make sense of them, they flittered out of her awareness again. She could only see William, and only hear the pulse of the music.

They were bathed in the swirls of sparkling coloured light reflected from a mirrored ball that hung high in the domed ceiling. As they danced, William ran his hand across her shoulder and lightly up her neck and into her hair. He leaned towards her and kissed her softly.

Not here. Not in this place.

The thought twisted up into Vreni's mind like steam rising from hot coffee, but then it faded and was gone, leaving her to return to her music and sink her face into William's shoulder. They danced. They kissed.

Not now. They're waiting. Rita's waiting.

'We shouldn't leave Rita sitting on her own,' she

whispered into William's ear. She turned and saw Rita lying sleeping on the sofa.

'Rita's not here, it's just us,' he whispered back.

She looked over her shoulder again and the sofa was empty. 'But ... of course, it's just us.'

She felt hints of something within her mind, but they were somehow hidden in a mist. She kept dancing and tried to sing along with the music, but each time she did the beat became arrhythmic and the words slipped, turning into something else, as though two songs were being played at the same time.

She shrugged and stopped trying, stopped thinking. 'I could dance with you forever,' she said.

'I'd like that,' William mumbled, squeezing her closer.

She felt something bump her from behind. 'Sorry,' she said automatically.

'How clumsy of us,' said a couple as they dancing past.

She snapped her head around, finally alert to the fact that things weren't right. She saw an old couple. No, she saw an old William and an old Vreni. *What's happening? What is this place?*

The music had faded a little, just for a moment, and she heard other sounds above the melody, voices singing and chanting. The sisters.

The chamber grants your wishes Vreni, Anna said loudly. *It tempts you, and entangles you in trivial desires like picnics and dancing, until that's all you can see.*

'What?' Vreni shook her head again. She felt confused.

The music in the room rose up once more, filling her

mind. She leaned into the welcoming warmth of William's body.

Anna called urgently. *Look into the shadows. Open your eyes, Vreni, and see into the shadows.*

For a moment Vreni rested her chin on William's shoulder and peered into the indigo pools of shadow at the edges of the room. She couldn't see anything so she tried again to ignore the insistent voices, but the chanting grew louder, blocking out the dance music.

Anna's voice was unrelenting. *Focus, Vreni, look harder.*

Vreni slowly rocked and waited for her eyes to adjust. She concentrated on the darkened pockets of the room. She thought the dim light and her fatigue were playing tricks on her vision. How could she be seeing what she was seeing?

Reluctantly she slid out of William's arms and walked into the darkness. Lying alone in the gloom was a skeleton. It looked like someone had sat down in the darkness and simply stopped living.

Vreni explored the other puddles of shadow and found two more reclining piles of bones. Each was draped with remnants of rotting clothing, but one also wore a heavy chain that was entangled in its ribs. On the chain hung a silver disc engraved with a spiral.

Vreni knew that pendants like these were worn by some of the Sisters. Her mind cleared instantly, as though a storm wind had blown through it.

Anna sobbed. *Ilona,* she said. *A sister lost is now found.*

Vreni looked around her. The coloured lights that had

seemed so real a moment ago were fading. The music was fading away with it. She felt confused, foolish.

What is your true desire, Vreni? Anna asked urgently. *Keep that desire foremost in your mind and it will give you the strength you need for this battle.*

Vreni wondered how this could be a battle.

We all have to battle false desires in this life, Vreni. What is your true desire? Anna repeated.

Vreni saw images of home and family flash through her mind. She remembered her desire to get the potion and free them. As those thoughts slipped through her mind one by one, they also appeared around her in the chamber.

The smiling faces of Rita and Mama, and the aunties. Papa appeared sitting on the sofa and disappeared again in a flash. Even the ponies flickered briefly into being before fading away.

The glistening bottle that held the sleeping-death potion sat temptingly close on the wooden chest. She lunged for the bottle and grabbed it. She waited for the dread to creep through the glass and seep up her arm, but there was nothing. It wasn't real. None of this was real.

She watched as one desire after another appeared to tempt her, but with each new illusion, the realisation solidified. Her true heart's desire was freedom for herself and her family.

Finally understanding the nature of the chamber, Vreni experimented to see if she could control what was happening. She thought of Rita, and Rita appeared. She thought of the ponies, and they appeared, tossing their heads and whinnying. Then Papa, just once more.

Now that she was sure the chamber would manifest her wishes, she focused her mind on her true desire for freedom and to make her own choices. It was the nature of this chamber to grant her desires and, seeing as her greatest desire was for freedom, it seemed that the chamber was releasing her.

Her head cleared and the confusion of the false visions dissipated.

William reached to offer his embrace again. She shoved him away, trying to bring him to his senses. He came towards her again. At least she knew without doubt now how he truly felt about her and that it wasn't just the magical work of the Sisters that made him have feelings for her.

'William,' she yelled, 'we have to leave.'

'But everything we need is here, and I have you,' he said softly.

Vreni groaned, feeling the frustration growing towards her lovestruck companion. 'We have to go,' she repeated, shoving him again.

Anna's voice came again: *Use his affection for you, Vreni, if that's all he has to offer you right now.*

Vreni pulled on the crimson ribbon and looked at the charms. She touched a shiny globe containing three dark brown cloves. *Cloves on the breath and your lover will do your bidding.* Vreni smiled, remembering the afternoons she had spent with the young sisters, blending herbs and making tinctures while they all played with the idea of what their new power could do for them.

She took the small ball and placed it in her mouth. It began to dissolve and fell loose from the ribbon. The heady fragrance of cloves filled her mouth and wafted up into her nose. She walked towards William, rising up onto her toes so that when she spoke he would breathe in her exhaled words. Then her every whim would be a command to his ears.

'We need to go. I'm leaving and I don't want to leave without you. We have to go *now*.' She pulled him by the arm.

He stared at her and followed, then hesitated. 'But ... we could dance.' He turned back towards the sofas.

She tugged harder, but he was frozen in place, eyes glazed. 'Now,' Vreni implored. She couldn't believe he might choose these trifling pleasures over her. 'We're going. Move!' she screamed, heaving him behind her.

He was like a dead man, shuffling as she dragged him along. They had nearly entered the passageway when the lights dimmed to create pools of colour and the music lifted again. William stopped in mid-step and swayed. He pulled against Vreni, trying to turn back again.

LAST TURN

When the songs of the Sisters fill your ears and your heart
you are never alone. So sing and join with the magic
of the music. Our power is borne on the song.
—Pratigs Māsa, Book of Wisdoms

***

She yanked William's arm fiercely towards her. Letting go of her frustrations, she punched him hard in the stomach. He let out a groaning breath. She used the last of the strength given to her from her frustration, tightened her grip on his arm, and at last managed to haul him from this strange chamber of desires.

They stumbled down the curving passageway. As she dragged him along, William trudged in a mist, mumbling about food and dancing. Her legs felt as though they were made of stone.

Memories from the chamber remained, and her emotions, a mixture of homesickness and heartbreak, overwhelmed her. The images of her family in the chamber had seemed so real. Apart from when her brother Peters had died and now the unthinkable loss of Papa, she had not felt such a sense of loss as this since she was small. At times back then, she sat next to her sleeping mother, lonely for her to wake up and take her in her arms.

The feelings that the chamber had conjured were holding onto her like an anchor. She had used all her strength to make herself move from the room, and now, along with the weight of remembered sadness, she carried the burden of a dazed William.

She lumbered along the anticlockwise corridor, William shuffling awkwardly behind her like a mindless zombie. The chamber of desires was consumed by the curve of the passageway. The further she got from the turning point, the lighter her legs felt and the clearer her thoughts became, more controlled. She hoped the lingering power of the chamber was leaving William, too, but he continued to shuffle on unchanged.

'So, do you feel like dancing?' she joked, hoping it might break William's zombie-like state. Nothing.

She continued pulling him forward, looking back at him every few steps. She wasn't sure what she was watching for, but checking every few metres became a rhythm, her gaze alternating from him to the stone floor. She trudged on along the curving passageway, her resentment towards William building with each step.

'Vreni, watch it!'

She turned quickly to face William and could see that his eyes were bright and wide, but looking past her up the passageway. He pulled her to an abrupt stop just as she ran into the wall. They had reached another turning already.

This one had no challenge, thankfully, as she hadn't even realised where they were.

'Are you all right?' William hugged her, rubbing her shoulders and checking to see if she was hurt. 'You must have tuned out. You need to be more careful.'

'Careful?' she snapped at him, her resentment bubbling up. 'Well, Mr Careful, what was the last thing you remember?' She shoved him in the chest with both hands, letting her frustration resurface.

'What do you mean, remember? You washed my face and we ... walked here.' William blinked rapidly, realising something was missing and trying to recall his recent memories.

Vreni stayed angry. She wanted to be alone. She wanted to be up in her tower staring out at the sea. Even now, everything about her life was controlled by someone else. She wanted to be able to make her own choices, and now this frightening place, filled with unspeakable dangers, was probably going to kill her and she wouldn't get a chance to have any life at all or make any choices except the one that had bought her here.

Her eyes burned with the tears of frustration. *How much more of a price am I going to have to pay before I get some control over my own life?*

She turned away from William and stormed off around the turn, veering clockwise again, almost running. Her tears flowed. She felt like screaming. Her throat was ropey with the effort of keeping the scream from getting out.

If there had been some way out of this place, she would have slammed through the door and run, and kept running. If she fell into long-sleep then so be it, let some curious scientist slice her open like they'd nearly done to Rita. Then it would all be over, all the complications and secrets no longer her concern. She stomped on, mumbling her tearful frustrations under her breath.

You're doing a difficult thing, Vreni, Anna said soothingly. *And this is the most difficult part of a difficult thing. You might not see your Sisters standing with you, but please believe us when we tell you that you are not alone.*

Vreni's ears filled with the hum of many sweet voices. The chanting was deep and rhythmic, slowing her angry heart. The harmonies surrounded her and for a while she felt enclosed by the music, protected. The enchanted sounds flowed through her, washing away her fierce frustration.

Her tears finally dried to salt on her cheeks. When the music faded, Vreni wiped her eyes and sighed deeply. She realised two things at almost the same time.

The first was that she did not want her life to be over, to be sliced up or any other thing. She was glad she had been chosen and given the chance to make such a change, to bring freedom for her family and for herself. Her life had already changed because of this, and that was worth the fear and the danger. She was one of many strong women. She could feel that inside herself now.

The second realisation came to her in slow stages. She had been almost running along this passageway and she had not reached another turning point yet. This curve was longer than any of the others so far, which meant it must be the last and most outward ring of the labyrinth.

She stopped, breathing hard. The next turn was up ahead. It must be the last turn and after that, they would turn towards the centre of the labyrinth and the vault that contained the AlGuild's most precious possessions, one of which had to be the potion.

She stood listening to her heart pounding. She tried to imagine the view from her tower, looking out over the tranquil sea. The imagined scene only calmed her heart a little.

'I'm sorry,' William said, walking up behind her. 'Whatever happened, I left you alone back there.'

'I wasn't alone,' she said, lifting the string of charms the Sisters gave her and rubbing them gently. 'It's all right. It wasn't your fault.'

She told him what had happened in the chamber of desires, or at least what she was clear about in her own mind. He looked bewildered and embarrassed. She checked the bandage she had fashioned from her scarf and saw that it was still in place. It covered more than half his face.

'Are you my mummy?' she smiled, kissing him lightly on his uninjured cheek. 'This is the last turn, you know.'

She leaned flat against the wall, wishing she could push herself through the stone and vanish. What next? What was waiting in the vault?

Anna's voice came to her quietly: *You, Sister Veronika, have come further through the labyrinth than any of us have ever done before. If someone is in the vault you will face great danger. If it is unoccupied, then fortune is smiling on you, but either way we're sure that what you see in there will be disturbing beyond measure. We have witnessed what those in the*

Alk̦imk̦i Gilde have put their evil hands to over the centuries. We have no reason to think that what lies inside the centre of the labyrinth will be anything less than the full measure of their capabilities.

THE VAULT

*The AlGuild assures that the highest ethical standards
are met in regard to production. All our clients can be
confident that none of our products are tested on animals.
—AlGuild guide to consumer information*

***

Vreni gulped a breath, but her lungs felt frozen along with
the rest of her.

Anna continued speaking: *All your Sisters are with you.
You have our charms, and they contain the spirit and sacrifice
of every one of us. The amulets allow you to use the power of
the earth to impose your intentions. The power is yours, Vreni.
You will be able to achieve what is truly your heart's desire. If
that weren't true you would already be lost to us, dead or insane.
Stand fast, gather your magic and be in control. Victory will be
yours. That is your purpose.*

Behind Anna's voice, Vreni could hear the Sisters singing. She knew they were weaving songs of strength and
protection. She stood tall. She had chosen to do this, and it
was what she had wanted, a chance to change things. She

felt tired and frightened, but she would not be a sleeping princess anymore. She laughed to herself.

'Time to go,' she said, touching the remaining charms that hung around her neck.

'What did they say?' William said, pointing to her ear.

'They said it would be dangerous, and frightening.'

'And what should we do?'

'Think quick, move fast.' She shrugged and smiled, thinking she sounded like an actor from an adventure movie.

'Okay, boss,' William said, giving a mock salute.

They walked the last few metres of the curving passageway and then turned right. The floor sloped downwards. Now the passageway looked older. It was more worn and uneven, like the stone floors in the alchemist's room in Vreni's grandmother's palace.

The rough downward passage stopped at a heavy wooden door. On the door was a strange symbol.

'Silver,' William said. Vreni looked puzzled, so he explained. 'It's an old alchemical symbol for silver. My father likes to collect old drawings. One like this and a few others similar to it hung on a wall at home. I hope this picture's not telling us that this is where they keep their treasure.'

'It depends on what they consider treasure.' She reached out and touched the door handle. It felt cold but smooth, as though worn down by countless hands over the ages. She hesitated.

William's hand came to rest on hers. They turned the handle together and slowly pushed the door inward. It moved with unexpected ease and silence.

The space inside was much larger than Vreni had expected. It was dimly lit by a round skylight at the centre of the high-domed roof, which was letting in the weak glow through heavy bars. The sky outside looked like late afternoon, but Vreni had lost track of how long they had been travelling through the labyrinth.

The room was circular, as she had expected, with high walls that were lined with shelves full of books and bottles and small chests. In between the banks of shelves, oil paintings hung in heavy gold and silver frames. There was a scattering of furniture. There were reading tables holding heavy leather-bound volumes, stiff-backed chairs and some low divans with rich velvet coverlets.

There was a raised platform in the centre of the room, directly under the light-filled dome. On the platform sat a large, gnarled tree. The tree was bare of leaves, as it would appear in autumn, although Vreni thought this one could be bare because it was old, its sap had dried up, and it was no longer able to sustain leaves or fruit.

She scanned the room more carefully now. She was thinking of the alchemist's room in her grandmother's palace, and the wolf that was held there and set loose to kill her. She didn't see any obvious sign of guards or defence, but then she saw something she could barely believe.

Her face flushed with an awful heat as she gazed upon three young girls. They were the same girls she had seen when she visited the dream realm, she was sure of it. The girls lay now as they had back then, heaped together on a low divan. They looked as though they were simply sleeping, but Vreni recognised them, and that meant they had been held by the sleeping-death for centuries.

She shuddered. These girls had been stolen away from their families and robbed of their lives, and were now imprisoned in the darkness at the edge of death. This would have been her grandmother's fate if it hadn't been for the Wise Sisters.

Wordlessly she squeezed William's arm and pointed. She walked towards the girls, scanning the darker places in the vault as she moved, half expecting some creature to leap at her from its hiding place.

She knelt beside the girls' wretched bed and brushed a gentle hand across their young faces. Their faces were soft, and so still, held slightly out of time. She felt like she had when she would sneak into Rita and Mama's bedrooms to spend time with them when she was very lonely.

Seeing the girls again, feeling their dusty hair and the brittleness of the cloth of their dresses, rotten with age, Vreni was fuelled with determination. She was so close to changing all this. She touched the vial of softening potion hanging with her other charms.

'I could free them now,' she whispered.

There'll be time for that later, Anna said.

'But if—'

Faith, Vreni.

'Yes.' She knew Anna was right. Why wake them now to face who knew what?

Vreni stood and moved towards the shelves to seek out the remaining sleeping-death potion. The Sisters had been sure that even a few drops would be enough for them to create a formula to fully reverse the curse and save Vreni, her family, and maybe, somehow, the sleeping girls. She was so close now.

Standing in the dim shadows cast across the shelves, Vreni reached out with her mind, to sense the potion. Its resonance had been gouged deep into her awareness when she touched it in the dream realm. She could still recall the cold dread that had seeped through the glass, and the feel of the terrible icy darkness that had crawled across her skin, as if the liquid inside the bottle were trying to find a place to enter her body. She searched through the shelves, reaching out with her awareness.

William moved around the tree on the pedestal, trying to find a better position from which to watch over her more closely.

On the third bank of shelves Vreni was instinctively drawn to an ornate silver box that was high up and almost out of reach. She opened it and removed the small, familiar bottle from its bed of decaying red velvet. As she lifted the thick glass of the bottle she felt the haunting cold rise up her arm, but this time the feeling of dread was mixed with relief. This was it. It would all be over soon.

There was a soft, rustling sound behind her. She jumped and the bottle fell from her hand, rolling away across the knotted wooden bench. At the edge of her vision she saw something move. Both she and William turned towards the central platform. It seemed as though the old, half-dead tree had moved.

'What was that?' she asked.

'I think it moved,' William said.

'The tree?'

'Maybe not.' Now he sounded doubtful.

Then a ripple of movement ran through the tree once more. William moved toward Vreni protectively.

The fading light in the room made it difficult for them to see the tree in any detail. It was swollen and stump-like, with only two branches reaching feebly towards the domed ceiling. One of the branches had sprouted an unusual taproot that trailed down and joined with the floor.

The tree didn't look as though it was planted in any soil. Its swollen roots seemed to spread out across the platform and disappear under a thick blanket of mouldering leaves, which lay all around it, cushioning its bulk. Resting at the top of the trunk, between the two uplifted branches, was a rounded, wrinkled stump.

The tree was topped with a spray of gnarled twigs sticking out at odd angles, making Vreni think of an ugly head with outstretched arms, but then all trees looked a bit like that, she decided, especially in winter.

The trunk of the tree was bulbous and distorted. It looked as though it was collapsing in on itself. The bark was murky and uneven. It warped and folded to accommodate the crooked shapes.

'I must've been seeing things,' William said quietly, and he turned back again to the job of scanning the room.

The tree shuddered once again, and the arm-branches stiffened, the tree's trunk appeared to swell and collapse again, and what sounded like a loud breath was somehow exhaled from it.

Vreni and William stared transfixed as two eyes blinked

open in the bark, which was now turning into a face on a stumpy wooden head resting limply on the right branch-arm. A small twisted mouth opened with a rasping yawn. Clearly visible were the features of the face within the crinkled folds of bark.

Glassy eyes the colour of autumn leaves stared out from their woody sockets. The eyes looked around without seeming to focus on anything. The branches rustled feebly again and Vreni realised that this was the face and arms, and the swollen curves of an old female body. Any legs that may once have existed had long ago been transformed into roots. This thing was made from wood, or had been turned into wood, but either way it had to be the work of the alchemists and their organisation, the AlGuild.

'What is that?' William asked.

'*Who* is that, you mean. What have they done to her, and how?'

'She's beautiful, isn't she?' said a deep, viscous voice from somewhere in the darkness.

Vreni felt her heart thump up into her throat. Her ears buzzed with the rush of blood as her heart pounded violently.

'Captivating,' added the unseen voice.

William was frozen in place. His face was the colour of stone. He was staring intently into the patch of darkness where the voice had come from.

'Can you see anything?' Vreni said.

'I think my mind's still playing tricks from before. I'm

sure that's all it is, it can't be ... anything else,' William whispered, and shook his head slowly, stiffly.

His breath shuddered and his shoulders hunched forward. He stared down, as if looking through the floor at something no one else could see. Rubbing the key amulet between his fingers, he turned to look at Vreni and his eyes were wet. He squeezed the key, digging it hard into his palm.

'What is it, William?' she whispered.

Leave it alone, Vreni, Anna said. *He can't say the words yet, not even to himself.*

'What words?'

You'll know later, Anna said firmly.

Vreni wished she knew what was going on.

'I like to watch her sleeping,' came the voice from the darkness. 'I wait for her to wake, longing to see those sparkling amber eyes.'

Vreni squeezed her trembling hands into fists. There were footsteps coming from where William had been staring.

Lights flickered on around the room. A tall gaunt man, more bone than flesh, walked slowly towards them, never once taking his eyes off the wooden woman on the platform. The bony man wore a look of love and longing that Vreni had sometimes seen on her father when he thought he was alone, sitting with his sleeping wife.

The strange thin man's gaze never faltered. He moved close to them and then walked past, appearing spellbound. He stepped up onto the platform and brushed his fingers tenderly across the rough, bark-encrusted cheek of the reclining figure.

'My Rozālija, I am here. I'll be here for you always,' he murmured.

William was shaking. His eyes were wide open and staring. His jaw was clenched.

Vreni came closer to William, trying to offer some comfort. This man seemed more frightening to him than anything else so far. What was it about him that had William in such a state? Right now she had no chance of finding out.

She took William's hand and squeezed it. 'I don't think he sees us,' she whispered.

'Yes, I see you,' the man said without taking his eyes off the Rozālija creature. 'As master of the guild, I have many ways of seeing and a plethora of other useful skills. And after I have gazed into the eyes of my love, I will show you some of those skills ... by killing you both.'

The words echoed in Vreni's head. Her hands shook as she played nervously with the amulets hanging around her neck. She could feel their power tingling against her skin.

You know about your grandmother's aunts, Vreni, Anna said. *They were all named for the most beautiful flowers. They were the first of the Wise Sisters, and Rozālija was the one that plotted with the alchemists to kill Ieva. We heard rumours that the alchemists had somehow used the sleeping-death potion to keep the old witch alive. It's hard to believe she's endured so long, and now she's this barely human thing.*

'This is Veca Tante?'

'Yes,' the Master said. 'Some people used to call her that, so long ago. Never us, never her loyal Alķimķi Gilde, but others, the witches, her sisters.' He paused and stroked the bark-encrusted face as if offering comfort. 'The stories were told and re-told until the world believed she was an ugly old witch. But as you can see they were all just stories. She is glorious. She is beautiful.' He leaned in slowly and kissed the wooden cheek with surreal gentleness.

The words the Master spoke filled Vreni's mind with an icy fog. She couldn't think what action to take. This really was Veca Tante. This wizened enchantress who had kept men imprisoned generation after generation, making them do her bidding. This husk of a man was her devoted servant.

Is Veca Tante really still waiting for the day when she'll defeat the Wise Sisters? Does she even know who she was, or what she's become?

Vreni had always thought of herself as some kind of freak for being a sleeper, but now she realised she wasn't a monster at all.

Vreni looked past Veca Tante to where the three girls were sleeping. She had heard what Anna said, but all she could think of was that if she was going to die today then she would at least release these three girls from their prison first. She started to move around the platform. Her fingers found the small vial of softening formula hanging among the charms. She edged towards the sleeping girls.

With incomprehensible speed the Master drew himself from his adoring trance and moved to block her path.

'You are a sister-witch,' he snarled. He leaned horribly

close, his face briefly brushing her skin, and sniffed her. 'No, you are a sleeper. Are you one of Ieva's daughters, a granddaughter? No matter, you will be just as dead, who-ever you are.'

He leaned over her and sniffed her face once more. 'Rozālija was right to believe the whispers about the sleep-ers and the sister-witches. How curious and delightful to see one of you after all these years, but you leave our little experiment alone.'

'Experiment!' Vreni exploded. 'This is *not* an experi-ment. These girls were someone's daughters. You fiends and that ... *creature* might have had some ludicrous motive for doing what you did to my grandmother, but why these girls? They offered no advantage to your cause.'

The Master moved back again to touch his beloved Rozālija.

Vreni edged closer to the sleeping girls. She felt a cold grip on her legs, freezing her in mid-step. She couldn't move. She felt as though there was a band of ice around her neck. Her throat was constricted and she pressed against the invisible, frozen collar, trying to loosen it.

'Now, now, young witch, the Alķimķi Ģilde didn't just play with daba like your sister-witches do. Your Pratigs Māsa,' he spat out the words, 'spent their time danc-ing around with nature and making magic to soften and manipulate, trying to do good.'

He flicked one hand and bunches of herbs lifted off the benches and flew into the air, whirling above their heads. 'The Alķimķi Ģilde uses magic as a science.' He gestured again, and this time a few leather-bound books lifted to join the swirling throng. 'We needed to have scientific rigor.' He sounded manic and patronising. 'All good science has to have sound experimental practice in place. These girls were simply an experiment—'

A strangled murmur came from the platform. The Master stopped and turned his gaze once again on the tree-witch.

Vreni felt the grip on her legs and throat release, and the floating objects dropped abruptly to the floor. She lunged towards the girls again, but somehow the old man was there to block her way. He leaned down and scooped up one of the girls with a single arm, obviously much stronger than he appeared. The girl hung there like a rag doll.

'We don't think of these specimens as actual people,' he said. 'We consider them to be useful laboratory rats, nothing more, and I'll still have two left.' He took a knife from his belt and plunged it into the girl's chest.

Vreni flinched. She felt the contents of her stomach rising into her mouth and swallowed hard. She waited for some reaction from the rag-doll girl. How could she not feel the knife in her chest, in her heart? But the girl just hung in the man's arms, undisturbed. No blood came from her wound. Vreni struggled to accept that this could be happening.

The Master casually dropped the girl back onto the divan with the knife still poking up from the fabric of her dress.

Suddenly the Master's bony hand took hold of her, wrapping tightly around her neck. William raced to help her, but was snared mid-step by the Master's invisible choke collar. He stood gasping for breath, struggling to reach her.

She pushed at the attacking arm, trying to get him to release her. She thumped and scratched, feeling the hard muscles flexing as his hand constricted around her throat. She felt crunching in her neck as he squeezed. Pain radiated through her jaw and up into her ears. Her lungs heaved uselessly as she struggled for air. A thunderous buzzing-ringing filled her ears, and patches of wild, fizzing colour blocked her vision.

The Master's face was so close to hers. He stared into her widening eyes.

'I have lots of dramatic ways to kill you,' he whispered, 'but I do enjoy the, personal touch.'

With the last of her energy, she kicked out at his legs and slammed her fists into the sides of his chest as hard as she could. He wrenched her off her feet. She could feel the weight of her body pulling on her neck as she dangled. As she struggled, she reached toward the divan with one foot, hoping to support her weight.

The pressure on her throat was complete, she had no air. As her world began to blacken and fade. She felt the Master's face touching hers.

'I like to collect last breaths,' he snickered quietly. 'I like to inhale the last breath a person will ever breathe. I have quite a collection.'

William moved again. The old man was too enthralled by the sight of Vreni dying to think about keeping him under control.

As though she was a precious object, the Master moved Vreni almost gently towards the divan to lay her with the others.

The knife! With her last effort Vreni stretched out her chin and bit into the Master's sallow cheek, clamping down with all the strength she had left. She could taste the salty iron of his blood in her mouth. He let out an angry growl, and slowly pulled his dagger out of the ragdoll girl. It came away clean.

'You're harder to kill than I expected,' he said. 'How delightful.'

Vreni felt his hot whisper in her ear. She saw the knife, held high. Then she saw William's reflection glinting in the metal of the blade.

There was a heavy grunt as air was expelled from the Master's lungs. Vreni wobbled as he regained his footing, and now she could feel the floor under her feet again. William's arm came up underneath the hand that held the knife, smashing the blade free of the Master's grip. It tumbled through the air and landed with a quiet snick of metal cutting flesh. Vreni dreaded to think which girl had been stabbed now.

The constriction around her neck was released and she collapsed to the floor, gasping hungrily for air. She scrambled blindly to get away from the Master, and didn't stop until she collided with one of the wooden shelves. She leaned back, trying to stifle her sobs, panting, trying to focus her blurred vision and clear away the blackness.

The room came slowly into focus. William and the Master were knotted grotesquely together, each gripping the other's throat. William was a full head taller than his emaciated opponent, but the Master was still able to lift William from the floor, as he had done with Vreni. William was planting violent kicks into the Master's legs, which caused the old man to lower him briefly so his feet could touch the floor, offering a precious second to snatch a breath. But William's colour was fading.

Vreni looked around at the malevolence and death in the room, and realised she would have to add to it if this was to be truly finished. *This has to stop.*

She reached for the charms. Finding a small sphere full of frogspawn, she placed it in her hand and whispered to the glass to melt. A moment later minute tadpoles swam around in the dish of her cupped palm. She chanted.

'Swim and grow, swim and grow,'
'You are no longer tiny eggs.
Lose your tails and find your legs.
Seek a hiding place, beyond the tongue,
Keep growing till his life is done.'

She shuddered at the command's intention, *her* intention.

When she had finished chanting, her hand contained seven shiny green frogs. They hopped gently down onto the stone floor and moved unnoticed to where William and the Master were still locked in battle.

William looked determined rather than scared, and he had a look of something else, as though this battle was his.

What had he realised that she had not? Vreni whispered her spell again, sending her frogs to obey her commands.

The frogs reached the heels of the Master's shoes. They started to climb up the back of his trousers, growing a little more as they ascended, their sticky footpads clinging to the fabric as they climbed.

William's eyes flickered when he saw them appear at the Master's shoulders. From there the frogs lolloped out along the Master's arms. Stopping at his wrists, they blinked serenely, and waited until the Master opened his mouth to roar another threat at William. Then the creatures leapt into the moist darkness and slipped easily beyond the Master's tongue, down deep into his throat.

The shrivelled man's grip on William loosened. William lifted his knee and rammed it deep into the Master's stomach. The man collapsed onto the floor and lay coughing. William stepped clear of the fallen man's reach and watched as he writhed on the cold stone. The old man's face was making shapes as if he was trying to scream, but no sound came out.

Vreni rose to her feet and walked closer to see the effects of her spell. She knew the frogs would continue to grow to full size inside the Master's throat and block off his airway. She knew this was happening because it was her intention when she chanted the spell. This was what she had wished for. For the Master to never be able to do harm again. *Is this who I am? A killer? Is this what I need to become to be Veronika, bringer of victory?*

William had become stone-like again. He stared down at the gasping old man.

'What is it?' she asked.

Leave him with his moment, he will tell you when he can, Anna said.

As the two men stared at each other, the Master's body started to spasm and jerk. His chest heaved as his lungs tried desperately to suck air through his amphibian-filled throat. He grabbed at his neck, trying to swallow. His sallow face turned grey. His lips turned blue, then a deeper blue again. His eyes bulged with the effort of trying to breathe.

Then his eyes could no longer stare at William. The dilated irises rolled upwards under his fast-blinking eyelids until they were gone forever, leaving just the yellow-white of his eyeballs, traced with a web of tiny red lines formed by bursting blood vessels. The Master's body heaved and arched. His hands clenched and unclenched, and his feet kicked out weakly at nothing.

Then everything was still. The old man lay on the dark stone floor like a bony blue ghost. The frogs had completed their task.

'What happened just then?' Vreni asked William.

'Tell you later,' he mumbled.

The Master and Veca Tante are a team, Anna said forcefully. *You need to act on the old witch as well. Soften her, Vreni. Use the vial.*

'But what about the girls?'

We can help the girls later, but take action against Tante now or we may still lose it all.

SOFTENING

All things that are begun will end. All things that are made
will be unmade and remade to begin again.
Then are beginnings endings or endings beginnings?
—Pratigs Māsa, Book of Questions

***

Vreni took the vial of green liquid from around her neck and jumped onto the leaf-strewn platform. Veca Tante made distressed mewing sounds as her eyes darted around the room, searching for her ensorcelled lover, and then they fixed on Vreni.

Do those yellow cat-eyes truly see me? How alive is she inside her wooden prison?

Vreni caught sight of the heavy silver spiral amulet hanging around the thick, inhuman neck. *How dare you wear the sign of the Pratigs Māsa?* Vreni gripped the pedant and yanked at it, snapping the ancient chain. Veca Tante let out an anguished cry.

Vreni broke open the small vial of softening formula and poured its syrupy contents onto the rough bark skin.

It dribbled into the folds of the witch's distorted cleavage and soaked quickly into her woody flesh. Veca Tante quivered, and a low gargling growl came from between her bark-covered lips.

Vreni shoved the old witch's amulet into her pocket and jumped down from the platform. She returned to William, who was still standing over the Master's fallen body. The blue lips twitched and rippled, and Vreni felt her heart gallop again. Surely he couldn't still be alive.

But no, the dead cheeks fluttered and the thin lips grimaced into a morbid smile as the frogs squirmed their way back out of their victim's mouth. One by one, the emerald frogs appeared through the Master's thin, blue lips. They glistened in the softening light of the room. All seven frogs remained on the dead face, their large eyes looking around, blinking slowly. They began to croak quietly.

Vreni reached out to William. He turned slowly from the face full of frogs to look at her. He appeared to thaw slightly.

From behind them there was groaning and wailing. They turned and watched as Veca Tante twitched and shuddered. Wordless noises, full of grief, came from her wooden lips. She sobbed as pieces of her crusty bark skin flaked away and fell to the platform.

There was a dull thud. They both jumped and turned to see that a small piece of decorative wood panelling had fallen to the stone floor. Their eyes tracked upwards to see where it had come from. The timber that panelled the ceiling was splitting and breaking apart. The domed-glass skylight began to sputter and crack as the ceiling warped.

Glass started to rain down across the platform, and needle-like shards pierced the tender flesh that had been exposed as the old witch's bark fell away. Now she howled and contorted.

The cracks opening up and down her body oozed a mucky-brown sap. Ripples ran across her wooden body, which undulated from the roots pushing the remaining sap upwards. With each pumping wave, the brown fluid oozed more freely from the cracks and wounds as it made its way to her head and moved up into the stunted branches that might once have been her hair. These thin branches sprouted tiny dots of green that budded with unnatural speed. Shining green leaves uncurled and grew. Buds appeared and swelled, and when they opened the flowers bloomed. There was a daisy, something that looked like mistletoe, and some chicory flowers. Last of all, one perfect red rose grew and threw open its petals.

'It's as though she knows this is her end,' Vreni said to William. 'All plants feel the harshness of winter coming and know they could die in the snow. She's setting seed. Seeds are the immortality of the forest.'

'Yes, this is her end,' William agreed. 'Look.'

As the bark fell away, soft spaces of flesh were left bare, filling quickly with a squirming sea of worms and beetles.

'She's doing what old trees should do,' Vreni said, almost reverently. 'She's composting and returning to the earth.'

The beetles and worms roiled over one another, feasting on the mushy wooden flesh. They multiplied and spilled out over the edge of the bark and flowed across the trembling body. Veca Tante opened and closed her mouth, but she no longer made sounds. A quivering wave of tiny creatures crawled across the old witch's face and entered her mouth and eyes. With one last shudder, she shook her head fiercely and crumpled. Her large bloated body sagged and collapsed inwards, pulling the face and the stunted arms down to form a pile of disintegrating humus.

All that remained on top of the rotting pile was the rose, the last three petals clinging to its red rosehip, which was swollen with seeds.

'It smells like the forest.' Vreni breathed deeply.

A second heavy wooden panel crashed down to their right. The ceiling was buckling and cracking open.

This place was held together by the old witch's magic, Anna said.

Vreni looked up, surprised to see the first traces of faint early-morning light glowing through the cracks in the roof. Another panel fell. Above it, the metal of the exterior roof screeched as it twisted.

'We have to get out of here.' William pointed to a door that had not been visible before. He pulled Vreni in that direction.

'Not without the girls.'

She shook off his grip and ran back around the platform to the dusty divan. She lifted the wounded girl into her arms. She felt as light as a baby bird. Beside her, William knelt and lifted the other two girls with a grunt, laying one over each shoulder.

They turned towards the door. Another piece of the

ceiling crashed down, falling across Vreni's shoulder. Her skin burned as the wood grazed its way down her back. A jagged nail sliced open the back of her heel.

'We have to get to the door,' William said. 'The roof won't last much longer.'

Around them the roof beams groaned, and heavy wooden panels peeled away from the walls like old bark. Sheets of metal swung from the disintegrating roof.

They zigzagged through the debris and finally reached the door. William walked through, but Vreni hesitated.

'Come on,' he said.

He laid the two girls down and turned back to help her. He took the wounded girl and started to pull Vreni through into the short and incredibly narrow passageway. She could see morning light coming through the door at the other end.

'No!' she yelled above the whining of the twisting roof metal.

She ran back into the crumbling room, circling to the right. She stayed close to the wall to gain some protection from the falling roof. Reaching the shelves where she had found the velvet-lined box, she remembered that the bottle had rolled from her grasp when Veca Tante had startled her. She quickly checked the bench where she thought it had gone, but it wasn't there. Throwing herself down on the floor, she thrust her arm under the bottom of the cabinet and groped wildly.

Her hand landed on the cool glass, and again she felt the creeping cold travelling up her fingers and across her palm. Blessings.

As she pulled the bottle out from under the cabinet, a large wooden beam came loose from the roof with a loud screech. She curled up her body to protect the bottle and its horrible–wonderful contents. The beam struck her back. Most of the beam's weight hit the shelf first, but it knocked the air from her lungs as it slammed into her shoulder and pushed her head into the heavy cabinet door. Her leg was pinned in place by the beam. She was trapped.

The bottle! She rolled it fearfully in her palm and smiled, it was unbroken.

'Vreni!' William called.

'I can't move.'

'On my way.'

There was another crash. The door was now blocked by a second fallen beam, with William on the other side.

'I know I'm not alone,' Vreni said, urging herself to stay calm and remember her powers.

You are never alone, Anna said. *Remember, you have all our love and our strength, always.*

Vreni tucked the precious bottle of sleeping potion into the silk pouch around her neck and felt for the glistening red amulet hanging among the remaining charms.

That contains a drop of blood from each of us at Mežs Mājas, Anna said. *Each drop has travelled through the heart of the Sister who gave it and contains the strength and love of us all.*

Vreni placed the glass bubble, full of blood, onto her tongue and concentrated, remembering the faces of her sisters and the sweetness of their voices as they sang joy-fully together. She thought of Rita, her mother, her aunties and the cursed girls, robbed of their lives. The bubble melted away and she tasted the salty-sweet strength on her tongue.

I am Veronika, bringer of victory.

Growing warmth spread throughout her body, and she could her sisters singing. She arched her back, feeling the jagged edges of the wooden beam digging into her skin. She inhaled deeply, smelling the blood of her sisters on her lips. She pushed with the force of many and lifted the beam. She quickly slipped sideways, freeing herself from the trap before it dropped back down.

She threaded her way through the destruction in the vault and back to the blocked door. She leaned her weight against the fallen beam that blocked the doorway and pushed hard. It scraped noisily as it slid slowly across the brass strap that banded the exit door.

Vreni could feel the borrowed power from the charm waning. She pulled at the door and managed to open it just enough to squeeze through. The door slammed shut behind her, knocking into her back. She stumbled towards William, who stood holding the two sleeping girls.

'We have to go *now*,' he urged.

All she could do was nod as she lifted the third girl into her arms. Feeling the last of the borrowed strength seep fully from her now, she leaned on William for a moment while her head spun. She breathed deeply and found a last vestige of strength from the charm.

'Thank you, my Sisters,' she murmured.

They turned and walked quickly down the passageway as the building disintegrated behind them. Pushing open the final door, they walked out into the morning sunshine and away from the collapsing ruins. The sun seemed a ridiculously normal sight after everything that had happened since they had seen it last.

Still watching for danger, Vreni caught sight of the guard standing dazed outside the building. He looked their way, but didn't seem to see them. He turned, as though he had heard something, and walked purposefully away from them, around the side of the building. They walked quickly out the front gate and into the empty carpark.

The guard watched, transfixed, as the building collapsed. He didn't even notice the unauthorised vehicle that entered the carpark, loaded its five passengers, and drove away.

DIMINISHING

Is it the raindrop that makes the flood?
Does an egg hold the bird's song? Is the tree hiding within
the seed?
—*Pratigs Māsa, Book of Questions*

***

The young security guard stumbled around the buckling metal shell of the building. Hour after hour, he circled the outer wall. He listened to the structure inside collapsing and crashing down, but he was listening for another sound as well. He was sure he could hear a cry for help, a plaintive call from beyond the warping steel walls.

He had seen them get out, hadn't he? He thought he remembered seeing someone, but the memory was unclear. All he knew clearly now was that he was needed by someone. He could definitely hear a voice calling—couldn't he?

Plumes of dust rose up with each crash. He walked around the building, tugging at each buckling window in turn. He slammed his fists against the glass, hoping he could break them. Each time he passed the front door he tried the security pad. Nothing. He slammed his shoulder hard against the door until he felt dizzy. Nothing.

He circled in this way throughout the day, swooning each time he heard a whisper of voice from beyond the bent walls. At sunset he discovered a place where the twisting metal had ripped apart, forming a ragged gash in the wall. He tugged at the sharp edges. Trickles of blood flowed across his palms. Finally, he made the opening wide enough to clamber through. The jagged metal caught on his shoulder as he passed, but the wound went unnoticed.

Within the walls nothing remained except piles of stone and rotting timber. The scene looked like an ancient ruin. He stumbled in and out of the detritus. He could hear the voice all the more strongly now. Its soft words filled his head and his heart.

He came at last to the centre of what used to be the building. The sun was setting and the last light painted the sky orange and red. He knelt among the shards of broken glass, and tenderly reached to pick up what remained of a rose from where it clung to a thin, twisted branch poking up from the rubble.

'You are beautiful, my beautiful rose.'

He held the rose gently in his bloody palm. Its three remaining red velvet petals quivered, and fell loose into his hand. The bulging rosehip shone a vivid crimson. He held the round seedpod to his heart.

'I'm yours, always.'

Holding the rosehip lovingly to his heart, he stood and turned then paused. 'Gold,' he mumbled, hefting a chest with the with a sun symbol carved in the lid. The handle of the heavy chest dug deeply into his palm as he dragged it, stumbling back through the rubble. Once outside he stared into the darkening red of the setting sun and started westward, looking for a place to plant his seeds.

HOMECOMING

Home is family and fealty, comfort and companionship,
acceptance and truth.
Home is a palace, a cottage, or a heart.
—Pratigs Māsa, Book of Wisdoms

***

As the car dropped down into the green, birch-filled valley of Mežs Mājas, Vreni finally allowed herself to relax. She had tried to whisper questions to Sabina, but her voice must have been too quiet, or Anna was making her wait, and the answers she sought would come later.

Vreni sat with the girls in the back seat of the car while William sat up front with the driver. She wasn't sure if he was really sleeping but that was how it looked, there were no answers from him either.

She rolled down the window and breathed in the cool fragrance of the forest. Home. William stirred in the front seat.

As the curved dirt road bought them closer to the cottages at the centre of the valley, Vreni could see Sisters standing on the verges, smiling and waving. When the car passed, they followed behind like they were joining a parade. The birdsong under the trees was gradually overtaken by the joyous chanting and singing, which intensified as each new voice joined in.

The car circled through the gardens, and as it passed in front of the lab building Vreni saw Sabina and Anna waving and singing among the cluster of happy faces, fully restored and as beautiful and radiant as she had ever seen them.

Now Vreni realised why they hadn't given her any answers on the trip home, the spell had been undone.

She wriggled her shoulder from under the sleeping girls. The car had barely stopped when she pushed open the door, scrambled across the gravel and threw herself at Sabina and Anna. Her legs buckled beneath her. Their arms encircled her tightly and held her weight as she nuzzled into them and let her tears flow. Pressed so closely between the two women, Vreni could feel the vibrations of their humming through her skin. As Sabina cooed quietly, the music surrounded Vreni and she felt her strength returning.

The bottle containing the potion pressed coldly against her skin. She slipped it from around her neck and handed it to Anna, who held the bottle high in the air.

'Veronika, bringer of victory,' Sabina announced.

Everyone cheered and crowded in around her, pulling William into the excited crescendo of celebration until they were standing close together. Vreni's mind swelled with questions again, but in the joyous noise, all she could do was smile and hug him.

'Thank you,' she managed to say as the music and laughter continued.

'Now, I must be indelicate,' Anna said, smiling, 'you two badly need a bath and a change of clothes.'

'Yes,' Sabina agreed. 'You need to clean yourselves up and get some rest, and tonight we'll have a feast in honour of your victory.'

The crowd thinned, and Vreni watched as the sleeping girls were carried into the laboratory.

***

It was late afternoon when Vreni walked out into the garden. Her bath had been fragrant and energising. She knew the water had been laced with restorative potions, and she was glad of it because she could feel her physical and emotional strength starting to return. The setting sun was painting crimson-orange light across the treetops as she walked slowly through the patchwork of flowerbeds and ponds, heading for the quiet of the pine grove.

Under the green canopy the air became cool and still. As her eyes adjusted to the deep shadows, she saw William. He was sitting down, leaning against the rough bark of one of the older trees. He looked refreshed and his wounds were covered with clean white dressings.

'Do you come here often?' she said, trying to sound cheerful although she was bursting with questions.

'I do.' He smiled. 'They have a great light show and the

girls are great dancers.' He stood up and bowed dramatically. 'Will you dance with me?'

'How could I resist?'

They curled into each other's arms and started to sway slowly.

'We did it,' she whispered, and felt his arms grow suddenly tense around her. Realising he wasn't going to say anything yet, she let it go. 'You're right, it is a great light show here.'

His arms relaxed and they danced until the light faded.

William led her out of the pine grove to the wooden bench by the pond. The light from the buildings created a shimmering patchwork on the still surface of the water. The noise of happy preparations echoed from the cottage windows.

Vreni softly touched the dressed wounds on William's face. 'I can't thank you enough for what you've done for me. I wouldn't have been victorious, or even alive now, if you hadn't been there.'

'You're welcome, but like I said before we entered the labyrinth, I was doing this for me too. I wanted some freedom, and now ...' He trailed off. He was rubbing the key amulet between his fingers.

'You don't need that key anymore,' she said.

'I never needed it, Vreni.'

'I don't understand?'

'It was a bio-lock, set to a DNA pattern.'

'But the key overrode the lock, otherwise only the Master could open it.'

William took a deep breath and held it for a moment. 'Or someone with very similar DNA.'

'I still don't understand.'

'The Master is, was, my father,' he whispered.

Vreni felt her throat tighten. 'What? That can't be true.'

'I know my own father's face,' he said slowly.

'You knew when you saw him inside the vault. Why didn't you tell me?' Hot tears rolled down her cheeks.

'Because when I saw that it was him, suddenly everything made horrible sense. I realised what he must have done to my sister and to my mother. He needed a son to follow in his footsteps. Once he had that—' William shuddered and released an anguished sigh.

'You should have told me,' she choked out.

'How could I have said that to you, Vreni? It made no sense to me. I could barely admit to myself.'

'But if I'd known …' She was trembling.

'If you had known, could you have done what you did?'

'I killed your father.'

The words crackled like lightning. She felt dizzy and couldn't breathe. Knowing she had ended the life of a cruel, half-human monster, a stranger, was bad enough, but now this anonymous stranger had become a person. *I have killed a person.*

'I'm sorry, but I needed you to do what you did. I *wanted* you to kill him. It had to happen for you and your family, but also for me, and for my mother. I believe he killed her once he had me to groom to one day take his place. He would have made sure I was held under the witch's spell, to be the next master. The alchemists made prisoners of us both. He was a monster, Vreni, he was never my father.'

Vreni pushed away from William and retreated to a tree at the edge of the pine grove. She pressed her face hard into the rough bark. An angry storm of questions brewed in her mind. *Did Sabina know about all this? Why didn't she tell me? Are we just puppets, dangling on the magical strings of the Pratigs Māsa?*

'We haven't been controlling you,' Sabina said quietly behind Vreni. 'We've watched as the succession of masters came and went over the centuries, so we knew who he was, but when you met William that was not our doing. That was your fate, and his. You were meant to meet each other that day. Love is far more powerful than all our magic.'

'You used him,' Vreni growled. 'You brought him here to get what you wanted.'

'When we knew who he was, we realised he could enter the labyrinth undetected, but the choice was always his. Always.'

'So are you really my Sister, my friend, or was that just to get close enough to secretly train me?' Hot tears rolled down her face. 'Did you train me to kill?' She was sobbing. 'And Papa? Did you do that to Papa to make me come with you?' Vreni struggled to breathe.

'I have known your father all my life.' Sabina's tears flowed freely now as well. 'I watched as he guarded you and protected you with all his love. I wished he were my father. I know the pain of your loss.'

Sabina took Vreni in her arms, and Vreni crumpled.

'Please believe me,' Sabina said soothingly. 'We saw the opportunity for real success when fate bought you and William together. But think back over what happened and you'll realise that William's feelings for you are real. Neither of you would have done anything against your will. Seek inside yourself and know that this is true.'

Vreni drew in a purposeful, calming breath as William approached. She looked from one to the other. She saw the truth in their connecting and unfolding stories.

There was the scuffle of gravel as Anna ran from the lab into the cottage, then a loud cheer erupted.

Sabina gripped Vreni's arm. 'That cheering means only one thing, Vreni. The potion will work. There will be a cure. You have done it,' she cried, wrapping her arms around them both. 'Come on, we have a victory to celebrate.' She guided them towards the festivities.

MY SOUL TO KEEP

The sleeping curse gave us purpose,
and made us who we were.
The cure has given us choice and promise,
and remade us into something we are yet to discover.
—*Pratigs Māsa, New Book of Wisdoms*

***

Vreni stood in her tower, staring out to the east, across the sea. The sun was sinking low behind her and the tower cast a long shadow across the garden and out to the edge of the cliff. The sea beyond was turning a deep purple, it would soon be swallowed by night time. A few stars were sprinkled across the evening sky.

Vreni thought of the long-ago times in her childhood when she had built rickety playhouses out of worn blankets. The light that penetrated through the holes in the blankets had been her make-believe stars and the moon she had dreamed of visiting. She wished she could still pretend and weave a world made of stories and un-truths, but she had truths now and she had come up here to make the choices she was finally free to make.

There were three truths that Vreni carried with her now. She opened her journal, hoping that her thoughts would become clear as the words tumbled onto the pages. Each sleeper would be offered a cure, she had a decision to make soon.

She wrote: *Truth: I killed a man. I did not hold a knife or brew a poison or shoot a gun, but I made my intentions clear. I wove the magic and gave instructions to the frogs. The frogs didn't kill him; they only did what I instructed them to do, what it was their nature to do—grow and hop and seek out a moist hiding place. I brought them to life and sent them down the Master's throat. I knew what would happen, and I still made it happen.*

Vreni stared out the window and wondered about her own nature.

Truth: I am a magical creature. I live by magical rules. Like Veca Tante, I have used a variation of the sleeping potion to travel through time. She used it wishing to live long enough to defeat us. I have used it and witnessed the wonder of change across my century.

Magic had saved them and imprisoned them all. William was meant to be the next placed under the old witch's spell, to adore her and serve her until he was used up. Isn't that what he would become if he chose to were the Sister's silver amulet?

Truth: the Wise Sisters have done what they promised and reversed the sleeping potion. Now all sleepers have a choice. When Rita, Mama and the aunties next wake they can choose to take the formula and be free. The new formula has worked, and the Sisters have woken two of the three sleeping girls. The last girl remains in the safety of long-sleep while they work on making successful repairs to her heart. She will be waking soon, when waking no longer means death for her.

Vreni laughed to herself. The girls were amazed to have woken up in another time and place. Their new world frightened and fascinated them. It was funny to see them fretting over the creatures trapped inside the television, just like Vreni had done so long ago. She knew she had saved them. If she hadn't killed the Master, they would still be lying in a heap like discarded rag dolls, perhaps forever.

She would teach the girls about their new world and their unique history. They could choose to sleep again, because the Wise Sisters now had complete control of both formulas.

These ideas swam in Vreni's head, making her dizzy. It was all over. She had won a victory for her family and herself. So why, with all this freedom, did she feel as though she was weighed down with lead? All she had ever wanted was to be free to live like everyone else, to travel and love, and to live free of secrets.

She flicked absentmindedly through the heavy pages of the family journal that lay open next to her own. The history it held was rich and powerful. The people held within its pages were exceptional and strong. They had spanned centuries and remained resilient against so many challenges. Vreni was proud of her unique history and her strength. Would the cure change everything?

Memories of Vreni's century spun through her mind: images of fashion, cars, technology. Her century had been a time of exponential change, and she felt privileged to have been witness to it. But what might the future hold? Maybe she could stay as she was and keep travelling through time. The thought was tantalizing. She loved the thrill of waking to new and marvellous things.

She looked up at the moon. *I would've thought that by now people would be able to visit there.*

Vreni's eyes refocused as William's reflection appeared in the dark mirror of the tower's windows. Something glinted. He was wearing an amulet like the one her father had worn.

'How can you be wearing that?' Vreni heart raced.

'Sabina said it was my decision.'

'But I haven't said I'll marry you. We've had *one* date,' she said incredulously.

'Love is the magic, Vreni, and I've chosen to do this, to watch over all this,' he said quietly.

'My soul to keep,' Vreni whispered bitterly.

'No, there'll be no *keeping*. I know how that feels, just like you do. But you'll need my help when everyone starts waking up, and I hope you'll still have time for dancing,' he added, smiling.

She smiled back. 'I'd like that, and I did promise you a dance.'

'Only one,' he laughed, and took her hand, spinning her around.

She touched the amulet. 'What about if, I mean *when*, I take the cure?'

'Then I take this off, I suppose. Is it *if* or *when*?'

'Honestly, I don't know yet. I need more time to decide.'

'Well, we have plenty of that,' he said, rubbing the amulet slowly.

'I'm not sure if I want to miss out on.'

'I know,' William said, smiling. 'The future's too good a place to give up, and now we can think about sharing it. No rush,' he said, squeezing her shoulders.

'No rush,' she agreed, looking up at the moon again. 'I always thought I'd get to go there.'

'Maybe you will.'

'Maybe I will.'

BOOK TWO

BOOK TWO

TALES OF BLOOD AND FATE

*The curse was cured, the truths were written into the
Wise Sister's Book of Wisdoms and we would like to say
they all lived happily ever after.
But Vreni was not the first to challenge the
alchemists' stronghold.
Other Wise Sisters had gone and never returned.
The tale of their fate was lost
within the circles of the labyrinth.*

PROTECTOR

*The old witch is not gone. I see her
sprouting like a bloom of choking mistletoe, pretty, so pretty as it kills its host.
Life from death. We think Veca Tante has
met her end, but nothing comes to an end.
Hatred, like love, can transcend the grave.
From death comes life. Veca Tante returns
from death into life. I am sure of it. I see
her. She is made new, woven from thorny
blossoms.*

~Sister Gizela's vision

* * *

A fierce shudder wracked Vreni's body. The air scorched
like flame as she breathed in. This first breath always
burned after her lungs had lain so still and cold during
the long-sleep. A raspy moan rose up, sounding distant
through her first clouded awareness as she whimpered in
response to the fiery pain.

Shallow breaths helped to diminish the burning, but
her lungs gulped hungrily, and her throat seared with

each new breath. *Patience, it will pass.* She focused on making her rigid body move. Eyelids, fingers, toes ...nothing could move yet. Her skin could not feel to touch or be touched. Her ears were filled with ragged breaths and the thumping of her heart as it strained to pump the long dormant blood around her body.

Am I alone? Am I safe? She had fallen asleep up in the tower. Was she still there or now tucked into her bed? Her father always watched over her while she slept and been by her side at each of her twenty-one awakenings. He was gone now. Her heart squeezed tight with fresh grief. How long ago had it been now since he had died? How long had she slept this time?

Vreni strained, struggling to make her body move. With every effort there was icy, burning pain. *I wouldn't have fallen into long-sleep and woken in this agony if I had taken the cure when the sisters had offered it. I'd be free of the curse, but I'd hesitated. Why?* She felt a cool tear as it rolled away from her eye. Straining, there was a flicker of movement. Her fingers burned as they twitched, still they could not feel and give clue to where she was.

With effort, there was more movement and less burning, but her prickling limbs remained wooden and stiff. Her litany would fill the time she had to wait to be fully released from long-sleep. She swallowed, pressed her lips together and began. 'I am Vreni,' she said, with only the barest scintilla of a whisper. 'I am sixteen years old —'

A wailing rose and quelled her words. Ribbons of darkness swirled in Vreni's mind. She braced herself to face the blackness of the curse's magic. Centuries ago, when

Veca Tante made the curse, she had intended it to kill. The Wise Sisters were able to soften the curse from death to sleep, but the dark menace remained on the edges of that softening and sometimes it encroached, with its swirling hatred and made her awaking all the more frightening.

Black tendrils crawled around Vreni's awareness. *This blackness will pass.* The tendrils wove closer, binding her until she could barely breath. *It's never been like this before.* Then the bindings released and Vreni's struggling breath rushed in her ears. The ribboning blackness rose and twisted in on itself. Taking shape, becoming Veca Tante's gnarled face. Vreni's heart thundered in her ears. Before now, the half-woken dreams had only ever been cold blackness.

Why is it different now? Why is Veca Tante here within my wakening when she is dead and gone?

Among the black mist, the old witch's sparkling yellow eyes stared at Vreni and her wooden lips creaked open. 'I am here because I dwell here now,' the old witch rasped, in response to Vreni's unuttered questions. 'You diminished me and put me here with your magic, but this place will not hold me.'

'You're not real. You were destroyed,' Vreni snapped at the vision.

The twisted, wooden face continued to stare, drifting closer, its lips creaked into a smile. 'I am as real as you and, like you, I dally here at the edge of death, but not for long.' The wooden smile splintered and broadened.

'I poured the softening potion on you myself and

watched you rot. You are dead, crushed inside the labyrinth.'

The old witch chuckled and wheezed. 'A dying tree will set seed when it senses the end coming.'

Vreni felt herself pulled through the swirling black. A chill crept across her face. She was back, standing in the labyrinth, watching the softening potion dissolving Veca Tante's ancient wooden body. The sweet smell of forest rot was thick in the air. Flowers budded and grew from the old witch's wooden head as she died. As Veca Tante rotted at Vreni's feet, the rose hastened unnaturally to bloom, and just as quickly it withered and died. 'Your seeds were crushed under the rubble of the ruined labyrinth.'

The old witch's voice trickled along the black tendrils. 'Death comes to all things that live, and life comes from death. The forest rot is the bed for the spring seeds,' she said. 'Soon it will be my springtime, and I will grow and blossom.' A gnarled wooden hand reached out of the swirling blackness. The long twig fingers wrapped around Vreni's throat. She couldn't move. Her breath burned and turned into sobs.

The creaking wooden smile opened wider and laughed. A gush of squirming, scuttling creatures poured out. Screams echoed inside Vreni's mind, but the wooden hand squeezed, imprisoning her breath. She could only clench her mouth closed as the creatures squirmed and scuttled across her cheeks, down her neck.

She wished her skin was still frozen. She begged silently that the crawlers wouldn't seek out her ears, her nostrils. She dared not breathe, then suddenly, it was all gone.

The face melted into the blackness and the waking dream leached away. The wooden hand released her throat. Vreni coughed out a breathless cry and gulped for air.

Her throat ached. The smells of wooden decay and mouldering flowers lingered. Where the hand had gripped her throat there was a burning chill. Waking had never been like this before. She lay there with her eyes still frozen shut, fearing that when they finally opened, she would see her flesh turned to wood.

The last shadows of black faded. She strained and flexed to waken her body and the familiar prickling fire flared with each effort. Her ears drummed as blood sped around her body. *It will pass.* She breathed deeply, ignoring the burning and the dark edges of the curse, she focussed on whispering her litany.

'I am Vreni, I am sixteen, almost seventeen, young and ancient, both together. My mother is Gaida, my little sister is Rita...' *No, Rita and I were the same age, and she was asleep again, so I am older now. Or has she woken? Did she take the cure? If she's now free from the sleeping curse, she'll be growing older. She could have grown old and died.* Vreni sobbed and thrashed wildly to shake away the last bonds of this accursed long-sleep. Her body stung with each exertion. *I could have taken the cure when I had the chance?* But she'd not been ready to make her decision, then long-sleep had claimed her, without warning as it always did.

'My mother is Gaida. My father is ... was Parvils. Papa rests in his pine grove now. William...'

William had not been part of her litany before now. He had not been part of her life until her last awakening. They had done brave and frightening deeds to help the Wise Sisters free Vreni's family from the sleeping curse. Their life was filled with fantastical things, the most fantastical of all, for Vreni, was that she and William had found each other. Because of their meeting, the family was safe, free, and the story of the sleeping curse was ending, but endings are not tidy. Vreni lay, half-frozen and remembered.

They had done sad and awkward duties, like attending to William's father's death report and his funeral. Artūrs, Vreni's uncle, had used the family *influence*, as he liked to call it, to ensure minimal questions were asked about the unexpected death. William's father, the Master Alchemist, had shown all the signs of having suffered a heart attack. Vreni supposed anyone would have a heart attack while choking as their throat was filled with magical frogs.

Vreni struggled to accept that truth about herself. That she chose to cast the spell that sent those frogs to kill a person. As she saw the relief in William's eyes when he knew he was free from his father's evil grasp, her guilt had eased in part. Thinking of William's relief made it easier to leave that part of her life behind and start a new story with him. They had spent many months together, getting to know each other, they'd filled this new chapter of their life with many happy and romantic moments before she had fallen into long-sleep. These memories flooded into Vreni's mind and she welcomed them, urging them to push away the frightful vision of the old witch aunty.

Over those months, they had the beach to themselves and spent many long days swimming and walking. On each visit, Vreni found a shell to add to the collection, as she and her sister Rita had always done when they were at the beach with Papa.

On warmer days, they took the ponies down to the water's edge and rode them in the shallows. Vreni thought she heard Rita's pony Fudge whinnying with joy each time William fell off her back into the water, which was often.

One afternoon, after spending time alone in the city, working with the lawyers to attend to his father's estate, William had arrived home with a large cardboard box and a huge smile. 'It is time for me to add my own touch of style to my new home. And it's too far to go every time.'

'Too far to go for what?'

'It's a surprise.' He'd smiled and walked into the conservatory. 'No peeking, you'll know when.' He closed the doors in her face, leaving her alone in the foyer. Vreni shrugged and smiled, turned to the stairs and climbed to the tower. She had barely reached the top of the twisting stairs when she heard music echoing up the tower. William filled the house with happy unpredictability, which she loved about him. When she raced back down the stairs to the ground floor. She pushed open the conservatory doors, there were swirling shards of light bouncing off the mirror ball onto the glass walls. That evening they enjoyed the first of many private dance parties.

These memories melted away the darkness. The burning cold of her strange waking dream was replaced by a vivid image of William. In those months before long-sleep had claimed her, Vreni had become sure she loved him, but she was not sure what words to add to her litany. What was William to her? 'William is —'

'William ... is waiting for you to wake up and come dancing,' said William in a soft voice. She felt his hands now, holding hers.

'Are you hungry? I was warned that you always wake up starving, so breakfast is ready when you are.'

Vreni's eyes finally opened and there was William, sandy hair formed into gravity defying spikes, a huge smile, sitting by her side as she lay safe in her own bed. 'William is my protector.'

'At your service, Lady Veronika.' Hearing William call Vreni by her full name, she drew in a sharp breath and let go of William's hands.

'What did I say?'

'Papa used to say something very similar at my awakenings.'

'I'm sorry.' William rubbed the amulet nervously between his fingers. 'This is all still a bit new to me.'

'Don't apologise. It's wonderful to wake and have you here. Papa used to always seem to know when one of us would wake.' Vreni struggled to sit up. William pulled her into his arms and wrapped her in a hug. The last chill of long-sleep melted into the embrace. 'Papa used to say he'd had centuries of practice at knowing when one of us would wake, but you haven't. How did you know?'

'I couldn't stop thinking of you, I mean, more than normal. Then last night and this morning I started doing things for both of us, two coffee cups, two bowls of ice-cream, which I had to eat by the way. And the amulet — it tingled? Like static. The same thing happened when Rita woke up...'

'Rita! Why didn't you tell me?'

'Rita's awake.' William smiled. Vreni thumped his arm and swung her legs out of bed, wiggling her toes in the shaggy rug. 'How long have I slept?'

'Nearly a year.'

Vreni felt a lump of guilt blossom in her stomach. She thought of her hesitation about taking the cure and chewed on her lip to stop herself apologising to William. 'Tell me about Rita?'

'She woke about five months ago. I was the last person she expected to see. Your mentor from the Wise Sister, Sabina, came to spend time with her as she grieved Parvils.' Vreni drew a shuddering breath at the idea of not being awake to comfort her sister after Papa's death.

'Does she know everything? About the cure? Do you think she will take it and give up being a sleeping princess?'

William squeezed Vreni's hand. 'You have a lot of catching up to do.'

Vreni's face drained and her green eyes widened.

'No, everything's fine. I'll go and make us some breakfast and bring you up to date while we eat.' He helped her to stand and held her until her legs stopped wobbling. Then he kissed her gently. 'Will you be okay?' She nodded. 'Take your time, there's no rush.' He walked to the door and turned holding it half closed. 'Two things,' he said pausing.

Vreni smiled back at him. 'What?'

'I missed you — a lot.'

'And?'

'And ... I really thought you'd have morning breath after sleeping for so long.' He slammed the door shut as Vreni threw a pillow at his disappearing head and laughed.

'William is my protector.'

She walked over to the window, pushed it wide open. The sea and sky stretched out until they blended in a blue haze at the horizon. Breathing deeply, she felt her stiff lungs crackle as they filled with fresh salty air. Her breath caught as she felt the wooden fingers tightened around her throat again. She heard a distant, echoed laugh and the smell of rotting forest returned. She coughed and reached for her throat to pull away the wooden hands, but there was nothing there. She gasped and leaned out her window. 'Enough bad dreams.' She looked out across the sea for a few moments, breathing in the salty air, then turned her mind to getting dressed and breakfast.

REUNION

Vreni has woken. We must warn her of my vision.

Be calm, Gizela. There's no blossom creature. It's the talk of death and loss that has you so troubled. Soon we'll gather to finish our farewells to Parvils. Vreni insisted his body be magically bound to wait for Giada to wake and sing her husband's soul to Vinsaule.

What of the others lost in the ruins of the labyrinth, Anna?

We'll search and bring them home. We'll bring Ilona home, and sing her across the cosmic sea, with all the brave Sisters who were lost.

Surely, we should warn Vreni of my vision?

We've kept our promise to the beauties, Gizela. There is nothing to warn Vreni about. Ease your mind and allow yourself some time to rest and commemorate.
~Wise Sisters Gizela and Anna in conversation

* * *

Vreni stood at the top of the stairs gripped the long banister rail. It was the same smooth curve she slid down after every wakening, but things were changing. 'Even though things change, I am still me,' Vreni whispered as she sat on the banister and let gravity take her. Speeding down the polished curve of the rail, she landed with a thud at the bottom of the stairs.

'Always an impressive trick.' William clapped from the open kitchen door. 'With that sense of balance, I see why I'm the only one who ever falls off the horses.'

'You'll get better at riding, and Fudge is very loyal to Rita, which makes her a difficult horse to deal with. I'll ask Artūrs to look into getting you a horse of your own.' She hugged him and stole a warm kiss as she twirled past into the kitchen. 'Breakfast looks wonderful, I'm ravenous.' Vreni put all her attention towards eating. Fruit, eggs, bread and cheese, milky coffee. Then she suddenly stopped as though a switch had been thrown. She sat staring at her coffee and spent many moments ripping a piece of bread into tiny crumbs. 'Tell me what I need to catch up on.' She stared at William.

'Oh, well once upon a time there was this amazing, heroic girl. Gorgeous too ...'

Vreni smiled. 'I'll be fine, just tell me what's happened while I was sleeping.'

'Nothing bad okay.' William rubbed his hands together. 'In short ... everyone's awake.'

'Everyone?' Vreni's heart clenched.

'Yep. Lucky for me, Rita woke first.' William squeezed his hands together and sighed. 'She was so sad when she found out about your dad.'

Vreni felt her stomach jolt. Her father's death was a wretchedness the all carried.

'I listened and did what I could to help her grieve,' William continued. 'Sabina came for her as soon as I let her know. They spent all their time together, talking, they went to the beach. I left them alone, but I knew Rita was feeling better when she started teasing me, especially when she saw the disco ball in the conservatory. I told her Fudge had thrown me into the surf a few times and that cheered her right up.'

'She was good at teasing our brother too,' said Vreni.

'Brother?'

Vreni nodded. 'We had a younger brother, Peters. He *was* our younger brother, then our older brother then...'

'The boys aren't sleepers?'

'No. He grew old as we slept. It felt that in the blink of an eye he was gone.'

'And Rita teased him?' William interrupted her thoughts.

'Every chance she got.' Vreni smiled and welcomed the reminder of happy memories. 'You said everyone is awake?'

'Yes. Your Aunts woke within a week of each other. I was in the city dealing with Dad's estate and I stayed away while Rita and Sabina explained what had happened while they had been sleeping. But Rita told me everything when I came home. Did you know, your Aunt Mila and Zana knew about your training?'

'What!'

'Sabina told Rita it was your aunts who saw that you had a magical calling. They'd told the Wise Sisters to watch you and train you, so Sabina was sent to be with you and Rita.'

Vreni pulled her hands through dark hair and sighed. 'How can one family keep so many secrets?'

'You're asking me? I'm the guy who found out a couple of years ago that his own father had a secret life and was some sort of ensorcelled love slave to an old magical tree woman.'

'A what!' Vreni laughed and started sweeping up the breadcrumbs.

'A little dark humour.' He shrugged. 'Anyway, Rita talked me up to your aunties. Told how I'd help keep Rita safe, and how we'd worked together inside the AlGuild ... the labyrinth. They were proud that you were talented enough to draw me away from Veca Tante's influence, well something like that. It was all a bit too abracadabra for me to follow. Anyway, after a while your aunties insisted, and Rita made me come and meet them.'

'It went well?'

'They love me. They spoil me rotten—'

'Mother?' Vreni interrupted.

'Your mother woke up a month after your aunts.'

The crumbs scattered back to the table. 'When? How long ago? I wanted to be there to ease her grief. She must be...'

'She had her sisters, and Rita and Sabina. They were all overcome with the loss of course, but they were concerned for you. They felt terrible that you'd been all on your own when Parvils first died.'

'I wasn't alone. I had you and the Sisters.'

'They know that now. It's been a comfort to them that you weren't alone.' He grinned, raising his eyebrows.

'How is this funny?'

'Gaida asks regularly if I am preparing wedding plans for the next time you wake.'

'Married! I'm so sorry. Please, you didn't take them too seriously, did you?'

'Hey, I get it. They're just doing their *last century* thing, or is it the century before that? I just kept changing the subject and telling them how amazing and brave you were in the labyrinth.'

'Do they already know about the cure?'

William took her hands in his. 'Vreni, they've already taken the cure. Your aunties, your mum, Rita, they're not sleepers anymore.'

Buzzing filled her ears, her head was spinning. Sucking

in a noisy gulp of air, she sighed it out slowly. 'All of them? It's only me left?' Her chest tightened. 'Where are they?'

'At Mežs Mājas. The aunties wanted to go back and take up their studies and examine how the cure worked. Sabina pleaded for Rita to come and help her with Nessa and Klara. They have so much to learn since being rescued and woken here. Sabina felt that no one would be more qualified and enthusiastic than Rita to train them for their transition into twenty-first century life. Gaida went too, she wanted to pick berries and mushrooms and spend a little time away from the grief. She knew when you woke it would be time to hold the ceremony for Parvils passing to Vin...'

'Vinsaule, the world after this one. It's tradition that he be sung across the cosmic ocean. It's simple, but important.' Vreni rubbed her eyes and spoke into her palms. 'It should've happened when he first died, but I couldn't bare the idea of Mama not getting to sing her husband across. I asked Sabina if the Sisters could wrap him in an ancient hold-safe spell so his singing could be delayed.' Her breath shuddered and she wiped away a tear. 'I cannot delay the farewell any longer.' William stood and gathered her up into a hug and she let herself nestle into the familiar warmth for a long moment.

He swayed. 'Do you want to dance?' he whispered.

'What.'

'Dancing always helps us when things are ... challenging.' He swayed some more.

Vreni laughed. 'I'd love to, but only if I'm all caught up now.'

William swirled her around the kitchen table and back to her chair.

'That's everything about your family.' He poured her more coffee. She sipped and listened as William recounted what he had discovered about his father. Before he died, William's father was all that remained of the Alchemist's Guild, known as AlGuild. Veca Tante ran this corporation with the least number of ensorcelled guards to protect her magic secrets. William's father managed substantial investments, preserving the appearance of a registered company, but he was always working as Veca Tante's puppet.

While Vreni had been in long-sleep, William had spent time in the city with his father's lawyers. Over the years, the law firm had been kept at a distance while they acted on the AlGuild's behalf. Now they were transferring titles and share portfolios to William because he was his father's only heir.

'I own the ruined labyrinth and the AlGuild Compound,' said William.

'Have people been out there? Sabina wanted it to stay a secret.'

'No. No one, except the Sisters, seems to have a clue that there is, or was, a building there. Even the lawyers weren't clear on much, except that Dad held the land title.'

'Have the Sisters started searching yet?'

'They're just guarding the site for now and still planning. I think they wanted you to be there.' Vreni shuddered at the idea. 'Is that really necessary?'

'It'll be fine. Anna says the magic died with the old

witch.' William said as he picked up their plates and walked to the sink.

The old witch's words twisted across Vreni's mind — *Seeds pull life from death and rot. I will return as sure as spring.* She felt the cold tangle of black tendrils from the dark dream.

Vreni's hand trembled making jumpy rings in her coffee. 'She's dead. How could she not be dead,' she mumbled into her coffee cup.

The sound of tyres crunching on gravel pushed the thoughts of shadowy dreams and staring yellow eyes away. One car, followed by a second. Vreni stared up at William who was smiling broadly. 'They left Mežs Mājas as soon as they heard you were awake.'

'All of them are here? Mama?'

'Not Nessa and Klara, but everyone else...'

Vreni left a puddle of splashed coffee as she dropped her cup and race from the kitchen. She pulled the heavy front door open and ran out into the morning sun. She leapt onto the driveway and wrapped her arms around her mother as she stepped from the car. 'Mama!'

'Salds meit ... sweet daughter.' Gaida whispered as her arms encircled Vreni. Everything seemed to freeze. Vreni noticed nothing outside the circle of her mother's arms. She breathed in her mother's familiar scent, but there were added notes. Since her training, Vreni recognised herbs and blossoms easily. This fragrance was also a potion, Agrimony and Balm of Gilead to counter sadness, Cala-mint and Carnation to strengthen resolve. This was an unguent worn to heal a deep grief. This was a widow's scent.

'Mama, I'm so sorry. How are you coping?'

'I will be fine in time.' She tightened her embrace and then released it and smiled. 'Time for those things later, for now the world belongs to *dzīve* ... to life. We should celebrate. Our family is awake and together, because of my brave daughter, and your meddling, secretive aunties who counselled the Wise Sisters to foster your magical talents.'

Vreni saw her aunts Zana and Mila standing with Rita and William. They drew closer forming a circle of embrace around Vreni and her mother. Beyond the happy crush, she saw Sabina, Anna and Gizela with a clutch of other Sisters, unpacking baskets and cases from the boot of both cars.

Vreni locked eyes with Sabina as she moved towards the front door carrying a large basket. Sabina smiled and mouthed, 'All this good is because of you.' Vreni felt she had heard the words in her mind.

'When are you and William going to be married?' Gaida asked.

The question bought an expectant silence from the circle. Vreni stared at William, who smiled and shrugged. Then Rita came to the rescue. 'This is the twenty-first century, Mama. You know how much things have changed in your two hundred years, well marriage customs have changed too. Couples sometimes don't marry for many years, sometimes not at all.'

'Love doesn't change.' Gaida took Vreni and William by

the hand and placed their hands into each other's. 'I can see the love you share. There is stronger proof of it in the magical way you found each other.' She touched William's amulet. 'This is the strongest proof of all. I know how deep the love needs to be for this magic to work, so that the amulet will slow time for you.' Her eyes clouded over for a moment, then she smiled. Vreni had seen it many times. The smile Gaida always had for her husband. 'Tonight we will gather to say our good-byes and burn the candles to light the way and show my Parvils the path he must travel across the sea of stars. Today we will celebrate our new life, free from the curse.'

Vreni stared across at the pine grove where Parvils lay, cradled in the earth and held-safe by the Wise Sister's magic. She knew she would not be able to persuade her mother to delay the singing. The singing would loosen the last of her father's bond to this world and guide his soul across the cosmic sea. Vreni was not ready to say this final goodbye.

'Walk with me in my lovely gardens,' said Gaida, as though she had not just announced her husband's funeral. She beckoned them all into the manicured patchwork of flowers and fruit trees.

'We will eat outside then,' said Zana. 'We bought a light lunch with us, so we were a surprise, but not a burden.'

'I made lots of William's favourites,' added Mila.

'This happy time will fuel us for tonight.' Vreni squeezed William's hand and they followed the surreal family parade out across the gardens.

VINSAULE

Tread lightly on your blessed path across the sky mountain,
to the pasture where you will dwell in the blessings.
May Saule lighten your steps and gladden your heart.
Be prosperous in your new world beyond this world.
Keep us in your heart and remember the path you took
across the river of stars, so that you may return to protect
us.

~Funeral Blessing

* * *

The house by the cliff edge had never been so filled with noise and movement. Parvils had built this ostentatious home for his family, with room to accommodate many people and host grand celebrations. How pleased he would have been to see those he loved gathered together. Vreni had seen the way her family used to offer hospitality and celebrate when she had travelled back into the Dream Realm and visited her grandmother, Ieva. In her grandmother's palace, all those years in the past, Vreni had witnessed the joy and generosity of her ancestors before the curse had forced them into a life of secrets and solitude.

Over the centuries, there had only been the Wise Sisters, the family and a few loyal caretakers. Vreni's family wasn't small, but she couldn't remember a time when everyone had been awake and together. Now, the house felt frenzied after living so many years surrounded by the hush of long-sleep. Vreni walked through the busy house watching her family. Except for her, they had all taken the cure. They would never again be held by the sleeping curse and the house would be like this from now on, happy and hectic like Grandmama's palace had been.

It was quieter in the tower. Tonight, Vreni and her family would celebrate her father's life and ready his soul for his journey to Vinsaule. Preparations for his feast started straight after the family picnic in the gardens, and the sounds of eager bustling drifted up the twisting stairs from the house below. Vreni was grateful to steal some moments of peace alone in the round glass room. Cool, salty air blew in through the windows and filled the space right up into the vaulted roof. She took a slow, deep breath.

Today the tower was her sanctuary not the prison it had felt like for so long before she had met William, nearly two of his years ago. That's when everything changed. She had joined the Wise Sisters, discovered her magic, fought alongside William against Veca Tante's evil. They'd retrieved the remaining drops of the original sleeping potion, from within the labyrinth, so the sisters could fashion the cure and free her family from the sleeping curse.

Because of Vreni, everything had changed for her family and for the Wise Sisters, but she had not taken the cure herself. She had still not changed. With each waking, for over a century, she had wished to be free of the curse. 'Why haven't I taken the cure?' A chilled breeze twisted across Vreni's shoulder and past her ear. She thought she heard a whispered chuckle. Her heart jolted.

Gripping the window ledge, she listened, nothing, perhaps just a shadow of her earlier dream. She shook her head and turned her attention on the scene outside the windows. The dazzling blue on blue of sea and sky that stretched out to the north and south and all the way to the horizon pushed thoughts of whispers and shadows from her mind. Vreni turned from the sea and the cliffs to look at the rest of her home. The gardens, the stables, the pine grove her father had planted to remind him of his far away home.

She released a long sigh. The pine grove was Papa's place now. This grove would become the gateway for his soul to return each autumn at Candle's Eve. The family would invite him back by burning the candles to light the way for a feast to celebrate the lives of those most loved and now departed.

Vreni, as a very young child, at a Candle's Eve feast, sat with her feet swinging under the chair, her chin on the table, staring at the dishes of delicious food, while everyone filled the room with song to welcome departed family members back. When the singing stopped, the adults took turns around the table to reprimand the dead, blaming them for any hard times during the past year. It had all been confusing for Vreni, but as she grew older, she realised that traditions sometimes felt both strange and familiar.

'We would not scold you, Papa,' Vreni whispered as she stared at his pine grove. 'In all those years, you never failed to protect us in this world, and we know you will be our defender from the next.' Her eyes stung and she blinked away the tears, tomorrow will be time for crying.

She returned her gaze to the sea and blocked out the sounds of preparation for the farewell she had not given her father when he died more than a year ago. No one had been awake except Vreni and there were other things to be done first. Artūrs had arranged for Parvils to be readied and wrapped and buried in the pine grove. Vreni asked the Sisters to help so that Papa's soul would be safely held, cradled and protected by the earth and their magic, until there were enough voices to raise song and guide him on his way.

The delay went against tradition, but she believed the curse would be cured and everyone would wake. She had insisted they wait so her mother could sing farewell to her husband. Tonight the family would gather and prepare to send Papa's soul on its way to Vinsaule where he would dwell in paradise. 'No one deserves paradise more,' she whispered and turned to join her family.

* * *

Though the house had a large grand dining hall, they decided to hold Parvils' funeral feast in the kitchen. Everyone agreed that this was his favourite place in the house apart from his library.

Having slipped in through the kitchen door unnoticed, Vreni stood for a moment enjoying this unfamiliar bustle. This evening would be filled with sadness, but it was balanced with the happiness of celebrating Papa's amazing, generous life. The air in the kitchen was warm and filled with delicious aromas. Traditionally, the feast for lighting the way centred on serving beans and peas, so green and full of life, but her mother and the aunties were busy adding their own touches to the tradition.

Watching the three sisters working elbow to elbow, chattering and laughing, Vreni saw what made them able to endure all the challenges. These women, the sleeping beauties, her family had withstood centuries of struggle, with faith and resolve to make the best of each moment together the curse allowed them to share. Since her time staying with the Wise Sisters, she had seen this conviction with adult eyes and she was proud to be counted among such strong women.

'Stay away while we are cooking,' called Aunt Zana without turning from her work. 'Help your sister with the table.'

'So, your magic eyes are still working.' Vreni smiled and picked up a basket of pine sprigs, breathing in the scent of Papa's trees. Exhaling a deep sigh. Her mother looked up at the sound of her sigh. Mama's gentle smile and nod was a private moment of comfort between them. The family had pretended for centuries that life was normal when nothing was. Today would be no different, so the small talk continued.

'Yes, the magic eyes still work just as well as they did

when you and Rita were little,' Zana said, still not bothering to turn from her chopping board. 'And they will be watching you and your William until you are married,' she added.

'You'll be watching for a while,' Vreni muttered.

'My ears are also magical.'

'Zana,' scolded Aunt Mila, 'enough about weddings. Rita explained that traditions have changed.' She elbowed her sister. 'Anyway, William wears the amulet, he is not going anywhere, and Artūrs has said that he has used *his* magical eyes while we were sleeping and he assures me they are abiding by courtship rules.'

'Courtship rules!' Had Artūrs really been spying on us? Vreni's face was bright red.

'Courtship rules, how last century,' said Rita.

'Or the century before,' Vreni added.

The aunties and Mamma were giggling like young girls. Vreni blushed again and retreated from the debate to help Rita who was laying a heavy linen cloth the long table.

Pine branches would offer protection to her father's soul as he travelled and make a strong connection between the living and the departed soul. Vreni arranged the sprigs of pine down the centre of the table. Rita placed tall cream-coloured candles amongst the branches leaving spaces for bowls and platters. They placed cloth napkins, the special bronze cutlery and the crystal goblets. Vreni held each one for a long moment before she set them down. These were the glasses they had used for the wine at supper, with William, the night Papa had died. She touched each glass gently, trying to feel which had been the one her father had been holding that night.

'Have you tried the candles?' asked Zana.

'Yes Aunty,' said Rita.

'They need to burn bright and long to show the way to the world of the dead, lest the tricky devils lead Parvils astray as he goes on his journey.'

'Yes Aunty, they are the best quality. I bought them from a special place on line.'

'What line did you buy them on?' Zana shook her head.

'It doesn't matter what line,' said Mila, 'as long as they burn bright.'

The chattered suddenly quietened. 'It is time.' Gaida caste a solemn smile around the room. 'Light the candles.'

The bowls and platters were placed within the pine sprigs. Everyone gathered in the warm circle of light. As they took their seats, each person placed a gift on the table. Talismans and tools that would be placed with Parvils to ensure prosperity in the afterlife.

'I offer this book that is a record of your deeds and service to your family and the Wise Sisters. With this, those in Vinsaule will know you as a wise and brave soul.' Sabina placed the small leather volume next to the centre candle and sat. Each of the Wise Sisters attending silently placed charms and oils Vreni recognised as protectors and healers.

Artūrs offered wine. 'We will share this together one day my friend,' he said quietly. The remaining house staff offered tools, a knitted scarf and many written messages.

William's hands shook as he held the magical amulet

he'd accepted from the Wise Sisters when he committed to being the new family protector. 'I only have a promise to offer ... I will keep them safe.'

'Papa, you always had time to play and make me smile.' Rita placed the faded old ball on the table. 'Peters will smile to see this again.' Vreni's eyes burned as she thought of her brother. She drew comfort from the idea that, because of those gone before, no one would ever be alone in the afterlife. The aunties offered bundles of food and teary well-wishes.

All the while Vreni's clammy hands gripped her offerings. Her throat was dry and she swallowed hard as she stepped closer into the light and opened her clenched hands. On one palm was a perfect shell and on the other a smooth, dark pebble. 'We spent so many hours walking hand-in-hand on the beach. You gave your gift of love and protection to me and to all of us in the minutes and hours, days, years, centuries you offered ... we have so much to repay you for. Take this stone and shell as talismans to guide you back to us each year at summer's end so we can hold your hand and walk with you on the beach.' She placed the pebble and the shell among the pine needles.

Mama held the amulet Parvils had worn. It was charged with her husband's love and was a symbol of the loving protection he had offered to her and the family. She did not speak as she placed it on the table with trembling hands. Her grief grew with each offering until it shrouded her and she was stooped over, weighed down by the burden of it. She was alone despite being surrounded by family.

Sabina began to sing quietly. The other Sisters and Vreni joined the song. Gaida remained hunched, her lips trembled with reluctant whispers of the song that was all about farewell. Ripples of chanting wove in and around the sung words until the music filled the dark places in the room and in their hearts. Gaida lifted her head and smiled. 'Thank you, my husband, for our life together.'

The Sister's song altered, turning from solemnity to celebration. Artūrs and the aunties started heaping food onto plates. The meal and many stories were shared late into the night as the candles burned, lighting the way.

As the candles started gutting, Vreni saw Artūrs and Sabina gather the offerings that Papa would take with him to the next world. Her heart squeezed tight, the charms and gifts were to be placed with her father's body, which meant the temporary grave was open. The keep-safe spell had ended. The offerings would be placed in the deeper, and permanent grave, dug by Artūrs in the little pine forest her father had planted and loved.

* * *

Early rays of sunlight crept across Vreni's closed eyelids. She turned from the bright intrusion and pushed her face into the pillow, hoping to return to her dream where she and William were dancing on the beach with tiny foamy waves rolling over their feet. The dream moon above them was a mirror ball casting multi-coloured flecks of light across the night-time sea.

Strong, sweet voices seeped in through her open window. All remnants of the dream were pushed away by the singing. She sat up stiffly and remembered the candles and the offerings from last night. It was morning, the singing for her father's journey had begun. It was said and believed that the gates of heaven were opened at dawn and remained open until the sun reached its zenith. The sun had barely risen over the cliff-top, but Vreni felt bad for having overslept. She scrambled into her clothes and raced to join the singing.

The cool green of the pine grove was striped with early morning light. Vreni crept up and joined the singers circled around Parvils' grave. Dark soil, that would settle in time, was mounded up where it had been replaced after Parvils and the offerings had been buried. The singers took turns setting flowers on the grave. The rhythm of the chant took possession of Vreni's heartbeat. She let herself be drawn into the comfort of belonging to a shared purpose, an essential way of being since joining the Wise Sisters.

Voices rose and fell and the cadence was layered with hummed melody and harmonies, then words of beginnings, endings and salutations to the traveller joined the joyous melody. The singers flowed from one song to the next with twists and turns but no pauses.

One song told the tale of the rivalry between two ancient crone sisters named Life and Death...

> *'I claim the earth.' Life sang to*
> *her rotted sister. 'For you can see*
> *there is no place on this earth where*
> *living things do not abound. In every*
> *corner and crevice, everywhere are*

*men and maidens, flowers and fruit,
birds and beasts, even the creeping, squirming things of the soil are
proof that I, Life, hold possession of
the earth.'*

*Death smirked and mocked her
sister, rattling with wet laughter,
her bent body buckled further, but
her words rang with truth and coun-
tered, 'Sister, you can believe as you
will with your eager faith ... tas viss
mirt ... but it all dies.'*

*The sister called Life smiled and
whispered, 'Mīlestība nav mirt ...
love does not die.'*

This song reminded them to accept the inevitable
struggle between life and death. More songs followed,
each blended into the next. Entranced by the voices and
the shared purpose, the morning melted away. As the
music faded, Vreni realised the noon sun was prickling
her skin. 'Take our love, Parvils, to sustain you until next
we meet,' Sabina whispered. 'Travel well and true.'

'Travel well and true,' they all echoed.

Everything had changed since her father had died.
Vreni looked at the faces in the circle. The curse had
challenged their lives over many centuries, but now it was
gone. All these people, including her, were now travelling into a life they had never envisaged. What would life
be like free from the curse? Whatever their new life was

like, the vow Vreni made on the night her father died remained. She would protect her family.

ILONA

Gizela continues to be troubled by visions of a frightening plant creature. I'm sure this manifestation is a response to the delay in recovering Ilona's remains from the ruins.
Holding her grief through all these years has taken its toll on Gizela and I'm sure that is the cause of these false forewarnings in her visions of sprouting, thorny demons.
~ message from Zana to Sabina.

* * *

A few cars and vans were scattered in the AlGuild carpark. Vreni lingered at the car, hesitating at the thought of walking into the grounds. Sabina squeezed her hand. 'The gardens are no longer a threat. The defences were diminished along with Veca Tante.' Sabina held the car door open for her and they crossed the carpark and walked on through the ring of dense green hedges to what remained of the collapsed AlGuild building and the hidden labyrinth crushed beneath the ruins.

Vreni's eyes widened as she scanned the devastation. She had not had the chance or any desire to look back when she and William had run from this place carrying the potion and the sleeping girls. She was shocked by the extent of the ruins. The remains of the building, that had concealed labyrinth, resembled a newly bombed war zone. Enormous, pretzelled iron girders twisted in and out of buckled sheets of steel and shards of glass jutted up from the mountains of rumble. The ground had been cleared to allow movement around the edge of the destruction, and a small temporary building had been placed close to the ring of trees.

Anna and some of the other sisters were walking the perimeter searching for the safest entry point. Each time Anna pointed to a potential path, her gesture was answered with the shake of a sister's head. Everyone had been waiting so long for the search and recovery work to start at the ruins. They were eager to find the secrets and answers that were hidden inside, especially the answers about Ilona's fate. She had entered the labyrinth so long ago and never returned. Anna, usually standing serene and tall, looked hunched and pale with the burden of deciding on priorities for the search.

'We need to ensure any secrets the ruins hold remain secret. We saw what AlGuild did with this knowledge and power. We need to make sure we collect everything so that it can never be used with evil intention again.' Sabina shuddered. 'We need anything that looks in any way malevolent removed and taken to Mežs Mājas where we can bind it so it never gets into the wrong hands.'

'I'm sorry,' said Vreni, 'I didn't think to take anything else when we fled. I just wanted to get the potion and, when we discovered the girls, we needed to get them to safety. I hope nothing has been taken already.'

'You have nothing to apologise for. Because of you and William, we have this opportunity.' Sabina smiled at Vreni, but as she turned back towards the ruin the smile faded away.

'You're thinking about Ilona?' Vreni asked softly. 'I know how important it is for Gizela, for us all, to get her back and send her properly over to be in peace with her ancestors.'

'Sister Ilona will have her peace.' Sabina sighed deeply. 'For now, our priority will be to work our way directly to the centre, to what remains of the vault. From what you described, that is where we will find any remaining workings of AlGuild magic that need our gravest attention. If we find Ilona on the way, it will be a blessing. If not, that will be our next task. We have this place to ourselves. We have time to search thoroughly now.'

'Perhaps less time than we thought,' said Anna as she completed her walk around the rubble. She held out a pale cloth handkerchief. It held a few red flakes.

'Blood?'

Anna nodded. 'We found the most likely passage into the rubble, and that's where we found this. It may be that we were not the first to be here.'

'So Gizela's grief-filled warnings might be true and —'

Anna raised a hand and interrupted Sabina's speculation. 'Gizela has been very troubled waiting for the return of Ilona's remains. This blood may just be from a bird or some other curious animal. I will analyse it to find out.'

'That creature we fought, the hoard, could it be its blood?' said Vreni. 'It was very strong. Could it have survived the collapse and gotten out?'

'We have kept watch,' said Sabina. 'Such a creature would never have gone unnoticed. We would know already if it had gotten out.'

'I'll get this tested now.' Anna hurried towards the carpark.

'Show me this possible entrance way,' Sabina said to the other sisters. 'We need to start the search without delay.'

* * *

Within days a small settlement of metal site buildings ringed the edge of the ruins. When Vreni had first gone to Mežs Mājas and joined the Wise Sisters to be trained and guided to know her magical nature, she had seen the skill, commitment and hard work offered to keep her family safe. Now, she found herself watching their demolition work from a distance and smiling with renewed awe at the versatility of her Sisters. Like a colony of worker ants, they scrambled to dismantle the ruins and expose its secrets. This was simple, un-magical work, but it was done tirelessly and with the same purpose as any of their other fantastical undertakings.

A little magic was required to baffle the truck drivers who delivered site buildings and equipment, and removed the rubble. The Sisters folded perception to make the visiting men see a half-built mansion instead of a shattered building. They had been working for more than a week, and had nothing to show except less rubble.

'Finally!' Sabina immerged from a dark knot in the wreckage with two sisters. They carried a large wooden chest. Vreni ran to them and helped with the load.

'I remember this chest. It's from the chamber that tempted us with visions of our desires.' Vreni stared up at Sabina. 'That's where I saw Ilona, laying at the edge of the chamber she can't be far from where you found this.'

'Leave the chest.' Sabina's voice was trembling. 'Vreni, in my satchel there is a blue shroud. Please fetch it and bring it to me.'

Vreni scrambled to get the shroud then ran to follow the others into the tangle of wreckage. 'No, Vreni,' said Sabina. 'You saved her already. Now we will bring her home.' Sabina disappeared back into the rubble, leaving Vreni to pace and wait.

The moment Sabina found Ilona's remains, Vreni felt it. The words of blessings echoing in her mind, growing as the bond between Sisters' reached from heart to mind. Vreni chanted and hummed blessings as she waited. Other Sisters working nearby joined her and added their harmonies. Sabina immerged from the ruin carrying Ilona, swaddled in the blue shroud, her song as one with the waiting Sisters. Ilona was carried free of the ruin, the Wise Sisters gathering to follow behind with the reverence of a funeral procession.

As Vreni expected, they had found Ilona's remains against the curved stone wall where Vreni saw her laying when she and William stopped in the chamber to rest on their way through the labyrinth. That chamber had been created to trap anyone who reached it by conjuring visions from deep within the victim's mind. Visions so real they would anchor the victim to their desires until nothing else mattered.

That was what had happened to Ilona, she had stayed spellbound by her desires. When Vreni had been in the chamber, seeing Ilona's remains slumped against the wall had shocked her enough to make her listen to Anna's warning. She fought the fantasies the chamber tempted her with, dragged William away, saving them both.

Sabina laid the blue bundle of bones down on the grass with gentle veneration. A yellowing sheaf of papers fell from the folds in Ilona's shroud. No one noticed it, and Vreni gathered the papers up. The hum continued, more Sisters gathered and joined in, lifting their voices in commemoration. Vreni glanced down at the papers. It was a letter or some kind of record written by Ilona. There would be time to look at it later. She tucked the rolled papers gently into her back pocket.

* * *

Anna, Sabina and Vreni returned to Mežs Mājas to sing Ilona across the sea of stars. After Ilona's remains were laid to rest and they sung her to her peace, Vreni revealed the papers to Anna and Sabina. The three took themselves away to sit at the edge of the large reflecting pond where Vreni had first discovered her magical powers hidden in a glimmer. They sat in silence and read the brittle, yellowed letter, passing the pages to each other as they were read.

Dearest Gizela,

I believe now seems the time to complete my report. I need to share what I know while I am still able to. I believe I am half way through the labyrinth, at the second turning point. This space is the home to a sad, blended creature. It is a rancid patchwork of limbs and flesh, dappled with so many sad faces and it is tormented beyond reckoning. It, He, paces and mumbles and weeps, screaming out at unexpected moments, begging for food or companionship. He apologises endlessly to someone called Mandy and another called Ralf. I doubt my chances of being able to pass by this creature with its desperate hunger and its many grasping arms. So, it is important that I write what I know so far for your eye to read.

We are right to suspect the surrounding gardens might hold enchanted defences. I met no defences as I approached from the north of the building. Through the dark I saw one guard silhouetted against the light from inside the building. I stopped to decide on what charm might be of greatest effect against him and that was when the ground beneath my feet began to quake and ripple.

The ground moved out from under my feet like sand washed away as the waves retreat. My feet sunk down into the earth and I felt a slithering flow move around my ankles. In the pale glow coming from the door I could see the ground had come alive. I was surrounded by a roiling mass of worms, and leaches and all manner of blind, hungry creatures that had squirmed up out of the warm dark ground as they felt my footfalls. I shuddered as the tangle writhed and flowed upward, then they bit into my skin, thousands of tiny hungry mouths sent to feed on me and make me into humus. I cried out and the guard was at my side and holding me before I could finish choosing a charm.

He flinched as he sunk into the wormy ground and I took that moment to choose a charm from my necklace. I pulled him close to me as I melted a fragrant orb in my mouth then I leaned in closer still and praised him for saving me. 'You are my hero.' I whispered. He wanted to be a hero. I could feel that about him. I whispered, again, making sure my lips brushed his and he breathed the vapours of the charm deeply, filling himself with illusions of passion. 'You are so brave ... so handsome.' We embraced and I allowed him a kiss as his reward. I pushed him down and he lay on the roiling ground and I lay on him still whispering charmed promises.

He did not notice when I slipped the key out of his pocket as we kissed. He did not notice the creatures from the ground had started feasting on him, clambering onto his body until he was held down by the weight of them. I left him to be

gnawed, consumed, turned into dark rich earth.
As I turned his key in the lock I could hear his
muffled cries, the cries faded and I could only
hear the hungry creatures, nibbling and swal-
lowing, pulling him down into the ground.

Once I had slipped inside the building, I trav-
elled clockwise at first and turned then ... here
I am at the second turning facing this ranting
chimera. I fear this may be all the information I
can gather and sadly I am still so far from the
centre and any chance of finding the potion. So,
before I attempt to pass by this creature, I will
send a note to you Gizela, and you will have your
eye back. Thank you for the sacrifice you so freely
gave. I will return your ear once it is used to send
my next message or ... when I have no use for it.
Blessings Ilona.

Vreni read along with Sabina and Anna. She tried to remain silent but curiosity was overtaking her good manners. 'Was this letter sent in the same way you watched over me and spoke to me when I was in the labyrinth?' she asked.

'Yes. Ilona had written this letter knowing that Gizela's charmed eye would read it,' said Sabina. 'And an account would be written in the Book of Records.'

'So Gizela had given Ilona an eye when she went into the labyrinth, the same thing you did for me when I went in.'

Sabina nodded. 'When Ilona had used Gizela's eye to

send the message the magic was undone and Gizela's eye was returned to her.'

'But if Gizela knew all this about the hoard, why wasn't it in the Book of Records? Why didn't she let you know?' Vreni's face flushed. 'If I had've been warned —'

'Ilona was our mentor,' Anna said firmly. 'We were very young and heart broken when she did not return. Gizela chose to withhold some of the details from the letter... as a kindness. So she folded it in a glimmer and kept it unremembered for many years. Because of that, Gizela had no knowledge that she had a warning to offer about the monster.'

'When you and William faced the hoard, Gizela's glimmer was ripped away and she was distraught at the thought of failing you,' added Sabina.

'I understand how strong a glimmer can be,' said Vreni. 'Please tell me she forgave herself for the oversight.'

'We hummed with her, and helped her to find that forgiveness,' said Anna.

'Once all was healed, and you were safe, she told us what she had hidden and forgotten inside the glimmer,' said Sabina. 'But to touch the paper ... it's very different.' Vreni reached for Anna and Sabina's hands and offered a hum of comfort for them.

'Do you know what happened to Ilona in the chamber of desires?' Vreni asked as her hum echoed and faded. 'Did she send another message?'

'The eye could only be used once,' said Sabina. 'It was a lesser spell. Ilona's magic was not as strong as yours. She wrote the letter so it could be read by the charmed eye.'

Anna held out a small silver ear shaped charm. 'I found this among the bones. It holds a message that was never sent.'

'So Gizela never regained her hearing?'

'She still had one very good ear, and we still never managed to keep anything from her.' Sabina's voice was light-hearted with the recollection, but her smile was false.

Anna placed the charm in Sabina's palm and their hands locked together, sharing a scintilla of grief. 'Gizela gave this charm, she will be the first one to hear the message.' Sabina nodded.

* * *

Gizela held the charm in her ancient palm. 'Ilona, your sacrifice is our endless blessing.'

The old Sister stared off, looking into her past memories and searching for the words that would release the charm to deliver its message.

'I have freely given, lent an ear as you travel alone. Listening now with my heart as the message returns home.' Gizela's face became frozen with intent as she moved to pick up her pen. The others stood at a respectful distance and strained to read the end of Ilona's story as the old Sister wrote.

> *I am through the second turning. I escaped the creature. The poor thing howled and shrieked when he saw me. His clawed hands swept towards me as fast as a darting robin and those claws pieced my clothing and deeply grazed the skin on my shoulder. He pulled me close, sniffing*

at me and licking his lips, so many mouths all licking and slavering. I was frozen with fear, my shoulder burned. It leaned in close, blinking its myriad eyes, dysrhythmic mismatched blinking. Then it sniffed at my skin. 'Mmmm,' it purred, as though I was a fine feast. Then it licked me. Its sticky, befouled tongue slid across my face. 'Mmmm,' it repeated, and raising its face to the domed roof, it sang out, 'Thank you, master!'

This creature was so anguished and pathetic, I could take no more. While the monster sang praise to the more monstrous master that created it, I turned and braced and bit deeply into the putrid flesh of his clawed hand. He howled afresh and lost his grip on my clothing. I leapt free, scrambling across the cobbled floor, out and away into the corridor.

The thing bellowed and shambled after me. I ran, crawled, fell, scrambled. Behind me there was a rattling of metal, a heavy thud. The creature wept and roared. 'Don't leave me! Hungry! Lonely! Don't!' He wept, yanking on the chain that was shackled to one of its many legs. I did not remain to see any more detail, I ran, the shouts fading behind me around the curve of the passageway.

So here I sit in the shadowy opulence of the next turning point. I've had my fill of the fresh, cool water that trickles endless and musically from the spigot into the font on the wall. And

*now you are all here to listen to my tale. I do
not have to travel alone any longer as my Sisters
have found me and we sing together...*

'She was lonely and missed the companionship of her Sisters,' whispered Sabina, 'And the chamber gave her what she wanted.'

'If it wasn't for Anna, William and I would have come to the same fate,' said Vreni.

*... I missed you so much. The journey through
the labyrinth has been such a challenge. I
couldn't imagine taking another step through
this monstrous place without my Sisters by my
side, and now here you all are. The herb poul-
tice is very soothing. Thank you for tending my
wounds, they are so painful and inflamed. The
cuts are so deep, if you had not come and aided
me, I'm sure they would have become infected.
You have bought food with you. Aahh! Such a
feast. Yes, we will eat and I will rest a while, then
we will travel on together. Mmmm, your song is
so soothing.*

*Thank you, I'm feeling rested but I have
woken, should we start on again? We need to go.
Yes, some breakfast before we leave is a delightful idea.*

*Yes, I would love to hear a story. How did you
know the tale of Pastaris and the Giant was my
favourite?*

I must still be weaker than I thought, but I am

awake again now, we should go. Yes, a little food
before we leave, for my strength ...

'She wasted away in that place,' said Gizela, putting down her pen. 'She thought we were there with her and she thought we were tending her.'

'The illusions were very convincing,' said Vreni. 'I could not see the falseness until Anna asked me to focus on my heart's desire.'

'Ilona's heart's desire was to be with us. The chamber fed on her desires until she was consumed by it,' said Anna.

'Through Ilona's eyes, she had us there by her side ... until the end.' Anna touched Sabina's shoulder lightly.

'A small comfort.' Sabina sighed raggedly. 'She is home now.'

LUNCH

Beware the well-trod path, for things can hide there in plain sight. The familiar can cloud your vision.
Your eyes are open without truly seeing.
Walk carelessly at your peril, else you be lost.
~Book of Wisdoms

* * *

William spent the morning trapped in a shag-carpeted, corporate hell. He listened to his new team of lawyers and accountants as they trawled through endless by-laws and clauses. To ensure Vreni's family's secrets stayed secure, he had recently transferred all his dealings to a new, up-and-coming law firm with no knowledge of his father's questionable dealings. The new team were impressed with the value of the portfolio. William knew he was their first *big shot* client. They were enthusiastic to be meeting with him in person and they were taking full advantage of his presence and combing through every detail of his portfolio. William wondered if it was possible to die of boredom, but it was important to make sure that all the details about the AlGuild ruin site were in order, and were organised in a way that would keep them hidden. 'So all the permits are in place for the development of the site?' asked William.

'The forms came back with all the boxes ticked. You must have picked a great property development firm for this project. I've never seen the inspectors so relaxed and agreeable. They usually question every detail just for sport,' said one of the team, in a brown suit, who's name William had forgotten.

'I guess my team must have the magic touch.' William smiled, placing his hand on his chest and felt for the amulet inside his shirt. Whatever the Sisters had done out on site when they were dealing with the inspectors, he was grateful.

'So that's it, no more paperwork or inspections?' William did not want anyone showing up at the ruins unannounced.

'No more inspections should be necessary until you call them out when construction is complete,' said the brown suit.

William knew there would never be a completed construction to inspect, but that was a detail he could lie about later. 'Right, in that case, thank you and good morning.'

'Well,' interrupted another man in a blue suit. 'There are just a few investments to review.'

William stifled a groan. As the brown and blue suits started shuffling papers and talking to each other, William tuned out. He had slept badly again last night. His father's empty apartment was convenient, but it had a congealed atmosphere. William always thought it was because his father's grief, but it had become a creeping darkness since he learned what his father had done, who he had really been. At least he only ever had to stay there for a couple of nights at a time, then he returned to Vreni's house, their house, at the cliff tops.

Twitching, restless, weary. He shook his head, touching the amulet again. 'Harden up, William,' he mumbled under his breath. Parvils had endured much more tedium than this in all the decades – centuries he had watched over the sleepers. These meetings did not compare with his sacrifice. William was the family's protector now and he was, pretty much, filthy rich because of all the wealth his father had amassed in AlGuild's name, on behalf of the old witch, so this was the trade-off. He yawned and started nodding and smiling as blue suit pointed to figures and clauses and told him where he needed to sign.

As the last document was signed, William was already standing and moving towards the door. He paused, suddenly struck by an impulse, and asked, 'Could you look into getting an appraisal on the apartment? Too many memories, I think I need to sell it and move on.'

'We can do that for you,' said the blue suit. Leaning forward he grabbed William's hand and shook it as he tried to reach for the door.

* * *

The busy street was a welcome contrast to the morning of legal tiresomeness. Avoiding the crowd at the crossing, he threaded his way through the lines of impatient cars and trucks all edging up in anticipation of the traffic lights changing to green.

Hunger nagged his stomach, he decided he would eat at Laima's café and he increased speed. This café used to just be a place with the strong coffee on his way to uni or to work at the hospital labs. Then, that night, he and Vreni had gone to the dance party, they'd kissed. Then Rita had collapsed, no pulse, and he'd witness Vreni's desperate weirdness at the hospital. He had helped Vreni steel away the sleeping Rita and they had come to hide and wait at Laima's café. That was the night his whole life changed.

He had not even known the old café owners name until he had been told she was part of a wide network the Wise Sisters had in place. At first, he thought the Sisters had put Laima there because of him, that, somehow, they had drawn him in against his control. But they had explained, or tried to explain, that things and people can't be forced, they are only drawn together because they should be together. It had sounded very abracadabra to him until he had spent time with the Sisters, learned the family history and felt the magic at work once he chose to wear the amulet.

William's stomach growled and he looked ahead to the faded sign above Laima's café. It was half way up the next block. He was jogging now, thinking of delicious lunch options from the café menu. He kicked something hard and heavy.

His attention returned to the street just in time to reach out and grab an overbalancing shop assistant that he collided with. Next, he noticed his leg was wet and realised he had kicked into a large bucket of flowers that the teetering florist must have been placing on the footpath. 'I'm so sorry!' He bent to pick up the flowers that were spread across the walkway. 'Are you alright?' He handed the bent blooms back to the florist. 'I will pay for anything that's damaged.'

'Thank you. That's very generous of you.' The young woman straightened up her display and then turned, walking into the shop, leaving William feeling damp, ridiculous and clumsy. This florist shop had been here for years and the flower displays always spread out onto the footpath. William loved the fragrances that put up such a good fight against the pollution stink from the traffic. He was surprised he hadn't noticed where he was. He followed the florist through the door.

Inside the tiny shop, every surface was loaded with potted plants, arrangements and buckets of lose flowers. More bouquets and plants sat on shelves that extended up the walls. Some of the plants grew up and around the shop, twisting and climbing from shelf to shelf reaching for the skylight in the ceiling. The walls had become a mass of thick green and blossoms. The air was warm and damp, and so thick with fragrance that William coughed and his eyes watered for a moment. 'Again, I'm very sorry. I was thinking about lunch instead of watching where I was going. How much do I owe you?'

'Where were you going to eat?' The florist slid a scribbled tally of the damages across the counter and William pulled out his wallet and paid her.

'I was going to Laima's.'

'Where?'

'The retro café on the next block.'

'Oh, you mean that scruffy old place?' The florist finally looked up from the flowers she had been arranging into a tiny posy and fixed William in a stare with her golden, hazel eyes. She reached over and placed the cluster of tiny flowers into the lapel buttonhole of the jacket William always wore over his t-shirt and jeans when he visited the lawyers. The fragrance of the small flowers cut through the cloying atmosphere of the shop. William inhaled deeply. It was such an unusual fragrance. 'I usually go to another place for lunch,' the florist said, looking down as she fashioned another tiny posy.

'Let me buy you lunch, at your other place,' William said suddenly. 'To apologise for being clumsy.'

'That would be lovely,' she said and pinned the other tiny arrangement to her dress. 'I'm going out to lunch,' she called to the back of the shop. A moment later a thin young man appeared through the door. He looked like he might have been recovering from a big night on the town.

'Okay, Bella, see you soon,' he said, nodding in slow motion.

'So, you're Bella. My name's William.' He reached and shook her hand, it felt cool and smooth. 'Show me this favourite lunch place of yours.' He followed her out of the shop, down the street and around the corner. They crossed the road and entered the park. Bella paused as they stepped onto the grass and kicked off her shoes, then walked up to a food vender's van parked under a large tree.

'This is your favourite place for lunch?'

'I spend so much time in the shop, so it's nice to be out-side.' Bella kept looking at the ground as she spoke. Her toes digging into the grass until they reached the dark soil underneath. 'Sitting out here, on the grass ... restores me.'

'What would you like?' William asked. He ordered a crusty roll stuffed with cheese and salad, some fruit and coffee.

'The usual?' the vendor said to Bella. She nodded. Bella's usual was a very unappetising looking hot dog without sauce or mustard or sauerkraut and a bottle of water.

'You really do come here a lot.'

'I love gardens. I'm very lucky that my apartment even has a roof-top garden, I call it my folly.' She smiled, star-ing into the distance for a moment. But I have to spend such long hours at the shop, away from my folly so this park has become a favourite place.' Bella walked over and sat between the raised roots of the tree and leaned into the trunk. William paid the vendor, grabbed their lunches and joined her.

Bella took the hotdog and nibbled at it then leaned over to adjust the flower in his buttonhole. 'Tell me about William who doesn't watch where he walks.'

'William Masters, studying science at uni. Well, I'm having a break this year. My father died a while ago and I've had to take some time to tidy up some family lose-ends.'

'That's very sad.' Bella's eyes became glassy. 'I also lost someone ... that's why I have the florist shop now.'

'The other guy, at the shop, is he your brother?'

'No, he came with the shop.'

'You inherited the shop and the guy, interesting Will and Testament.' William laughed and saw that Bella didn't. 'Sorry, sometimes my jokes have very bad timing.' He offered an awkward smile. 'You chose to keep the business going instead of selling up?'

Bella chewed before answering. 'The shop is important to my family and I'm the only one in a position to carry on the family ... traditions right now.'

'I know what you mean, sometimes you need to stand by the people that are important to you. Even if you are in danger of being bored to death by your lawyers.'

'Is that why you look so tired?'

Now William chewed before answering, not wanting to say something lame like, my apartment is spooky at night. 'I'm staying in my father's home. It's full of memories and I'm not sleeping very well.'

'I know what that's like, memories can be very haunting. Do you have to live there?'

'Funny, I decided today to get my lawyers to look into selling it so I can maybe get a new place.'

'Lawyers.' Bella exaggerated the plural. 'I would guess that having many lawyers means you also have many dollars, and that would give you many options.'

William felt suddenly self-conscious. 'I guess I do have options.' He brushed his hand across the bump of his amulet. 'Everything changed suddenly about two years ago and the changes seem to have kept coming since then. I'm probably still not quite up to speed with the new situation.' William's phone vibrated in his pocket.

'Hi, Rita.'

'Hi, invisible guy. Where are you?'

'Oh no, we were meeting at Laima's ... I'm running a bit late.'

'Well, we're here waiting. Nessa and Klara are very excited about visiting the city, and all they've seen so far is views from the car window on the way in. Klara drove Artūrs crazy while he was driving us here. He didn't stay to see us into the café. Now, the girls are staring at the street through the café window and shouting about every new thing they see. I need you here before Nessa and Klara get any more excited. You promised them a tour and lessons on city life. While we've been waiting, they've practised ordering coffee, so hurry before they order another cup, more caffeine will make for an interesting afternoon.' Rita hung up before William could say anything else.

'I must apologise, again,' said William, slipping the phone into his pocket. 'I have forgotten an appointment. I have to go.'

'You haven't had your coffee.'

'I know, but I better go.'

'It sounded like family.'

'My sister,' William said as it was simpler than trying to unravel his family dynamics with a stranger. 'Let me walk you back to your shop.'

'Thank you but no, I'll stay here a while longer.'

'I'm sorry again about the flowers.'

'No harm done.' She leaned in close. 'About your apartment. I saw a gentleman from some real estate firm in my building. I'll check and see if there is anything going up for sale. It's a unique building.' She adjusted the posy in his buttonhole. William breathed in the fragrance and his thoughts swirled momentarily. 'Drop by the shop again and I'll tell what I find out.'

'I will,' said William standing up. 'Nice to meet you. Thanks for the flower.'

'Bye for now,' Bella said. Closing her eyes, she leaned back into a crook in the tree trunk.

William took off running towards Rita and the girls waiting at the café.

HOARD

We will create a hunger, a craving, so large and an
emptiness so deep, then blend it with a loneliness
that will claw at the heart and soul.
We will weave these things into the young man's very being.
When the weaving is complete, the new creature's
body and mind will be ours to control.
And it will adore us even while it abhors us.
~Alkimki Gilde (Alchemist's Guild)
Book of Agonies.

* * *

During the Wise Sisters' exploration, the ruins had offered up some mercies and some secrets, but the search was progressing slowly. Vreni hugged herself against the early morning chill and stared at the remnants of the building, remembering what it had been like to walk through the circular stone passageways before they had collapsed.

Today should be a day when Vreni was fully focused on her and William. She had counted the days she had been awake, the way her and Rita had always counted them to calculate their birthdays. Today it had been three-hundred and sixty-five of Vreni's waking days since she and William had met in the city and danced together in the pulsing forest of light at the dance party. Of course, only she could still count time this way. For William, the time had been longer. He had chosen to wear the amulet as her father had done for her mother, so doing, he was tasked with waiting for her to wake. Rita and all the other sleepers had taken the cure, so time did not detour through the darkness of long-sleep for them anymore, but for Vreni, today was their anniversary.

Her thoughts should be focused on William, but she couldn't stop thinking about the hoard creature. It had been chained to stand guard in the second turning point inside the labyrinth and it had captured William. Vreni remembered its many arms, clawing and slashing and its tangle of miss-matched legs. She flinched as she recalled its patchwork of twisted, sagging faces, singing and howling. If she hadn't managed to rescue William and escape, the creature would have eaten their flesh to satisfy its hunger and then, by some magical means, whatever remained un-eaten would have become part of its body.

She shuddered at the memory the dog's tail wagging against the creature's bloated flesh. Echoes of the hoard's lonely pleading filled her thoughts. Its desperate screeching as it tugged to be free from its chains as Vreni pulled William away along the curve of the corridor. The hoard creature had struggled and survived for so long imprisoned in the labyrinth, she realised she was wracked with an unexpected concern for it. Its life had been an unending horror. What if the poor thing was still lying trapped and alive in the ruins? It, no he, he must once have been a person before the Alchemists changed him. He could still be trapped in the labyrinth, alive, in pain, hungry, lonely?

'Take care, be watchful,' Vreni called as Sabina gave instructions to a pair of Sisters who were going into the ruins to assist Anna.

'They're all being careful, Vreni,' said Sabina.

'I was thinking of that hoard creature. It must have been kept prisoner at that turning point for a very long time.'

'And you're wondering if it is still in there somewhere?'

'He, it, was incredibly strong, what if they stumble over him and are unprepared.' Vreni cleared her throat. 'It wasn't his fault he became like that. What if he, it's trapped in there, and in pain?'

'Do not apologise for your compassion, Vreni,' said Sabina.

'We should look for him and ... end his suffering if we need to.'

'We will not need to,' said Anna, appearing out of the ruins carrying a stained, tattered bundle. 'He has been found, and he did not survive.'

'Was he still chained there?'

'He was, but they will remove his chains. We will bury him at Mežs Mājas.'

'You aren't calling him it,' said Vreni.

'We can't any longer. These are his possessions.' She lay the bundle down. 'This appears to be his journal.' She opened the stinking cloth and lifted a ragged pile of stained papers, holding them gently in her hands. 'He had a name. He was Jeremy, and he wrote about his life in these pages.'

'Can I have them?'

'Only if you share the reading with another Sister. His story can't have been good, so you will not read it alone.'

'I will share it with you,' said Sabina. She took the papers from Anna. They moved inside the office cabin and spread the curled pages on the table searching for the earliest date and began reading Jeremy's journey to hoard.

* * *

January 17, 1972

I'm having a great life! Jeremy Rush MSc —that's me. I'm the first person in my family to graduate university. I am a scientist. Unbelievable! And not just that, Professor Norwich came up to me at the graduation and asked if I had a job yet. I told him I've had some interviews, but its early days. Trying to sound as professional as I could. It was better than saying 'well Professor, I've only done two job interviews because I couldn't resist spending the summer surfing.'—which is what I had actually done. Then, he offered me an interview. He said a colleague of his at some company called AlGuild was looking for someone just like me to head an experiment they were keen to succeed with—after that I missed the other details, I was too busy cheering inside my head, so I only heard a splash of words—biochemical—grafting—behavioural— whatever, I have been offered an interview. Apparently, I am just the type of person this scientific corporation is looking for.

February 14, 1972

It may be a bit cliché, but today I asked Mandy to marry me. Romantic restaurant, massive bunch of roses. I hid the ring in the most beautiful blossom—nice romantic touch. I could barely speak enough to ask her the question. I was so nervous. She said yes and cried, and then I cried. The waiter had to help me get the ring on her finger, then we were all crying—smooth. But now I am engaged to be married to the girl I have loved ever since the day we saw each other lining up to schedule classes on the first day of uni—way back.

Life's sweet, I got the girl and I got the job at AlGuild. The interview was not what I expected and I had to do a medical as well. They said lots of corporate places had the same policy about health checks, anyway, it was no big deal, just some tests and I gave I little blood, had a couple of vaccinations, Mandy said that was pretty standard too.

March 20, 1972

I started at AlGuild last week. I'm still not feeling really confident. I don't want them to think I don't know what I'm doing, but I don't really understand what I'm working on. They have me identifying proteins and setting up growth mediums in dishes, but none of what I'm doing seems to be connected to the stated hypothesis. I can't see the work I'm doing leading to any big picture outcome, but my supervisor, Nathaniel, aka Mr Creepy, says he's pleased with my progress.

March 25, 1972

Damn, I fell asleep at work. After lunch today, I must have nodded off. When I woke up I felt strange, scared almost, and hungry. I was starved, in fact I'm still eating as I write this—three meals later and I'm finally starting to feel full.

March 26, 1972

God I miss Mandy. I haven't seen her for two days. Come on, I've got to get over it, it's just two days, I usually go away surfing for weeks. But of course I'm lonely, why shouldn't I miss my fiancé.

March 28, 1972

Mandy's a bit cheesed off with me. She said I'm being too clingy. That I never leave her alone, and she's right. Last night I showed up at her place, hugging her so tight we both heard her bones creaking. Then I wouldn't leave her alone, I couldn't, I followed her around, kept grabbing her hand, then I kept making excuses and delaying when it was time for me to leave. She didn't know it, but after she shut the door I just stayed there, outside her door for a long time. I really wanted to knock and go back in and be with her. When I finally managed to walk away, I went for a run for two hours around the darkened streets until I could stop fixating. Then I was so hungry—must have been all my nocturnal running.

April 1, 1972

Well I'm the April fool, double shots of coffee and I still fell asleep in the lab. Today was the third time I've slept at work. This time Nathaniel found me, drooling on the lab bench. He was cool though, but he insisted on a quick check-up. How could I say no. I'd woken up hungry and I couldn't hide how badly I had the munchies. Nathaniel just seemed to laugh it off, he even sent for a tray of food, which I ate while he poked at me and mumbled to himself. I am eating ridiculous amounts of food.

April 15, 1972

I've blown it. Mandy wants me to give her a couple of weeks' peace. Of course she does. I'm still being all lonely-desperate and she's got a lot of big stuff happening at work. She really needs time to write reports and prep, and I'm acting like a needy baby. So I'm running more and eating much more. It's a good thing AlGuild pays me so well.

April 16, 1972

If I have to leave Mandy alone for a while then I'll get a dog, a lonely needy dog that likes lots of hugs, and likes to run.

April 17, 1972

My new, needy dog is called Ralf. I picked him up from the shelter today. He's shaggy, like a dish-brush with four long legs. He'd been homeless for a while before the shelter, so he is hungry for company, and won't leave me alone. I like that. We went out for a run and he didn't pull on the lead at all, just stuck with me like glue the whole time. He will do fine as my buddy while Mandy has her break. God I miss her. I'm still stupidly hungry all the time and I have a slightly embarrassing confession to make. I ate some of Ralf's food, it was delicious. He looked confused, sitting there wagging his tail and waiting to be fed while I scoffed his doggie-chow. I'm so glad Mandy didn't see that. She thinks I'm strange enough. By the way, I think she's ignoring my phone calls.

April 21, 1072
Things have been weird the last couple of days. I think I'm blacking out. At work, Nathaniel has been concerned, he gave me some more tests. And at home Ralf has been licking me to wake up and then going nuts to get food or attention or go for a run. I haven't been running. All I can think about is eating. The food runs out really fast, but Ralf has a large sack of delicious doggie-chow and he likes sharing it with me.

April 23, 1972
I swear I had just bought a fridge full of food, before I blacked out. Ralf just woke me and I went to the kitchen

first thing and there was a mess everywhere and no food left. Not even doggie-chow. When I asked Nathaniel if he knew what might be causing the black-outs, he drew some blood and said it might be a good idea if I stayed at the labs until they figure it out. I can't do that because of Ralf and because of Mandy. How long has it been since I've seen her? I have to see her. I'll run there with Ralf and introduce them to each other.

April 24, 1972

Oh God. Mandy is dead. I woke up with Ralph licking me and someone thumping on the front door. It was the police they said someone had been in her apartment. The place was ransacked, food and furniture everywhere. They found her in the middle of the mess. They say she asphyxiated, not strangle or anything, more like maybe smothered, she died because she couldn't breathe, but the police can't figure out what might have happened. Oh my God, they said she had bruises around her body like maybe she'd been hugged too tight. Who could have done this to her. My beautiful Mandy. The police said one of Mandy's neighbours told them I'd been there yesterday, with Ralf. I don't remember anything about going there. The police were firing questions at me and asking me if Mandy and I had been fighting, the neighbours said they heard yelling. I don't remember anything. She's dead. What am I doing to do? I just want to hold her tight and never let her go. Before the police left they told me to 'be available' to help with the enquiry. I slouched down onto the floor and cried into Ralf's fur and hugged him tight until he nipped me and clawed his way out of my arms. Damn this hunger, how can I be eating like this after hearing about Mandy. Ralf and I ran and got more food and doggie-chow.

April 25, 1972

What the hell is going on? Mandy has just died and all I can think about is food. I blacked out again and when I came to the kitchen was totally trashed. Ralf won't come near me. When I go to pat him he whimpers and backs away. And I need to hug him so badly, hug him and never let him go.

I blacked out again, not sure how long for and I can't find Ralf. His doggie-chow bag is ripped to shreds and empty and there's a dark stain on the kitchen floor. I'm so hungry, all there was to eat was some mouldy bread and I ate it. I went to the front door, hoping that I might have let Ralf out at some point in my black-out. I opened the door and called for Ralf when I did I felt a strange sensation on my back. A tickling scratching. There's something weird stuck on my back. It makes no sense. God I feel hungry. I miss Mandy so much, and where's Ralf? What the hell is happening. The tickling, scratching what is that. The last thing I need now is some hairy lumpy growth.

I have to write this, it can't really have happened. Maybe if I write it, that will make me come to my senses. Maybe it's all an hallucination. Here goes, I was worried about the hairy growth thing, so I went to the bathroom to look at it in the mirror. I was so hungry I ate the soap.

I twisted and turned until I could see the weird growth thing was in the mirror. It's a tail—dog's tail—Ralf's tail. It wagged. I screamed and yanked at it. Pain seared across my back. I vomited up the soap and staggered back to the lounge.

Now it's written but nothing changed. I looked at the stain on the kitchen floor.

I vomited again, but I'm hungry. Ralf.

I can feel the tail squirming behind me and trying to wag. It's stuck, it's part of me.

Nathaniel came. I remember that. He banged on the door and I remember howling at him trying to tell him everything and asking him to help me.

I'm here, AlGuild I think, but not the labs. I have my journal and my tail. I'm hungry. I'm lonely. . .

Book good. Hoard has stories—not so lonely for now.

Words hard—stories hard—so hungry—I'm lonely—I have Ralf with me—want more ...

* * *

The stained pages were darkened with tears. Vreni wiped her palms across her wet cheeks. 'They took everything from him,' she said quietly. 'They transformed him into a monster.'

'His suffering is at an end.' Sabina gathered the curled pages together. 'We will lay him to rest and honour him.' Sabina was humming. Vreni felt the wretched sadness, the residual frustration and unfairness she had absorbed from Jeremy's story being drawn from her.

Sabina wrapped her in a gentle hug and she gave in to

the sadness, the pain escaped in racking sobs. When it had faded, she joined Sabina's hum.

'I haven't eased the burden of your sadness,' Vreni said to Sabina.

'One of the other Sisters will help me disperse the negative energy. Your turn will come when younger Sisters look to you for your strength to ease their sadness.'

Vreni held Sabina's hand. 'What else do you think we'll find in the labyrinth?' Vreni recalled her dream about the old witch, her wooden face smiling, saying she was on her way back. 'Is there any chance, Sabina ... any chance Veca Tante isn't dead?'

'She survived for centuries, so her magic was more enduring than we had imagined possible but you watched her Vreni. She was unmade by our softening potion. You saw the worms dominate her flesh and the earth claim her back.'

'I just feel ... something.' Vreni badly needed to see the place of the old witch's destruction. To know with absolute certainty that the old witch had been obliterated.

'Tell me how you are troubled.'

'I had a dream as a was waking from long-sleep. I was trapped in vines and small creatures were slithering all over me. Veca Tante was staring down at me, she said she was coming back.'

'You know that sometimes waking from long-sleep can be frightening,' said Sabina.

Vreni's interlocked her fingers, clenching them tight. 'Sometimes I wake in the night feeling bugs on my skin. I brush at them and there is nothing there, but then I see the yellow eyes, and the vines wrap around me, squeezing. Then it's gone.'

Sabina stared into the distance as she listened. 'Gizela,' she whispered under her breath.

EVICTION

Honey-suckle and sweet star-weed to attract
the one you seek. Ambergris, so he turns his
gaze to see only you. Orris root to break any pledged
bond of love he may have with another.
~Pratigs Masa Book of Secrets

* * *

'Thank the goddess you're here,' said Laima, looking up the stained and tattered newspaper she had been trying to read. 'I have never heard any human ask so many questions.' She raised an eyebrow towards Rita, Nessa and Klara who were sitting in the booth at the window.

'Sorry I'm late, Laima. I had an unexpected morning. Can I have coffee or are you too cross with me?'

'If I make coffee for you, you must drink it quickly.' She looked at the chittering girls again.

'William! William, William, you're here.' Klara, came bouncing across the café and hugged him tightly. 'Cold shirt,' she said noticing his t-shirt.

'Not cold, cool,' Nessa corrected. 'Klara, come and sit down. Calm yourself.'

'Cool shirt.' Klara slouched back into the booth and glared at her sister. 'Gorgon?' Klara read the word printed on William's t-shirt. 'Why do you have such a strange thing on your shirt?'

'Not gorgon,' Nessa corrected again. 'Jargon?' she turned to Rita for confirmation.

Rita nodded. 'You're learning really fast, Nessa.'

'I learned a lot from my time sitting in the college rooms with Uncle and the other alchemists before...' Nessa fell silent and stared out the window. 'Before we went to sleep and woke up here, four hundred years later.'

'Nearly four hundred, but now you have so many more amazing things to learn,' said Rita, deflecting the conversation away from the sleeping curse. Knowing her uncle had used her and Klara to experiment on had been a difficult truth for Nessa to accept.

'But why do you have this strange word on your shirt?' asked Klara.

'I had it especially made for the days I have to spend with the lawyers. Jargon, lots of tricky words, is part of their job, they have no choice. The t-shirt reminds me that they're not really trying to bore me to death. And it's all worth it, because soon the Sisters will have access to all the resources the guild had.' William yawned.

'You look tired,' said Rita. 'Still not sleeping well?'

'It's only a problem when I stay at my old place ... Dad's place. By the way, I've decided to move. I told the jargon boys, the lawyers, to look into putting the apartment up for sale.'

'Then I ... we won't have anywhere to stay when we come to the city.'

'Don't worry, I'll get another place. I met someone today who told me there are apartments for sale in her building. It sounds like a funky old place, so I think I'll take a look. I can definitely afford to do some renovations now I'm corporate.'

'If what I heard Artūrs explaining to Mama about the wealth you inherited, then you could buy the whole building.'

Laima bought William's coffee over.

'Can I have more coffee please,' asked Klara.

'*We* have had enough,' said Nessa, laying her hand on Klara's.

Klara huffed. 'When are we going? Are you still going to show us the palace gardens we saw on Rita's instant-net?'

'It's internet, Klara.' Rita said.

William sighed. These months since the girls, Vreni's mother and her sisters had woken had become a clunky, ad hock introductory course on the twenty-first century. William was constantly explaining new things to Gaida and the aunties. Rita was a self-appointed expert, passing on what she had learned on the internet about their new century to satisfy Klara and Nessa's rampant curiosity.

'Yes, I'd planned for us to walk through the gardens, but there is no palace, well there is a large building, but it's not a palace.' He shook his head and smiled. 'I'll explain about the architecture when we get there.'

'Will there be shops?' asked Klara.

'You've been hanging out with Rita too much.'

'Oh no! Not a hanging.' Klara looked pale.

'Rita, I'll leave that one for you to explain later.' He turned to Klara and smiled. 'My favourite *cool* t-shirt shop is not far from the gardens. We could get you a shirt with something printed on it.'

'I wouldn't know what to choose. Will you help me?' Klara asked. William nodded.

'I will get a shirt that says, *tomorrow*.' Nessa smiled.

'Why?' asked William.

'Because I fell asleep by my uncle's side that day and I woke up in the most unbelievable tomorrow.'

'William.' The faded bead curtain in the doorway swung wildly and rattled as Bella rushed through the door. 'Pardon my intrusion, but I just found out about the building.' She stopped for a moment catching her breath.

'Hi, Bella.' William stood to greet her, then turned and introduced her to everyone. 'Rita, Nessa, Klara, this is Bella. She's the one I mentioned, that told me about the flat for sale in her building.'

'That's what I need to tell you.'

'Sit down. Do you want coffee?' Bella shook her head and slid into the booth next to Klara. She sat very still for a long moment, turning her head slowly, looking from Klara and Nessa, then she shuddered slightly and reached out her hand across the table to Rita. 'Nice to meet you.'

Rita shook her hand lightly. 'Don't you work at the flower shop down the street, Bella Rosa?'

'That's the shop, and that is me. I was my uncle's favourite niece so he named the shop after me.' She turned and took Nessa's hand. 'What an unexpected pleasure to meet you.' She squeezed Nessa's thin hand and released it. Then she turned to Klara. 'Klara. You must be Nessa's sister. You look so much alike.' Bella leaned in close to Klara drew in a long, deep breath. For a moment her eyes glazed over.

'What did you want to tell me?' William slid into the booth next to Bella.

'Oh yes. When I got back to the shop, I saw an email from the building manager. They are selling the building and they won't guarantee the rental agreements will continue after the sale.'

'That's bad timing, I liked the sound of that place.'

'It is a shame. I really like living there. I'm so lucky to have my lovely roof-top garden.' She turned and adjusted the flower in William's buttonhole. 'I grew these flowers up in that garden.' She lifted the posy closer to his nose for a moment.

William breathed deeply. 'Well, if you do have to move, I'm sure we can help you with re-potting the plants in your garden.'

Bella smiled up at William and giggled in a way that made Rita feel like tipping William's half empty cup of forgotten coffee into her lap. She let her own cup drop heavily onto the saucer. 'It was so nice to meet you, Bella, but we have places we need to be. Don't we William?'

'Yes William, you promised to help me get a *cool* shirt.'

'Oh, do excuse my intrusion.' Bella pushed into William, almost nuzzling him. He slid off the seat and let her out of the booth. She took his hand and touched the flower once more. 'Drop into the shop again and I will know how things are progressing... about the building I mean. It's such a shame that a stranger will buy it.'

Rita glared, Bella was holding William's hand way too long. 'Klara, where would you like William to take you first?' she said loudly.

Klara jumped up and pushed between William and Bella. 'I would love to see more of those wandering musicians. Will there be some in the gardens?'

'Buskers.' William let go of Bella's hand. 'There usually are a few in the gardens.'

Bella turned and left without saying goodbye.

* * *

The gardens were a patchwork of flower beds, squares of smooth lawn and clustered displays of plants. Pathways meandered through stark arrangements of gnarled desert plants, then between tall groves of bamboo that formed archways of green, and on through to tangles of jungle.

Rita walked with Nessa, answering questions about the gardens and their new life in this century. Klara ran from statues and fountains to buskers, brushing her hands along everything green and growing in between. Klara appeared so different to modern girls her age. She was still so playful and childlike while Nessa, just slightly older, seemed to have slipped fully into adulthood already.

William was quiet, he looked tired and preoccupied, but he did rouse himself to answer all of Klara's incessant questions. Rita was glad to have a break except it gave her time to stew a little about the way Bella had flirted with William. The flirting wouldn't work. William wore the

Wise Sister's amulet, and the magic of the love bond and the oath binding him to Vreni was intricate and strong. A little flirting was nothing against the powerful magic held in the amulet. Rita relaxed and focused on the gardens.

The path led to the centre of the gardens, where many radial paths converged on a large, circular parkland with an imposing stone building in the centre. The building was now an art gallery and it was surrounded by a series of large ponds that were bursting with lilies, reeds and exotic water plants.

'These ponds remind me of the pleasure gardens that surrounded the labyrinth before it collapsed. At least the water here isn't trying to kill me.' said William, seeming more like himself at last. 'I wonder how things are going out at the ruin?'

'You can ask Vreni all about it at home tonight.' Rita waggled her phone at him. 'She just messaged. She's heading home, she misses you and the beach. She says she has a surprise for you.'

'Then I need to answer all Klara's questions about the *palace* here and we need to buy some t-shirts and get home.'

* * *

William played the role of personal shopping assistant perfectly. Nessa got her t-shirt with *tomorrow* printed in blue. Klara still couldn't decide. William thought a shirt with a huge orange question mark was the most appropriate for now, considering how many questions she always asked. He chose to have the word inertia printed on his shirt and asked for a second jargon shirt. Rita refused to get involved, saying t-shirts were just not stylish.

They stood at the parking station desk, waiting for the attendant to bring William's car down. 'I've got an idea,' said William looking excited, buoyant. 'I'm going to look into buying that building.'

'What building?'

'Bella's apartment block.'

'You only need one apartment, William.' Rita felt suddenly warm.

'Yeah, but I'm *corporate* now. And they might only be small apartments, we could use more than one if we're all staying in town together.'

'What about looking around at some other places?'

'At least I can go and check it out, talk to the lawyers and see what they say.' The car arrived and they all got in. He drove without speaking for a few blocks and then blurted out an afterthought. 'I'll call the lawyers now and get them to contact Bella before she closes the shop and find out about contacting the owners.' William shoved in his ear buds at the traffic lights and called his lawyers.

Rita was relieved William wasn't going to see the flirty flower floozy himself, but she still felt a twinge of concern. He was not acting like himself, switching from tired and quiet to brash and excited in seconds. The William she knew was always steady. On the way home, she listened to his side of a conversation about property values. During the discussion, someone in the law office had done some searching and contacted Bella at her shop and it sounded

346 - MARTII MACLEAN

to Rita that the person on the phone had confirmed her building was actually for sale.

ANNIVERSARY

The amulet is our most powerful magic.
It holds power against time itself.
Extending life over many lifetimes.
The bond is made with love and by the free
will of he who wears it. If that bond should somehow be
broken by means other than choice,
it would be death to the wearer.
                       ~Pratigs Masa Book of Wisdoms

* * *

Sabina had done what she told Vreni she would, and gone back to Mežs Mājas to seek Gizela's counsel and cleanse herself of the deep sadness they had found in Jeremy's journal. Before she left, she'd made arrangements for Jeremy's monstrous remains to be loaded into the truck to return with her. The Sisters would ensure he received his blessing and, though it may not have been his tradition, he would be sung over the sea of stars to his peace. Every living thing deserved its peace.

Anna had not yet seen the journals and she insisted on taking Vreni home to continue her cleansing if need be. She knew Vreni would get little time for peace with Rita and the girls spinning through the house. Vreni and William took their responsibilities of caring for the family quite seriously, but Anna knew it was also important for them to have time to be young and in love. They deserved the normal life they had risked everything for, but sometimes love needed to get a reminder. 'This morning, I heard you say that today was a special day,' said Anna as they pulled the car into the gravel drive, stopping in front of the house.

Vreni smiled broadly. 'It is a special day.'

'What's so special?' asked Anna.

'It's sort of an anniversary. It's hard to explain.'

'Like the way you and Rita calculate birthdays?'

'You know about that?'

'Sabina told me about it decades ago.'

'Did she think we were foolish?' Vreni blushed.

'Sabina was pleased that you could still enjoy these normal happy occasions in your lives.'

'I want to make a special meal for William and me, but I should make food for everyone before they get home.' She pushed the car door open.

'I'll help you.' Anna smiled to see Vreni feeling happy again, and followed her inside.

* * *

By the time Vreni heard the crunch of tyres on the gravel driveway again, the kitchen was full of delicious aromas. She ran to the front door, Klara and Nessa were already half-way through it.

'Vreni, I'm so glad you're home,' said Nessa.

'I've missed you.' Klara wrapped her arms around Vreni. 'Have you found any treasure in the ruins?'

Vreni felt a twinge as she remembered the latest discovery. *What other horrors may lay at the centre?* 'No treasure today, Klara.'

'And Liga is well?' Nessa always asked this question about her sister.

'She is resting,' Vreni said, as she always did. Liga had been resting for four hundred years. They couldn't wake her when they woke Nessa and Klara. They were waiting until arrangements could be made to find the right kind of medical help. Help that would not ask questions about why a girl who appeared dead needed to have knife wounds in her heart repaired. When the repairs could be made Liga would be awakened and finally be reunited with her sisters.

'Everything smells delicious,' said Klara pushing through the kitchen door.

'Remember your manners, sister,' Nessa said following her.

Vreni turned back to the open door and William was there smiling at her. She hugged him and pushed him back out onto the veranda, where there was privacy for warm, quiet kisses.

'It was a *jargon* day today,' she said rubbing her hand across his chest. She noticed the odd flower pinned to his lapel. She sniffed and twitched her nose at the acrid fragrance.

'I was with the lawyers all morning.' William sighed. 'It

seems the asset transfers are almost finished, but I'll need to keep meeting with them until it's all done and the Sisters can take over properly. I bought another jargon shirt just in case it drags on.'

'How was it with the girls this afternoon?'

'Busy, noisy. Laima nearly wouldn't give me coffee because I was running late to the café and she was stranded at the mercy of Klara's questions. We visited the gardens like I promised and we all got t-shirts.'

'Not Rita?'

'No, not Rita.'

'Style issues?'

'Yep. How are things at the ruin?'

Vreni reached up and gently touched the scare that ran across William's cheek. 'Hoard is dead. We found its, his remains and —' She stared out across the garden towards the sea. 'I can tell you all that later, for now, I've made plans. Anna and I have cooked a feast for the girls and I have prepared a picnic for us. We're going to the beach. The moon isn't full but it will be nice to watch it rise this evening and be normal and ...'

'And what?'

'Today is a special day.'

'I'm intrigued.'

'So, you should be.' She touched the flower. 'Go and hang your jacket and come and help me with the picnic food.'

* * *

They moved through the gardens, lit by the last rays of

coppery sunlight, then stepped into the tumbling green shadows on the path leading down the cliff to the beach. The evening was filled with fresh salt air and the gentle rumble of the sea below. The waning, crescent moon climbed higher into the sky, reflecting soft, creamy light. Patches of pale moonlight fell on the path, lighting their way. They walked in silence down the steep track, enjoying the simpleness of being with each other.

Vreni stopped at the bare cliff-edge, half way down the path. She put down her basket, wrapped her arms around the spindly tree and leaned out over the edge. A wave slammed against the rocks far below and a plume of sea-spray pushed up the cliff-face dampening her skin.

'You're not in that big a hurry to get to the bottom,' said William.

She laughed and swung back up onto the path. 'I wonder what other magic is in that amulet?'

'Why?'

'Papa used to say almost exactly the same thing when I'd stop here.'

'Sorry, I didn't mean to —'

'It's fine. I love that I get reminded of him. Let's hurry, before the moon gets too high.'

* * *

The sand still held the warmth of the day. Vreni twisted and squirmed her feet down deep and the sand squeaked. The moon made ribbons of light on the water that rolled in and out as each wave pushed its way to shore. The bubbling foam glistened on the shiny, wet sand as the waves receded.

'The moon looks so close,' said William.

'Its orbit path is closer to Earth lately.'

'Magical knowledge?'

'Scientific ... astronomy.'

'Well, however it works I'm grateful, it looks amazing.'

'The next full moon will be a blood moon,' said Vreni. 'A total lunar eclipse, the position of the umbra, the shadow, makes the moon glow red. They're spectacular.'

'It sounds like you've seen heaps of them.'

'Just lucky I guess.' She smiled. 'It's been a long century.'

'Look at that!' William pointed down the beach to where a luminous cloud of algae filled the dark water with glowing sapphire brilliance.

'Another beautiful thing that's just for us ... for our special night.'

'I'm getting very curious about what this special night is.' William wrapped his arms around her. 'Don't keep me guessing.'

'It's our anniversary,' said Vreni.

'This may sound like an excuse to have not gotten you a present, but you slept through our anniversary, months ago.'

'Haven't I explained how Rita and I calculate time, the sleeper way?'

'Pardon me?'

'We only count the days awake, so it's been three-hundred and sixty-five *awake* days since we met and danced and Rita fell into long-sleep and made you help me rescue her and you brought us safely home ...' Vreni was silent for a moment. It also meant that tomorrow would, for her, be the anniversary of Papa's death, but they had celebrated and honoured his life already. *I need tonight to be about happy things.* 'We should celebrate. Put your basket down and come with me.' She took his hand and led him to the damp sand near the water's edge. The water sparkled, reflecting the moonlight. She bent to pick up a shell from the sand, putting it in her pocket to add to the collection. 'First, we dance.'

They folded into each other's arms and danced to the soft rhythms of the waves lapping around their toes. The moon rose higher into the sky and cast soft light over them as they twirled and swayed. No one else mattered. It had been a weird and stretched out, almost two years, with so many changes, but the things that really counted were right here, unchanged, Vreni and William, dancing together.

The night breeze chilled Vreni's skin and she shivered. William pulled her close to him. 'You're hot,' she said.

'Thank you for noticing.' He let go of her and smiled, flexing his muscles. 'I've been working out.'

'No. I mean yes, you look wonderful.' She touched his forehead with the back of her hand. 'You just seem hot. Are you feeling unwell?'

'Not really. A bit tired, but the lawyers always make me feel like that, and I never sleep well when I have to stay in the city.' They walked back up the sand to the baskets.

'You should think about getting a new place,' she suggested.

'Funny you should say that. I found out about a place today that is coming up for sale.'

'What's it like?'

'Well, it's more a *they* than an *it*.' William spread out the blanket on the warm sand. 'Let's eat and I'll tell you all about it.'

They ate as William told her, how much the lawyers thought his father's penthouse was worth and he told the story of the florist shop and meeting Bella, who told him there were empty apartments in her building.

'When I was at Laima's, meeting Rita and the girls, Bella caught up with us and told me she'd found out the whole building was for sale. I think she was worried that she might have to move out when the new owners took over.'

'So, you missed out?'

'Well, no. On the way home I phoned the lawyers to find out the details and see if I could afford to buy the building once I sell the penthouse. They laughed at me and said I could buy a few of those old blocks on the east side of the park for the money I'd get from selling Dad's … from selling the penthouse.'

'So, you're thinking of buying a whole building?'

'Yep. The lawyers are going to check it out for me.'

'You're a scientist who likes dancing. How does that qualify you to be a building renovator?'

'Well, I've got to live somewhere,' William snapped.

'I thought you lived here?'

'I can't stay at the penthouse anymore.'

Vreni laid her hand on William's chest. The amulet he wore was hot through his shirt. 'Maybe it will be good to have a spare apartment in the city, now that everyone is awake.'

'Yeah.' William seemed distracted. 'Bella will be able to stay there too. She was really worried about having to leave. She has the flat on the top level. It leads out to a roof top garden. She calls it her folly and she was quite upset when she got word the building was for sale. Maybe she thinks the new owners might have wanted the top floor for themselves.'

'You seem to know a lot about this ... Bella?'

'After I knocked over all her flowers and apologised, I offered to buy her some lunch. We ate and talked for a while before I had to race to meet Rita. Bella came to Laima's and told me she had just found out about her building.'

'Strange coincidence,' said Vreni.

William shrugged. He was quiet, almost sulking for a while. 'Maybe I attract coincidences. I met you by chance.' He scratched at his chest and winced. 'Something must have bitten me.'

'Maybe it's a reaction to the flower.' Vreni reached out for the wilting boutonniere that William had moved from his jacket and pinned to his shirt.

'I don't think so,' said William, covering it with his hand before Vreni could touch it.

She lay her hand on his chest. He was still hot, maybe even hotter than before. 'Okay, maybe we should head back up the path and get away from the bugs.'

The magic of the amulet William wore was strong. Maybe it was too strong and affecting him in some way, making him sick. He had worn it for nearly two years already, surely any issues would have arisen by now. Vreni decided she wanted to have Anna look at him. 'Anna has some great cream for bites, we'll get some from her when we get home.'

* * *

An angry looking rash spread out from two places on William's chest. The first was the place where the small, strange smelling posy, he was given by the florist Bella, had been pinned to his shirt. The second, most severe and more worrying place was in the centre of his chest where the amulet he wore to slow the effects of time, was touching his skin. Hot red lines of inflammation were radiating out from both sites and trailing across his skin. Vreni scanned along the red lines, and she looked up to see Anna was also trying to assess the extent of his condition without alarming William.

'I think we have discovered a new thing that you are allergic to,' Anna said casually. She picked up the flower to identify it. 'The rash should start fading now you're not in contact with the flower.'

'But I like it. It has an unusual fragrance.' William reached out swiftly and took it from Anna. 'I'll keep it in water.'

Vreni flashed Anna a worried glance.

'Very well, if you insist, but take this.' Anna handed William a small vial. 'It will ease the itching and calm your fever.'

He laid the flower on the table and took the vial. He swallowed it down and grimaced. 'That was horrible.'

Anna raised a surprised eyebrow, but just said, 'It's better to find out things like that after you have done the swallowing.' Anna reached towards the flower, but William's hand was on it again before she could pick it up.

'If you must keep it, promise you won't wear it.' Anna said, then she fixed her face like a mask and looked out at the crescent moon rising high in the sky. 'It must have been such a nice night for my little love birds, picnicking down on the beach under the moonlight.' She put and arm around each of them. 'I'm sorry to bring your evening to a close, but it's time for William to rest.'

'I'll walk you to your room then get you some tea in case in you can't sleep,' Vreni said taking William's hand. He held the posy tightly in his other hand.

'Go on, you love birds and say your romantic good-nights somewhere else, or I'll be jealous.' Anna gathered them in another quick hug and shoved them out the door.

* * *

'I took him the tea but he was already asleep,' said Vreni as she sat next to Anna at the kitchen table. 'Now tell me, what was all that kissy-kissy talk about? Love birds? Romantic good-nights?'

Anna was examining a tiny piece of petal. 'Oh, the love-bird thing.' Anna laughed quietly. 'I needed to distract him so I could get this. I also put a small counter-charm in place. I know it sounded melodramatic but it was the first thing I could think of.' Anna offered Vreni a cup of tea.

'A counter-charm for what?' Vreni felt that twitching hunch that she had felt at the beach return. She took the cup and sipped at the warm sweetness.

'The posy is a charm. I'm very sure of it.' She poked at the tiny piece of petal. 'I'll need to test this at Mežs Mājas, but—'

'The smell and the ... it feels like it has a presence.'

'And the way William guarded it,' said Anna.

'When I went to take him his tea, he was asleep but holding the flower again.'

'You didn't take it?'

'No. I put it back in the vase.'

'Good, we need to be casual about this until we know more.'

'So, the red trails across his skin and the fever, they're not an allergy?'

'I might have said yes if it wasn't for the marks where his skin is reacting to our amulet.' Anna gazed into the distance as if seeking an old memory.

'You didn't say anything to William about the rash caused by the amulet?'

'No. He didn't seem to notice and until I know more, I want him to think we believe it is just an allergy.'

'What difference would it make?'

'Did you see how obsessive he was about the flower?'

'He let me put it in water before he went to bed.'

'And then he was compelled to hold it again.'

'This is so strange.' Vreni's mind raced. 'What's going on?'

'I don't know why or how, but William's sickness is linked to the amulet. This is somehow about magic.'

'But we are the only holders of the magic. We destroyed the labyrinth and the master and Veca Tante.' For a moment Vreni saw smoky ribbons of blackness at the edges of her vision. She felt something skitter across the back of her neck and her heart thumped. 'It can't be the old witch, I watched her rot, and we have seen no trace of anything in the ruins to even hint that she might have survived.'

'Rita told me about the girl who owns the florist shop. She gave William the flower.'

'What about her?'

'She gave William the flowers, and he reacted strongly to them.'

Vreni shuddered. 'Did Sabina tell you about my dark dream when I woke from long-sleep?'

'It has been mentioned.'

'In that dream, Veca Tante said she was coming back. Something about seeds and springtime.'

'Seeds.' Anna stared into the distance again.

'There would have been seeds left when she diminished. Maybe this Bella —'

'No. You can't grow a person from a seed.'

'You can't turn yourself into a tree and live for four centuries either,' said Anna, 'But Veca Tante found a way to do it.'

'Even if somehow the witch could regrow. It can't be *this* Bella. She's more than twenty years old. It's been less than two years since the labyrinth collapsed, and you can't grow a twenty-year old person in two years from a seed,' argued Vreni trying to convince herself more than Anna.

'The Wise Sisters have seen and done many things that shouldn't be possible over all the centuries,' said Anna.

'But William's reacted more to the amulet. It could somehow be that.'

'The amulet is very strong magic. It works because of the loving commitment William made to be your protector. If something is trying to taint the amulet's power, William could be suffering because of the conflict.'

'What will happen if this conflict continues?'

'Anything I say will be a guess. William chose freely to wear the amulet. It does not control him. We know of other charms, that we do not use, which compel those who wear them to act against their will. A struggle between such charms would be exhausting.'

'Nessa's father, and then her uncle had died unexpectedly,' said Vreni.

'Yes. Veca Tante's charms would have made them do things they found detestable.'

'Like testing the potion on his own nieces?'

'Yes, and the conflict must have destroyed them.'

'So, something could be causing conflict with William's amulet.'

'I fear it may be.'

'We should try to find the source of the conflict.'

Anna took Vreni's hand. 'Today has been a long one for you, so I took the liberty of mixing a special blend for you.' She pointed to the cup. 'You will sleep well, and in the morning, we will work on this together.'

'But William ...'

'I'll check on him later, but first I will call Gizela and get her to look for some answers in the Book of Wisdoms.'

The tea had given Vreni dreamless sleep and she was aware of nothing until the morning sun shone across her face. She went straight to check on William. His room was empty. The flower was gone. William had left a note under the empty vase.

Thanks for the surprise picnic.

I'm heading back into the city to get things moving with the apartment building.

Another jargon day and I might need to stay in the city tonight but it will be

worth it to get out of that horrible penthouse.

xx – W

'He's gone,' said Vreni as she entered the conservatory.

'I know. I checked on him earlier and saw he had left. Don't worry, Laima has called already. He's having breakfast at the café and talking her head off about buying the apartment building while he waits for the solicitor's office to open.'

'So, he's alright, feeling better?'

'Laima says he seems back to himself.'

'What about the flower? It wasn't in his room?'

'I asked, and Laima said there was no sign of a flower.'

'I should go in to the city and look at this building with him. Maybe Rita could drive me?'

'You are already anxious enough. Do you really want

to go driving with Rita?' Anna smiled and poured herself more coffee. 'I know you want to be with William, but I have had a call from the ruins. They have reached the centre of the labyrinth and they've found things they want to show us both, as soon as we can get there.'

'But William was so sick last night.'

'I'll make sure he's watched over.'

RENOVATOR'S DREAM

A bird is too wise to build its nest on a rotting branch,
but mistletoe looks lush and alluring as it rots the limb
away. The bird thinks of feathering its nest and
gathering berries for its babies and doesn't
feel the branch trembling as it rots.
~Pratigs Masa Book of Wisdom

* * *

William stared out at the people bustling by Laima's café. He startled, splashing cold coffee onto the table as his phone vibrated in his pocket. He mopped the spill with a napkin as he opened the message. It was from Bella. William couldn't remember giving her his number, but he shrugged and read it.

> Your lawyers made contact
> about the building, exciting — B

Yes, I'm going to see them now - W

> Did you enjoy your flower? If
> it's dried up,

> I have made you a new one.
> Come to the shop -B

363

William pulled the dry flowers out of his pocket and rolled them around in his fingers. As they crumbled, they released an intoxicating fragrance. He breathed deeply, shoved the crumbling bouquet back into his pocket then lurched out of the booth and strode across the black and white tiles.

'What, only one coffee?' Laima called after him as he swept the bead curtain aside at the door.

'Oh, yeah.' He turned back and put some cash on the counter. 'Thanks, Laima, busy day, gotta go.' He stepped out into the morning sunlight and turned towards the flower shop.

Bella was waiting for him on the footpath. 'Here's a fresh boutonniere. It will bring us luck today.' She pinned the small, sweet-smelling posy to the lapel of his jacket and smiled. 'If my little bit of magic works, then by the end of the day we will both be getting what we want.'

The fresh flowers had a rich spicy scent. 'That sounds great, but I should see this place before I sign up to buy it.'

'Of course. Would you like to go there now?'

'Sounds great.'

'Harry!' She called to the ragged looking shop assistant. 'I'll be gone for a while. Look after things.' He nodded drowsily and turned back to moving the bunches of flowers.

'He looks like he's been up partying all night,' said William.

'He hasn't been feeling well lately,' said Bella. 'I'm sure the problem will resolve itself soon enough. Let's go.' She took William's hand and led him around the corner towards the park. 'We can stop for breakfast on the way.'

'I've already had breakfast, at Laima's.'

'Oh, you've already been there.' She squeezed William's hand tightly. 'Maybe just juice for you or coffee.'

'Coffee sounds good,' William said, as they walked towards the food van in the park.

'The usual?' asked the smiling food vendor.

'Please, and coffee for my champion.' She touched William affectionately on the chest and her hand paused on the amulet. 'Your skin feels quite hot. Are you unwell?' Her hand grasped the amulet through the shirt fabric. She reached up with her other hand and rubbed the flower lightly and it released a fresh waft of fragrance.

William inhaled deeply. 'No, I'm feeling fine.' He placed his hands over hers.

'Your heart is racing,' Bella said, brushing her fingers across the amulet again.

'It's an exciting day,' said William. 'I'm going to see the place that might be my new home.'

'How do you like it, mate?' asked the food vendor.

'I like it fine,' said William in a haze.

'Your coffee, mate?'

William shook his head and smiled. 'Black will be fine.'

Bella took the coffee, bottle of water and a hotdog in a white bag from the counter.

'You eat hotdogs for breakfast?'

Bella shrugged. 'I didn't have time to eat at home. I wanted to get in early, I had a feeling you would visit.' She shrugged again and smiled. 'And ... I like hotdogs.'

'Should we sit at your tree.'

'How sweet, you remembered.' She sat and leaned against the tree's trunk. 'Your coffee is very hot. Let me put some cool water in it for you.'

'Would you please get me a paper serviette from the van.'

As William walked to the van, Bella took a sachet of sugar from her bag and quickly added it to William's coffee, then she poured some of her water in and replaced the lid.

'Here's your napkin.'

'Thank you. Here is your coffee.'

'Thank you.' William sipped his coffee and coughed. 'Obviously that guy's hotdogs are better than his coffee.'

'It's not good?'

'A little bitter.' He shrugged. 'I've had worse.'

'I have some sugar.' She dug into her bag, swiftly took William's coffee and added another sugar sachet before he had time to protest and handed the cup back.

'Thank you.' William coughed as he sipped. 'It's no worse.'

'You're welcome. It pleases me to give you that little something extra.' Bella smiled, pulled a piece off her hotdog bun and nibbled at it. 'When you are living with me ... well in the same building, you will get plenty of chances to do kind things for me.'

'All you'll have to do is ask,' said William.

'I'm sure that will be so,' said Bella quietly and she leaned back against the tree's smooth trunk and closed her eyes.

William stared at her and sipped his bitter coffee. He smiled. 'I've never known anyone like you,' he said.

'Perhaps you have.' She opened her eyes and leaned closer to him. 'I hope I have a chance to show you how unique I am.' She bought her face up close to his and brushed her hand across his chest, touching the amulet through the fabric of his shirt. He drew in a deep breath. She smelt of flowers, spicy, mossy like a forest. William dropped his coffee cup. 'You are unwell?' Bella reached her arms around him as he swayed.

'I'm okay, just a little dizzy. I think I'm a bit like Harry, not getting enough sleep.'

'Oh, I hope you are nothing like Harry.' She laid her cool hand across William's forehead. 'That wouldn't be good at all.'

'Everything will be fine when I don't have to try and sleep in my old place anymore.'

'Yes, everything will be ... fine when you are living at my ... your new *place.*'

'So, should we go now?'

She kissed his cheek and stood up. 'Let me show you your new home?'

'Can't wait.' William sprung up, wobbling slightly.

'It's not far from here. We can walk, if you like.'

William nodded and Bella took the empty cup and the rest of her breakfast and threw it all in the bin. She took his very warm hand in her cool hand and they walked through the park towards the rising sun.

* * *

The building was tall and narrow. The exterior was clad in small dark bricks. There were shiny letters above the double doors in the centre of the building—Seventy-One. Tall leadlight windows flanked the doors, and matching glass motifs repeated in the windows on the two levels above. A row of wider windows spread across the fourth level. Above them, was a mass of reflection that ran the width of the roof.

'Is that a glass atrium? Is your garden glassed in? How cool!' William squinted and craned his neck to see the roof-top garden in more detail.

'Yes, my little folly is covered in glass. Parts of it can open to let in the rain and on very warm days to accept the cool breezes. I value my plants tremendously and take very good care of them.'

'I can't wait to see it,' said William.

'I must warn you. The building is in a state of disrepair.' She came close and whispered. 'I feel self-conscious, showing you my tumbled down home right now.' She trailed her fingers gently along the line of his jaw. 'I would rather wait ... tidy up a little, and show you my apartment and my garden later.' Her fingers trailed from William's jaw down the side of his neck. 'Then you will know all my secrets.' She giggled softly.

'I'm sorry I shouldn't have imposed. I'm sure I don't need to see everything to get an idea about how much repair work it will need.'

Bella smiled and hugged him. 'You are such a gentleman. The lower apartments are vacant and unlocked, you can see those for now.' She stared up towards the roof garden for a moment. 'Will you be going to the lawyers today to finalise details of the sale?'

William's eyes sparkled as he gazed at the building. 'I'm sure I will.'

'Let me show you the lower apartments.' Bella turned the key and pushed the heavy front door open. They walked into the dim foyer space, lit only by the morning light coming through the rippled glass in the doors.

William saw a door on each side of the hallway, with a tarnished brass 1 and 2 on the dark wood. Further back in the foyer was a spiral staircase with the metal railing snaking up into the dark upper levels. 'It's a little gloomy,' he said.

'Yes, with only me here the owners have let things go a bit. But I like the peace and quiet.'

'I love the metal staircase and the tile-work on the floor.' William walked over and touched the twisting banister, looking up to the darkened levels above.

'Let's start with apartment two,' said Bella, wrapping her fingers around William's arm and pulling him away from the stairs.

They looked through the ground floor apartments, both had two small bedrooms, a tiny bathroom and one larger room that was a combined living and kitchen space. Both flats were decorated with decades old tiles and had gaudy wallpaper that was peeling away in heavy curls. William stared at the retro stylings. Everything was in need of repair and so different from his father's penthouse. 'With some fixing up, this place will be perfect.' He sighed, smiling.

'That's wonderful! I'm so happy.' Bella threw her arms around him and kissed him.

William kissed back, taking her in his arms. He held her, pushing his face into her spicy smelling hair, he breathed deeply.

'You must go now,' Bella said pulling out of their embrace and leading him back the building's front door. 'Go to your lawyers now and sign the real-estate papers before you change your mind about this ... renovator's dream.' She laughed stiffly.

'Renovator's dream. It's definitely that, but I'm not changing my mind.' William looked at his watch. 'I'll go and get the paperwork done now.'

'I feel so anxious about these arrangements. My fate rests with you.' She stepped close again and fussed with the posy on William's lapel. He breathed in the fragrance. 'Please come back here and tell me you have finalised everything with the sale. I have something special planned... a celebration.' Bella's phone rang. She looked at the screen. 'I must take this phone call. She kissed him forcefully, opened the door and pushed him out into the bright morning sun.

* * *

The rest of the morning was filled of suits and signatures, but it was all done. The lawyers already had a generous offer for the penthouse. Settlement would be fast with both properties. He had been told by the suits to consider the apartment building already his. Now, he stood on the opposite side of the street and stared at the place that would soon be his new home. He looked up wondering if he could glimpse inside Bella's apartment. The midday sun was glaring off the top floor windows and showed only reflections of the city roof line.

He crossed to the building, stood on the wide step and knocked on the glass door. There was an intercom panel next to the entrance. As he scanned for the button for Bella's apartment, the front door opened and she smiled out at him.

'Am I congratulating my new landlord?' Bella asked.

'Yes, it's all done. The seller even lowered the price to persuade me to move faster on the sale.'

'How wonderful.' She hugged him tightly and pulled him inside, locking the door behind them.

It seemed less dull in the building's foyer now. William was surprised to see Bella had set up a picnic on the tiled floor. 'Is my celebration feast a good surprise?' She pulled him down onto the rug and opened the basket.

'It looks wonderful, but why not up in the roof garden?'

Bella poured a glass of sparkling red wine as she spoke. 'I knew it would be easier for you to find me here. We will eat and drink then I'll show you the rest of your new home.' She leaned and kissed him on the cheek. 'Again, congratulations.' She handed William the wine.

William scratched at his hot inflamed skin through his shirt as he took the glass.

'Are you troubled?' asked Bella.

'I may be allergic to these flowers.' He touched the posy. 'I'm sorry.'

'I'm not offended. Even florists can be allergic to some flowers. I have some cream that should help your skin.' She bought a blue glass jar out of her bag and edged up very close to him on the blanket. 'You enjoy your celebration wine and I'll sooth your discomfort.' She reached up under his shirt and started rubbing the ointment on his hot skin. He shivered at its surprising coolness and smiled as Bella's hands made light feathery circles across his chest and his back as she applied the cream. She poured more wine and offered him some food. The wine and the lack of sleep made the picnic ripple and blur.

Bella's voice wavered, fading and surging. Then she was holding his arm tightly. 'Watch your step...' The narrow spiral stairs twisted up through the musty building. He looked down at his feet, willing them to tread carefully on the wedge-shaped metal steps. Had he really had so much wine that he was unsteady on his feet. Surely, he'd had only one glass. He couldn't remember. The steps spun and spiralled under his feet. Bella's words faded and twisted as though they were caught in cobwebs that hung in the stairwell. '...my apartment is bigger. I hope you won't be jealous...' The wine and climbing the stairs made him sweaty. The cobwebs felt sticky on his skin. There were voices singing 'We'll weave bolts of gossamer silk...' The old building clicked and creaked around William, then everything became bright. 'Do you like my folly, my delicious garden?'

William was surrounded by a quivering tangle of green

and blurred bursts of floral colour. The midday sun was blinding through the glass roof and William felt hot and itchy in the close humidity of the glasshouse. Bella's words sounded distant, and his own words sounded even further away. He was dazed by a cascading rush of spicy, sweet fragrance and the wet peppery smell of the soil after rain. The air was hot and steamy, and his ears filled with a buzzing murmur of frenzied insects.

'Come sit with me by the pool.' Bella's voice echoed in and out of the hazy green tangle.

'Your garden is lovely,' he finally managed to say with tremendous effort.

'Lie back and rest,' she said. He was sure she had kissed him again. 'This is your place, William. You belong here now.'

* * *

William woke, feeling the floor, hard and cold beneath him. He was back in the foyer. He looked out through the front doors. The brightness of the midday sun had faded. His head felt heavy like he had slept very soundly. He smiled at finally being able to sleep so well even if he had fallen asleep in the middle of ... He struggled and remembered lunch, the celebration and the visit to the garden. He recalled feeling itchy, but his skin was calm now. Bella had administered her special cream. William smiled again as he remembered how delicate her touch was.

'This is my place now.' He stretched and his hand brushed against a flower laying near him on the floor. Under the flower was a note.

W —

Look, you are already sleeping soundly in your new home.
I left you in peace to rest. Harry needed me at the shop.
Please don't go exploring the building on your own
(the wine made you very clumsy on the stairs)
Let me know when you will be moving in.
-B

'Too much wine, how embarrassing.' William sat up, picking up the posy. He saw the one Bella gave him that morning had already dried up. He was no longer itchy, thanks to the cream, so he replaced the dead flower with the fresh one and breathed in its heady fragrance as he re-read Bella's note. He stood and thought about going back up the twisting stairs, but instead he picked up the dried posy and placed it in front of apartment two. 'I think this will be home for now.' He pushed open the heavy front door and walked into the fading afternoon light.

BOOK OF AGONIES

The past is filled of treasure and joys that lift us like clouds,
but the past also holds sorrows that are stones,
too heavy to be carried alone.
~Pratigs Masa Book of Wisdoms

* * *

Vreni's life, waking and sleeping, over almost a century held unique struggles, but she had always had the support and protection of her family and the Wise Sisters. During her last awakening, everything about her life had transformed. The changes had been surprising and magical, frightening and sad, but through it all, William had been by her side. In the last two days she had experienced something she had never known before now—insecurity.

She and the other sleepers had been the unpredictable ones and everyone else around them, her father, the Wise Sisters, were reliable, dependable. And so was William, but now he was not acting like *her* William. She wanted to know what was going on with him in the city, to know more about this building and the girl, Bella, but she needed to be patient and trust in the bond she and

William shared that was held within the amulet. *Faith.* She and Anna walked from the car park towards the AlGuild search site.

The twisted pile of ruins had grown smaller as the Sisters had picked their way to the centre. Until now they had only found answers they had already partially known, Ilona's observations and the illusions that were her downfall, Hoard—Jeremy's tortured life. Vreni recognised items from the vault in the centre of the labyrinth, furniture, art, books and arcane equipment. Most of these were sitting scattered on the lawn inside the thick ring of hedged trees that surrounded the ruined building. Sabina was looking through the salvaged items and directing the Sisters as to what to do with them.

'Quite a collection,' said Anna as they drew closer.

'There are some surprisingly old things here, but I doubt we will be able to use anything,' said Sabina. 'These objects have spent centuries surrounded by dark happenings. I don't believe any of us could spend an extended time near these things without suffering ill effects.'

'We will never be able to let them out of our possession,' said Anna. 'The darkness weighs so heavily on these objects they will need to remain hidden.'

'So, we are still guardians.' Sabina stood and beckoned them to follow her through the path in the wreckage to the centre of the ruin.

They ducked under bent steel and stepped around piles of wreckage that had once been stone walls. The charred remains of a door leaned on the last wall left standing. This was the door that had appeared as the old witch was decomposing. The door Vreni and William had escaped through carrying the sleeping girls. This had been the Master's chamber in the centre of the labyrinth.

Vreni remembered the roof beam dropping down against the door. She had been pinned by it and heard William fighting to get back through the door to save her. Then she recalled the salty, sweetness of the strength charm melting on her tongue. Her head and heart filled with strength of all the Sisters and she pushed through the wreckage. Carrying tiny Liga in her arms and running with William down the narrow passage to escape as the building fell around them. 'Endings and beginnings,' she mumbled, leaning against a twisted girder.

'This place is full of difficult memories,' said Anna squeezing Vreni's hand. Vreni squeezed back and looked across the circular space. There was an ancient reading table and two curve-backed chairs, looking surreal arranged amongst the rumble. Three items had been placed on the table. Two wooden chests and a large leather-bound book.

'Why have these been left here?' Vreni asked.

'We wanted them to be touched as little as possible,' said Sabina.

'Why?'

'You know how you felt after reading Hoard's ... Jeremy's journal. The residue of his sadness was almost debilitating.' She paused and reached into her pocket and took out three charm sachets. 'Angelica, strong protection against negatives energy.' She handed then to Anna and Vreni.

'You believe we will need this protection?'

'Indeed, we will,' said Sabina. 'This is ... one of the old witch-aunty's books. I believe it is a record of things that have been done at her bidding since she started on her chosen path.'

The leather on the book's cover was stained dark by centuries of hands opening it to add to the agonies it was likely filled with. Vreni reached out and touched a corner of the book's thick spine. The leather was not stained there. 'I saw this book, when I travelled in the dream realm and went to her rooms in the old palace to search for the potion.' Taking her hand from the book, Vreni rubbed her cheek, remembering when Veca Tante's nails scratched across her face.

Next to the book was a wooden box. She reached to lift the lid. 'No. Not yet, Vreni. I want our full attention on the book first. And our united energy to deflect its harm.' No one sat, and each of them stayed their distance as Sabina reached and opened the cover.

Inside, in faded brown lettering, on the yellowed pages, was written:

Viņi ņem no manis, es ņemšu no viņiem.

'They took from me, I will take from them,' whispered Vreni.

The words were fine and detailed like inked filigree and they were framed in ornate illuminated designs of painted vines and twisted branches. Looking more closely, at the page's boarder, they saw the branches were thorned brambles and the flower buds were sculls and tortured, tormented faces.

'This was the vow Veca Tante made when she was the

young Aunt Rosalija,' whispered Sabina. 'All those centuries ago, when she was over looked and old Peters gave your Grandmother Ieva rule of the principality. When she chose to tread her hate-filled path of revenge.'

'This is no Book of Wisdom,' said Anna. 'It will be filled with torment and anger just as Rosalija was through all those long centuries.'

The pages turned, heavy and crumbling. Each new page held notes written in varying hands. Much of what was written was smudged and hard to read. There was list of men's names, a list of the original alchemists. Next to each was a date and then further across the page, another date with *miris*, indicating the man's death. The men on the list barely lived for months between the first date and the date of their deaths.

'This must be a record of the men that she tried to control,' said Vreni.

'It has to be very powerful magic to get the men to be so totally obedient,' said Anna. 'Many of them would not have survived its potency.'

There were pages containing detailed lists of these short-lived men, with dates spanning almost a century. After that, the list of the quickly-dead gave way to a much shorter list of longer-lived alchemists, who were given the title of Master.

'The entries change here,' said Vreni. 'Now the records include women and children.'

'All the women appear to have died in childbirth or soon after, as did their daughters,' noted Anna.

'But their sons did not die so readily,' said Sabina.

'At least not until they became young men.' Vreni shivered. 'Then the lists of the dead expand all over again. What is this?'

'It's a breeding program.' Anna's breath shuddered. 'She was trying to find companions, men to control.'

'Like William's father,' whispered Vreni.

'We saw what the Master was capable of because of Veca Tante's control, even in her diminished state,' said Sabina. 'The magic would have had to be very powerful. Many of her acolytes would not have survived the enchantment.'

'That enchantment was powerful enough to make William's father turn against his own son, to conspire and prepare him to be next in line to be a prisoner of the old witch,' said Vreni.

'It's recorded here,' Anna started turning the brittle pages. 'The means she used to try and achieve control over her acolytes and other creatures that would serve her purpose.'

The pages were filled with illustration after grotesque, cruel illustration. Smudged annotations recorded the experiments and unimaginable blendings. Detailed annotations recorded the tormented creatures that resulted from the experiments and the damage the creatures inflicted. The dates of the creation and death of the tragic beasts were scattered among grimy pages.

'This is the one I saw, the wolf creature Veca Tante called Bruno, the one with the singing children captured in its fur.' Vreni shivered. 'She has written how she favoured him as a pet. She wrote that he lived a very long while. It would have been a tormented life, haunted by the voices of every child he had been compelled to kill.' They leafed through more of the grimy pages.

'There are notes about poppets,' said Anna. 'That's how she controlled the alchemists so thoroughly.'

'Poppets were to be used only for protection, for healing,' said Sabina. 'Never for control.'

'They can be used for control. The maker of the magic can place whatever intention she desires on a charm— even on a poppet,' said Anna. 'But there is very little detail written about how she created them.'

'There is much written about how the alchemists believed in the vigour and strength, support and protection that Rosalija's protection charms would bring them.'

'They must have all believed the charms and poppets were protecting them?'

'It's human nature to be scared of illness and death and to desire strength and success. It was a very common practice to offer protection by way of a poppet,' said Anna. 'The young alchemists would have freely given a lock of hair, a finger nail, even a few drops of blood to be woven into the poppet charm as a small price to have such protection.'

'Then she used the poppets to control them?' asked Vreni.

'It seems so, though it isn't evident anywhere in these pages how she did it,' said Sabina.

'The truth about the poppet magic could not be recorded in this book or the Masters would have seen it,' said Anna. 'Surely, even in their captivated state, they would still have had their enquiring minds. She couldn't risk them seeing her notes, on the conjuration of her poppets, in case they discovered their true fate.'

Vreni shuddered as she looked at page after page. The centuries of agony stretched out from one monstrous experiment to the next. The alchemists were committed and loyal but over time they had their curiosity and intellect twisted into something depraved. They followed Veca Tante's bidding to weave nature and dark magic. They experimented, transforming the long line of acolytes and their doomed children into monsters, or corpses as the experimentations failed.

One page bore an elaborately decorated title: Silvia. On these pages, Silvia was recorded as a daughter of one of the masters. The records showed that soon after she was born, the mother and Silvia had both died from the same fever, but Silvia's story continued.

The page was filled with detailed diagrams showing transformations. The first was of a small child, perhaps old enough to be toddling, sketched wearing a simple night-gown and bonnet. Next to the drawing, some notes had been written. It looked like a list herbs and elements, but they had become unreadable over the centuries.

The rest of the page was filled with more drawings recording Silvia's transformation. Slowly, over the course of the few months, the drawings showed Silvia's soft, smooth baby skin started to darken and become leathery. Her little round toes fused together, connected with wisps of webbed skin.

In the next drawing, her feet were lost altogether as

leathery fins grew out from the tiny toddling feet. With each drawing the poor little child continued to change, until her legs and torso were covered in shiny, dark skin that was textured with raised ridges, and her feet ended in translucent paddles.

A shiver rose up Vreni's spine. 'This tiny child would have become a lonely thing of legend, a river nymph. If she was allowed to live, she would have lived alone and lonely forever, yearning in the river or like Jūraté in the old mythology, weeping amber tears into the water to have them flow down into the sea.'

The miserable parade of grotesquery and cruelty continued throughout the pages. They found the notes on making a hoard creature and saw that there had been many such addled monstrosities used as guards over the centuries before it was to become Jeremy's fate.

The pages turned and Vreni felt she would drown in the thoughtless cruelty of it all. Another page was turned and she was fully submerged as she read a less faded word —William. What followed were entries that were all about William and his mother. The records told of how strong William's father was to not perish under the magical control. The notes told of testing the young William with positive results and of the plans for him to follow in his father's fate.

That was not all that the pages contained. Vreni stared at the details about William's mother and *two* older sisters. William had only ever mention one sister. How will he react when he knows this truth? She read and re-read notes about potions and doses until tears blurred the words and hot disbelief grew into anger at the fate of these innocent lives.

'It is all so much uglier and crueller than I could have imagined.' Vreni's breath shuddered.

Sabina lifted the lid of the smaller chest as Anna closed the book full of agonies. 'This is the poppet box,' she said, sounding exhausted. She lifted the lid on the second box. She glimpsed inside and closed it quickly. 'I think this is for William to open. It looks to have belonged to his father.' She closed her eyes for a moment. 'Clouds and stones,' whispered Anna. 'The contents of this box may offer him great solace through mementos, photos or these things could make it all infinitely harder for him to bear.'

'Maybe he should not have to bear it,' said Vreni. 'Their fate can't be changed by him knowing it.'

'William has a right to know what really happened to his mother and his sisters,' said Anna. 'You would want to know if it were your family.'

'You're right, but this would be best coming from me.' Vreni gathered up the box of sadness and went to call William to arrange for him to come to the ruin.

FAMILY ALBUM

Truths can be many things.
They can be great wealth or a great burden, a lush
orchard of sweet memories or a desert of endless despair.
Our truths, become whatever we choose to take from them.
~Pratigs Masa Book of Wisdoms

* * *

William drove to the ruins, impatient to see what was in the box that Vreni believed had belonged to his father. She had rung him as he stood in a daze on the front steps of Bella's — his apartment building, trying to piece together his foggy memories of the day. Vreni said she had been in the centre of the ruined labyrinth. They had found the box there, but they had not pried any deeper into its contents. It should be left for William to investigate. At first, he was reluctant to go, feeling a deep sense of dread, but it was mixed with curiosity and he decided the drive might help to clear his head.

By the time William pulled into the deserted carpark at the front of the AlGuild ruins, his memories of the day were drifting even further away. He opened the car door and got out then hesitated. Bella's flower was on the lapel of the jacket he wore for the lawyers. He took off the jacket and laid it gently on the passenger seat and reached for his old worn coat from the back seat.

'How did everything go with the apartment?' Vreni smiled as he shrugged into his coat, walking to where she stood at the gate.

'It went really well.' He gave her a quick hug. 'It's all cool.'

'Tell me more?' She took his hand and led him into the gardens.

'The lawyers are working on the details,' he said vaguely. 'What did you want me to look at?' Vreni dropped the subject of real estate for now. William squeezed her hand and shuddered as they walked towards the tree arbour. 'It feels surreal, walking out here in the gardens again.'

Vreni did a little heavy-footed dance as they passed under the arbour. 'See, no flames,' she joked. 'All the garden's defences were unmade when the old witch died.'

'What,' mumbled William. He was scratching and fidgeting as they walked, and he had hardly said anything since he arrived.

'I said, it's nice to walk through here without getting set on fire.'

'Yeah.'

'Or mashed or smothered or turned to crystal ... or stolen by trolls or eaten by giants.'

'Trolls.' William nodded robotically as they continued across the wide band of green lawn, now free of the deadly smother-fly plants that almost killed William the day they had first walked through these gardens to get to the labyrinth.

'William, are you alright?' Vreni squeezed his hand, it felt hot. She took both his hands, stopping, and turned to look at him. At first his eyes were glazed and staring. He shook his head slightly and his eyes cleared. As he focused on her, his expression brightened and he looked more like her William again.

'I'm fine,' he said giving a smile that looked forced.

'You seem ... preoccupied.'

'There's a lot going on ...' He trailed off without finishing.

She reached out and touched the amulet through his t-shirt. This charm was her reassurance. *Reassurance about what?* William was tired, busy, preoccupied. 'If you want to talk, I'm all ears. Well, not in the Hoard way.'

'Groan.' said William.

'Sorry.' The apology was for the joke and for poor Jeremy, but Vreni was unsettled by William's actions.

His stiff posture finally softened and he wrapped his arms around Vreni and kissed her. His skin felt unusually warm. 'What did you find that you felt you needed to show me?' he asked.

'First tell me how things went with the apartment?' Vreni wanted to focus on positive things before making William face the sad memories that awaited him inside the box.

'Not just an apartment, the whole building.' William smiled. 'I spoke to the lawyers this afternoon. They had spoken to a real estate guy, but that's all details and jargon. The important thing is that the deal is being done. The penthouse went on the market today and someone has already made an offer. The sellers of Bella's apartment building are very interested in my offer, well the offer the lawyers negotiated for me.'

'That was very fast. Did you even look at the place? What's it like?'

'I met Bella there this morning and had a tour, sort of. I got to see inside two apartments and Bella says all the others have the same floor plan, except for hers. She has the penthouse with the roof garden.'

'That sounds lovely.' Vreni realised she was feeling jealous. 'What does the roof garden look like?'

William had only fragments of details about going upstairs and he didn't mention drinking too much wine. 'I only had a quick look upstairs. Bella was in a rush to open the shop.'

'So, you are buying a whole building that you haven't really looked at.'

'I know it will take a lot of work, but I'm getting a great deal, and they say I'll have plenty of funds left over once Dad's ... the penthouse is sold. All six of the lower apartments are empty right now so we can have our pick.'

'We may need them now that everyone's awake, and Rita keeps encouraging everyone to enjoy city life.' Vreni laughed and kissed William. 'Congratulations.'

'Thanks.' He smiled and squeezed her hand. 'Now what did you need to show me?'

They walked on through the gardens until they were at the ring of ponds. These too were safe now. No more enchanted water and the crystal statues had melted away with the witch.

'Let's sit down.' Vreni indicated for William to sit next to the wooden box she had carried from the wreckage. She had bought it out here so William could react to what he might find inside in private. She took a deep breath and sat down next to him.

'We found this in the centre of the ruin. I'm sure it belonged to your father.'

'Right.' William went to lift the lid then pulled his hand away.

'It contains letters and photos.' Vreni wanted to warn William, but she knew it wouldn't ease his pain. 'Sabina only opened it for a second. She saw there were pictures, maybe of your mother. She said there were cards, note-books maybe.'

'Really?' William drew a shuddering breath. 'Why were they hidden away in there?'

William slowly lifted the lid. He stared in at the jumble of yellowed paper and curling photos. 'So, you already know what's in here?' William sounded angry.

'No, Sabina only saw enough to know this is for you to explore, and maybe to discover the things you have wondered about for so long.'

'I don't think I really want to know. It felt so good to finally be free from him. I'm even moving out of his place to the new building and now I have to face him all over again inside this box.'

'You can choose not to look,' Vreni said. 'We all have choices.'

'And if I choose not to look, if I choose to set the box on fire and never look.'

'I will respect and support your choice, without question.' Vreni wrapped her arms around him. She felt his heart hammering in his chest. 'For so long we were both stopped from making our own choices, I know how precious having a choice is.' His heart slowed a little. 'You have been so patient waiting while I decide about when to take the cure ...' William kissed her and gently twisted a lose curl of her hair around his finger as he stared across the still pond.

'I need to know what's in here so that it can all finally be over,' he said.

Inside the box were layers of joy and sadness. Photos of happy family scenes. A photo of a small crowd gathered for a wedding, photos of William's mother and the growing bump of her belly that would become one of his sisters. Vreni's breath caught. Surely the truth about his second sister would be in here somewhere.

'The people at the wedding must have been Mum's family. Dad didn't have family,' William made a sad laughing sound. 'Well, we know why.' He softly touched the photo of his pregnant mother, smiling and happy, and then the next photo of her holding his sister and glowing with pride. 'This must be Maggie,' William whispered.

'Have you never seen a picture of her before?'

'No, I believed she was a sickly baby and I thought it must have been too hard for Dad to look at images of his ill child, but she looks healthy here, and cute.' He smiled and riffled through the photos finding another pink-faced baby picture.

Vreni's stomach flipped. William held both photos and turned them over. The dates on the back were just over a year apart. He turned them back and they both looked at the differences between the photos. Both were of sweet little faces in pink bonnets. In the first picture his mother glowed, but in the second she looked frightened, cautious, and desperate.

'Two sisters. How could two babies be dead?' William started digging wildly through the contents of the box and the layers of happiness and sadness lay scattered around on the grass. Smiling babies and funeral cards. Tiny pink bootees and notes made by family as to why they were too busy to visit and then he found his mother's tattered journal. So much apprehension and confusion as she waited for her third child to be born. The pages were full of hope and gripping fear.

> I didn't think I could live through discovering a third baby lying still and cold in the crib next to my bed. I had said no more children, but I was convinced by Alfred, somehow, he persuaded against my heart's will and now I feel the energetic little legs kick me. This baby feels so strong, kicking and squirming. But that's how it was with my other two, my lovely daughters and now they're dead ...
>
> It's a boy, a son. William is strong, and he will be fine and healthy. Alfred took him to have special tests, he assures me our son is perfect and fit for anything that lies ahead for him ...

They flicked through the rest of the journal, sharing the happiest and saddest pieces of William's family's history through his mother's eyes.

> *I am so happy. William has grown tall. He laughs and sings garbled, happy songs as he toddles around on his chubby feet. Today was the first day that I didn't wake and run to his crib expecting to touch his cold face. Things are going to be fine.*

Then there were no more entries. Sometime after William had been walking and singing, the diary stopped.

'I thought she had died because of complications during my birth. Father said she had weakened and withered and died that same night.' William voice shook. 'But I was a toddler, I knew her.' He stared off as if trying to see old memories. 'I don't remember anything.' Tears brimmed over and trailed down his cheeks.

'She loved you. She was so proud of you. You made her so happy.' Vreni hugged him tight. His tears dampened her shoulder, and she could feel his quiet sobs.

'He killed her,' William mumbled into Vreni's shoulder. She began a gentle hum to sooth him. 'He waited until he knew I was strong enough to follow in his fate and then he killed his own wife.' William's voice was sour with betrayal. Vreni held him closer and filled her hum with kindness and comfort. He sat stiffly as she crooned, then finally the comfort of the hum soothed his heart and he sagged into her embrace.

They sat together until the reds and oranges of the late afternoon sky were mirrored in the still water of the pond. William straightened up and drew a heavy sighing breath. He reached back into the chest and took out the photo of him cradled in his mother's arms. 'I had a mum that loved me,' he said quietly as he tucked the photo into his inside coat pocket. 'You know what I said about making my choice,' William said.

'Yes. It's yours to make.' William pulled a lighter out of another pocket. 'You have a cigarette lighter?'

'I'm a scientist, I conduct experiments. Sometimes that involves combustion.' Vreni nodded. 'I've made my choice. I'm burning the box.' He patted his coat pocket. 'I have all the history I need right here.'

He leaned in, touching the lighter's flame to the curled memories in the box. Then he walked around picking up the scattered items and throwing them into the flames.

The red-oranges of the fire joined the glow of the fading daylight and the pond water danced with colour. They stood staring as the flames consumed William's sad history. Vreni was relieved he had no desire to explore further and perhaps discover some other horrid details of manipulations and potions that the Master, Alfred, his father might have inflicted on his tiny, cursed family. William had proof that his mother loved him and he was closing the old chapters of his life once and for all.

Everyone but me has now started their new story. I haven't had the courage to take the cure and start the new chapters of my life.

A voice came out of the darkness. 'Is everything well?' It was Sabina.

'It's fine,' said William. 'Thank you for showing me my past.'

'I see you have decided to leave your history behind you.'

'All except the important things.' William showed Sabina the photo. 'I can't remember her, but I believe her love for me was huge.'

'The good in you, and the strength you had to resist your father, is proof of the effect of your mother's love had on you,' said Sabina.

William went quiet and stared into the darkening sky. His eyes were cloudy again. He scratched at his arms. He wrapped his arms across his chest and stood stiffly. 'I'm heading out.'

'Good idea. Let's go home and walk on the beach.'

'No. I'm going to take one last look at the penthouse and drive by the new place, just to make sure it's all real.'

'I'll come with you,' said Vreni.

'No. I want to spend some time on my own. Don't wait up, I'll see you at breakfast.' He gave Vreni a quick kiss and strode off into the darkness.

'What was that?' Vreni shrugged.

'The truth about his family was a big thing to accept,' said Sabina. 'He deserves a little time. Did you hum for him?'

'I did.'

'Does he know about the book filled with the agonies, and the potions his father used?'

'No, he never asked' said Vreni.

'Good, and anything else that may have been dis-covered in the box is gone, so all will be well, when it is.' Sabina took Vreni's hand and they walked slowly through the moonlight garden.

WILLIAM

As you travel, beware of the false map.
It may guide you to many places,
but in each one you will be lost.
Let your heart be your map and you will be found.
~Pratigs Masa Book of Wisdoms

* * *

The musky, spice of the dried posy filled the air inside William's car. He took it from the jacket and pinned it to his coat. As he drove back towards the city, thoughts about the contents of the box unravelled and he allowed fresh anger to swell.

Over the past two years he had accepted his father had been ensorcelled by strong magic and been compelled, beyond his control, to manipulate William's life, and lead him into a life of slavery at the hands of Veca Tante. But to know his father had killed his own daughters, because they didn't suit his purposes, was unthinkable. 'I had sisters.' A hot tear ran down William's cheek. 'Mum sounded so retched and frightened in her journal. And then she had been hopeful when I was born.' He gripped the steering wheel tightly. 'She loved me, and I don't even remember her. Then, when *he* finally got the son he needed for the witch's purpose, he killed her.' William was drowning in a hot storm of rage. He had been robbed of ever knowing his mother or his sisters. His tears welled up and blurred the road ahead. He quickly squeezed the tears from his eyes and the road came back into focus.

Vreni had offered him the box and helped him discover this tiny heart token, it was the one remaining treasure from a life he had never known with his mother. The curled photo was inside his coat pocket. He pressed his hand against the curl of it and, as he did so, he brushed his hand across the flower. He inhaled its fragrance deeply and coughed. Vreni had bought the box to him and made him choose. Because of her, the last illusions about his family had crumbled. She tricked him into facing this dark, unthinkable truth. Vreni had caused him to feel this pain. His sweaty hands gripped the steering wheel and he sped on.

Weaving impatiently through the city streets, William considered, then drove past many possible destinations. Finally, hoping that a walk would ease his anger, he pulled his car into the curb at the edge of the park. He didn't have any other real options for now. Earlier today, had enthusiastically thrown the penthouse keys at the lawyers and asked them to arrange people to clear the place out. It was full of his father's possessions and he wasn't interested in keeping any of it.

He could get a motel room for tonight. Why bother, he doubted he could sleep. He trudged on through the semi-darkness of the park. The green-black was lightened with patches of orange glow from street-lights and small path-lights casting creamy circles around the garden beds.

His mind churned—where to go next? Home. Back to the beach? He touched the crumpled photo. He couldn't go home while he was feeling like this. He pulled the amulet out of his shirt and held it tightly, squeezing it until it dug into his palm. 'Why am I angry with Vreni? She didn't do any of this to my mother, my sisters. And I love her. The magic in the amulet works, so there's no doubt about my love for her.' He suddenly felt a wave of dizziness, his skin flared with heat, and he started scratching again. He staggered slightly and sat on the edge of a garden bed to wait for the dizziness to pass.

'Oy! Find your own spot, mate,' grumbled a voice as the shadow came to life next to him.

'Sorry, I didn't realise anyone was there.' William put his face in his hands. 'Just feel a bit off, that's all.'

'Here. Have a drink.' A hand reached out of the darkness holding a bottle of water.

William hesitated.

'It's just water,' said the homeless guy. 'We have to stick together you know.'

'But I ... that's very kind.' William sipped at the water until his head cleared.

'You should see someone about that rush, or whatever it is you're scratching at.'

William realised he was still scratching and his skin was now burning. 'Thanks for the water and the advice. I know exactly who to see to fix this rash.' William stood slowly and turned in the direction of Bella's place ... his place. He stopped and reached into his pocket. 'Please let me repay your kindness.' He shook the homeless man's hand and pushed a wad of notes into it, then turned and strode out of the park towards Bella and more of the cream she had given at lunch time.

When he arrived at the apartment block, the building was in darkness. The front door was locked as he'd expected. There was a glow from the roof garden, but the rest of the top level was dark. He paced up and down the footpath looking up at the glow on the roof-top and wondered if he should ring the buzzer. He was still scratching and feeling light-headed again. His skin burned and images of his mother and his sisters swam in his mind.

He crossed to the opposite side of road to get a better look at the glowing glass of Bella's folly. His chest ached with the strain of holding the new sadness about his lost, murdered family. His eyes burned with tears, and he crumpled, sitting in the gutter with his knees tucked up to his chin like a lonely child. 'I want Vreni. But she did this,' he mumbled as the wept. 'She showed me the truth that took everything away from me.' He raked his finger nails across the enflamed skin on his neck. He felt a coolness as the evening air chilled the blood rising on his skin. 'I just want to be better. I want to feel good.' He sobbed and caught the musty fragrance of the posy. He took several slow, calming breaths. Then he stood, walked across to the building and pushed the buzzer marked Bella.

'Who is this?'

'It's William.'

'Why are you...' There was a brief, brittle laugh. 'Are you moving in already?'

'No, I'm sorry to bother you so late.' His voice shuddered. 'I need more of that cream.'

'There is something else, tell me.'

All at once William was a flood of words. He held the intercom button down and blurted out all the shock and agony of his discovery and his conflicted feelings about Vreni. He scratched and wept. 'I just want it all to go away. I need help to make it all go away.'

'I'll come down.'

'But —'

'The electric lock is broken.'

He released the button, wobbled, slid down the wall and sat on the top step.

It took longer than William expected for Bella to walk down from her apartment. The door opened and then closed again behind her with a heavy click. 'I thought you'd invite me up?'

'I didn't think you could wait. Here drink this.' She handed him a glass bottle and he realised how thirsty he was. He gulped down the cool liquid. It tasted of spice and fruit. She handed him a second bottle. 'Drink this one more slowly while I rub some salve on your skin.' She slipped her cool hand under his shirt and the burning stopped immediately where she touched.

He sighed and he felt his muscles start to unknot.

She dabbed the ointment onto his neck then caressed his cheek, moved closer and kissed him lightly on the lips.

'You have had a very happy day and a very sad day.' She removed the dried flower and replaced it with a fresh one.

He breathed the familiar, comforting fragrance deep into his lungs.

'Finish your drink.' She pushed the bottle back up to his lips. 'Do you really want me to help you make the pain go away?'

He swallowed and nodded.

She smiled in the orange glow of the street-light. 'You might think me foolish, but my family has a silly old tradition, my old aunty used to say it was magic. Maybe it was, but it always seems to work. She would make a little doll creature, a poppet. She said, that with some of her special magic, she could take of all the bad feelings you were having and send them to stay in the poppet's heart instead weighing down our own heart. She said the little creature could protect us from illness and give us strength.'

William listened and nodded. His mind was full of warm images of Vreni's magical aunties and all their comforting mumbo-jumbo. 'I know a little about old aunty magic,' he mumbled. The cream and the drink allowed him to finally feel calm, comforted. 'What harm could it do.'

She smiled. 'So, you consent to my magic,' she asked again.

'Yes, I consent to your magic.' He laughed softly. The street-lights pulsed and danced. Bella touched his face softly again.

'I will need some small tokens from you for the magic to work. I little hair, some nail clippings.'

'Very abracadabra,' he mumbled.

402 ~ MARTII MACLEAN

'What?'

'I mean ...um...'

William slumped against the rough brick wall and watched the street-light wavering as he luxuriated in the feeling of her cool hands touching his fingers, tickling his scalp as she ran her fingers through his hair. He dozed and roused when he heard Bella speak. '...once apart you are now joined ...' He stared at the street-light surrounded by its orange cloud and his eyes were heavy again. '... you are it and it is you, bound as one ...' He breathed deeply and his ribs crackled and expanded. He sighed and dozed. '... be strong, be loyal, be dedicated... smitten...mine...' Bella was silhouetted by the cloudy glow of the street-light. '... eyes for me ... deeds for me ...heart for me ...only me...'

William shuddered. He rubbed his hand across his chest feeling for something but the was nothing there. 'It's gone.'

'What's gone?'

'A thing ... I'm not sure ... it feels hollow.'

'You feel unwell? Are you in pain?' Bella placed her cool hand on his. 'I will get more cream.'

'No. No pain.' William shook his head. 'Thank you for helping me.'

He felt a kiss. 'My beautiful Bella,' he whispered. Warm darkness closed in around him.

NOWHERE

Once they are in my grasp, they will know nothing else in life
but to adore and serve me.
They will love me until they are consumed.
Their last words, with their last breath will be of me.
Their souls will be lost and seek for me, and without me,
pine for eternity.
~Alķimķi Ģilde Book of Agonies.

* * *

'It's been days and he's nowhere.' Vreni was frantic, almost tugging Rita along the crowded footpath.

'Vreni stop shoving me. You've never been to the flower shop, so how about you let me lead the way.' Rita pulled them over to the edge of the path and took her sister's hands gently. 'We will find him, Vreni.' She squeezed her hands. 'Artūrs is going to see the lawyers and we will see if they know anything at the flower shop.'

'I shouldn't have let him go away on his own after he found out about his mother and his sisters.' Vreni drew a sobbing breath. 'I hummed to sooth him, but it mustn't have been enough and he has been so unwell, the fever, the rash.' Tears streamed down her face. 'I thought he needed to see what was in the box and now I have caused all this sadness. When I try to do good things, they become something bad.'

Rita held Vreni firmly by the shoulders. 'Enough.' She took one of Vreni's lose dark curls between her fingers and twisted it in the way she always soothed her when she was troubled. 'You've done amazing things, Vreni. You rescued us. You changed everything for all of us. You cannot make yourself responsible for the horrible events that happened centuries before you even existed.'

'But I've asked so much of William, and then I showed him his family's heartbreaking past when I could have just—'

'Stop. If you keep dwelling on these things, then you will have nothing to offer to the magic. You need to be strong and focused in case we need your magic.'

'I hoped we don't. Maybe William has just changed his mind … about me.'

'The magic of the amulet would never have worked if he didn't love you deeply. Wait until we know something before you …' Rita stopped and stared, then looked up at the sign with the words Bella Rosa fashioned out of twisted vines that were dotted with tiny rose buds. The sign was as Rita remembered, but everything else looked very different from the last time she had walked past the flower shop.

The buckets on either side of the door were full of drooping blooms and green, brackish water. Dying leaves and petals laid crisp and browning on the footpath. The door was open. They stepped slowly into the small, sour smelling shop.

'Hello!' Rita called. Vreni started pounding on the tiny service bell on the counter. There was a shuffling in the back of the shop. 'Excuse me,' Rita called again and placed her hand over Vreni's.

'Yes, may I help you?' mumbled a voice. From out of the shadows at the back of the shop, a grimy, dishevelled man shuffled towards the counter.

'It can't be.' Vreni gasped. 'Harry?'

The dark, sunken eyes of the shop assistant looked towards Vreni, struggling to focus. 'May I help you,' he said leaning heavily on the counter as he spoke.

'This is ... I know him. It can't be.' Vreni grabbed Harry's hands. They felt hot and his skin was flaky. 'Where is Bella?' He gazed back at her and started nodding slowly. She shook him. 'Where is she?' she shouted.

'Vreni, enough.' Rita took her hands off the trembling Harry. 'What's all this about?'

'This is Harry. The Harry I told you about.' Rita shrugged.

'Hello, I'm Harry,' he said then sagged onto the counter-top.

'This is the guard from the AlGuild building, when William and I went searching for the potion. I tricked him with a false voice so we could get in. We thought he must have been killed when the building collapsed because he never showed up anywhere or went to the authorities.'

'So?

'So, he's here. This Bella ... Bella Rosa must be connected to AlGuild somehow.'

'My Bella Rosa.' Harry seemed to revive. At the side of the counter there was a photo of a pretty, brunette woman holding flowers. He reached and gently touched it, 'She's so beautiful.'

Vreni ran around the counter and grabbed the swooning Harry by the shoulders. 'Where is she?' She shook him. 'Where is Bella Rosa?'

Harry wobbled like a rag-doll and collapsed onto the floor. Vreni toppled over with him. 'Where is she?'

'Working with a new assistant,' he mumbled. 'Preparing him, she said no interruptions. She said wait here with the flowers.' Harry's lips were turning blue. He was struggling to breath. 'I miss her,' he whispered. He looked small and broken.

'Where does she live?' She shook him. 'Where?'

'She lives in a beautiful garden,' he croaked, smiling. 'She is the queen of ... all the blossoms.' He was gasping.

'Tell me, where is this garden?' Vreni tapped on his face to rouse him. His skin was burning.

'It's up in the sun ... up high ... with the spiders ... blossoms ... she is so many blossoms.' He coughed and wheezed. He closed his eyes and went very still. The wheezing stopped.

Vreni heard blurred words, Rita was talking. She was talking on the phone. Vreni stopped listening to the one-sided conversation and instead listened hard to hear if Harry was breathing. He remained silent. *I have shaken the last piece a life out of this poor wretched man and I still know nothing.* Her tears fell onto his gaunt, grey face.

'We need to go.' Rita placed a gentle hand on Vreni. 'Artūrs said he will meet us at Laima's and tell us what he has found out.' Rita placed her hands under Vreni's arms and lifted her from the floor.

'We can't leave him here.'

'No, we can't. Artūrs said he will see to it that Harry is taken for his blessing.' Rita urged Vreni through the front door. She shoved the buckets of dying flowers back into the shop, flipped the sign on the door from open to closed and locked the door behind them.

'Another funeral, because of me.' Vreni leaned hard against the wall.

'This was not because of you, Vreni.'

'I shook his last breaths from him to get answers.'

'He was wretched before we came.'

'He sounded infatuated with this Bella ... like William's father did with Veca Tante. Harry was a young man and now he's dead. What happened since I saw him guarding the labyrinth? Could Bella have done something to him?'

'Maybe it's a coincidence. Harry may have been going to parties, living a wild life and making himself very ill,' Rita said.

'The other possibility is impossible. I watched the old witch die with my own eyes. I watched the worms and beetles and maggots roiling in her woody flesh. She decayed into forest litter, she cannot have somehow regrown and be alive.'

'If she can't, then she isn't.' Rita tugged Vreni up the street.

'Even if she had the power of the forest to sprout and regrow, how could she be more than a child? It's only been two years. Even with magic humans don't grow that fast.'

'Then it's not her.' Rita pulled Vreni into the café.

'Maybe there is something ...' Vreni remembered her vivid, frightening dreams and thought of the horrors in the book full of agonies. *What if it's not over?* She shivered.

* * *

The coffee swirled in a milky vortex as Vreni stirred it, counting each slow circle the spoon made inside the cup. She counted the two-hundred and three black tiles on the café floor before the coffee had arrived. She had turned the spoon eighty-seven times in the cup. What was taking Artūrs so long?

'Hello. Coffee please,' said a mild, familiar voice from the counter. Artūrs crossed the floor with his usual unreadable calm and sat in the booth opposite Vreni and Rita.

'Did you get the address of the place he was buying?' Vreni blurted. 'Have you been there? Is he there?'

Artūrs smiled and held up his hand. 'I know where the building is. I went to take a look. It looks quite deserted, rundown but I saw a few traces of something interesting.'

'What did you find? Is William there?' Vreni's coffee was splashing out of the cup.

'I found some things outside the building.' Artūrs patted

his pocket. 'Gizela wants to see them before we make any more decisions about what to do next.'

'But William may not survive waiting for us to decide what to do. Harry is dead, in the flower shop. He was hot and looked like something was wasting him away. William may perish the same way if we don't hurry.'

'Sabina wanted me to remind you that William had his own magical traits. He was selected and bred by Veca Tante for his strength as his father was.' Artūrs reached across and took her hand, it looked so much like her father's hand. She gulped down a sob. 'None of us want to wait, Vreni. We want to go there and bring him home now, but we should make sure we are prepared first.'

'They have arrived,' said Laima, interrupting the conversation. 'At the flower shop.'

'Rita, you go and help the Sisters to prepare for Harry's farewell,' said Laima. 'Clean up the shop and put an out of business sign on the door.'

'What will I do after that?' Rita asked.

'Drive home,' said Artūrs. 'I will go to Mežs Mājas with these found items.'

'Please tell me where William might be,' Vreni begged. 'I need to undo this.'

Artūrs took her hand. 'You will be undoing this thing, but you are one of the Wise Sisters. You will start the undoing by coming with me and making preparations as Sister Anna has requested.'

Laima bought Artūrs his coffee and looked deep into Vreni's eyes. Vreni felt a warmth between them and remembered the thick ties that bound her to the Pratigs

Masa. She felt suddenly foolish to have overlooked the tenet that gave the Wise Sisters their power — unity. Artūrs swallowed down his coffee, with a nod of thanks he walked out of the café. Vreni squeezed Laima's hand and followed Artūrs to the car.

DECISION

All things have their beginning and their end.
They are born or grown or are fashioned by heart and hand
to exist until they no longer exist.
Everything that is made can be unmade. To unmake
something,
it is necessary to understand the nature of its making.
~Pratigs Masa Book of Wisdoms

* * *

'I've decided it's time for me to take the cure.' Vreni pushed into the room with such conviction and determination that the stained-glass doors were still swinging wildly.

'Sister Veronika.' Gizela looked up for the discoloured pages of the newly discovered Book of Agonies and acknowledged Vreni with her formal name as she always did. 'What has bought you to this decision?' Sabina watched, but didn't include herself in the exchange.

'That.' Vreni pointed at the tattered and bloodstained pages of the Alchemist's Book. 'And what Rita and I saw at the flower shop. Everything has changed since William disappeared. That dead person at the shop is, was Harry, the guard. The one I saw before I went into the AlGuild building.' Vreni was shaking.

'You could be mistaken about that poor young man. William's behaviour has upset you very much,' said Sabina.

'That was Harry. Somehow Veca Tante is still alive. I saw her in the dark edges of my last awakening from long-sleep, it felt so real.' Vreni touched her hand to her throat and continued. 'She said she would return like spring. Now I'm seeing shadowy glimpses of her, hearing mumbled words, feeling ribbons of cold, even when I'm awake.'

'From death comes life,' mumbled Gizela. 'The seed makes the blossom. The blossom makes seed.'

'Harry talked about blossoms too. Just before he died, he said Bella was full of blossoms.'

Sabina watched as Gizela mumbled quietly to herself. 'We are struggling to make sense of what's happening, but we have some suspicions we cannot ignore.'

'So, William is in danger?'

'He could be,' said Sabina. 'But it could just be his reaction the strength of the amulet's magic.'

'With what we've learned so far from that.' Vreni jagged a finger towards the Book of Agonies. 'We know we are just starting to understand what the old witch was capable of. What if, somehow, she is young and strong again? What might William be facing? I was there when she was diminished. I saw her rotting body bloom and set seed, but I didn't take the seeds when they fell. I could have stopped this.'

'It had been centuries. None of us had even imagined

Veca Tante could be alive when you entered the labyrinth,' said Sabina. 'How could you have known to do anything with the seeds.'

'I do know that I have to be the one to bring William back and I cannot risk falling into long-sleep unexpectedly. Give me the cure.' Vreni's eyes were glassy with brimming tears.

'You have waited to make your decision about the cure long after all the other sleepers have done so.' Gizela voice was stronger. 'You have waited for some reason, maybe there's a reason for your hesitation you don't even realise. Are you sure that you want to rush the deciding now?'

'The decision needs to be about the sleeper, her life, nothing else,' Sabina added.

'I'm not doing it because William needs rescuing. I'm doing it because if we don't stop her, Bella, Veca Tante, then it starts all over again. She will be able to write another volume of her Book of Agonies and the ugliness will continue, for me and all of us.'

'Your reasoning is sound, Veronika ... bringer of victory.' Gizela's voice rung with pride.

'Before you take the cure,' said Sabina, 'can we ask you to do something for us. Doing so will contribute to your success at freeing William.'

'Doing what?'

'We need to learn exactly how she controlled the men, and may be controlling William,' Sabina said.

'The old witch wrote about using the sympathetic magic of poppets,' added Gizela.

'I remember having poppets when we were young.' The

memory made Vreni smile. 'When we went into the forest back in Varve to search for mushrooms, the governess, the Sister, showed us how to lash twigs together with ribbon and make stick-dollies. She taught us which herbs and flowers to tie on them to keep us safe from the wild forest creatures. She said the dollies would also help us understand the birds.'

'There were more details in the Book of Agonies about making *little men*, to strengthen and protect the alchemists. The other box we found in the centre of the ruins was filled with wax and clay, sticks and twine,' said Sabina. 'There was a small package of relics, hair and nail clipping and a glass vial that was labelled as tears.'

'What does that have to do with William?'

'If she used these poppets over the centuries to control the alchemists, then it stands to reason that Rosalija, Bella, is going to use one now to control William,' said Gizela.

'To unmake something, you need to know first how it was made and there are no details mentioned in here.' Sabina touched one finger on the putrescent volume. 'We know the components, but only Tante or Bella would have known the workings of the magic. We want you to enter the dream realm and journey back to find out how she did it.'

'The Sisters have made the stick dollies for centuries. Why can't you use an unmaking from the Book of Wisdom?'

'These poppets were very different from ours. We need you to learn the details of her making and then you will know the unmaking. If she is controlling William this way, nothing else you do will free him.'

'How will it help to send me back to see Grandmama lying in her death-sleep?'

'We will send you to before that time. To the time just after Ieva inherited her title. Rosalija was just starting to build control. She would have been creating her heart binding magic. We need you to get close and watch what she does,' said Sabina.

'But she will recognise me like she did last time.' Vreni touched the scar on her cheek. Veca Tante had slashed Vreni with her clawed fingernails, then licked the wound, and tasted the differentness of her sleeper blood.

'You will go to a time before that time, when Veca Tante will not be at her most powerful for some years to come. She will not yet recognise you because she has not yet created the magic that links you to her.'

'And what magical defences will I have this time?' Vreni brushed her hand over her scared cheek once more.

'It is an earlier time for the Wise Sisters as well, so they, we, are not what we will become when you visited at the time of Ieva's cursing. All you have in your defence this time is your familiarity for the palace and a knowledge of how to act like you belong there.'

'You will appear as an unremarkable house girl again,' added Gizela. 'But this time, you have a valuable knowledge of the palace corridors.' The old sister smiled her encouragement.

'You said you want me to go into the dream realm

before I take the cure.' Vreni turned to face Sabina. 'What are you not saying?'

'Ah that nimble mind,' said Gizela and she laughed gently. 'That's why she was the one.'

'We have observed that sometimes after the sleepers take the cure, they suffer some degree of insomnia,' said Sabina. 'Simply, if you take the cure now and the sisters can't sing you to sleep then you can't travel in the dream realm.'

'I'll do it. But when I get back, I'm taking the cure. It's time to end this.'

'We will prepare the dream room and you will travel to-night.' Sabina hugged Vreni quickly and pushed through the stained-glass doors.

* * *

The moon dappled the courtyard with creamy light, mixing with the warm glow spilling from the windows and doors of the buildings that surrounded the garden. The evening air was still and thick with fragrance, geranium, rosemary, violet. Vreni stood in the doorway looking at her shadow stretching across the cobbles. She looked across to the shadowed alcove that marked the entry to the stairs that spiralled down to the dream room. She forced her feet to step out and walk across the cool stone. Her fingers trailed the tops of the plants as she wove her way slowly to the arched alcove and pulled the door open.

The flickering golden light of the candles in the stair-way played against the stone spiral of the stairs, Vreni imagined being inside an enormous twisting sea-shell. She leaned out over the stone banister and looked down into the creamy-pink helix that led deep into the earth to the dream room. Voices rose up, pulling her to join them. Her heart shifted its rhythm to match the chants of the Sisters waiting below.

The twisting of the stairs and the force of the chant on her heart, left Vreni lightheaded. As she reached the bottom step, she braced herself against the banister and caught her breath. Gizela and Sabina stood inside the door and beaconed her to enter. At the threshold of the dream room, Vreni felt the web of energy enfold her as she stepped inside.

Nothing seemed to have changed since she had been here the first time. The platform in the room's centre surrounded by Sisters, singing and chanting rhythms. The curved walls still glowed with colourful murals of gardens and the forest, filled with berries, blossoms and birds. The painted women are dancing through the painted landscape, holding their hands high in celebration with their eyes gazing upwards. Again, Vreni followed their gaze to the room's ceiling, midnight blue with a spiralling trail of sparkling light that started at the door and coiled in on itself until it reached the glowing crystal in the centre.

Allowing herself a brief private ritual, Vreni walked around the room. 'Now I lay me down to sleep.' She whispered, brushing her fingertips along the curving wall, watching the jubilant, painted women. 'I pray the lord my soul to keep.' The Sisters remained circled around the centre platform, but their magical song was reaching out to Vreni, drawing her towards the platform where she would embark on her travelling dream. She could no longer resist, turning away from the painted ladies, she turned towards the centre of the room. 'If I die before I wake.' The Sister's rising cannon drowned out her words. 'I pray the lord my soul to take.' The circle of Sisters opened. Vreni walked through and lay on the warm stone platform.

Harmonies wove and tangled within the chant. The music pulsed deep into Vreni's flesh, pushing everything else out of her awareness. She stared up, the crystal in the centre of the blue spiral rippled and pulsed, then it and singing faded away.

DREAM REALM

Blood holds its humours, its biles and its phlegm.
Her blood holds an unfathomable gift. Within its elements
float the seeds of fate.
Magical seeds from which I will grow my revenge.
-Alķimķi Ǧilde *Book of Agonies*

* * *

The waking was as it had been when she had entered the dream realm the last time. There was no burning breath, no drowsiness or lingering dreams, but nothing else was as Vreni had expected it to be. She woke instantly alert, but confused and suddenly frightened. She expected to wake in the fire-lit gloom of the kitchen, surrounded by chatter and the aromas of cooking food. Instead, bright light flared through her closed eyelids. Bees were buzzing close by and she could smell moist earth. There was a weight on her chest. Something was on her. Some creature, too small to be a wolf. *But what?*

She pressed her eyes tightly closed and lay stiffly at attention, waiting. The weight of the creature shifted, it moved across her body, then it was gone. She let out a long-held breath. Then the thing was back, on her arm, her shoulder. *Move. Run.* Fear held her. A rasping, wetness dragged across her cheek. Vreni remembered when Veca Tante had licked her face, to taste her blood. The witch auntie's tongue had felt rough then, scraping across her skin, as this did now. Vreni heard herself whimper.

'Meow.' The creature licked her cheek again.

'Cat?' The word came out as a laugh. The creature that was now a cat and not a demon, shifted and settled itself in the centre of Vreni's heaving chest. She flicked open her eyes and looked into a pair of deep amber eyes, that stared down at her from a round blue-grey face.

'Meow.'

She reached up and scratched the blue fur face.

'Meow.' The cat purred and a contented vibration rumbled deeply into Vreni's chest. She patted it as she looked around, realising she had woken in the kitchen garden. In the same circular herb garden, where she had hidden during her last visit to Grandmama Ieva's palace. Last time she concealed herself while she rifled through the Wise Sister's box of charms. There would be no magical charms to aid her this time, as she had travelled back to a time when the Wise Sisters barely existed. All she could hope for was that the old aunty, now the young Rosalija, was truly weak in her magical abilities and that she had not yet taken control of the alchemists.

The purring rose and fell in waves as Vreni discovered the cat's favourite scratching places, under the chin, behind the ear, on the little patch between its big golden eyes. The sun was high, and she was surrounded by fragrant bushes of herbs which were setting seed.

'Zils Zens.' The cat looked in the direction of the voices calling him then he turned back for another pat.

'Zils Zens. Where are you?'

'Blue Boy. Is that you?' Vreni sat up and the blue-grey cat slumped down into the folds of her skirt in her lap. She was wearing a long woollen dress similar to what she had worn the last time.

'Zils Zens.' The cat answered to its name with a yipping meow and moments later, the herb bushes shook, and the bees lifted in a disgruntled buzz, as Vreni's small hiding place was filled with little girls.

'There you are,' said the larger of the three girls, with dark hair and a serious, gentle smile. She glanced at each of the smaller girls then released their hands and turned her attention back to the cat. Vreni lifted him up and offered him back to his owner. 'Mama has told you to eat the mice.' She scolded the cat. 'But you're out here bothering the birds again.'

The other two girls stared at Vreni, and she braced herself, waiting to see if they would declare her a stranger and raise the alarm, but the middle-sized girl only glared at her. 'So Zils Zens isn't the only one hiding in the garden and not doing his chores,' she finally said. The tiny girl just nodded as she spoke.

'Hush, Klara,' said the older girl, 'It is not your place to be so bossy. Uncle has warned you about being gracious.' She shoved the blue cat into Klara's arms. 'Take Blue Boy back to the kitchen and point him at the mice.'

'Who's being bossy now, Nessa.' Klara stuck her tongue out and stomped off.

Vreni's heart galloped. She must have misheard. 'Nessa. Klara.' Her throat squeezed closed around the words.

'And Liga.' Added the smallest girl as if she was missing out on something. Vreni stared at her, frozen. She had never seen Liga's eyes open. They had not yet been able to wake her from the curse. Her heart was not repaired yet. These girls were young compared to the girls she knew now, the girls they had rescued and woken.

Vreni's mind scrambled to put the pieces together. The girls would be much older when Veca Tante decides — decided to trial the potion on them. They would fall asleep here. They would be hidden and moved to far-away places as she and her family had been. Everything they knew and loved would be gone. Then, in hundreds of years from now, *I find them, rescue them. The Wise Sisters would finally wake them, but not Liga, if she was woken before she was healed then her life would be short and painful. Maybe I can stop it happening...* Her breathed shudder. *No, I have no effect here. I am but a shadow.*

'Liga,' Vreni whispered and stroked her hand gently across the little girl's cheek. A sobbing sigh escaped Vreni's lips.

'Are you feeling well?' Nessa asked. Vreni could only nod.

'Don't be sad,' said Liga. 'We will help you pick the herbs for the kitchen.'

'Thank you.' Vreni willed her breath and heartbeat to calm and stood, her legs unsteady.

'I apologise for Klara's terseness,' said Nessa. 'We all have our chores and I love to sit out here myself, spending time amongst the herbs.'

'Klara says we're special,' blurted Liga. 'Because Uncle has his new position in the college, and we can visit there sometimes.'

'Hush, Liga,' said Nessa. 'Stop your boasting.'

Liga huffed and reached into the pocket in her skirt to pull out a pair of small shears. Nessa did the same. Vreni pulled up her apron to form a shallow well to hold the clipped herb sprigs.

'You must be proud of your uncle?' Vreni enquired as they worked.

'We are proud and grateful.' Nessa looked down at the ground for a moment. 'Ieva has always been good to our family. She will never let us go through difficulty, but since Papa died last winter, Uncle has been helping us, so his new position at the guild college helps us too.'

'Now I must apologise to you,' said Vreni. 'I spend a great deal of time in the kitchen, gossiping if I was to be truthful, and I have heard little about the guild college. It sounds grand.'

'It is,' Nessa gushed. 'There is a great library with books on the new disciplines that have been bought by the traders from up and down the rivers. The students of the college, like Uncle, study these fantastic volumes and discuss the various fields of alchemy.'

'You sound as though you have learned much yourself.' Vreni smiled. 'Not like me and my knowledge of gossip.'

'Uncle has let me listen,' said Nessa. 'I don't understand very much, but I love sitting in the college rooms.'

'These college rooms sound beautiful.' Vreni shuffled the load of herbs in her apron.

'They are, especially when the afternoon sun is shining through the tall windows. We sit under those windows on the divan and listen to Uncle and the others talking. I try hard to understand and remember the things they say.'

The divan. Vreni shuddered remembering the girls, older, lying trapped in the sleeping death on that divan. *On the west side of the palace.* She knew exactly where these chambers were. She had been there already, but that time hadn't happened yet.

'I should go. Thank you for your help, Nessa and yours, Liga. You are very lucky to have such a wonderful uncle.' The last words burned in Vreni's throat as she said them. She could only imagine it would be just a matter of time, a few years until their wonderful uncle would be drawn far enough under the old witch's control to allow the experiment to take place and that would seal the three girls' fate.

I am just a visitor in this time. I can have no effect here. Vreni would go to the guild college room and hopefully be able to learn the secret, magical workings behind Tante's control over the men of the college. She needed to find something to help her free William. Vreni pushed out of the circle of herbs, waved goodbye to Nessa and Liga, and walked towards the kitchen door.

Rich aromas filled the kitchen. Women, with plaits coiled up like crowns, heavy skirts and stained aprons, chattered and bustled with their chores. Pots bubbled on hearths at either end of the long, cobbled room. As Vreni turned the herbs out of her apron onto the heavy wooden table in the centre, a stout, happy-faced woman shoved a warm pastry into her hand.

'Paldies,' Vreni mumbled. 'Thank you.' She bit into the smooth warm dough. The peppery filling of the pīrāgi was steaming hot. She whistled and puffed little breaths to cool her burning tongue. The pain reminded her of the Sister's warnings. Although she was a visitor on the edges of this time and place, she was still present enough that any injuries done here were real and could be deadly. She brushed the scar on her cheek.

'And something else.' The pastry cook stared into Vreni's eyes and placed a small pouch into her palm. 'An incense,' she whispered, her eyes glowing in the kitchen's gloom. 'Burn a little of this and people who inhale the smoke will barely remember your comings and goings ... and that is best when the person coming and going has no place being here.'

'How do you—' The stout woman pressed a hot finger to Vreni's lips.

'You have things to do, and we Sisters have secrets to keep.' She squeezed Vreni in a half hug. 'Finish your food,' she said, and walked back to the oven.

Vreni rubbed her thumb across the small pouch. *This is the very beginnings of the Wise Sisters.* Struggling to swallow the last of the pīrāgi, she placed the pouch in the pocket of her dress, picked up a bucket and rag from the corner and went in search of the college rooms. Nessa had said they received the afternoon sun, so Vreni was certain they were the same westerly rooms she had visited last time. If she was lucky, she would be able to get inside and see what she could learn about how Veca Tante, young Aunty Rosalija, was establishing control over the men in her influence.

Vreni knew from the height of the sun and the bustle in the kitchens, that it was almost time for lunch. If she could get to the western rooms as they were leaving for the midday meal, then she may be able to spend some time in there undisturbed. She moved through the stone corridors with an air of purposefulness, trying to look as though she and her bucket had been summoned for some important task or other, but as she went on, she realised she was unremarkable, one among the many girls cleaning and scrabbling at their errands throughout the palace.

The dinginess of the corridor was striped with bands of light shining in through the narrow slits in the stonework. Ahead of her, the way curved and started feeling frighteningly familiar. Rounding the bend, she came to a door. The handle and the metal strapping were smoother and shinier than the last time she had seen it, but she knew this was the door leading into the west facing rooms. The rooms she had visited last time in this place's future.

Hesitating, she leaned against the cool wood and breathed deeply. *There is no other way to find out how the old witch does her controlling magic than to go inside. I will be nothing more than the girl sent to clean.* The door was every bit as heavy as it had been when she had opened it last time. She turned the cold metal handle and pushed the door open just enough to squeeze through.

Three broad bands of light stretched across the chamber's stone floor. Dust swirled in the sunlit air. Vreni glanced to the left of the door, to where the wolf, Bruno, had been when she was here last. Thankfully there was no cage and no such sorry beast anywhere to be seen. The divan, covered in tapestries and cushions, sat under the tall windows. The shelves lining the walls were half-filled with the books Nessa had spoken of. The reading table and the central bench were where she remembered them, but they appeared less worn. Barely any of the alchemical equipment, vials or bottles were present, but in the centre of the bench were an array of small boxes.

Vreni shivered, her skin suddenly chilled and clammy. The boxes were newer, but identical to the ones that had been uncovered in the vault. She was sure they held the tokens offered by the unwitting men. Inside would be a collection of the hair and finger nails and any other physical tokens that would form a sympathetic bond between the poppet and the man. They were gathered from whoever it was the old witch wanted to control.

There were footsteps outside in the corridor. Vreni moved back towards the door, positioning herself as though she had just come through it. A woman walked into the room with her head bowed. She was preoccupied with a leather-bound volume and had not even acknowledge Vreni's presence.

'I am sorry for the delay.' Vreni feigned, trying to sound obedient and purposeful while her heart was slamming inside her chest. 'I came as soon as Uncle sent me,' she said, hoping those in the guild rooms had paid little attention to Nessa and her sisters when they visited, and would believe Vreni was one of them.

The woman looked up at Vreni with annoyed disinterest. 'Why?'

The woman was beautiful. Tall and slender with chocolate hair held in a lose plait and emerald eyes that flickered with bright amber flashes. Vreni stared, struggling to speak. She recognised this woman. She had seen a photo of her, on the counter at the flower shop. This was Bella. *Rosalija—Veca Tante—Bella.*

Run! All Vreni could think of was that she wanted to escape. Her body flooded with heat. She wanted to leave this place and run, then somehow will herself out of the dream realm and go back, leave Mežs Mājas, get back to William in the city and ... and what. The room spun around her. She squeezed her hands around the bucket's coarse rope handle. *I need to stay. I have to find out about her magic so it can be unmade.*

Vreni stared down at the bucket and fidgeted with the rag until she could slow her breathing. 'I didn't mean to disturb you, Lady Rosalija,' Vreni ventured. 'Uncle said the books should not sit in dust.'

The young Rosalija looked at her fleetingly. Vreni held her breath, waiting to be seen for who she was. But to this younger Tante, their last meeting had not happened yet and Vreni was just a cleaning girl. There were no sleepers yet and no potion. This young witch was only beginning to grow her power and who knows if the plan for the sleeping potion was even a thought in her mind yet.

'Clean if you must. There is warm water on the fire.' Rosalija looked back down at her book and turned her attention to the boxes on the bench. 'It will be easier soon,' Rosalija mumbled to herself. 'When self-important uncles and the other alchemists will do what I say and do less thinking of their own.' She placed the book onto a carved book-stand in the centre of the bench.

Forcing her legs to move, Vreni took her bucket and rag and walked to the reading table. She watched Rosalija working and wondered why she hadn't hidden the book. Then she realised how rare it was in this time for people, especially girls, to be able to read. To Rosalija, Vreni posed no threat of reading and revealing any of her written secrets.

Vreni took a pinch of the ground herbs the cook had given her from the pouch in her pocket and sprinkled them into the candle flame on the reading table. A thread of blue smoke rose into the air and expanded into nothing.

Vreni heard Rosalija take a deep breath as the vapour reached here. If the herbs did their job, then this young Veca Tante would have only a vague recollection that someone had been here at all.

Rosalija gathered an array of tiny twigs and leaves and was arranging them thoughtfully on the bench. Vreni strained to see over Tante's shoulder. The page of the open book, propped in a carved wooden book-stand was filled with a drawing of stick-dolly. This strange little creature looked almost alive, like it had been grown in the forest.

It had stiff limbs and a rigid body that seemed fused to a stubbled face with two dark pits for eyes. The dark eyes seemed to stare out of the page and lock Vreni's gaze. She shuddered. An uneven collection of sticks protruded from the creature's stumpy head.

For a moment, Vreni thought of the tree creature that Veca Tante would become, did become, under the effects of her own magic for so many centuries. Everything that came in contact with her magic became ugly and tortured. Vreni had already seen how heartless and self-serving the old witch's control would be. Her hate-filled purpose blinded her to the pain and cruelty she inflicted.

The Wise Sisters possessed equal knowledge and power in using the qualities of nature magic to change circumstances or strengthen people, and to offer protection. They could even wield some influence over another person, animal, or insect, but that influence would never be used to make them act counter to the creature's nature or against the person's will. This ruthlessness gave Rosalija great power. If Bella was using these same methods, she would have the upper hand unless Vreni could find out how she made her controlling magic.

Feigning her cleaning tasks, Vreni moved around the room silently, to get a clearer view of the book and the content of the boxes. The hollow-eyed little doll, similar in size to the ones Vreni and Rita had made with their governess when they were little, lay on the table top.

It looked different from the dolls that protected her and Rita as children. These were made of roots and wood, all sharp edged and hollow eyed. Vreni repositioned herself to study the pages more clearly. The poppets also had a hollow in their chests. Now she could read part of a spell.

This new and loyal heart holds remnants, freely given and the yearning of your soul.

As these pieces of you are bound, so you are bound to me. New heart, new life.

This new bound heart, loves only me, loyal to me and obedient of my every word...

Rosalija worked intently, shredding herbs with the same type of tiny sheers as Nessa and Liga had used to help Vreni pick lunch herbs in the garden, but these herbs were not culinary. Vreni could see and smell, Bat's Head and Bedstraw, Crowfoot for making a strong binding and Belladonna to make past memories and loyalties fade away. All these herbs lay in a small pile on a strip of purple cloth. Vreni smelt the tang of Iron-weed and Knot-weed powder, and finally the stinging acridness of Paprika to strengthen the spell.

The young witch aunty made a little hollow in the pile of herbs. In the cavity, she placed finger nail clippings, then she took a small crystal of agate and wound a lock of hair tightly around it. This would be strong, old magic. Was it really strong enough to make these men kill their wives and children at her bidding?

William's father had been so removed from himself and so under the old witch's control, he had been lost to William, a stranger to his own son. William was starting to lose himself. Vreni felt certain this was the same magic. It was fighting the magic of the amulet the Wise Sisters gave him. If it wasn't for the strength of the amulet, perhaps William would have already been lost to her.

As Vreni moved behind the witch, pretending to clean, she read all she could of the spell and the list of requirements. She watched as the sticks, roots and twigs were woven and twisted together. There, on the wooden bench, laid an ugly stick body, with hollow soul-less eyes staring at nothing, and a gaping cave in the centre of its chest.

Next the young witch finished binding the lock of hair around the crystal and sat it within the herbs then wrapped the bundle up and bound it tightly and pushed the purple bundle into the cavity where the poppet's heart should have been. 'Tonight, I will complete the binding and we will see if this alchemist is strong enough to survive under my control. If not, I will search until I find the man with the strength to tolerate the binding and hope that he has sons.'

Nessa's father was dead. He must have been a victim of this control? Poppets were only ever meant to be used for protection. Perhaps Nessa's father had died fighting against the sympathetic control? Vreni got a glimpse of the last part of the spell.

With this made and charmed heart you are bound to me.

Until your flesh or this charmed heart are unmade you are bound to me.

Unmade. The word filled Vreni with hope. She would find William's poppet and unmake it. Break the bond and free him, but first she needed to get out and get home. She hoped the incense was still present in the air. She walked to the door, pulled it slightly ajar and was just slipping through.

'Oh.' Rosalija looked surprised to see Vreni at the door. She looked her up and down for a moment. 'I need your help, girl.'

'Of course,' said Vreni, continuing her deception as a helper. Head bowed, she walked over to the bench. 'How may I help you?'

Rosalija took Vreni by the hand and smiled. 'What I need ...' There was a flash of movement and Vreni felt a searing pain across her palm. 'What I need is blood,' she said coolly. 'The binding requires it.' She squeezed Vreni's hand hard and the blood beaded on her slit palm. Rosalija tilted Vreni's hand, holding it tightly she placed a metal bowl underneath to catch the trickling blood.

Vreni tried to pull her hand away. 'Stop fighting child, you have plenty of blood to spare and a little scar on a house-maid's hand is nothing.' The blood dripped from the edge of Vreni's palm. She watched the drops fall in a fast slow rhythm as the wound was squeezed to encourage the bleeding. Each drop added to a small circle of splatters that splashed out to the edges of the small bowl. Vreni concentrated on the patterns of circles and tried to ignore the stinging and burning as Rosalija continued to squeeze. All at once the young Tante sniffed at the air and released Vreni's hand. She picked up the bowl of blood and sniffed again. 'Curious.' She stared into Vreni's eyes, looking puzzled.

There was a loud knock at the door and the stout cook appeared. 'Lady Rosalija, the midday meal is being served.' She gave a little curtsy. 'Is the girl still here? I need to show her how to work faster. Come with me girl, there are things to be done in the kitchen.' The cook bustled forward and swept Vreni out the door before Rosalija could protest. She slammed the door shut and they walked swiftly away.

'She cut me.' Vreni held up her wounded hand and allowed herself a sighing sob. 'She put my blood in a bowl.' The stout cook went pale and tripped over her hurrying feet.

'Your blood shouldn't be here.' She wrapped Vreni's bleeding hand in a cloth and tugged her towards the kitchen. 'The end should never meet the beginning,' she mumbled as they walked.

When they reached the kitchen, the cook signalled to another woman and showed her the blood-stained rag. 'The aunty has her blood.' They both looked stricken.

'What do you mean my blood shouldn't be here?' As Vreni asked the question, the woman started humming. In turn, every woman in the busy kitchen began to hum. The hum grew until it filled the room, then softened and as it diminished, the women and the kitchen faded from view.

* * *

All around and inside her head, there was humming and gentle words. As Vreni became more aware, she felt soft hands cleaning her wounded palm, applying ointment and a soft cloth covering. 'My hand,' she choked out the words and sat up, her head spinning.

'It is deep but it will be fine, Vreni,' said Sabina. 'How did it happen?'

'Bella did it. I mean Veca Tante, she was different, younger.' There was a flood of panicky recollections as Vreni remembered what happened. 'She was young, and looks just like Bella, the florist, who lives in the building William wants to move in to. She wasn't destroyed by the softening potion. Somehow, she got out of the ruins, the old witch has resurrected, regrown. She has power over William, I know it for certain now. I saw the poppets, but nothing like the ones we used for protection. These ones have a strong binding.'

Vreni froze. She looked at her injured hand and re-membered the thick drops of blood the young Tante, Rosalija, collected in the silver bowl. She had said she needed blood to do the binding. 'She cut me and took my blood. She noticed something. She sniffed at it. Why did she do that?'

'That blood should not be in that place or time,' Gizela whispered.

'That's what they just said. Last time I was in the dream realm, Veca Tante had tasted the magic in my blood. This time she smelled the magic. What if she somehow knew or felt ...'

'What did she do with the blood?' Sabina locked eyes with Gizela.

'She collected it in a silver bowl.'

'I can see the consequential path from there to here ... from then to now.' The old sister sighed. 'Every tree must grow from a seed. I fear the blood she took from you was that seed.'

The room felt chilled around Vreni. 'By going back in the dream realm this time, I started all this.' Vreni gulped for air and tried to make sense of what she believed had happened. 'My blood completed the poppets and allowed the black bond that trapped generations of alchemists, generations of William's descendants to a half-life of slavery and misery.'

Sabina said something, but the words were lost behind the sound of Vreni's heart drumming in her ears. 'When I left my blood there, the magic looped back and enabled the sleeping potion to be made in the first place. The magic we had worked so hard to diminish is will start all over again ... because of me.'

'Vreni, by going back in time you now know how the poppets were made.'

'They were made because of me, my blood.' Vreni sobbed. 'Then somehow Veca Tante used it, or will use it, to curse Grandmamma.'

'Vreni, we have cured the curse. That part of the story is over. Your blood will soon also be free of the curse'

'My blood is a curse. It seems now that it always has been.'

Sabina held Vreni's hands firmly. 'If your blood and the magic it contains was used as the binding agent to work the poppet magic, it stands to reason, that when you take the cure, your blood will be the agent that can sever the bond and set William free.' Sabina looked at Gizela and the old Sister nodded.

'I want this wretched poison out of me, before I can hurt anyone else I love.'

The hum started building again. Vreni felt herself calming. 'We will give you the cure, but first, two things,' said Gizela. 'You need to rest and the cure can make it hard to sleep, so you can take it in the morning.'

'You said two things.'

'Your blood is full of magic young Sister.' Gizela hesitated and looked to Sabina who nodded. 'We ask you to give some of your magical blood, before it is changed.'

'My blood is a curse,' mumbled Vreni.

'Your blood is the last of the ancient magic and it is mixed with your magic, which is the strongest the Sisters have seen. We would like to preserve some of it.' Vreni nodded in drowsy consent. The blood was drawn. The night closed in around her and she slept a dreamless sleep.

MADE AND UNMADE

The fates are a serpent eating its own tale.
The ending of a thing becomes the beginning of the next,
and then those beginnings are remade as endings
to be reborn as beginnings
as the serpent twists and squirms through the world.
~ Pratigs Masa Book of Wisdoms

* * *

Everything looked unfamiliar when Vreni woke. Her mind was weary and clouded. She scanned the room, rough creamy plaster walls, wooden beams, small panes of rippling glass nestled deep into the thick walls and a small posy of flowers at her bedside. Of course, she was at Mežs Mājas.

Stretching, she pulled the feather quilt up around her chin and opened her senses to the familiar morning activities. The smells of breakfast cooking nearly pulled her straight out of bed as her stomach protested with emptiness. She listened to the music of her forest home. Somewhere, a Sister, perhaps two, were humming as they worked, lacing a little magic with their hum. The birds in the forest that surrounded the cluster of stone buildings were joining the music, responding to the magic in the harmonic phrases. It was one of the greatest pleasures she had known since joining the Wise Sisters, to be part of the magic that was created through the unity of many voices. All the Sisters, sharing intentions and weaving the spell-work into song. This unity added strength to the magic.

The hum built and resonated in Vreni's chest as she added herself to the union with the birds and the voices. As the music twisted up from her chest into her mind, its presence opened a pocket in her awareness ... memories of last night and her trip to the dream realm started flitting into her consciousness. This hum had been a glimmer, just a small one, but it had enclosed her memories while she slept. Vreni shivered under the warm quilt as the glimmer broke open and released the knowledge of her time in the dream realm back into her mind.

Zils Zens, the little blue faced cat, Nessa and Klara, much younger, and Liga alive and well, with her lovely blue eyes open. The gift of the herb pouch. Walking on the smooth stone passage-ways through the castle that led her to the much younger Veca Tante. The young Rosalija, the angry maiden aunt, who was aggrieved at not being chosen to rule the principality when Vreni's grandmother, Ieva, was chosen in her place.

The alchemists' chambers had looked like a library and the alchemist thought they would work with Rosalija to learn and grow wise in the ways of alchemy. They could never have guessed their fate was to be bound in magical slavery until they perished.

Vreni shuddered and cried out as the last memory was released from the glimmer. The blood, her blood. She felt the burning pain as the knife sliced across her palm. She watched with her mind's eye as Rosalija squeezed and the drops of blood trickled from the cut into the silver bowl and she saw how she had responded to the blood, feeling the magic in it. Rosalija, despite all of her books and her alchemists, had not been able to make anything like the magic in Vreni's blood, and she may never have been able to, but Vreni had given her all she needed in those drops of blood.

Hot with guilt, Vreni flung back the quilt. 'My blood started it all.' Tears flowed down her cheeks and dropped onto the bandage wrapped around her injured hand. She sobbed. 'The magic in my blood allowed Veca Tante to control the poppets, and all the alchemists throughout the centuries right up to William and his father. And she was able to make the sleeping potion and control us all.' Vreni's breath came in wracking sobs. 'I made all this happen.'

'You made all this go away when you bought us the old potion,' came Sabina's gentle voice as she and Gizela walked into the room.

'You didn't intentionally give the blood, Vreni.' Gizela sat close and took Vreni's hand. 'You were playing the role of obedient house-maid, so you could leave with the knowledge we sent you to gather.'

'It was not even Veca Tante's intention to extract magical blood,' said Sabina. 'But it was her intention to do evil or to learn how to do evil.'

'Fate is a powerful thing, Vreni, as is love,' said Gizela. 'Though fate is harder to see. It is love's shadowy sister, but they are both woven into our lives, sometimes for us to control and sometimes they control us.'

'I need to get the magic out of my blood before fate gives me any more surprises. When can I take the cure?'

'There is just one more important thing you need to do first.' Gizela's eyes sparkled and the old sister's gaze made Vreni's heart skip.

'Another task.'

'An important one ... breakfast.'

Sabina smiled and shook her head. 'Gizela used to play the same tricks on us, before we got to know her trickster ways. She is right about breakfast, eat and meet us in the lab afterward. Then you can take your dose of the cure.'

'That's it? Just take the cure and that's it? No singing, no ceremony?'

'The singing and ceremony all happened as part of the cure's production, but I'll explain more about it later.' Sabina and Gizela left, closing the door behind them.

Vreni spent a moment staring at the tiny speckles of dust dancing in the column of morning light pouring through the small window. *This is the day, after so many other days of waiting and wishing and striving and sacrificing. And after my hesitation, today I will take the cure, just like that.*

After the glimmer had revealed its hidden memories from the dream realm, the idea of eating breakfast felt like a chore, but the cook filled the table with food and hovered around looking stern and nodding as Vreni ate. Bread, egg, porridge, pastry, and coffee. As Vreni went to pour a second cup of milky coffee, the stern cook's face broadened into a satisfied smile, and she disappeared back into the kitchen. Vreni stacked her plates on the trolley and walked out into the gardens.

Her footfalls crunched on the gravel path. She stopped, and stood staring at the lab building. Whether she got to the lab quickly or slowly, this was the day that everything about her would change. She turned away, deciding to walk the full circle of the gardens before going to the lab.

She knew everyone except Liga had already taken the cure and that her strong desire to be cured had made all this happen, but she still felt minutely hesitant. She stood looking at her reflection in the still water of the large pond.

After I take the cure, I will be normal, not a sleeper any more. The Sisters will not need to watch over me. William will not need the amulet anymore and we will age together. If we stay together. Unless it is just the magic that holds us together.

* * *

Inside the lab, Vreni smiled as she looked at all the white coated workers that were sitting hunched at the wide benches. She remembered sitting at those benches, with the gaggle of young Sisters when they had trained with potions and amulets and had joked about using magic on boys. It all seemed so long ago.

Sabina and Gizela sat at the far end of the room. There were piles of old yellowed books on the bench. Vreni shuddered, the Book of Agonies lay open among them.

Next to the books was an array of equipment that looked just like the items Vreni had seen in the dream realm. The young Rosalija had these things gathered together on her wooden bench in the same way when she was working on her poppets.

'I know you are in a hurry to be a normal girl,' said Gizela. 'But can we impose on you to help us with the poppet work for a small while before you take the cure?'

'I just want take the cure so I can go and find William.'

'This is important work,' said Gizela. 'We need to do all we can to ensure your success.'

'Of course, it's the least I should do to help undo this situation and bring William back.'

'This situation which is not your fault,' said Sabina as if she was reading Vreni's mind.

Vreni smiled. 'Couldn't I take the cure and then work?'

'Everyone who has taken it became a little sick and muddled while the cure did its work,' said Sabina. 'We need to have you clear headed. Is it too big an imposition?'

'Working together makes us strong and successful. It is no imposition.'

'We know that any physical token from the subject, needs to be offered freely to allow the poppet to work,' said Gizela.

'What tokens?' asked Vreni.

'Clippings of fingernails, a lock of hair, a few drops of blood.'

'I gave her my blood.' Vreni's heart squeezed. 'Could she have control over me somehow?'

'She would have no way of connecting you to that

cleaning girl all those centuries ago and besides, you didn't willingly offer the blood,' said Sabina.

Gizela spoke, diverting them back to the work. 'These poppets were only ever sanctioned to be used for protection and healing. All magic works because it is part of the will and intent of the people it is to affect.'

'No one would refuse magical help to be healed or be protected,' said Gizela. 'So Veca Tante would have only had to offer a proposition to give health and protection. These gullible men would have willingly and eagerly offered a lock a hair, some nail-clippings, blood or tears in exchange for the promise of vitality.'

'They would never have realised what her purpose was, but their willingness would have resonated in the tokens they offered. That was all she would have needed to strengthen the poppet's bond to the men,' added Sabina.

'The book shows a few types of poppet.' Gizela pointed to the pages. 'Vreni, we need your fresh memories. Describe what you saw the witchling working on when you visited her yesterday.'

'To reverse the poppet's magic, we need to balance its making with a strong unmaking,' said Sabina. 'If you can remember the recipe that you saw we can design a counter-measure.'

Vreni looked at the faded drawings. 'It was like that one. It was made from vines and sticks woven together.'

'Do you know what plants were woven?'

'I saw many bunches of herbs and willow stems on the bench. There were tiny pebbles of red crystal and amber. Tante took the crystal and wrapped it in a tiny piece of parchment, which had a word written on it, but I didn't get to see the word, she wrapped it before I saw what she had written and then bound the tiny parcel in purple cloth.'

'She would not have used the amber,' said Gizela looking somewhat triumphant. 'Amber has an ancient intention for protection and healing. Amber is the blood of ancient trees. It flows through them and if they are cut or a limb breaks under the weight of winter snow, it seals them against harm. Amber contains the magic and wonder of those mighty ancient trees. It has travelled down from the deep magical places through the rivers to the sea. It holds all the hidden magic of those places in its heart. Amber could never have helped the witch do harm to her victims, but it will help us in the unmaking.' Gizela walked over to the corner of the lab and retrieved an ancient wooden box from the cupboard.

The box was lined with velvet the colour of mid-night and within the dark blue folds of fabric laid pieces of amber in all shapes and sizes. Some were the colour of fresh cream, others looked like dark speckled globs of honey. Vreni reached out and felt their warmth. They seemed to vibrate at her touch and for a moment she would have sworn she could hear a quiet hum rising from the cluster of golden stones.

'Amber will be our first curative,' Gizela said, placing her gnarled hand into the box. 'Soon the right piece for the task will make itself known to us.'

'Wait,' said Vreni. 'As she wrapped the crystal, she placed seeds and herbs inside the bundle with it.' Vreni paced slowly and opened her mind and her senses to draw up the memories. 'Apple seeds, Nightshade.'

'Those herbs would make the victims forget their old lives and believe everyone they had loved to be dead.' Gizela mumbled something under her breath and scratched some notes in her journal.

'I smelt the sourness of Adderwort and the spice of Arnica flowers,' Vreni continued.

'They would form a strong spiritual and psychic bond, linking Tante to her alchemist. I see now why there was such compliance from these men throughout the centuries,' said Sabina.

'Mice,' mumbled Vreni as she paced. 'It smelt like a mouse nest ... Hemlock. Tante bruised the tiny flowers when she placed them on the parchment and the stench of them stung my nose.'

'Hemlock will hold the victim frozen to the binding of the spell. Well done, you are a skilled observer, Sister Veronika.' Gizela patted Vreni warmly on the shoulder. 'Now stretch your perception. Was there anything else in this conjuring?'

'Knotweed, Rhubarb flowers.' Vreni sniffed the air as though she was back in the alchemists' chambers. 'Paprika,' she added finally.

'Knotweed and rhubarb for a binding fidelity and Paprika to strengthen the magical blend.' Gizela continued to mumble and write, then she wandered off and started gathering jars and vials and placing them on the bench.

'Good work, Vreni,' said Sabina. 'Your recollections are vital. Veca Tante never recorded her spells in the Book of

Agonies. She wouldn't have dared. Even addled as the alchemists were, they were still curious about the alchemy. They would have seen the powerful magic in the spell and asked too many questions.'

Gizela did another mumbling sweep of the lab and returned with bunches of herbs. 'Vreni, you need to make this charm.'

'But you have so much more experience,' Vreni argued.

'No one loves William as much as you do,' said Gizela. 'Your love and commitment to him will strengthen the unmaking.'

'Tell me what to do.'

'Basil is first. It will dispel his confusion and strengthen his will. It drives away hostile and evil spirits. Sabina, gather some brimstone to burn away the poppet's power.' She placed some small bowls on the bench.

'Caraway.' Vreni chopped and inhaled the freshness of the seeds.

'They will remind of his passion for you.' Sabina smiled.

Vreni Blushed. 'Dill to push away the dark forces. Elder will release the enchantment.'

'Just placing this charm on William is only half of the task,' said Sabina. 'The poppet will still need to be unmade and spoken over for him to become fully free. You will need to find the poppet.'

'It could be anywhere. Hidden.'

'It won't be far from either of them,' added Gizela. 'She stopped abruptly in front of the box of amber. 'There you are.' She selected a smooth almost triangular piece of golden amber and rubbed it gently between her palms.

She smiled, as though the stone had given her a secret. 'Vreni, place this near your heart as you work.' She gave Vreni the warm piece of amber. Vreni blushed again as she placed the stone down the front of her bra.

Gizela placed a few more herbs on the counter. 'Chop these finely while you think of your love,' she said. Then she shuffled and mumbled her way to the stained-glass doors. 'Gather some Witch's Burr please, Sabina, and some Ague,' she said and then disappeared through the door.

Sabina walked out and Vreni was left with the bench full of herbs that released a heady fragrance. As she chopped, her heart and mind filled with wonderful memories of William. She worked her intension to release him from the binding of the poppet magic into every fine flake of herb. The amber grew warmer as she focused on the charm.

When Sabina returned the last of the herbs were chopped and made ready. Gizela placed a small piece of thick paper on the bench in front of Vreni. 'You need to write the word that will give the charm its purpose.'

'How do I know what it will be?'

'Search your heart. It will need to be a word that is significant to you both. Don't tell us what it is, just write. If only you know the word it will help you to know when the unmaking has worked.'

Vreni choose a word then wrote it. The herbs and volatiles were blended and placed on the word with the very warm amber nestled in the centre. As Vreni wrapped and bound the bundle with pale blue thread, Gizela and Sabina took the remaining herbs and brewed a tincture filled with the will and strength of all the Sisters.

The bundle containing the charm sat next to the brown glass vial holding the strengthening infusion. Vreni would need to get the charm around William's neck and get the liquid into his mouth. The charm and the bottle looked so small and ordinary. 'Faith,' Vreni whispered.

'Like the bird who sings before dawn, having faith that the sun will rise,' added Gizela. Vreni let out a ragged sigh and smiled at the ancient Sister's strength. The strength and the shared intentions of all the Sisters was in this magic. *Faith.*

Sabina walked back from the cabinet holding a small blue glass bottle. 'Here is the cure.'

Vreni's hand trembled as she reached to take it. There was a picture of a bird taking flight on the tiny paper label. 'So, this is it? This is what you created from the drops of old sleeping curse potion I retrieved from the labyrinth?'

'Yes, Vreni. We had tried so many times to make a cure and failed until you bought us those last drops of the original potion. Now you will be free from the curse of long-sleep forever.' Sabina beamed with pride at their accomplishments. 'We have kept our promise, and we are still exploring what else we might create with the drops that remain.'

'I just swallow this and it's over?' Vreni asked.

'We have seen, with Rita, Giada and your aunts, that there is a little more to it than that,' said Gizela. 'It seems that when the cure takes away the long-sleep, it also takes away all your sleep, but just for a while. Be prepared for a couple of sleepless nights as your body transitions.'

450 ~ MARTII MACLEAN

Vreni was suddenly hot with concern. 'Will I still be magical? I need to be able to defeat the poppet and ...'

'The only thing that will change is the long-sleep,' said Sabina. 'Your Aunt Zana was magical as a sleeper and she is still magical after she took the cure, though her magic does not compare to yours.'

The blue bottle felt cool in Vreni's hand. She removed the lid and sniffed at the contents. It smelt like the air before a storm. Her lungs drew a deep breath almost on their own. 'Endings and beginnings,' she said with a sigh. 'Now everything is over and yet it is starting anew.'

She placed the cool glass to her lips, tipped the liquid into her mouth and swallowed. It tasted alkaline, like an absence of flavour. It was cold, but it burned as it made its way down into her stomach and from there, out-wards. Travelling through arteries, veins, every thread of capillary felt frozen and singed both at once. She leaned heavily on the bench. Gizela and Sabina were at her side, holding her up.

The frozen scorching passed. Vreni stood tall and took a deep breath. 'That's it, I'm cured now.'

'Yes, but remember your body will take time to adjust, you may not sleep much until it does.'

'Use the time to work on your charms, Vreni,' said Sabina.

'Haven't we just done that?' Vreni pointed to the vial and charm on the bench.

'Those are for William,' said Gizela.

'But I want to get started, head into the city—'

'First you will need to make charms to help you as

you are helping him.' Gizela pointed a crooked finger at the window. 'The day is almost done. Make use of your sleeplessness to make your charms and we will start to-morrow.'

MONSTERS IN THE MIRROR

The fates sing their messages in the garden of dreams
and we spin in destiny's dance as we are swept and swirled
in fate's tangled tales.
~Pratigs Masa Book of Wisdoms

* * *

As the evening drew in close, the Sisters shared evensong and drifted off to their rooms to sleep, Vreni felt no sign of drowsiness. She sat by the dying fire and opened the blue leather-bound journal that held all she had learned in the magical lessons from before and since the glimmer. Charms and potions for protection and persuasion, spells for far-sight and clear-sight. Hums and songs to calm, strengthen and compel. She felt a pang of guilt, for her to make the charms, the Sisters would need to make sacrifices as part of the magic.

When Vreni had entered the labyrinth, Sabina and Anna gave an eye, an ear, lips, so that they could see what she saw, and Vreni would be able to talk with them and not have to travel alone. She had quailed at the sight of their beautiful faces, deformed by their sacrifice. Gizela had lent her ear to Ilona so long ago, when she travelled the labyrinth before Vreni. Ilona had died with the magical gift and Gizela's ear had not been restored for decades until Ilona was found and blessed.

Searching her own heart, Vreni found the unity the Sisters shared and she felt the promise they had each made down through the centuries. To give freely and add their strength to the magic was not a sacrifice to them, it was a privilege.

Crick-crack-break-your-back-burn-your-house-to-cinders.

Vreni looked up from her blue book to listen more carefully. It was an unusual chant. One she had not heard the Sisters share before. Who was up at this late hour, singing this odd children's rhyme?

Pop-and-crackle-make-us-cackle-when-we-scorch-the-cat.

'What?' Vreni peered into the dark shadows, she couldn't see anyone. 'Thank you for filling my sleepless hours with a little amusement,' she said into the darkness. 'But I have my charm work to keep me occupied.' No one answered. 'Would you like to join me for some tea?' Vreni leaned towards the silver teapot she had left warming on the stone hearth.

Warm-the-tea-for-you-and-me.

She dropped the teapot and it clattered to the stone. In amongst the coals, little licks of flame were chanting from tiny burning mouths. *Tea-tea-for-you-and-me. Scorch-the-cat. Black-the-hearth. Burn-your-fingers. We-all-laugh.* The small orange-red figures of flame, wavering in the coals were doubled over, chortling out a staccato, breathy laugh.

Vreni stared, then squeezed her eyes shut and went to look again. When she opened her eyes the dancing flames were still there, swaying back and forth. *Burn-true-is-what-we-do. Crickle-crackle-crickle-crackle.*

The room felt suddenly hot. Vreni slapped her book shut and burst out the door into the cool night air of the garden.

Vreni's heart thumped as she stepped across the gravel driveway towards the central garden beds. She stopped and held the blue book tightly to her chest. It had been a long day and it was late. She had taken the cure which was, at this moment, changing her blood. She was no longer a sleeper. *Where do the little dancing flame sprites fit into this?* She took a breath to calm herself and chanced a look back through the window. The fire had died away to dull coals. *I must really need some sleep.*

The moon was just rising over the ridge of hills that surrounded Mežs Mājas. The flowers and plants started showing shadows of their daytime colours in the pale light of the almost full moon. Vreni decided a walk would help make her tired and ready for sleep. A stork rustled up in its nest and Vreni startled again. She walked with deliberate slowness, choosing to circle the large pond at the centre of the garden. She would spend time there looking at the moon's reflection and then, if she was still not sleepy, a little time in the lab.

The fine gravel crunched as she walked. Vreni reached the rose bushes and bent to smell a partly opened bud. It twitched. She gasped and pulled away. The rose petals unfurled, becoming wide wings and it lifted from its stem.

'Smother-flies!' Vreni covered her face and ran. Stumbling, she fell on the gravel path.

She looked back, straining to see in the moonlight. How many more of the deadly creatures had felt her presence and lifted into flight? She saw only one, flapping gently in the air, its wings beating slowly in a way that made Vreni think of breathing. *How could the Sisters allow these creatures to have infested our gardens?*

'These creatures belong to me.'

'Who's there?' She looked towards the voice, but only saw the blood red smoother-fly hovering and blinking, staring at Vreni. Then it faded away, turning into moon-lit mist. There was not even a petal laying on the path to show it had existed.

Vreni's hands stung from where the gravel had cut her skin. Her legs trembled as she stood up. The words had sounded real, but there was no one to say them. She drew a ragged breath and checked again for more of the creatures, then continued walking on the circular path.

The moon had risen higher, and its milky reflection filled half of the pond's surface. There was a rustling behind Vreni, off towards the darkness of the pine grove. She spun to see the cause of the noise. A night bird rose into the air, silhouetted as it flew across the face of the moon. Vreni smiled at her jumpiness and stared up taking purposeful breaths to calm herself. 'Soon, lady moon, you'll be full and round,' she said. 'But I'm glad you're not glowing red yet, I'm jumpy enough already without the blood moon shining over me.'

There was another noise. Footfalls on the gravel. Vreni

strained to see into the patches of shadow cast by the trees. Something was moving, with slow soft, purposeful steps. Not frogs or something small and fury. It was a person. 'Hello.' Vreni said quietly into the shadows. 'You're up late,' she continued when there was no reply. 'Couldn't you sleep either?'

The person stepped out of the shadows, her head bowed, picking flowers. It looked like Nessa. No, Klara was smaller, it had to be Klara. That meant Rita had arrived while Vreni was busy working in the lab.

'Klara, I didn't expect you to be back here so soon. I thought you were enjoying Rita's lessons about city life.' Klara didn't answer. 'Klara.'

'I'm Liga,' a small voice said, as she turned from the flower bed. Liga smiled crookedly and stared with chalky white eyes. Vreni saw moonlight reflecting off the steel blade imbedded in her chest.

'This little one belongs to me.' The whisper came from nowhere, everywhere.

Vreni's stomach lurched, and she swallowed down the roiling bile that pushed up into her mouth.

'Liga,' Vreni gasped out the name. 'But you can't be here, you're ... sleeping.'

'I'm not tired at all,' said the crooked lips. 'And I'm all on my own.' She stepped towards Vreni. 'I'm all on my own because of this.' She lifted her hand and twisted the knife back and forth, the fabric of her gown twisted as she did. 'All alone because of you.' Liga pulled out the blade, it made a sighing sound as she drew it from her chest. 'You made the Master angry and he did this.' She pointed the knife at Vreni and took a step closer. 'Now I can't be with my sisters.' Vreni took a step back, lifting her blue book instinctively as a shield.

'You can't be here.' Vreni shook her head, this can't be real. 'The knife is still in the ruins...'

Liga stepped closer and Vreni turned and ran. Her head spun as she raced around the back of the hedge and past the secluded seat where her and William liked to sit, out of view of the main house. As she turned at the end of the hedge, she crashed into someone.

'I'm so sorry, I was startled. Did I hurt—' She turned to check on whoever it was, but there was no one there. She bent to pick up her blue book. There was a pile of bone and rag on the ground. Something glinted within the pile. It was the spiral pedant. 'Ilona?' Vreni stammered and her dizziness was swirled with disbelief and confusion.

'This one belonged to me too, for such a long time,' the nowhere voice whispered. 'But you took her from me. You took many things from me, but I'll take them back soon.'

The pile of rag and bone quivered and started to rise up. It was re-making itself bone by bone, until it stood, stooped, and draped with its shredded clothes and the pendant clinking against its ribs. Vreni begged her feet to move, but she stood frozen with bright splotches of colour flashing on the edges of her darkening mind.

A bony hand reached up and took her arm in a tight grip. The skeleton that could not possibly be Ilona, pushed her towards the stone bench at the edge of the pond. The skeletal arm seemed to beckon Vreni to look into the water. She had looked into the pond once before, to open the glimmer that had hidden her magical nature. What would she discover when she looked this time? She struggled to make sense of what was happening. The creatures, the voices. Every time her thoughts formed, they slithered away like eels.

The impossible Ilona rattled as she sat down next to Vreni on the bench. 'The mirror will show the monster,' she said in a voice like winter wind through the pine trees.

'I don't understand.' Vreni's words squeezed through her clenched throat.

A bone finger pointed to the water again. The moon reflected on the far side of the pond, but on this side, the water darkened, and an image started coalescing. The skeletal Ilona was now flesh, young and beautiful. She smiled at Vreni out of the water. 'Thank you for bringing me home,' the reflection murmured.

Vreni swallowed to loosen her throat. 'You deserved to be back with your sisters, you did a courageous thing.' Vreni stared at the pond. Her reflection was twisted by tiny ripples on the water's surface. *Ilona does not look like a monster in the mirror of the pond, it must be me.* She half closed her eyes, too scared to see what her refection would show when the ripples settled. Her blood had put all these fates in motion.

The ripples glowed and took form. They shone so brightly the moon's light paled. Then Vreni saw herself, radiant and strong. 'Why don't I appear as a monster after helping Veca Tante create the potion and our curse?' Vreni slumped and the parade of tragedy passed through her mind. 'Father, Liga, William's mother and sisters. Even you.' She pointed to Ilona's reflection. 'You gave up your life to try and save me and my family from a curse that I started by giving the young witch my blood. Everything I do is surrounded by death.' Her eyes burned. Warm tears wet her cheeks. Her chest heaved and she sobbed.

The skeletal arm rattled as it reached around Vreni's shoulder, but she felt the warm comfort that matched Ilona's fleshy reflection. 'You did courageous things, young Veronika, and you will do so again.'

Her beautiful image faded. Vreni turned to see the skeleton had vanished from the bench. 'Look into the water,' said Ilona. 'The mirror will show you the monster.' Her voice softened until it was nothing but a night breeze.

In the water next to Vreni's glowing image, a leafy, wooden creature rippled and sharpened. A bush, no a tree. Its eyes burned golden and stared out of the dark pond.

'Veca Tante,' said Ilona's distant breathy voice.

Vreni's heart flailed. Apart from the staring eyes, this leafy apparition looked nothing like the gnarled tree creature the old witch had been before she was destroyed. Ilona had not really been here so this image must be a dream. *I must be sleeping and dreaming all this. Wake up.*

The dream persisted. Vreni looked at the leafy creature. It was a mish-mash of plants, flowers and herbs with rough barked branches and budding fruit. The pond rippled, and the verdant shapes smoothed, became neat topiary, changed again, shaping itself into a person, a woman with pale green skin. The woman stood tall, looming over Vreni reflection and smiling with rose bud lips.

In the reflection, the woman moved towards the edge

of the pond. She stepped up out of the water and Vreni felt a cold splash on her leg. A long trailing skirt, woven from vines and willow tendrils scraped over her feet. The green-skinned woman glided across the garden towards a small table and two chairs, lit by a single candle at the table's centre.

Two men were seated at the table talking. The tree woman was now carrying a small tray. Vreni recognised it as the tray Artūrs used for serving at home. There were two glasses of red wine on the tray, and she handed a glass to the first man.

'Thank you, how gracious of you,' said the man using Papa's tone and Papa's words. Vreni couldn't breathe.

'I've missed you so much my darling.' The green woman's golden eyes stared longingly as she gave the wine to the other man. Then she leaned towards him and pressed her flower bud lips to his and kissed him.

'I have missed you too, my beautiful blossom,' said the Master.

This couldn't be, the Master was dead and here he was, drinking wine with another dead man who could not be here. Vreni's throat strained to scream, but no sound came out.

'How are you fairing?' the dead Master asked.

'I have been so lost and lonely without you, my darling. But now I am grown again.' As she spoke, she changed. Her green skin glowed fair and creamy, and her vine hair became dark and lustrous.

'Bella!'

The woman turned and smiled as Vreni spoke her

name. 'Soon I will have another loyal companion and then I will never be lonely again.' She twirled, her verdant skirt lifted up and out as she spun. 'He is strong like you were and he is almost ready, see.' She pointed into the gloom at the edge of the pine grove, where a tall thin man was wrapped in vines and bound to a broad trunk. He fought against the bindings and tried to cry out, but the vines covered his face and muffled the cries.

Bella flicked her vine skirt and flounced over to the bound man. She parted the vines on his face to kiss him. It was William.

'This one is nearly mine.' There was a whisper of laughing words in Vreni's mind.

Forcing with all her effort she moved towards William intending to free him from the bonds. She hesitated. Her heart tugged her to go towards her father. 'You can't be real.' She wanted to stand near him, smell his cologne and touch his soft dark hair. Then he was gone. The Master, the table, all vanished, and Bella melted into the shadows of the pine grove. Only William remained, struggling against the bonds.

Vreni ran to his side. The vines writhed and fought as Vreni struggled to free him. When the last of the bonds were wrenched away, he fell into her arms and they collapsed together onto the cool carpet of pine needles at the base of the tree. She held him tight, his skin was cool against hers. He was quiet, everything was quiet. The gentle darkness of sleep closed in around her.

LOST AND FOUND

Little putniņš, little bird, safe in your tree,
Why are you so restless, to fly and be free?
Wait and the mother bird will guide you from home,
The forest has dangers for a bird all alone.
                              ~Aunt Mila's Rhyme

* * *

Sabina and Gizela discovered Vreni laying asleep and chilled to the bone at the edge of the pine grove. She shared her frightening visions from the night in the garden. Sabina and Gizela counselled her to follow her instincts and consider what the visitations had told her. How those visions might guide her as she made her magical preparations. Vreni worked anxiously throughout the morning to make the charms, not wanting to delay a moment longer than was needed before she returned to the city to find William.

Now, Vreni sat in a square of afternoon light shining through the window in the booth at Laima's café. The string of charms laid heavy across her sweaty palms. She stared down at them, evoking each one's purpose in turn.

There was a collection of ants frozen inside a golden drop-let. Vreni's own blood had played a huge part in the family story since the very beginning and her instincts told her it still had a part to play. The sphere containing her blood felt warm against her skin. Next to it, was a silver orb full of songs and hums, then an orb filled with tiny shoots of green choke-weed that squirmed, waiting to be released and run rampant through a garden. There were other globs of potions and creatures held inert, waiting to be used if they were needed.

The string of spheres shimmered with the magical energy and intent they contained. She thought of who and what had been sacrificed, even for a short time, to give the charms their potency, and was overwhelmed with grati-tude for the compassion and unity she shared with the Wise Sisters. Her fingers stopped on one charm, a sphere filled with a rich golden-brown liquid, within it, a single clove floated. She smiled and remembered, the time when she first went to Mežs Mājas, and Emma's words as they laughed and made potions 'The scent of cloves on your skin will make your love do whatever you ask him.' Vreni felt the wrapped bundle in her pocket, the charm and the potion made to free William from the bond cast on him by the poppet. She hoped the clove oil would help her get the charm in place and persuade him to swallow the potion.

Regardless of Sabina's urging, Vreni had refused to take anyone's eyes or lips with her, but Gizela strongly insisted she would lend an ear once more. 'I had lived with one ear for so many years, a day or two more is nothing,' she said.

Vreni had finally conceded and now she stared at Gizela's perfect ear, held in miniature within a pearly sphere.

Vreni insisted on starting the search immediately and alone. Sabina relinquished and arranged a car to bring her to the city. So far, she had searched all places William might be, places they spent time in together. Even though she believed he would be at the apartment, she had promised to stay away from the building until the Sisters made final preparations and joined her.

Squeezing the necklace tightly, Vreni slipped the ribbon loop around her neck and tucked the charms out of sight inside her t-shirt. She stood and started pacing the floor, wishing it was somehow all a misunderstanding and that she would never need to use the charms.

This café was William's place. He always came here. It was a place where he just showed up, why not right now? She imagined him pushing through the tattered bead curtain with his coat flapping behind him. Then they would go home and finally have their ever-after. That was all she had ever wanted. To be normal and mortal, not to be some kind of hero. They would sit up in her tower and watch the moon rise and plan their university studies and plan for the day Liga would wake, healed and whole.

Laima pushed her half-read newspaper away, poured fresh coffee and shuffled out from behind the counter, interrupting Vreni's pacing. The old brew woman, this kind old Sister, wrapped a protective arm around her shoulders and squeezed gently, as though she was a little bird. 'Sit a moment, putniņš.' She nudged Vreni back toward the booth.

Vreni had sat here, two years and a lifetime ago, trying to eat burgers before going to meet William at the dance party. Later that same night waiting, with Rita in long-sleep, Vreni had sat counting nervous sips of coffee and wondering the consequences of divulging her family's deepest secret to William who she barely knew. Now, even Nessa and Klara called this place William's café when they planned their days with Rita in the city.

Regardless of the café's familiarity, it seemed that every time Vreni had been in this place she had been nervous, stressed, panicked, or heading somewhere she had not been before. Waiting. She seemed to always be waiting, all her life, asleep and awake and this place was where the waiting congealed and became a physical discomfort. The need to take action made her muscles ache.

'Wait a little longer,' Laima urged as she pushed more coffee across the old linoleum tabletop. 'Sabina said they're on their way. It won't be long now.'

'I can't wait any longer. I did what Sabina asked and took time this afternoon to look for him, and I went everywhere he might have been. The park, his t-shirt shop, the street markets, he's nowhere. I'm going to the apartments.'

'You have no key. You will not even be able to get into the building.'

'I will find a way, I have to.' Vreni's eyes brimmed with tears. 'At least I will be there, close.'

'Sorry putniņs, I didn't want to make you sad. I just worry that my little bird is in too much of a hurry to fly from her safe nest and into the darkness of the forest on her own. Just have some coffee first.' Laima looked at the wall clock, as if willing the hands to circle faster.

Vreni pushed the cup back across the table, causing a brown splash as she stood. 'No more waiting. Sabina will catch up soon enough.' She strode to the door, pushed through the beads and stepped out into the city crowds.

The streets were filled with knots of diners clustered around food vendors, so many busy, happy people who blocked the path or seemed to be moving in the opposite direction to Vreni. She tried to pick up her pace, but each time she saw a clear track it would collapse in on itself and she would start weaving again. She checked her direction hastily on her phone, Bella's apartment block was to the east, three blocks, maybe four. After many zigs and zags and apologies, Vreni saw a large patch of green ahead. The east side of the park. She checked the direction on her phone once more and broke into a jog, heading across the grass. Just beyond the far edge was a street block filled with older tenement buildings. One of them would be the apartment building.

Poor map reading caused Vreni to take the wrong street. She walked from building-to-building searching and checking her phone and her frustration grew. At the third corner she stopped and focused on clearing the clouds of negative emotion from her mind. She would not be able to signal her intentions to the charms if her mind wasn't clear.

She felt so lost. Not because of the map and being in this strange part of the city, but because William was not being William. Her funny, argumentative, dancing funny-man had become a robot, a zombie, and now he had disappeared. He had worn the amulet for less than two years, he was young and fit, but the dark magic that was being woven was fighting the amulet's magic, and the two sets of intentions had William trapped in the middle.

Vreni breathed away a tide of panic. Reaching for the ribbon of charms, she rolled them between her fingers. They tingled and vibrated. Her hand was drawn to one in particular. It was cool then warmed rapidly as she held it, she smelt ... dragon's blood, bergamot, something citrusy. A calming diffusion. She inhaled slowly and her heart was no longer a panicked bird.

The street was quiet. Vreni saw the green of the park at the end of the street and realised she had almost circled the block while she searched. She walked on with renewed focus. There were a few parked cars, and scooters on the footpath. The buildings on this street butted up next to each other with only an occasional narrow alleyway between them. They were built of stone, darkened by time, some tinged with moss or ribboned with ivy.

Vreni scanned the numbers and names on the buildings as she walked. Ahead she saw large metal letters glinting above the door two buildings from the corner, Seventy-One, this was it. She was caught off guard by the ordinariness of the place. Was she expecting turrets, gargoyles? It was a narrow building, dark brick. It was taller than the buildings on either side by two storeys. Each of the bottom three floors had pairs of identical lead-light windows, but on the windows the fourth floor were smaller and ran in a row across the entire upper floor.

Between the windows on the ground floor, heavy glass front doors, flanked on the left side by a rank of mailboxes and on the right side by an intercom panel. As Vreni walked closer, she saw faded names next to each of the six call buttons and BELLA written in bright, clear lettering on the seventh.

Vreni stepped up and tried the door. It was locked. She moved over to the intercom panel and hesitated. She would not have the element of surprise if she announced herself. Then she remembered the conjured voice she had used on Harry when he had guarded the labyrinth. She focused her intention and readied her voice to sound like someone she was not. She pushed the button, there was a long pause. She buzzed again.

'Yes.' The voice sounded surprised.

'It's Harry,' Vreni said. 'Will you let me in please.'

'Oh. Harry. I expected you to be … you have been so unwell … never mind. Make your way up … be careful on the stairs.' There was a pause, a barely heard laugh. 'It is very dark on the stairs and you might come to harm.'

'I will take care.' Vreni answered in Harry's exhausted voice.

There was a mechanical buzz and a stiff clunk from the lock. Vreni turned the handle, pushed, and stepped inside. The door locked itself behind her with a loud click. In the foyer, the bright heat and burble of the street was replaced by a cool greenness. The air was damp, it reminded her of the forest. Everything was still and noiseless.

As Vreni's eyes adjusted to the sudden gloom, her attention was drawn to a flickering safety light at the rear of the foyer. It flicked with a faded red glow over a collection of rubbish bins tucked behind the curve of the stairs. The doors leading into apartments One and Two were on either side of the foyer space. Cobwebs feathered the doorframes. The building certainly looked abandoned and poorly maintained. Vreni thought this explained the musty, earthy smell.

Her eyes grew accustomed to the poor light, and she saw a cast-iron helix of stairs twisted up through a central vaulted chamber. At the next level, the stairs paused at a triangular landing and a narrow bridge-like path connected the stairs to the equally narrow balcony that ran along outside the apartment doors, one left, one right. The gloom and cobwebs above, obscured the third level. The stairs curved upwards and disappeared up into a webby, green twilight above.

When the apartments were first built, the twisting ironwork of the stairs and balcony rails would have been considered luxurious. 'How opulent.' Her words reverberated in the stairwell. Up above there was a quiet rustling in response. Vreni shivered and listened intently for a few moments. The only sound was her heart thumping in her ears.

She walked the few steps to the base of the metalwork spiral and placed her hand on the banister. From above she heard rustle—click. The banister rail felt cool and downy, coated with some silky growth. Her damp palm smelt of the forest floor, like she had been picking mushrooms. Rustle—click. The building had no tenants apart from Bella, but what other things made their home here?

Had Bella conjured them? And for what purpose? Vreni swallowed and, stepping lightly, started up the stairs. There was more scuttling from above and the banister rail shuddered with each sound.

As she completed the first rotation of the helix of stairs, the cobwebs had increased until they formed an eyrie lacework blocking the way. Vreni swiped at them to clear her path. They resisted more than she expected they should. She pulled and a long tear opened in front of her and as it did a large piece of web came lose and draped over her arm. Clumps of heavy gossamer stuck to her sleeve as she pulled it away. It did not look like any spider web she had seen before. It did not have the usual radiating, circular design. Instead, this web appeared to be spun in even rows, the silken thread forming loops and twists and knots. Vreni looked at the larger curtain of web, hanging across her path, she thought she saw a pattern repeating itself.

The clicking sound started again, this time it took on a regular rhythm. The sound reminded Vreni of an old memory, of times sitting by the hearth, when she was young. This familiar noise was from then, but Vreni's memories were muddled after taking the cure and last night's strange visions. She stood for a moment remembering. *Knitting. Bone needles and shuttles click-clicking like when Mama and Zana and Mila would knit, crochet and weave on tapestry-looms by the fireside in winter.* The idea of knitting did not fit into this place. 'Knitting is not a defence,' she whispered. 'What type of guard would defend their post with knitting needles?' She thought of the smother-flies in the pleasure garden and knew that the best defence is one that is not expected.

From above, Vreni heard humming. The tune had fallen into time with the click of the rhythm.

WARP AND WEFT

"Will you walk into my parlour?" said the Spider to the Fly...
... the way to my parlour is up the winding stair ...
...there are pretty curtains drawn around; the sheets are fine
and thin ...
                              ~a child's rhyme

                    * * *

There was no sound coming in from the street. The air was
still. The curtains of web hung motionless. The clicking
and humming seeped down from somewhere above. Then
the humming formed into a delicate song and the words
filled the vaulted stair chamber with a hypnotic canon.
Come sit by me, I ask of thee,
Soon I'll be a bride so fair.
We'll weave bolts of gossamer silk,
And stitch the gown I'll wear.
Come sit by me, I ask of thee,
Come close and do not quail.
We'll spin silk threads and stories fine,
As we weave my wedding veil.
The sing-song chant whispered around inside Vreni's

head. It felt as though the cobwebs were within her mind. Her feet moved on the stairs almost without her bidding, stepping in time with the clicked rhythm. The heavy lacework webs shifted to make the way easier as she ascended to the second floor.

The second landing was thickly shrouded in cobwebs. They were draped on the twisting metal railings and they carpeted the narrow gantry bridges that led to the landings outside the apartment doors. Vreni looked up through the folds of web. The source of the clicking and the chanting was not on this level. Vreni looked up through the sticky curtains, straining to see what was in the gloom above. She stepped towards the next twist of stairs. The singing stopped. The clicking ceased. There was a leathery rustling.

Now the song had ceased, the mental cobwebs quickly cleared from Vreni's mind. *What thing as Bella created to guard this place?*

Before Vreni could imagine any gross possibility, the thing dropped down from the darkness above. There was no time to prepare a charm or even reach for her knife. It landed soundlessly on the gantry. No—it didn't land, it hadn't jumped from above, it had lowered itself on a web.

A spider, immense and dark, with legs like leathery, gnarled branches. It was draped all over in the same patterned web that hung from the banister railings. Vreni stumbled back and fell against the stairs. She took hold of her knife and prepared for the attack.

'Come sit by me, I ask of thee.' The huge black spider jerked its pointed legs, tapping on the stairs as it sang. Six long, jointed legs stood on the landing, but the two front legs and the web-veiled head reared up. The legs were arms, pale skinned arms that ended in human hands. The hands reached up and smoothed out the patterned web that was draped around the creature's abdomen. As the folds of lace settled the surreal picture completed itself. The creature was wearing a silken gown.

'Soon I'll be a bride so fair.' The hands reached up to the creature's head and brushed a tangle of auburn hair away, revealing a pale-grey human face. Black, glistening eyes stared at Vreni for a long moment. Then the thin lips stretched into a crooked smile.

The sound of Vreni's stricken heart thrashed in her ears. She stiffened and pushed away from the smiling creature. She felt the metal treads of the steps dig into her back, as she struggled up and backwards on the stairs, not taking her eyes off the smiling monster.

It stood still and continued its song. 'We'll weave bolts of gossamer silk,' it sang as it reached a hand to somewhere within the gown at the back of its body and drew out a thread of fine silk. 'And stitch the gown I'll wear.' The spider-creature's delicate hands worked deftly on the thread. Vreni was held spellbound by the action of the weaving. The thread was becoming a fine and intricate lace cloth.

'Come sit by me I ask of thee, come close and do not quail.' The spider-bride beckoned Vreni closer.

Vreni sat forward and then stood. Relaxing her grip on the knife.

'We'll spin silk threads and stories fine, as we weave my

wedding veil.' The spider-bride reached behind herself for another silken thread and offered it to Vreni.

As Vreni took a step forward and reached out her hand for the tread, she felt a burning, quivering at her throat. She reached up automatically and placed her hands on the charms. Her fingers landed on an orb, it opened at her touch and a pungent aroma released into the air. She was compelled to breathe deeply, and the acrid vapours stung her nostrils making her sneeze.

Her thoughts and vision cleared instantly and the compulsion to weave with the spider-bride left her. All that remained was revulsion and fear and ... pity. This poor creature was straight from the Book of Agonies, like the hoard, it had been left monstrous and wanting. Vreni decided to try and appeal to the bride within the monster.

'Congratulations, on your engagement. You're getting married soon?'

'Thank you. Yes, very soon, when my Brian, my fiancé, when he returns from... well he is away, but he will return soon.'

'You spin beautifully.' Vreni touched the delicate web that hung from the unseeable levels above.

'You're so kind. But I still have so much to do before Brian and I can be married. Will you help me?' She reached out the thread to Vreni again, but now her face looked more spider than bride.

'Come into my parlour,' Vreni whispered.

The spider bride giggled and took a clicking step forward.

'I would love to help you,' said Vreni stepping backwards. 'But I have to go up and visit with Bella.'

'No ... it's time for weaving.' The spider-bride flicked a long silky loop over Vreni's hand. She shook her hand to remove it, but it stuck and clung to her skin. She stepped back, surprised at the strength of such a fine thread and how well it bonded with her skin. Pulling again, she was free.

She remembered the bundles of spider silk she used to see when she walked in the forest. They were little woven coffins for creatures that were not quite dead. Poisoned by the spider's potion—venom, the victims lay sleeping and awaiting death, trapped.

Another loop of gooey silk wrapped around Vreni's hand. Yanking her hand back, she watched the thread stretch and pull tight, then finally break. She turned and scrambled up the steps.

There was a strange, barely human screech from the spider-bride and more thread flew towards her. She ducked behind a curtain of web and watched the thread stick fast on the lacy drape. The clicking of the creature's legs echoed on the metal grate work. 'Come sit by me, I ask of thee...'

Vreni searched her charms, feeling with her mind and her heart for which one to use.

'Come close and do not quail.' The bride's voice was a strangled squeal.

'Spirals within circles, within circles making spirals, dreams circle our hearts and spiral from our minds.' Vreni sang the only thing that came to her clouded mind. She needed to fill her ears and mind and leave no room for the spinster's song to think clearly enough to choose the right charm. 'We spiral within so we may circle without. Journeys within journeys, endings and beginnings.'

Her fingers stopped on a gobbet of amber, inside were tiny white speaks, hundreds of them. *Ants—bull ants.* In nature, a battalion of bull ants could overcome a spider and this charm contained hundreds of ant eggs. There was nothing natural about this enemy, but Vreni had to have faith in nature's power. She whispered.

'Be my defenders, be my army, and march on my foe.

Strike hard, be fierce, free this wretch from her woe.'

The gobbet dissolved on Vreni's palm, and the eggs cracked open in the tiny puddle of nectar.

The spider-bride sang on and took more, spindly steps towards her.

Vreni cupped her palm, took a step backwards and crouched on the stairs. 'Grow strong. Grow quickly,' she urged. The tiny quivering larvae began wriggling in the stickiness. Eating the syrup. They grew and changed as she watched. Soon the tiny warriors darkened and their armour hardened. They began posturing for battle and testing their strong jagged mandibles.

Long, sticky loops of web fell across Vreni's face, then across her shoulders. As she tried to pull them away she became more tangled. 'Hurry,' she whispered to her tiny army, and she lowered the handful of ants to the step. Her skin prickled as they marched down her fingers. 'Be my defenders, be my army, and march on my foe. Strike hard, be fierce, free this wretch from her woe.'

'...while we spin my wedding veil.' The spider's song ended and the clicking steps stopped at the bottom of the stairs. Strings of web rained down on Vreni, covering her face, her eyes. She gritted her teeth and breathed shallowly through the sticky death mask. More threads fell on her shoulders. The webs tightened. The spider-bride pulled on her web to draw Vreni closer. 'Come sit by me, I ask of thee. Soon I'll be a bride so fair.'

On the stairs, Vreni twisted, trying to turn and crawl away. The threads were wrapping around her chest. She tried to cry out through the thickening mask of web. She thrashed against the stricture around her chest. The spider-bride tugged on her web rope and Vreni thumped down one step then another. She pushed her feet against the banister and fought to keep her ground.

'Come sit by me, I ask of thee,' The spider-bride took the last few clicking steps towards Vreni. 'Come close and do not—' The song stopped, and the creature stiffened and made a strange questioning sound. The tugging ceased and Vreni took the opportunity to push herself back and away. She ripped a small hole in the web and could see again. The ants marched up the creature's legs.

The web tightened once more and Vreni scrambled to find a new position to brace her feet, but the spider-bride was not pulling her in. The web rope was jerking as the monster twisted and scuffled around looking for the source of her new discomfort.

She yelped and Vreni imagined the ants had now found those hidden vulnerable places between the spider-bride's leathery armour and were sinking their serrated mandibles into her flesh. Vreni knew this to be true, as this had been her intent when she chanted the ants into life, ordering them to distract and disable this poor tormented creature so that she could escape. Vreni knew it was these ants' nature to attack and keep attacking until their prey was dead. She tried to push this idea from her mind. She would add this new intention to kill to her list of truths later, if there would be a later. Vreni wept as she listened to the screeching and begging of the spider-bride.

'But I am to be a bride,' howled the veiled creature as it, she twisted, click-clicking, on the metal landing. She shrieked and pulled her many legs up and away at strange angles and kicked out stiffly at nothing. The dark human eyes searched frantically for the source of the burning pain. 'Brian!' The desperate screech echoed, bouncing around the empty stairwell.

Vreni squeezed her eyes shut. This poor wretch had no more asked for this than any of them who had suffered at the hand of Veca Tante and the alchemists over the centuries. The only one with choice had been the old witch aunty and now she was Bella, still choosing to torment and torture. And William was next.

Vreni wept as she listened to the screeching and begging of the spider-bride. She covered her face to stop herself from witnessing what her magic, her intentions, had put in motion.

A growling hiss from the spider-bride made Vreni look up, the tears had dissolved her web mask. While she wept the creature had transformed itself. The pretty pale maiden's face now had long curving fangs that pushed out from a jagged, dark mouth. The fangs dripped with venom as she twisted her head frantically searching for her attackers. The wailing shrieking cries joined together into a long dirge of agony. Vreni looked up into stair well, fearful that the noise would announce her arrival. Then she remembered Bella telling the false Harry to be careful on the stairs. Surely, she would think all this commotion was poor Harry's last moments and not bother to come down and look.

The spider-bride reared up. 'Brian!' she called to no one. The rest was screaming. She danced frantically, stiffly, circling, and searching. She bit at herself where the ants were attacking her, then she screeched afresh. The circling dance grew more frantic. The bride thrashed from the railing to the wall, and then to the stairs.

Vreni retreated further up the curved steps and the bride stumbled towards her.

Click-click. She turned and fell again, sobbing, whimpering, howling.

Vreni's own tears turned her view of the scene into a surreal water-colour.

The spider-bride tried at last to retreat back up her web-strings to the safety of her nest. She lifted free of the metal landing and hung screeching and panting on the end of her web. Her legs bumped together stiffly like dead branches in the wind. Her body convulsed and started to spin slowly on the gossamer strand. Then she fell, her howl descending into the green-dark space of the foyer below.

Taking shaky steps towards the landing, Vreni looked

down. From this distance, in the darkness, she could pretend the giant creature was smaller. It looked like any other insect, curled in death, except for what remained of the pale grimacing face. Dark liquid flowed out of the bride's body, pooling on the marble floor next to the collection of garbage bins. Vreni thought she saw a trail of ants marching away towards the door, but all she could really see was the pale face. Then there was a thud from somewhere up above.

FOLLY

Shy hearted, dryads hide, watching and waiting
within the green upon green of the secret wild.
These nature nymphs are friends with time,
strong as the trees that birthed them,
they dance across the seasons.
~Pratigs Masa Book of Wisdoms

* * *

The veil of web hung like lacy, wedding bunting all around the banister rails on the third landing. It glistened, catching the shreds of light that struggled down from a small window at the top of the stairwell. Suspended in the vaulted space between this level and the top most floor, was a tangled mass of web. Vreni climbed up a few more steps to examine the tangle more closely. This was the spider-bride's nest.

A knitted hammock hung in the centre of a radiating pattern of sticky threads that stretched out across the stairwell and disappeared into the dusty gloom of the vaulted space. Dangling from the ropey strands, three bundles of web, cocoons that held ... something. In the gloom, one of the bundles twitched. Vreni shuddered and looked away. *I cannot pay attention to this yet.*

The web was thinner where it crossed the stairs. It must have been ripped open and mended every time Bella had come and gone from her apartment above. Vreni squirmed through the looping tunnel of web, and climbed the last few curving stairs.

She stopped on the last step. Everything was so still. A cool draft was leaking in through old windows that lit the landing. Curls of pealed painted twisted in the draft on thin tendrils of web. The only door on this level was right in front of her. Cracked paint showing the antique wood beneath. A dull metal number seven hung by one screw. It looked as Vreni expected an ordinary old, run-down place should look, but she was sure nothing behind the door would be ordinary. There was another thud from inside.

The doorknob felt cool in her hot hand. She turned it slowly. Another thud. She pushed on the door. It wasn't locked. Her hand was sweaty and the doorknob slipped. She leaned close to the narrow opening in the door to listen. As she did, the strong scent of forest wafted through the opening. It smelt similar to her hand when she had touched the banister at the bottom of the stairs. The air in the stairwell was filled with mildew and dust. The spider-bride and her web smelt buttery and rancid. This rich freshness coming from inside was unexpected.

Vreni breathed deeply, and her thoughts drifted to forest walks. There was another thud. She held her breath and listened. Two more thuds, sounding like a door somewhere being moved by a breeze and banging randomly.

She pushed the apartment door open slowly and stepped into the room, leaving the door open behind her. She now saw why the scent of forest was so pungent here.

The room was furnished with large old sofas and chairs, tattered carpet, heavy tables and bookcases, and across every surface there was a layer of green. She stepped towards a chair and touched the fabric, it felt downy, as the banister rail in the foyer had felt. The chair was covered in a velvety coating of moss. She reached for the sofa. It felt the same. As she walked, her feet slipped on the damp, moss covered carpet. The bookshelves looked like tall, rectangular tree trunks, encrusted with lichen and ribboned with trails of ivy.

At each of the windows stood rusting planter stands holding glazed pots. The plants cascaded out of the pots and trailed across the furniture and the floor. Other tendrils had twisted up seeking the sunlight and formed looping curtains of green that tangled with the ruins of old lace curtains. The air was moist and smelt of the sweetness of the deep forest in summer. Vreni peered in the low gloom between the mossy tables and chairs. 'Mushrooms.' The word sounded loud in the stillness, and she froze waiting to be discovered. The thudding continued. Now it was more frequent, still dysrhythmic and more urgent.

The thumping grew louder and Vreni could perceive a direction now. The thuds sounded like footfalls from above. William had spoken about the apartment having a roof-top garden. Of course. She scanned the green tangle of the lounge room looking for the stairs that led up to the roof, nothing. She chose a door she guessed led to the kitchen and entered with caution. Scanning the room, she saw moss and green tendrils on nearly every surface, covering the gaudy multi-coloured tiles on the walls and benches. This room smelled danker than the lounge and the floor was covered in green wetness from the mosses having been trodden into slime. She slipped as she stepped on the slick tiled floor, but didn't lose her footing.

The footprints crushed into the moss made a trail across the floor to a spiral staircase in the back corner of the kitchen. Vines and blossoms spilled down through the opening in the ceiling and tangled through the banister and the stair-treads. The thumping was louder now.

Vreni rushed for the stairs, forgetting the mossy floor. She slipped, falling heavily on the hard tiles, and clenched her teeth to stop from crying out. She crawled across to the stairs and clambered upwards using the tangle of vines for hand and foot holds.

As she reached the top of the stairs, she slowed, panting and looked out into the garden. The light was fading. Above, the latticework of metal framed the glass roof Bella's folly and, beyond that, the sky was filling with the reds and oranges of the early evening. Vreni lowered her gaze, scanning across the garden she could see a tall shape moving.

It was William. She recognised the silhouette of his long coat flapping. He had his back to her, and she watched as he lurched and rocked. She smiled. He was okay. She knew these movements ... he was dancing? It was not the dancing they did together, more like the dancing he did for Klara, to make her laugh.

Vreni craned her neck and scanned around the overgrown garden. She couldn't see Bella anywhere, but she was sure she was here, hiding somewhere like a dryad. She had buzzed the fake Harry in and Vreni knew this building was too old to have ever been required to have emergency exists. *Maybe Bella is behind me, watching.* Vreni froze and forced herself to look back down the stairs. The kitchen was empty.

All that mattered was that Bella was not here right now. Vreni had to act quickly so she and William could get out. She stepped through an arched gateway into the garden. It was warm and everything glowed in the fading light. The domed space was teaming with green upon green. The air was moist and filled with hundreds of fragrances. Vreni found herself breathing deeply and being distracted by a desire to identify each new scent. The entire roof space was a walled tangle of green dotted with bursts of vivid colour. She stepped onto the narrow gravel pathway, and saw that the plants were beginning to encroach here as well.

William continued his lumbering dance. As she got closer, he mumbled some unmusical wordless tune to himself. *Somethings is not right.* She tapped him on the shoulder. He didn't notice her. She slipped the golden orb of the clove spice love potion onto her tongue and rolled it around until it melted and broke open. Then she tapped harder. He started to turn.

'Would you like to dance?' She breathed the words out hard, and he reeled around, jerking as his feet landed heavily on the path. He stared out past Vreni as if she wasn't there. 'William.' He breathed in the fragrance of her words, but his eyes wandered around as he searched for the sound of the voice. 'William,' she said more urgently as she rubbed her hand across his chest. The amulet was gone.

She almost fell backwards with the discovery and, without thinking, she immediately started searching the ground for it. *It must have fallen off.* Then she stopped herself. It had not fallen off, ever, in the two years he had worn it. He was here and he had not called her. The amulet had been taken off.

She grabbed his hands and yanked him closer. 'William.' Her whisper was a hiss. 'What are you doing?' His eyes looked straight through her. She could not see any traces of the William she knew in his lifeless, unseeing eyes. She had to use the unmaking charm now, while she still had hold of him. She reached into her pocket and fumbled with the bundle, pulling the charm free and unravelling its string. She tugged hard on his coat, pulling William's jittering body closer and slipped the charm around his neck.

He stood frozen for a moment. She took the opportunity to drop the charm inside his shirt so that it would be in contact with his skin. As she did, he shuddered violently and dropped to his knees.

From the darkening green tangle at the rear of the garden, Vreni heard a gurgling moan. Then words that hissed from everywhere at once. 'He is mine ... he is mine.'

Vreni scanned the garden searching for Bella, braced for an attack. She could not see her anywhere, but she saw

William's amulet. It was hanging from a bramble which looked out of place in all the lushness of the garden. As she stepped closer to retrieve William's amulet, she saw another object, hanging on a silver chain that was also tangled in the bramble. It was a poppet. A tiny hollow-eyed man made of sticks and vines. It stared out at her as unseeingly as William was.

Vreni seethed. 'He will never be yours,' she hissed into the darkness. The moan came again and swelled until it was a snarl.

'Bella.' William answered the strange sound.

Vreni turned William. 'It's Vreni. Will you dance with me?' She pulled him to his feet and held him close. A warmth built where their bodies touched.

'Vreni?' It was a miniscule, confused utterance. For a moment, he had recognised her.

'He will never be yours.' Vreni whispered. She turned William, trying to dance them back towards the top of the stairs. His movements became less juddering, but his arms still hung limp by his sides. She had to get him to take the infusion, or she would never get him down the stairs.

Taking hold of his coat, she pulled William closer. He thrashed to free himself of the coat and it fell to the grown. He over balanced and she gripped his arm tightly, supporting his weight. He swayed and started to mumble again. She dug into her pocket for the vial of infusion that would strengthen the charm. How could she hold him up and get him to take the potion?

She loosened the cap of the vial and poured the liquid into her own mouth. Then she pressed her lips hard against his. They felt cold and wooden. She waited. His lips warmed, opening slightly. She spat the mouthful of infusion into his mouth and pressed her lips harder onto his, sealing them.

She held their lips together and remembered their first kiss, at the dance party. She remembered not wanting that kiss to stop and now she did not want this kiss to stop, not before William had swallowed the infusion. She thought of how magical it had felt when they had danced together that night. She wove those memories into the intension of the potion and the kiss. He started to move. She swayed and turned when he did, as though they were under their mirror ball in the conservatory at home. She needed William to feel the memories she had held in her heart, adding the power of those memories to the charm and the infusion to break the bonds of the poppet magic.

The muscles in William face and throat finally moved, and he swallowed. His lips seemed to waken, and he returned her kiss. He was returning to her, but she knew she would still need to destroy the poppet for him to be truly free. She didn't even need to search for it. It was hanging right in front of her, and she would easily be able to unmake it. The garden all around them seemed to rumble and moans rose up around them. The ground, the floor beneath them swelled and shifted.

'What was that?' William said, sounding like her William, raising his arms around her protectively.

'We have to get out of here,' Vreni said, knowing William would not retreat unless he thought they were both leaving. She guided him to the top of the stairs. He looked around trying to make sense of their surroundings. 'What ...' He stopped as though he didn't know what questions to ask.

'I'll explain soon. Let's get inside.' She guided him towards the stairs. As they walked, she removed a charm from around her neck and hummed it to life. The hum took on form and shaped itself to became shimmering copy of her. The conjured Vreni took William's hand and led him downward in to the kitchen. Vreni looked down, watching him stumble down the stairs and saw the other Vreni help him sit at the mildewed kitchen table. The false Vreni's hum grew louder. Her shimmering hand stroked William's hair. He laid his head on the table and closed his eyes. At the top of the stairs, Vreni hesitated, watching for a moment, then she turned and ran for the bramble to retrieve the amulet and unmake the poppet.

The floor bucked again and Vreni thought of the Al-Guild building crumbling as the old witch's magic was unravelled. 'Maybe the new witch's magic is weak and would collapse.' In response, the ground began undulating, rippling. The plants quivered, restless, enchanted and more alive than nature deemed plants should ever be. Vreni knew the Sisters used magic to hold the fruit trees at Mežs Mājas in perpetual enchantment of summer-time, so their branches would always be laden with blossoms and fruit. She had never seen them use any magic that enabled the trees to move.

Vreni clambered to the bramble and untangled William's chain from where it hung on a barb. She shoved the amulet into her pocket and fastened it closed. The other silver chain snapped as she tugged the poppet from where it hung. Its wooden body chilled her hand. She breathed in deeply to prepare herself for the unmaking.

Fumbling with the knot securing the dark ribbon around the poppet's chest. She began unravelling it from around the small stiff body as she chanted quietly.

'Your honoured work is now fulfilled,
Your purpose ends as it is willed.
With thanks and love your task is ended,
I sever now what once was blended.'

As she finished the words and removed the last of the bindings from the charm, she dropped the dark ribbon to the ground. The plants and the floor reared up beneath her feet. A ragged howl wailed up from the ground all around her. She steadied herself and tried to calm her thumping heart.

With her lips up close to the hollow-eyed little poppet, Vreni chanted her unmaking spell again. The words honoured and thanked the man-shaped charm for its completed task. This was what should happen. It was not the poppet's fault that it had been used to harm instead of heal. Vreni needed to release the bond thoroughly so William would be free.

The howl formed into words. 'Mine!' The floor bucked and started to rise, forming swollen hillocks that twitched and collapsed again. 'Mine!' The words were coming from everywhere.

The poppet charm was almost fully undone now. Vreni whispered the spell of unmaking once more and felt what she had been waiting for. The bundle containing the crystal heart of the poppet dropped out onto her cupped palm, leaving a hollow in the tiny chest. 'It is just a husk now,' Vreni whispered, but she could not leave it behind. *Things that are left behind, left for dead are not always as dead as they appear.* She would not take that chance with this charm. She dug her figures into the bound heart and pulled at the thread. It snapped and the ground gurgled. She unwound the fabric package and shoved what remained of the unmade poppet into her pockets. She would check on William and then figure out what had happened to Bella and stop her.

Vreni turned, the floor rose again and it took shape. The shape of an enormous arm which was woven together from branches and vines. At the end of the verdant arm was a huge hand. It was reaching towards Vreni.

BLOOD MOON

The seed holds the universe of the tree in its heart.
Do we blame the seed if the tree grows gnarled and twisted?
The seed is just a seed.
~Pratigs Masa Book of Wisdoms

* * *

The giant hand slammed down on Vreni as she tried to throw herself out of its reach. She scrambled out from under the pressing bramble fingers and ran towards the light coming from the top of the stairs. The ground heaved as though it was drawing a breath. Vreni stumbled for a moment. How long before William would be back to himself? She had been relieved when her projected-self had hummed him to sleep so that he could rest and heal after his ordeal, but she feared she would need him very soon.

A second verdant limb appeared, rising from the tangle of ground cover. 'He's mine!' The words boomed, bouncing off the glass dome.

'Is that all you can say?' Vreni slowed, she thought of Veca Tante, who had been turned into a tree by centuries of her own magic. Thoughts and theories were forming in her mind and her curiosity was winning over her fear. She scrambled away and hid herself in a dark corner of the garden, crouched behind a dense bush and watched.

The two huge, green bramble arms had grown out of the low, hidden parts of the garden. The ground heaved another breath. Vines, flowers and brambles began to grow at the place between the two arms, forming shoulders, a chest.

Vreni watched as a mound of leaves and vines twisted upwards from the shoulders, forming a neck of branches. Atop the neck, the ball of twigs and blossoms grew, shaping itself into grotesque, oversized details. Eyes, a nose, a mouth. There were matted tresses of dark hair woven amongst the twigs, framing this monstrous face.

'I have found Bella.'

The arboreal mouth opened, and the growling voice bellowed out. 'He will be mine!'

Vreni could only watch in disbelief as this flowery face mewled and hissed and demanded. The tales of Bubak the scarecrow and Blodeuwedd frothed into Vreni's mind. Blodeuwedd belonged of the Welch histories and was a gentle goddess creature, woven from the wonders of the forest. She did no harm, living in harmony with nature. But the stories of Bubak were all about fear and cruelty and loss.

Aunt Zana had felt it her duty to teach caution, mostly frightening Vreni and Rita with tales of the things that hid in the shadows and lurked after sunset. She would lower the lamps, and in the red glow of the fire she would start her tale. 'Do you hear that scraping, girls? It is surely Bubak, out to gather fools. Fools don't last long in this world. My lovely nieces are not fools, are you?' Vreni and Rita would hold each other's hands tight and shake their heads. 'Because if you are foolish and wonder away on your own, Old Bubak will jump out of the shadows, as quick as a bitter wind, and he will bundle you in his sack and steal you away. So, my sweet nieces, ignore calls from the darkness, even if they sound like Aunty or Papa. Old Bubak uses false voices to lure the unwary away and weave their souls into his coat.'

This new grown Bella conjured a body of forest things, like Blodeuwedd, but her enormous face hissed and screeched full of anger and hate, worse than any version of the Bubak that Vreni had ever imagined from Aunt Zana's frightening tales.

Behind the transformed Bella creature, the full moon was rising. A blood-moon. Swelling up over the wall of the roof-top garden, it flooded the courtyard with an eerie red glow. The shiny leaves on the monstrous face gleamed with flecks of red.

Vreni held her breath, frozen with fear, as the creature lifted itself up growing out of the substance of the garden all around her. Regret crept into her dizzied mind. She had been the fool in Aunt Zana's story and gone off on her own. She had rushed away to unmake the thing that she felt so responsible for creating. Unity and the sacrifices the Wise Sisters made for each other always made their magic stronger. By running off alone Vreni had shunned that strength and unity. *My truths are full of selfish and rushed decisions.* She released her breath as a groan.

The ground rippled behind Vreni, and she was shoved in the back by something sharp. She was flung out of her hiding place, twisting through the air towards the monster. Sharp twigs stabbed into her skin as she landed. The beast's chest rose and fell under her. The vines and branches creaked and rasped as they rubbed past each other while the creature took form. Vreni looked back to see what had shoved her and saw an immense foot moving out of the shadows as an enormous leg stretched out towards the gate.

The foot kicked the gate at the top of the stairs slammed shut with a force that rattled the whole roof. Her hope of William waking and being able to help her, were dashed. *And if I don't defeat her, she will start all over again.*

The creature continued to grow. Vreni had landed on the surreal bracken cleavage of the giant forest woman's bosom. She looked down, the Bella creature was only half-grown yet and still attached to the undergrowth. Vreni rolled down across the abdomen to the ground, clamber-ing to her feet she scrambled away. She needed time to decide on a charm.

Her intention was clear, she had to obliterate this new form of the old witch and end her evil magic forever. Vreni skirted around the edges of the blood-lit garden, she touched each of her charms in turn, reaching out with her intuition to sense which to use.

The moon rose higher and Bella was nearly grown. Tendrils crept out from the edges of her body, twisting through the garden, gathering all manner of green things and drawing them close to be woven into her. The last branches and vines plaited themselves, becoming green flesh. Then the giant strained and lifted herself upright. The sound of rustling leaves and the grating of wood accompanied the cumbersome movement. Reminding Vreni of weaving baskets in that long-ago place, last century. Twisting supple twigs together and hearing them squeak as they slid into place. When the baskets dried and hardened, they'd hold mushrooms and berries gathered from the forest.

The weaving of this creature was mesmerising. Finally, the squeaks and shivering ceased and the creature stood, tall and glinting in the light of the blood-moon. Her head almost reaching the garden's glass dome.

In the red of the blood-moon, the monster looked as though she was burning. Vreni wished it was true. If it burned there would be nothing left, not like the seeds that Vreni overlooked. Those seeds had whispered out and ensorcelled poor Harry, who had found and nurtured the seeds and this thing had grown.

Vreni would make sure that nothing would be left. Her fingers fell on the charm needed, choke-weed. The virulent weed would follow its nature and take deep root in what remained of the garden beds, then invade the blossom monster's body and anchor her in place. *When she is trapped, I will burn her.*

The bubble of resin that held the twisting choke-weed warmed in Vreni's fingers and melted away. The enchanted vine coiled restlessly in her hand as it started to grow. She held the weed in her closed fist and edged closer to the creature. Tendrils of the weed twisted out of her closed hand, eager to grow and invade.

'Spread your tendrils twist and squirm,
Anchor the monster and hold her firm.'

She whispered her intentions and drew back her hand to throw the weed. As she did, an immense hand reached and closed around her, squeezing until she could do nothing except struggle for air. She fought to free herself from the grip, but it grew tighter.

The hand lifted Vreni into the air. The whole round moon glowed like a ball of fire in the dark sky. Suddenly she realised how high up she was and strained to twist around, looking to see if the dome vents were open. She imagined being thrown out into the night sky to land, crumpled and broken on the street below. *Would Rita be down there to see me land? Was Sabina at the door, working to get inside because I left them behind?*

The wicker-work hand lifted Vreni higher until she was gazing into its huge dark eyes that were made of creatures that had squirmed up from the wet, hidden places of the garden. The hand held her there a moment longer, as the eyes writhed and stared at her.

The mouth opened. Vreni braced herself for more screeching moans and more demands about possessing William. The mouth remained silent and opened wider still, until it was an enormous green maw, rippling and quivering with more dark, alive things writhing inside.

The hand holding Vreni moved closer to the mouth. It opened even wider. The crawling creatures dripped down inside the dark orifice, then twisted and wriggled to find a new latch-hold on the woven tongue. Vreni thrashed and kicked at the giant hand. Her mind flashed bright and dark as she struggled for breath.

The smell of forest came from inside the mouth. A sweet dampness like earth after rain. She tried to think of those happy times in the forest, to keep herself calm and focus on her charms but the hand's grip would not even allow her to draw breath, she could not move enough to reach her charms.

The wetness of the giant mouth closed around her, and the grip of the hand was replaced by the pressure of the tongue and jaw enclosing her in its slimy basketwork cage. Vreni gulped a breath. Then she was squeezed, her new prison creaked and rustled and she was tumbled by the raking tongue as the toothless mouth chewed her. The noise and the tumbling stopped, then there was a pulling constriction. Sticks and stems grabbed at her like a rippling wave of clawed fingers and pushed her down the dark throat as she was swallowed. She gulped breaths between each constriction and with each tightening of the throat, she was scratched by the interwoven branches. Her skin burned anew as the cuts and abrasions scraped along the sharp protrusions of wood. The wriggling creatures crawled on her grazed skin, attracted by her blood. *They are waiting for me to be dead to turn me into compost.*

Vreni felt a rise and fall, heard air rushing and rasping through the gaps in the grotesque wicker-work body. There were waves of coolness across her skin. As the Bella creature breathed in and out, the night air chilled Vreni's blood-dampened skin. Each false breath carried scents of the hidden places in the forest where things grew that could not be identified. The air seeping out from Bella's fleshy insides soured. Vreni breathed in the acrid mist and coughed. Her mind began to spin. She would be poisoned by these fumes, digested, and composted by the tiny gnawing creatures that inhabited this cursed miscreation.

There was a cool, wet slithering around her wounds. She remembered this sensation from walking the rainforest path that twisted down the cliffs to the beach at home. Almost every time she walked the track, she had become the temporary feast of the leeches that would blindly search for the warmth of her bare skin and gorge themselves on her blood before they would drop away fat and bloody.

The wiggling stopped and she knew they had started their blood-feast. Then she felt the flip-flop wriggling of the engorged bodies against her skin and the familiar sting as the leeches left her to roll away fat and sated filled with her blood. 'They are clever, these little thieves.' Papa used to say. 'You do not feel them until they have taken what they want.' Vreni smiled for a moment and was confounded that this memory, among the horror, was a comfort to her.

The squeezing continued to push her downwards. She coughed violently as her lungs tried to expel the foul gases. A wave of nausea overtook her, and she retched violently. A sour, coffee flavoured muck trickled from her mouth and slid down her chin. Now there was a slithering movement on her face. The little creatures had come, gathering together to collect this discarded piece of her.

They wriggled across her chin, sucking, nibbling at her skin with their tiny mouths as they supped on her vomit, eagerly collecting this small morsel as a first course while they waited to feast on the rest of her.

The creatures slithered closer to her lips, following the trail of the coffee spittle. She spat and forced out rushed puffing breaths, hoping the expelled air would make them back away. She screamed through clenched teeth and breathed hard forcing her sour breath through the tiny slit she dared to open between her lips.

The little creatures moved away from the sour screams, creeping around and across her lips moving upwards until she felt them tickling the edges of her nostrils. She huffed savage, wet puffs of air out of her nose to dissuade their progress.

She screamed, thrashing to shake them off. Straightening her body, she pushed against the edges of the tight space and heard the twigs snapping and crackling. The thorny tube of spikey bramble pushed back with such force that her legs were buckled. Her head and shoulders were shunted by the thorn wall behind her, and her legs were shoved up towards her chest with such force her knees smashed into her forehead.

The prison of twigs and branches squeezed in, holding her firm, rolling her into a ball of bones and flesh. Trapped on all sides by the vice of tangles of sticks and vines. There was a slow pulsing pressure, as the sides of this tunnel squeezed. The sticks pressed into her flesh. They felt like needles, knives, piecing her skin. The creeping came again. The little feet skittering and the things with no feet, slithering across her skin to feast on her blood. *At least the blood has tempted them away from my face.*

Trapped, Vreni could do nothing but think. No part of her could move. She barely had freedom to breath in this briar trap. She felt her clenched fist and realised she still held the magical choke-weed in her hand. She felt it straining to be free. She chanted her intention into the choke-weed once again and the pressure built inside her closed fist.

'Grow strong, be bountiful tiny weed,
Reach out with tendrils as fine as smoke.
Weave and tangle, grip and strangle,
Bind this creature in your green death-cloak.'

The weed swelled and grew, writhing against her palm, wrestling to be free. Vreni's hand was pressed between her chest and her legs. The strength of the growing weed pushed her fingers open, and she felt it uncoil and spill out of her hand. The sprouts twisted passed her trapped legs and across her bare, bleeding arms, slithering away, prising themselves in between the thorns and barbs that imprisoned her.

She waited, struggling to draw shallow breaths, and repeated the charmed words, urging the weed to grow out and strangle this creature. To weave into the monster body, prizing it apart until Vreni could fight her way out of the trap.

The smooth, cool leaves of the growing choke-weed slid across her skin. She felt its tendrils thickening and coiling past and she imagined it weaving its way in and out of Bella's plant body, tangling and twisting, then bursting out of her, growing and flowing until she was dressed in a shiny green death cloak. Then once it was woven into every hiding place within her it would squeeze and strangle, thickening and growing until it wrenched the plant woman apart. Vreni kept her intention strong and focused on this undoing. It was all she could do.

A growling moan echoed all around. Vreni's prison shuddered and constricted. The thorny walls stabbed into her flesh. The shuddering ceased and the spikes withdrew. Vreni's skin burned and stung, then there was a coolness as the evening air, twisting through from outside, touched her bloody skin. Then the slithering, skittering creatures returned, drawn by the smell of blood to continue their feast.

Vreni could no longer feel the choke-weed growing and swelling. 'Weave and tangle, grip and strangle.' She sobbed. Her chant had turned to begging. 'Bind this creature in your green death-cloak.'

Her skin was blanketed in writhing movement. There was nibbling, sucking, licking as her blood was slurped and supped upon. The creatures moved on to her face. A wriggling smoothness pressed down on her eyelids. Something tickled her nostrils. She huffed out forceful breaths to clear her nose and clamped her mouth tightly shut. Her chest ached with the sobs trapped within her held breath. Tears flowed, the creatures wriggled away from her eyes and retreated from her face to avoid the saltiness. *Blessings.* She slowly opened her mouth and felt around with her tongue to ensure they were gone, then drew in a gasping breath and the sobs poured out in shuddering waves.

There were new noises now. Vreni calmed herself to listen. There were echoing moans all around and a squeaking, like wet branches scraping on the roof during a storm. *Please. This must be the choke-weed forcing the un-weaving.* Surrounded by spikes and feasting creatures, Vreni still couldn't move. All she had now was her thoughts, her memories. *I am doing this for them, all of them, so they can be safe. My blood started this, and it seems I will give my blood to finish it.*

The squeaking continued and now there was cracking and creaking. The space around Vreni shuddered and contracted again. The crackling around her reminded her of another noise and she withdrew deeper into her memories.

She took herself to a time when they were young and had been with Aunt Mila in the forest. Rita had tripped and fallen on the berry basket and the woven sticks had cracked as it crumbled. She was covered in crushed berries and Vreni had laughed and teased her as she helped her up. 'You look like the juiciest berry in all the forest now. Watch out or the mother bird will sing to her friends and they will all swoop down and take you back to feed to their hungry babies.' Rita had cowered, whimpering and Vreni had laughed harder still. Aunt Mila had patted Rita's hand and glared at Vreni. 'Don't be unkind, Vreni. You are just jealous that the birds will be singing about Rita and not you.' Rita had nodded and stuck her tongue out. *I miss my sister, all my Sisters. I shouldn't have come alone.*

There was a pained moan, a shudder and the pressure of the thorny walls withdrew. Vreni fell to the bottom of the enlarged space and as she landed, spikes dug deeply into her back. She rolled cautiously, trying to find relief, thorns and brambles still surrounded her, but they were loosening. The woven fabric of the creature was unravelling. Red moonlight was entering Vreni's prison through the widening gaps. She looked around her and immediately wished for darkness. The creatures that had retreated away into the brambles were tempted out again by the smell of Vreni's blood and they were hanging above her, their shiny dark bodies reflecting the red of the moon. They wriggled and started dropping down like black rain. Worms and centipedes, leeches and beetles fell onto her, squirming to right themselves as they landed. Vreni re-coiled, whimpering. She felt them crawling and slithering through her hair and slapped them away widely, trying to shield herself from the squirming torrent.

There was another spasm, an angry growl that came from everywhere at once. A wave of beetles and spiders scurried down the woven walls and out as though they were running from something bad. Mice appeared out of the gaps and holes, their eyes glowing red in the moon-light. They jumped. Vreni closed her eyes and flung her hands up again to protect her face. They landed with a squeal and dug their claws into her skin. Vreni cried out, batting them off frantically. But they were not seeking her, just running over her to get away.

Vreni managed to get to her feet and balance inside the swaying monster. She could see the choke-weed now. It was still growing, weaving in and out making larger and larger holes. Soon they would be large enough for her to crawl through. She chanted to the weed again and squeezed her hands into fits, trying to be patient. Then it all changed. There was an angry growl and the choke-weed simply stopped. 'No.' Vreni chanted her spell again.

The charmed weed turned brown. 'No!' Then the walls rippled and started moving closer. Vreni covered her face with her hands as the walls of the prison slammed back in on her. Her skin burned where the thorns ripped through her clothes and pierced her again.

Through the brambles, Vreni thought she heard words. Now the Bella-monster was moving, swaying. Every move-ment caused Vreni's flesh to grate against the sharp walls. Every step Bella took caused more wounds, more bleed-ing and now the centipedes, the worms, the leeches, all those wiggling things that did not have the sense to flee, returned to feast. Vreni thrashed against the thorns and screamed into her hands.

The swaying was becoming jolted. The woven walls spasmed in and out around her. *Maybe William is doing some-thing out there?* The growling moans turned to screams, the Bella-monster thrashed around. Vreni was being tumbled into the thorns. More rips, more cuts. She tried to hold on to save herself from more damage. The piece of wall she held broke away in her hand. She grabbed a new place, and it came away too. With each dislodged handful, the creature screamed out. Something had happened. Vreni was hopeful, energised. *Maybe all my charms broke open, maybe something in them did this?*

She grabbed handfuls of the woven creature and ripped them away. The walls were becoming thinner. Red moonlight flooded in. It matched with the red on her hands and soaking through her clothes from her wounded skin. She was covered in her own blood from head to toe. *I will not die inside this monster.*

Bella bucked sideways and Vreni flew across the crumbling cage. As she fell against the barbs, blood flowed. Bella screamed. *I am causing her pain.*

Vreni ripped at the brambles until there was a hole to climb out through. As she clambered the creature swayed. 'No, no, no.' Vreni struggled to get outside as everything tilted sideways and she crashed down onto the gravel with the full weight of the verdant carcass on top of her.

Everything went still around her. She lay blanketed by twigs and vines, but they were no longer moving. The evening air cooled her bloody skin, her face tightening as her blood congealed.

She began to rip through the bracken walls. As she did, they began to crumble. *It can't be this easy.* She braced herself for the next bout. The creature convulsed and quivered as Vreni pulled clumps of sticks and twisted vines away, but there were no more attacks.

* * *

Vreni burst from the side of the collapsing monster and jumped away. It lay crumpled across the garden. Thick fronds of dead, brown choke-weed jutted out from Bella's dismantled body. Her woven face looked tortured, eyes wide, staring at nothing. She had been a creature of blossoms and shiny leaves that reflected the crimson moonlight, but what remained was gnarled and stiff. Once green leaves now looked like bloody scabs on infected wounds.

Vreni dared to reach and touch a leaf. It was shrivelled and coated in a dry red film. *My blood?* She plucked a leaf and touched the red smudge to her lips, tasting the coppery familiarity of it. It was blood, and the only one bleeding had been Vreni. *Somehow my blood has become a weapon.*

'She regrew once. I will leave nothing of this creature, no seed, no shoot. The witch will not regrow again.' She raced to where William's coat lay and rifled through the pockets. 'Fire.' She found the lighter and smiled, feeling her stiff face sting as she did.

She walked back to the giant corpse and touched the lighter's small flame to the protrusions of brown choke-weed setting fires where she pleased. The flames sputtered and leapt, dancing blue across the film of her blood on the leaves and igniting deep inside the monster's body and burning a deep orange.

Vreni had to step back from the heat as the flames consumed the woven forest monster who had been Bella, who had grown from a seed that had come from Veca Tante, who had been once, so long ago, an angry, aggrieved maiden aunt.

Over the crackle, Vreni heard noises behind her in the garden. An icy panic filled her. She tensed and reached for her charms, ready for what would come next.

'Vreni, what's with all the combustion? Are you alright?'

She turned and saw William rattling the jammed gate.

Running to him, she wrenched it open and threw herself into his arms.

'What happened?' he asked.

'I'll explain soon.' She returned her gaze to the fire, not willing to stop watching until there was nothing left but ash.

They watched until the flaming body collapsed in on itself, sending a spray of sparks up into the red sky. Vreni would not take her eyes from the monster until every stick was destroyed. She took William's hand and found a place to sit. As she watched the fire do its work, she told him everything that had happened since their anniversary, which was where William had lost the thread of the tale.

After a long while William only had one question, 'What was the word inside the charm?'

Her face flushed hot. If he was no longer controlled, he would know the word.

'I gave you the thing you value most,' Vreni said. 'I wrote that thing in the charm.'

William held the charm in his hand, turning it over in his hand. 'Choice,' he said quietly.

Vreni took the charm from him and unravelled it. She let the piece of amber and the desiccated herbs fall into her hand and showed William the word—*Choice*. 'Having a choice was the most important and the most potent force in your life. Bella had taken that away, so I made the charm to restore that choice to you.' Vreni held the soot covered, silver amulet in her hands. 'You will always be free to choose,' she whispered, staring at the amulet.

William reached and took it from her. 'I already chose, long ago. Nothing has changed.' He went to place the chain around his neck.'

Vreni took his hands and stopped him. 'Something has changed.' William looked grave. 'No, nothing bad, just new. I took the cure. I'm not a sleeper anymore.'

ENDINGS AND BEGINNINGS

The mystery at a story's beginning
can be a truth when the tale is told.

~ Book of Truths

* * *

Vreni stood in her tower, staring out at the ocean. She ran her hand over her smooth and mended skin. The Sisters had healed her. Sometimes the memories of the fight inside Bella, played tricks in her mind, but these frightening ghosts were fading from her memory.

Out beyond the cliffs, the sea was turning purple as the day faded to night. The fate-filled blood moon had waned and there had been two ripe and creamy moons since. Tonight, was a new-moon and the night would be dark, but they would be celebrating, so the darkness would be filled with the glow of the love that bound Vreni's family together.

There was so much to celebrate. So many new tales had started since Vreni had helped the Sisters free her family from the curse of long-sleep. Now the sleeper's centuries old story could be put to rest and become nothing but a magical myth to intrigue a young heart.

Rita had big plans to open a shop, to sell only the most stylish fashion. 'To save the world from people making poor style choices,' William had teased. But Rita had done it, the store would open soon and Klara couldn't wait. Nessa frowned and reminded her of the importance of lessons and responsibilities. Klara hadn't really listened.

Nessa could not resist the offer the Sisters made for her to study at Mežs Mājas. She was thrilled that in this century anyone could choose any path, and she didn't have to steal books to learn as she had to do a few years, no, a few centuries ago.

Mama and the aunts were happiest to be at Mežs Mājas too. Zana had encouraged the Sisters to see Nessa's magical potential, the same way they had been shown Vreni's. Mila was busy, along with Mama, finding ways to boss everyone around, though they liked to call it influence. Vreni smiled. Mama and the aunts still put most of their *influence* into trying to get her and William to marry. They would take much longer to get used to the way things were in this century.

She stared at the pages of her journal, her book of truths. New truths had been written there since the time of the blood moon.

Truth – my blood started this family's story so many centuries ago. When the young Tante cut my palm, my blood became our fate, all our fates. Without it, there would have been no curse and no Wise Sisters. I would not have ever become what I am without that story starting.

Truth – there would be no more incarnations of Old Aunty, no more regrowing. After centuries, the old monster's accursed life was finally defeated. My blood was stripped of the evil by the cure and that cured blood became a weapon against the witch.

William and Vreni had started their own new chapter. William had surprised Vreni and told her he'd asked Artūrs to use his *mojo* to get Vreni the documents she need to attend university, now they could study together.

'Will the university accept me?' Vreni had asked. 'What if I can't do it? Am I old enough?'

William had laughed. 'So, after battling for your life and mine, twice, you are worried about coping with university?' He'd hugged her. 'And you were born in what 1904, I think you are old enough for uni.'

Truth – the end of the curse was not the end for the Pratigs Masa. The Wise Sisters, still had the promise they made to each other centuries ago and they had a new purpose and a series of new beginnings.

William and Sabina were very excited about the developments with the new drugs that came from the old curse potion. This new chapter of the Sister's lives was properly open. With all their hard work and the new funds from the old AlGuild coffers, they could commit to developing these amazing new medicines.

The apartment building would come in very handy once it was repaired and renovated. With Rita's shop in the city and William and Vreni studying, the building will be buzzing with new, non-monstrous residents. And having a city home will let them escape from Artūrs' supervision. Mama appointed him chaperon until there was some sign of wedding plans.

Truth – I was kept away from the world by the sleeping curse, then I chose to stay away from the world by not taking the cure and holding myself responsible for the fate of everyone I loved.

'I know where I belong now.' Vreni whispered and closed her Book of Truths.

'You belong with me.' William slipped his arms around her waist and squeezed her close. 'And you belong downstairs, everyone is here and hungry. Gaida sent me up to tell you she needs you to set another place at the table.'

She turned in the circle of his arms and kissed him. 'I know how many people are in our crazy family and there is a plate set for everyone.'

'Are you sure?'

'Liga!'

William nodded and kissed her. 'She's healed and awake.'

She hugged him so tightly he groaned. 'Now all the tales are told.'

Acknowledgements

Book 1

Thank you to Yvonne Mes, Monique Moy and Isabella Maher for your writerly support. I'm pleased you shared the journey with me.

Declan and Trae Allen are the best monster wranglers, I'm so glad I had their creativity and insight to keep all my scary creatures from getting out of control.

Thank you to Penny, Anthony and the team for your professional insight and guidance on my journey from writer to author.

Book2

To my amazing and talented colleagues from Rainforest Writing Retreat, thank you for giving me a welcome space to share my nutty ideas, and for the creative support and inspiration that makes my stories possible.

Thanks, and hugs to Chris Radge for revisiting my weird, fairy-tale world and help untangled me when there were too many twists in my tale.

Thank you to Gina Pinto for her creative insights, attention to detail and outstanding editorial support.

Shell Watson offered her skilled artistic stylings to perfect my cover ideas and taught me invaluable lesson about the blessings of collaboration. Thank you so much.

About the Author

Martii Maclean lives in a tin shack by the sea, catching seagulls she uses to make delicious pies, and writing weird stories. She likes going for long bicycle rides with her cat, who always wears aviator goggles to stop her whiskers blowing up into her eyes as they speed down to the beach to search for mermaid eggs.

To find out more about Martii, and explore the free resources for kids and teachers, visit **martiimaclean.com**

Martii writes offbeat and fantastical tales for adults as **Rita Maclean.**

Rita's first anthology, **Tales from the Edge of Maybe**, will be available in early 2024.

Other titles from Martii Maclean

Stories for Kids

Weird Weirder Weirdest: A Collection of Quirky Tales
Come this way ... meet a whispering cat, write with a magic pen, use a watch to stop time, take a step in magic shoes and meet the patchwork girl ... it's not too far, just beyond the here and now.

Creepy Creepier Creepiest: Another Collection of Quirky Tales
Come this way if you dare ... find out what's slithering in the dark water, what happens to the chosen when the moon is full, rescue a fading girl, make an impossible phone call, follow the ghostly boy ... it's not too far, just beyond the here and now.

Strange Stranger Strangest: The another-est collection of quirky tales.

Come this way ... help teach the mermaid to ride a bicycle, re-boot the Cat-bot, discover who is sneaking around the Christmas tree, dare to take a bite of the apple, visit the weird drive-in on movie night, battle the mutant duck, discover the bizarre stuff happening at the skate-park and meet the surfers who can stay under water forever ... it's not too far, just beyond the here and now.

The Adventures of Isabelle Necessary

A gutsy girl, a cool beach town, awesome friends and oodles of adventures. Come adventuring with Isabelle at Saggy Beach.

Young Adult Novels

If I Die Before I Wake

The sleeping curse is genetic and hereditary, passed down from mother to daughter for centuries. Vreni is fifteen and has vowed to free herself and her family from the evil magic, and defeat the cruelty of the curse.

We of the Between

The world is poisoned, the seas flooded. When Trin sees blue people rise from the ocean she is destined to be drawn into the magical and dangerous place between two worlds.

Unreal Time

Time-loop traps, mutant marsupials and cyber-teen renegades: the future will never be the same again.

Stories for Adults

Tales of Murder and Mystery
In 'Mile High', no one chooses to leave the floating city and struggle to survive in the down-under. She stands unmoving, sealed inside the waste pod. No one can release her. Within minutes the hatch will open and she will plummet to her end. Who locked her inside?

Read this and other chillingly entertaining tales in the Oz Tales short-story series.

Tales of Forests and Fantasies
In 'The Clockwork Prince', an invincible steel warrior is built with a heart that does not want to kill. He reluctantly agrees to fight in exchange for freedom and a clockwork bride. Betrayed and broken-hearted, he fights for vengeance.

Read this and many other fantastical tales in the Oz Tales short-story series.

Short Stories of Ghosts and Graves
In 'Two Glasses', Lara's boyfriend is gone and now she is on her own in the cottage they shared for years. She feels very alone, but it seems she isn't alone anymore. Lara hears music, objects move by themselves. It could be stress playing trick on her mind, but what if it isn't?

Read this and many other fantastical tales in the Oz Tales short-story series.